RAPTOR 6

THE QUIET PROFESSIONALS
BOOK 1

RONIE KENDIG

SHILOH RUN  PRESS

For more information about Ronie Kendig, please access the author's website at the following Internet address: www.roniekendig.com.

Cover Design: Kirk DouPonce, DogEared Design

Published by Shiloh Run Press, an imprint of Barbour Publishing, Inc., P.O. Box 719, Uhrichsville, Ohio 44683, www.shilohrunpress.com

Our mission is to publish and distribute inspirational products offering exceptional value and biblical encouragement to the masses.

ecpa Member of the
Evangelical Christian
Publishers Association

Printed in the United States of America.

DEDICATION

To the U.S. Special Forces Community—
known as the Quiet Professionals.
You are warriors with humility and ferocity.
You possess courage and generosity.
You fight for freedom and those who cannot fight for themselves.
I pray this series honors the work you do, the men you are,
and your families who so tirelessly support you!
With a grateful heart. . .thank you!

ACKNOWLEDGMENTS

Special thanks to:

The Special Forces veteran who posed on the cover—thank you, sir, for your service and for the sacrifices you and your family have made as you have served. May God richly bless you!

Former Special Forces operator Jonas Polson for your service to our country and your vigilance over freedom. Thank you for your help and kindness with elements of this story.

Admiration and thanks to other Special Forces veterans who gave tips and tried to educate on the minutiae of all things SF. Clearly, I still have a lot to learn. Thank you, sirs!

Thanks to Colonel Dean (retired) for help with cybersecurity. Well, as much as you could give without making it necessary to have me killed (just kidding. . .mostly).

Thanks to Kirk DouPonce, who accepted the challenge to take this Rapid-Fire Fiction novel to the next level with an über-amazing cover! Thank you!

Thanks to my agent, Steve Laube, who remains steadfast and constant in an ever-changing industry. Thanks for keeping it real, Agent-Man!

Allen and Kellie Gilbert—thanks for your helping with skydiving information!

A million thanks to Julee Schwarzburg—editor extraordinaire!

Bethany Kaczmarek—girl, you got *skillz*! Thank you for your constant and incredible help in making this book stronger. You're amazing!

Rel Mollet—Where would I be without you, friend? You keep me encouraged and laughing when, really, I just want to puddle up and cry. You're one of the truest and most genuine friends I've ever had!

Thanks to the Barbour Fiction and Sales teams, relentless in their efforts to make our books successful: Shalyn Sattler, Annie Tipton, Rebecca Germany, Mary Burns, Elizabeth Shrider, Laura Young, Kelsey McConaha, Linda Hang, and Ashley Schrock.

LITERARY LICENSE

In writing about unique settings, specific locations, and invariably the people residing there, a certain level of risk is involved, including the possibility of dishonoring the very people an author intends to honor. With that in mind, I have taken some literary license in *Raptor 6*, including renaming some bases within the U.S. military establishment, creating sites/entities that do not otherwise exist, and other aspects of team movement/integration. Also, some elements of the story are pure entertainment and as with any work of fiction, demand a level of suspension of disbelief. I have done this so the book and/or my writing will not negatively reflect on our military community and its heroes. With the quickly changing landscape of combat theater, this seemed imperative and prudent.

GLOSSARY OF TERMS/ACRONYMS

AAR—After-Action Review
ACUs—Army Combat Uniforms
AHOD—All Hands On Deck
ANA—Afghan National Army
CIC—Commander In Chief
CID—Criminal Investigations Department
DIA—Defense Intelligence Agency
Glock—A semiautomatic handgun
IED—Improvised Explosive Device
Klick—Military slang for *kilometer*
M4, M4A1, M16—Military assault rifles
MRAP—Mine-Resistant Ambush-Protected vehicle
MWD—Military Working Dog
ODA452—Operational Detachment A (Special Forces A-Team)
OPSEC—Operational Security
RPG—Rocket-Propelled Grenade
RTB—Return To Base
SAS—Special Air Service (Foreign Special Operations Team)
SATINT—Satellite Intelligence
SCI—Sensitive Compartmented Information
SFOC—Special Forces Operational Command
SOCOM—Special Operations Command
SIPRNet—Secret Internet Protocol Router Network
TEDD—Tactical Explosive Detector Dog
UAV—Unmanned Aerial Vehicle
WMDs—Weapons of Mass Destruction

CHARACTER LIST

Dean Patrick "Raptor Six" Watters (Captain)—Raptor team commander

Brian "Hawk" Bledsoe (Staff Sergeant)—Raptor team member; coms specialist; rank – Staff Sergeant

Eamon "Titanis" Straider (SAS Corporal)—Raptor team member; Australian; engineering specialty

Fekiria Haidary—Zahrah Zarrick's cousin; teacher

Kamran Khan—Taliban member

Lance Burnett (General)—Raptor's commanding officer; attached to Defense Intelligence Agency

Lee Nianzu—assassin and associate of Zhang Longwei, son of General Zhang Guiern; Chinese

Mitchell "Harrier" Black (Sergeant First Class)—Raptor team member; combat medic

Peter "Z-Day" Zarrick (General, retired)—served as commander of Coalition Forces; Zahrah Zarrick's father

Rashid Mustafa—brother of Ara, one of Zahrah's students

Salvatore "Falcon" Russo (Sergeant First Class)—Raptor team member; team sergeant, aka team "daddy"; expert in ops/intel

Todd "Eagle" Archer (Staff Sergeant)—Raptor team member; weapons expert; team sniper

Zahrah Zarrick—a missionary teacher; daughter of General Peter "Z-Day" Zarrick

SUNDRY CHARACTERS

Amelia "Amy" Celine Archer—Todd Archer's wife

Ara Mustafa—sister of Rashid, one of Zahrah Zarrick's students

Ashgar Asad—drug dealer Majorca

Atash Mustafa—Rashid and Ara's father; husband of Razia

Behrooz Nemazi—Pashtun

Boris/"Scythe"—hacker/spy

Specialist Bramlett—female MP at sub-base

Brie Hastings (Lieutenant)—personal aid to General Burnett

Candyman—callsign for Tony VanAllen, former Raptor team member

Chris Riordan (Lieutenant Commander)—Navy SEAL

"Cardinal"—a spy who works with General Burnett

Collin Ramsey (General)—Commander of the Coalition Forces

Ddrake—Tactical Explosives Detector Dog

Desi Watters—Dean Watters's estranged sister

Donny Watters—Dean Watters's brother

Ellen Green (Specialist)—female soldier who was captured with Dean during the ambush ten years earlier

Sergeant Elliott—mentor to Dean; police officer and former Army Ranger (Vietnam)

Grant Knight (Sergeant)—Ddrake's handler

Hafizah Haidary—Zahrah's aunt and Fekeria Haidary's mother; has dark eyes

Ismail Sidiq (Colonel)—colonel in the Afghan National Army, Regional Command, North

Izzah Zarrick—Zahrah Zarrick's mother

Jahandar Haidary—Zahrah's uncle, father of Fekiria

Jahandar Peter Zarrick—Zahrah Zarrick's brother

Jeffrey Bain—American journalist

Mr. Kohistani—director of Kohistani School; older; has a long, graying beard; brown eyes; 5'5"

Razia Mustafa—Rashid and Ara's mother; not much older than Zahrah, married to Atash Mustafa

Sadri Ali—a known opium supplier

Sajjan Takkar/ "Variable"—an operative; a Sikh

SPECIAL FORCES PRAYER

Almighty GOD, Who art the Author of liberty
and the Champion of the oppressed, hear our prayer.

We, the men of Special Forces, acknowledge our dependence upon
Thee in the preservation of human freedom.

Go with us as we seek to defend the defenseless
and to free the enslaved.

May we ever remember that our nation, whose motto is "In God We
Trust," expects that we shall acquit ourselves with honor, that we may
never bring shame upon our faith, our families, or our fellow men.

Grant us wisdom from Thy mind, courage from Thine heart,
strength from Thine arm, and protection by Thine hand.

It is for Thee that we do battle, and to Thee belongs the victor's crown.

For Thine is the kingdom, and the power, and the glory, forever.
AMEN.

Written by SF Chaplain John Stevey,
the 7th SFG (ABN) Chaplain, 1961

CHAPTER 1

Present Day

Can't breathe. Can't breathe.

He sucked in a hard breath. Fabric drew against his nostrils. Hot. *Can't breathe.* No air! He thrashed, searching for freedom, for air. . . *I'm going to die!* At the thought, he jerked.

Where am I? A bounce smacked his head against something hard. Metal. Captain Dean Watters groaned. Opened his eyes. But couldn't see. The meaty rumble of an engine warned him he was in a vehicle. The tail of one by the roaring sound and steel digging into his shoulder. The way his breath coiled back at him told him he had a hood over his face. Mouth taped. Hands taped. Feet—he tested his leg—taped.

Get out or die! Dean kicked. Tendons strained against his effort.

Brakes squealed. Gravity shifted and tugged him. *Rounding a corner.* Again the engine roared.

Where are they taking me? Where's Z?

Recollection swarmed him in a thick cloud of defeat. She'd walked out. Willingly. He couldn't blame her. They'd been through the fires of hell and back since they were captured. The enemy had broken her. Gotten into her head and convinced her that helping them was the smart choice.

A sudden lurch made him slide.

Hands pawed at him as shouts erupted.

He was lifted. . . .

The truck bounced.

Gravity pulled him left again—another corner. The truck must've turned. Then spinning. . .

Still blind and bound, Dean felt himself flying. Through the air. Unrestrained. He tensed, no idea where he'd land. What he'd hit. Or in what. And he prayed—*begged*—God to let him live. He had to live. Had to find her.

Down. . .down. . .

Crack!

He landed with a thud. White-hot fire shot through his shoulder and arm. He groaned around the tape over his mouth. Shoved aside the pain, reoriented himself. Brightness speared his eyes. Specks of light glittered through the thick fabric. He scrambled to his knees, desperate to know where they'd dumped him.

A siren wailed.

Shouts.

He knew those sounds, the shouts. The base. His captors had thrown him at the gate of the base. Armed with that knowledge, he remained still. Anything to let those with the weapons know he wasn't a threat.

"Stay where you are! Hands in the air. Hands. In. The. Air!" The command came in English, Pashto, Dari, then Farsi.

Boots shuffled closer, along with more shouts to get his arms up. One service member came very close. It took everything in Dean not to move. One wrong twitch, and they'd put him down like a sick dog. A beam of light struck him. So much like the light torture.

The light vanished. "Dude's tied up." The voice was right over Dean. "Hold up."

"Careful," came another voice. "He could be rigged."

Right. Why hadn't Dean thought of that before? *Am I?* Mentally, he patted himself down but felt nothing strapped to him.

Whoosh!

Glaring white seared his corneas. He grimaced and ducked. Dean squinted rapidly, trying to force his eyes to readjust.

A Marine frowned at him as several others gathered around, business ends of their weapons aimed at Dean's head. The lead Marine pointed to the tape as if asking permission.

Dean nodded and his body swayed. He jerked straight. Then his body pulled him backward. Dizzy. . .so dizzy.

The Marine ripped off the tape.

After a moment of prickling fire, Dean stretched his jaw. "Watters. . ."

Breathe.

"He needs water!" a grunt shouted.

"No." Dean shook his head. Wet his lips, which tasted of salt and blood. "Watters, Dean. . . Patrick. . .captain." His vision was ghosting. "Four f–four—" His body surrendered.

CHAPTER 2

Undisclosed Location, Six Months Ago

Speed.

Surprise.

Violence of action.

The three principles necessary for successful engagement of an enemy in combat. Many times these three words carry through the grainy feed of the hidden camera. The men moving beneath the staticky image, unaware of the listening ear. Unaware of their vulnerability.

Their mission is not so different from mine, from those I fight for and with on a daily basis—to act without hesitation and with fierce action so the enemy can be caught unaware.

After verifying once more that the feed has gone live, I adjust the volume, punch the RECORD button, then settle back with my hot cup of tea to watch these elite special operators betray their every secret. Six men—only five in the room as of yet. I wait for their leader before putting on my headphones. The reception isn't the best in the sub-base command center, but I worked out all the kinks, navigating the complications and smoothly rerouting around their jamming technology. Still there is an annoying static hiss I'd prefer to go without for as long as I can.

They really should update their systems. Then. . .*then* they might have a chance. But the orders to cut spending—well, any tech-savvy person knows cybersecurity is one of the first things in budgets to get axed. That right along with breakfast. No more promise of three squares when these idealistic punks joined up.

The whole thing makes me laugh. Why would *any* country cut its defense budget? Were they really that arrogant? They are the only country dialing down their military armaments while the rest of the world is ramping up.

Another man enters the command center. "And cue the entertainment." I slip on my headphones and sip my tea. *Raptor Six himself.* Not real sure how he got that—Special Forces isn't known for using the six designation on team assignments. Must be a personal thing with our fearless leader. Either way, it feels stupid to me. I mean, they sound cool—Mercy Six. Rainbow Six. Halo Six. Whatever. The military and their numbers and acronyms. . .

"So. Raptor team." A guy with light brown, almost blond hair grins. He has this pretty-boy thing happening. Sort of reminds me of that guy who hunts demons with his brother on that one show. . .whatever it's called. "I like it. Chicks'll dig it."

That's Brian Bledsoe. Staff Sergeant. Now code-named Hawk—ha! Easy one to remember—Squawk Hawk. The guy quick with his tongue and his Glock. Not sure one could call him arrogant. He just isn't afraid to voice his opinions. Which are many.

Their team commander, Captain Dean Watters, glares at the younger Green Beret. That's something the team commander does quite well—glare. He isn't big on words, but the dude can put some serious action behind the few words he utters. I wouldn't want to meet him in a dark alley. Or any alley for that matter.

"This isn't about chicks." Sergeant First Class Salvatore "Falcon" Russo—the meanest guy on the team—snarls. All bark, but I'm not sure he has much of a bite. Must've had a bad childhood or something to be that grouchy all the time. But he is a top-notch soldier. Holds his own. Watches out for his team. I guess that makes him an asset. The team's Italian Stallion studies the documents on the table.

And with a twitch of this dial and a flick of that one, I zoom in and join them studying those documents. That's what I do after all—study what they study.

Ah. Readiness profiles. Good to know.

"We have to assume these identities, the new roles in moving out of being Green Berets, out of liaising with villagers and into black ops."

"It's not about us." Captain Watters leans forward, his fingertips pressing to the table. "This is about freedom, about securing innocent lives. Doing violence on their behalf."

Cue the American national anthem. Or should that be anathema? Aren't Americans pretty much *eating* their young back on their own soil?

"Think this is right?"

See? This guy I like—Sergeant First Class Mitchell Black. Which is weird—he's not black. He's as white as they come with some good ol' sun bronzing, compliments of the Afghan deserts. They're calling him Hairier. Wait. Scratch that. Harrier. Birds of prey. Not hairy men—even though his thick, light brown hair is longer than most of the guys on the team. But look at him—picture of calm assurance sitting in a chair, his elbows on the table as he takes in the documents. You wouldn't guess that since the guy had only joined the team in the last six months. Next to the captain, I think this guy could be the biggest threat. What's the phrase—*it's the quiet ones*?

"I mean, can we do this?" Black looks at the others. "Can we shift our specialties and work on a level we've never fully executed before?"

"We have," Russo says as he folds his arms over his chest. "We did it with the MWDs and handlers."

I grab my pen and scratch out a note to self: *Research MWDs.*

"Harrier wasn't with us then," Hawk says. "They stole one of our best guys out from under us." Bledsoe huffs as he drops into a squeaky office chair. I think the dude could bench-press an oil tanker if he tried with the way his muscles tear at the desert-camo sleeves.

"No, terrorists did that"—Captain Watters the purist, the patriot—"when they blew his leg off."

"Yeah," Bledsoe says. "And that's when they saddled us with the Aussie newb."

"Oy, mate."

Laughing loud doesn't alert anyone to my presence, and that makes me laugh louder. Bledsoe is not afraid of anyone. And Aussie—I grab my notebook and flip back a few pages and find his name: Eamon "Titanis" Straider—is nobody to sneeze at. They call him newb mostly because he's not American. That guy is as tough and rugged as they come. I mean, check out the black high and tight. Strong jaw and eyes that don't miss a thing. He's a close equal to the captain, but I'm not quite sure he's there yet. Still, nobody in his right mind would refer to Australian Special Air Services corporal as "newb" to his face. Except Bledsoe.

Lifting my cup of tea toward the staticky screen where Bledsoe stands tall at six foot, I toast him. "Your funeral, not mine."

"Mate, I'm not your enemy." Ferocity laces the words of the Aussie, who'd received two Victoria Cross medals. Three if you count the one inked over his left pec—not that I've seen it myself, but that's what his dossier says. That Oz native is as hardcore as they come.

"There is opportunity here," Straider goes on. "To act swiftly and do justice. You're a fierce fighter. Focus that energy on the combatants, Bledsoe. Not on me."

Electric tension crackles through the command center and the static—but only I notice that part.

Because it's a feed.

Nobody hears the feed. Except me. . .cuz I'm here in this tin can of a trailer.

Bledsoe comes to his feet. "I don't take orders from you, newb."

"Oh. Oh!" I lean forward and set aside my tea. The two are ready to go to blows. A match, right here on Sub-base Command Live Feed? Be still my beating heart!

"Enough." Watters saves the day. Again. And makes my duty here boring. Again. "Straider's right."

"Why is he here anyway?" Bledsoe asks. "We were fine on our own."

"Were you?" Straider hasn't earned his nation's respect and devotion by being afraid of confrontation. And he clearly isn't going to start today.

"Come on, c'mon." With a fake left cross, I beg them to duke it out. "Give him a what-for, Straider. Level the guy. Teach him a lesson."

"Do you want to run through the AAR with me on that?"

Watters straightens, his shoulders squaring as he plants his hands on his tactical belt. "Look. This is a change, but it's right up our alley. Right where we were headed. We've been in field long enough to know what needs to be done. It's second nature."

With a huff, I slump back in my chair. Disappointing. They always have to be so civil. Rules of engagement and all that. Well, Raptor team needs to hang up their raptor wings. Playing fair wouldn't bring a win. It'd bring death.

I smirk. "I'll make sure of it."

CHAPTER 3

Balkh Province, Afghanistan
01 May—1423 Hours

Bloody and angry, the sun dipped into the horizon, overtaken by the darkening day. Crimson clouds stretched their long, thin arms over the village. Dean shifted, staring down the optical of his M4 Carbine at the huddle of tents peppering the rugged landscape. Years of fighting scarred the land and its people. Evidence of the 115-degree heat warbled around the structure pocked from withering heat and bullet holes.

Grape huts.

Dean resisted the old urge to curse. Had to be a grape hut—a structure made of mud and stone. Even worse, complicating matters—the back had been built on to. Intel stated hostile combatants held Raptor's objective there. An American journalist. The killer was the two-foot thick walls with narrow slits. Perfect for snipers.

Raptor team had a sniper, too, but if they didn't proceed with extreme caution, they'd get picked off like vultures. Two hours in position and they'd verified location, number of hostiles, and likelihood of taking fire: 100 percent.

Sweat dropped into Dean's eyes as he peered through his reticle, tracing the scraggly trees and shrubs. Then back to their target location. "Colonel, what do you think?"

Colonel Ismail Sidiq of the Afghan National Army's Regional Command, North peered through binoculars. "Definitely *mujahideen*." The curl of the man's lip could be heard in the way he spat his response. "A thorn in my side, Captain Dean."

That the muj were Islamic fighters, many of whom the U.S. would declare terrorists, Dean didn't need the colonel to tell him. He'd had one encounter too many with the vicious fighters. "Think they have our package?" That was the question—had they tracked the right group of muj?

"Yes." Rocks crunched against dirt where Sidiq lay. "There is Azzam."

Dean lifted the thermals from his pack. Seeing Azzam, a fierce muj fighter, was yet another confirmation they were in the right place.

"That middle hut. See the blue pakol? That is him."

Scanning the unique hats, Dean pinned down the position. Staring through the sight, he eyed the grape hut again. Six or seven muj loitered near the door, one visible only by a leg that stretched into the light. One propped against the retaining wall. Two reclined on the ground, legs crossed. Another in a chair.

They'd seen two others enter the structure twenty minutes earlier. "You're sure?"

"Absolutely."

Dean had to ask. It wasn't that he didn't trust the Afghan native. He needed to make sure the colonel understood what they were about to unleash on this campsite and people. Death. If he had any doubts, now would be a great time for the colonel to speak up.

Dean looked to his left. "Let's do it."

Falcon gave a sharp nod. As team sergeant—or "team daddy"—he held a fierce dedication to ensuring the safety and protection of the team. He'd led the team, inspired them, on those missions when Dean had to liaise with the brass.

Dean keyed his mic. "Mockingbird," he said in a low tone, "this is Raptor Six Actual. Do you read?"

"Raptor Six Actual, this is Mockingbird," came a tight, controlled female voice through the radio. "I read you loud and clear. Over."

"We are in position, targets sighted."

"Copy that, Raptor Six. We have you on Halo Three, over."

A weird buzz flickered down the back of Dean's neck. Being watched from thirty-thousand feet—and knowing they could see the pakols just as clearly—would unnerve most men. For him, it meant an added layer of insurance. And that's where the payload would launch from.

"The eyes that see but don't get seen," Falcon said with a toothy grin.

"Glory One, this is Raptor Six Actual." Dean spoke to the Black Hawk that should've left Camp Marmal and headed their way by now. "What's your ETA for extraction? Over."

"One-four minutes. I repeat, one-four minutes. Over."

"Start the extraction on my mark." Dean pressed a fingered glove against his watch. "Three...two...one, mark."

"Mark. See you in one-four, Raptor Six Actual. Over."

"Okay, let's move." Dean glanced over his shoulder to Eagle, their weapons expert and, at thirty-four, the oldest member of Raptor. An irony that never lost its humor on Dean since the guy had him by a mere four years. "Eagle, paint that truck," he said, thumbing down the slope toward the rusted-out vehicle beside the hut where the pakols bobbed in and around buildings. "Once we're clear, call it."

Shoulder supporting the stock of his M24 Sniper Weapons System with its Leupold scope, Eagle gave a firm nod. "Roger, Captain." Protective Oakleys shielded eyes that Dean had come to read like words on an after-action review. A reddish-blond beard could not hide his set jaw.

After slapping Eagle's shoulder, Dean pushed up and skirted the ridge they'd taken cover behind. With Raptor team and the colonel's half-dozen ANA soldiers, Dean had a small army with which to snatch back the American journalist held for ransom.

Light seeped from the sky, yielding its power to the stars as their team descended with stealth. Adrenaline heated his gut and back as he inched closer. Sounds roared though only a whisper. The thud and crunch of boots seemed to shout. Crazy since the sound should be indecipherable with the wind and din coming from the camp.

As the steep path gave way to a small knoll, Dean went to a knee and held up a fist. Carbine at the ready, he eased his head to the side, exposing his face only as much as necessary, to peer around the lip of a rocky edifice. He scanned the mujahideen. Still talking. Laughing.

Clock ticking, Dean lowered his chin toward the stock, taking a bead on the closest fighter. He signaled the colonel to the other side and forward. As the team followed the colonel, Dean covered.

Adrenaline jacked, danger breathing down his neck, Dean never felt more alive.

Once the team was clear, he rushed left to join them. Bound and cover. Lather. Rinse. Repeat. With two fingers, he sent Harrier forward. Dean covered his six, walking backward, knowing they covered the front.

A shout stabbed the thick air.

Dean swung right.

Wide brown eyes bulged.

A hand clamped around the man's mouth as steel glinted. Blood chased the blade in a broad stroke along his neck. He breathed his last and crumpled back against an ANA soldier, who lowered the dead fighter to the ground.

Dean puffed out a stale breath—the one that could've been *his* last had it not been for Sidiq's soldier. Dean nodded his thanks then rushed around the corner.

"Captain, you have trouble."

Eagle's words held him fast. Dean waited, tension knotting at the warning. Trouble. And he stood within line of sight on the hut.

"Fighters pouring out of a tunnel a hundred yards to your seven."

Dean keyed his mic and whispered, "Copy." His gaze struck Falcon, who'd stepped into the role of his team sergeant when Candyman lost part of his leg in an ambush last year. Was that happening again—an ambush?

Falcon lifted a flash-bang from his vest.

Dean nodded.

After he plucked the rings, Falcon nodded his readiness.

To his left, kneeling behind some brush, Harrier stood ready with another canister. Dean lifted his own. After a quick check of the remaining men under his command to ensure they were prepared, Dean mouthed, *One. . .two. . .go!*

Leaning back, Falcon flung the flash-bang through a window.

Harrier lobbed one to the other side.

Screams knifed the merriment. Shouts. Thuds of boots.

The door flung back.

Dean rolled his flash-bang right under the gap in the makeshift door. He spotted another fighter just outside the threshold.

Boom! Crack!

Light flashed through the camp.

Boom!

Smoke and gas plumed through the air, dancing in victory. Panicked mujahideen bolted, tripped over their own feet. Clapped hands over their eyes. Screamed. Stumbled on top of each other. Fell. Coughed.

He counted. Worked it in with the recon they'd done. That hut should now be empty.

ANA fighters offered suppressive fire as Raptor whipped into the open, fast and furious. Dean locked on to his goal: retrieve the objective. He rushed toward the hut. He stepped in, a vacuum of darkness and haze swallowing him as he swept his raised weapon along the corners and shadows.

"Clear," he called into his coms as he hurried forward to the rear room. There, he shouted, "U.S. military! Jeff Bain. Jeff Bain!"

A man sat bound in a chair, coughing. "Here. . ." Gagging. The sound was wet, soft.

Dean took a knee beside Bain, who hauled in a greedy breath of oxygen.

Hawk appeared at the man's side and knelt, going to work with his combat medic skills. Darkness hid a lot, including the man's less-visible injuries, but no chances would be taken.

"Mr. Bain," Dean said. "We're getting you out of here, but I need to verify your identity."

The hostage nodded, his chin banging his chest as he coughed.

Dean used his KA-BAR to cut loose the cables. "Can you tell me the name of the first paper you worked for, Mr. Bain?"

"Star News." The cords slumped to the ground.

Dean worked the leg ties. "What is the name of your sister's dog, sir?"

"Diamond." His voice was stronger, even beneath the muffling of the mask.

"Let's get you home, Mr. Bain." Dean gripped the man's bicep and helped him to his feet.

Bain stumbled.

Harrier hooked an arm around the man's waist and hoisted him onto his toes. Air ripped a hot trail past Dean. The tiny explosion in the wall registered just as he felt the primal scream of the bullet. Felt another year of his life shave off. Directly in front of them, Falcon covered their egress.

They slipped out the front and to the right, hustling Bain away, his feet barely touching the ground. Thunder roared in the distance. The helos were closing in. It felt like hours had passed since leaving the relative safety of the ridge with his team and the ANA.

Bain went limp.

"His heart's weak," Harrier shouted.

"He'll make it," Dean said through clenched teeth. Sweat poured down his back, neck, and temples. *We'll make it. We better.* "Not losing my life for a journalist." Even one who'd spent weeks as a hostage. Having been in the man's shoes, Dean had more sympathy for him than he probably would've for a nosy journo.

"You and me both," Hawk said, as he and Falcon took Bain.

They escaped the small cluster and rushed to a small slope. Dean keyed his mic as they half dragged Bain to safety, to the extraction point. "Mockingbird, this is Raptor Six Actual, we have the package. En route to extraction."

Hawk and Falcon kept moving with their objective.

"Copy that, Raptor Six. Glory One is relieving herself."

On a knee, Dean stared back at the small encampment and village as shapes emerged—the rest of ODA452 and four of the ANA soldiers. He stilled. Shadows flitted and danced beneath flames in the village. Puffs darkened. Wait. . . *Too many.*

Dean snatched his Beretta and took aim as his men slid to cover beside him.

A fighter lunged into the open with a spray of bullets.

Another came from the right. Dean twisted and angled, firing as the scene went hot again.

"Wanna tell your friends to back off?" Hawk shouted, providing additional cover fire as the team raced for safety. "We already won this fight."

"My friends?" Dean growled past a smile as the crackling and popping of weapon fire was drowned by the inbound chopper. "Don't you remember?"

"That's right," Hawk yelled over the rotor wash as Harrier moved in and applied a butterfly stitch to the journalist's temple. "You don't have any."

"If the Army thought I needed friends—"

"They'd have issued them. Yeah, I know."

Dean shot a glance to the Black Hawk as the wheels touched down. He stepped aside as two Marines jogged over, loaded Bain onto a litter, then hurried him back to the bird. Trailing them, Dean climbed into the jump seat and let out thick breath. Boots skimming the warm Afghan air as they sped back to the base, he eyed the horizon. They'd retrieved the objective. His men were alive and uninjured. The ANA's team was with them, though a couple now sported extra holes. Another mission.

Another deadly mission. Another deadly *successful* mission.
So why do I feel empty?

—⁓—

Kohistani School, Mazar-e-Sharif, Afghanistan
25 May—0845 Hours

"Assalaam alaikum."

Zahrah Zarrick looked up from her laptop. *"Wa 'alaikum assalaam."* She shook her head at her cousin easing into the room. "You know he was only flirting with you."

With a cheeky smile, Fekiria Haidary giggled. "Oh, I'm aware." Her green-brown eyes sparkled. Then she wrinkled her nose. "He's too old."

"Your *madar* would not agree."

With a groan, Fekiria dropped into the chair beside her. "You must rescue me."

Another laugh nearly choked Zahrah. "Me? You're the one who insisted it was good to marry a man established in the community."

"Yes, established but not with ten grandchildren!"

Zahrah could not help but smile. She adored her cousin, even with her *laaf*. Exaggeration was a way of life here in Afghanistan, and her cousin heaped hers in mounds. Zahrah, on the other hand, was too sensible and too Western to let her family decide who she would marry. But she also respected her *kaka* and *khala* enough not to interfere with their customs. "He has *one*," she corrected her cousin.

"The man I marry should not have any! I am only twenty-one." Fekiria moaned. "Why can't I draw the attention of American soldiers like you? I served in the ANA and have just as much strength as you do!"

The words pushed Zahrah's gaze down and filled her cheeks with heat. She turned and lifted the math books from the shelf, using the move to hide her embarrassment. But it was true—speaking English as fluently and clearly as she did Pashto and Farsi ingratiated her with the American military, who had used her as an interpreter. "Your parents would never approve—and they didn't approve of your being in the army."

"I am well aware, but that has nothing to do with marrying a grandfather!"

"Fekiria, in this, I think you won't begrudge my American up-bringing, yes?"

She pouted as her gaze traipsed the small classroom. "I like our customs. They have worked for thousands of years. . . ."

A deep quiet settled in as Zahrah laid out the workbooks for the students who would return after their lunch break and the *zuhr*. Though she loved the mode the *muezzin* used for the noon *namaz*, she ached for her mother's people to know Isa—Jesus.

Silence gaped, drawing her attention back to her cousin. Fekiria never sat still. Never stayed quiet. In fact, a weight seemed to settle on the face framed in a vibrant teal polyester/cotton *hijab*. "What?"

Fekiria blinked and straightened in the chair. A weak smile flickered across the beautiful lips that Zahrah had often envied for their natural pink hue and fullness. "Nothing." She pushed to her feet and went to the window, where a dingy, striped, cotton curtain vainly attempted to shield the classroom from the sun. With two fingers Fekiria tugged aside the material.

Laughter pealed through the day, bringing joy to Zahrah's heart that matched what she heard from the children. So good to hear them laughing and playing. Not screaming. She shuddered as the memory of the attack two weeks ago stomped her mood. Only then did she also notice the merriment in the courtyard warred with Fekiria's expression.

Zahrah went to her cousin and touched her shoulder. "You wear the weight of the world. What's wrong?"

Though Fekiria softened beneath the words, she did not look at her. Finally, she sighed. "You came here—why?"

Zahrah frowned. "You know why—what my madar went through when they moved to America. . ." She shook her head and watched the boys playing soccer in the courtyard and the girls huddled to one side. Her mother had done the same thing, but not just around other kids—she huddled in life. Feeling alone, isolated, and excluded because she did not speak English, did not dress like Americans, and was poor, her mother had become a virtual recluse. "I never want anyone to experience what she went through. If I can help just one. . ." Saying the words reinfused her with determination. "Why are you asking?"

Shoulders slumped, mouth pouting, Fekiria sighed again. "I feel lost, Zahrah jan."

She still loved the endearments used in Pashtun and other Arab cultures. "Lost? How?"

Her cousin had lived in Balkh Province her entire life. Though

Fekiria's father had wanted to leave with his father and sister—Zahrah's mother—his ties to Afghanistan were too strong. A prodigy in science, Jahandar Haidary had been scouted by Afghanistan right out of secondary school. When Zahrah's grandfather escaped to America, Kaka Jahandar stayed behind for two reasons: fear of being captured and his love for the woman who would become his wife.

Shouts arose from the courtyard, and Fekiria stood straighter. "They're back."

Zahrah flicked her gaze to the school's front gate. Her simple lunch of hummus and vegetables curdled in her stomach at the sight of a military armored vehicle lumbering into the yard, followed by a canopy truck. "What are they bringing in here?"

As the vehicles glided by, Zahrah and Fekiria tucked themselves aside to avoid being seen. Once the diesel sounds rumbled past, Zahrah again peered through the curtain as the vehicles vanished into the old gym. Doors slid open and the gymnasium swallowed the vehicles.

"I don't know." Fekiria eyed her. "Think we should go see?"

"Are you out of your mind?" Zahrah shook her head. "No, we need to stay right here. No need drawing attention to ourselves."

"Must you always play it safe?"

"If we are killed or sent away, who will watch the children? Who will teach the girls?"

"But if we let them bring trouble to the school, they put the lives of everyone in danger—that includes you, Zahrah. And me!" Fire lit through her cousin's eyes. "I'm going to see what I can find out."

"Fekiria!" Her hissed admonishment fell flat in her cousin's wake. With a huff, Zahrah turned back to the window. She slid a hand along the long gray tunic of her perahan tunban then placed that hand on her stomach. She willed herself to have nerves of steel like her cousin.

After pushing herself out the door, she looked both ways down the short hall. The corridor seemed ominous with its dirty walls, cracking paint, and crumbling plaster. She went right, toward the main entrance.

A wall of flesh rammed into her. Hands held her.

Zahrah jerked back with a gasp, wresting from the man's hold. *"Zeh mutaasif yum!"* As her apology hung between them, her gaze hit his for a brief second, but it was enough to stab an icy feeling down her spine. "Sorry." She dropped her gaze, sensing his strong disapproval for looking at and speaking to him.

As he and a group of other men stalked into the sunshine, Zahrah worked to steady her breathing. Who was *he*? She hadn't seen him before. Too old to be a student. Another teacher? God forbid a man like that should teach children.

Only then did she notice the door Director Kohistani had insisted remain barred stood ajar. As she considered it, two more men emerged. Their fierce expressions urged her back.

The men breezed past. A shoulder hit hers—intentionally, she was sure. Her heart hammered, fear a familiar friend in recent days. Most Afghan men were kind and just like any other men, but a few made her want to flee back to America.

Shaken, she turned and walked after them into the courtyard to look for her cousin. *Father, I know You're with me wherever I go. . . .* The silent prayer stirred peace in the recesses of her soul. Playing it safe, cool, she strode to where she'd seen Fekiria disappear.

"Miss Zarrick! Miss Zarrick!"

The shout jolted her. She glanced back.

Eight-year-old Rashid waved as he hurried out of the building—but just as fast, a hand clamped on his shoulder. Hauled him back, Rashid's legs kicking up as his eyes widened. The tall man from the hall held Rashid against him, his tan *chapan* a sharp contrast to Rashid's blue.

Zahrah's heart plummeted.

"Who is this woman, boy?"

Rashid yanked away from the man, scowling. "My sister's teacher." He rubbed his shoulder and started for Zahrah.

The man's gaze drifted purposefully to the gym-cum-warehouse. "Tell the teacher to keep to her books and students." Then to Rashid. "If she values those she teaches."

His threat hung in the air. Zahrah scooted the boy around her. At the same time the man spewed more hatred, a melody and sage voice smothered those words. Afternoon namaz.

Thank You, Lord.

Swallowing hard, Zahrah bent to Rashid as the call to prayer sounded across Mazar-e. In her periphery, she saw the man stomp back into the building. She drew in a shaky breath and patted Rashid. "You should go to prayers."

"But I saw them, Miss Zarrick."

"I know. I saw the men, too."

"No! Not them."

She frowned. "Who?"

"American soldiers. In the hills."

The beautiful mode used by the muezzin carried heavily across the city as it fell quiet, for the most part. As the zuhr began, Zahrah remained still and respectful of those who held to the Islamic traditions.

"Hurry." She managed a smile. "To namaz before Director Kohistani notices you missing."

"But the soldiers—"

"Are doing their job." She touched the side of his face. "You must do yours now." She gave him a nod. "Go. We'll talk later." As he darted off, Zahrah straightened, threaded her fingers in front of her kaftan, and looked toward the sloping rise of earth.

"I will lift up my eyes to the hills—From whence comes my help? My help comes from the LORD, Who made heaven and earth."

If the soldiers were close, in the hills, then that meant. . .

Zahrah looked back toward the gymnasium, mentally considering the vehicles. The strange men. "Trouble's closer."

CHAPTER 4

Sub-base Schwarzburg, Camp Marmal
Mazar-e Sharif, Balkh Province, Afghanistan
27 May—1045 Hours

Go in early—break up your routine to avoid an ambush."

Palms on either side of the laptop, Dean looked down at the monitor that held the grim visage of General Lance Burnett. The live feed between the Pentagon and Northern Afghanistan came through surprisingly sharp. Had the man's gray hair gone *grayer*? They'd been through a lot in the last three years of working together. Dean guessed he probably had a few grays already, too.

Dean gave a slow nod, but something about the way the general said that made his nerves jounce. "Something we need to know, General?"

"Yeah," Hawk said, chomping into a muffin then talking around it. "That sounds a lot like, 'We know something you don't know.'"

"Like talking with your mouth full is rude?" Harrier shot back.

"And disgusting." Falcon eased into view of the camera. "General, if there's trouble—"

"You're in the middle of a war zone, Sergeant—of course there's trouble!"

Falcon straightened and shifted aside.

"Look, there's nothing we can put our finger on. But I have too much invested in your team to lose any of you." General Burnett slurped a soda and slammed down the can. "Now, get your sorry carcasses out there. Early."

"Yes, sir." The connection canceled and Dean nodded to his team. "You heard the man."

It took an hour to gear up and get the appropriate supplies for Harrier to work his medic magic in the village. Another thirty minutes spent rumbling over the brutal Afghan terrain and toward the village that hunkered at the foot of the mountain, east of the bustling Mazar-e

Sharif and west of nowhere. The village had just come into sight when Falcon eyed him from the driver's seat. "You feelin' it?"

"Every day."

"Right?" Falcon cut right around a hut with a burned-out roof and carried the team down the main street—"paved" with dirt pounded into a hard surface by years of foot traffic, beasts of burden, and vehicles.

Dean's mind buzzed with the unspoken warning Burnett had given by suggesting an early ETA. They'd been working with the villagers to provide medical care for the last several months. Alternating arrival times to avoid stepping into a pile of trouble. But for Burnett to suggest it—well that *suggested* anticipated danger.

Stretching his jaw, Dean scratched his beard. Just another few weeks and he'd shave it for his leave Stateside. Mrs. Elliott didn't like beards. But then, she didn't like that she now stood nearly a foot shorter than the young man her husband had taken under his wing. He smiled, remembering her taunts and teasing, but mostly—her love and prayers for him.

"Thought we'd stroll into Mazar-e on our way back."

Dean snapped his attention back to the Falcon. "What?"

"Hooah!" Hawk shouted from the back. "Get me some girls!"

Dean would scowl at the live wire, but it'd only fuel the fire. He thumbed toward Hawk. "That'd be a bad idea, unleashing him on an unsuspecting city."

"Need to get him one of those choke collars," Harrier put in.

Laughter trickled through the mine-resistant ambush-protected vehicle.

"Hey." Titanis eased forward, stabbing a finger toward the front, between Dean and Falcon.

Dean squinted past the glare the sun cast against the tan paint to see what the Aussie indicated. "What?"

"Trucks. I just saw trucks."

He shot a questioning look at his engineering sergeant. "You sure?"

"I know what a truck looks like, Commander."

Relatively new to Raptor, Titanis didn't have the casual comfort Dean had with the other members of the team. But his intensity, his penchant toward perfection and accuracy, brought a much-needed element to the team since losing Candyman.

"Pull over." Dean pointed to a street two blocks north of where the team normally conducted the clinics. "Eyes out." With that, he climbed out into the sun-drenched afternoon, lifting his M4 from the strap and cradling it as he scanned the street.

"Anything?" Falcon asked.

Tracing the buildings' walls, doors, shadows, Dean didn't detect a threat. But he also couldn't ward off the foreboding sense prickling the hairs on the back of his neck. "Nice and easy," he said as he walked the narrow road.

"This sucks." Hawk walked a cautious but steady pace.

"Quiet." Dean advanced, taking everything in. But that was just it. The streets should be filling with people heading to the clinic. Instead, only dust and dirt clogged the streets.

"I should be a half mile out and a dozen feet up." Broad-chested and well built, the team sniper seemed tense. More so than usual. Then again, Eagle always preferred higher ground and laying prostrate with his sniper rifle. But the threat level didn't warrant that. "You know what. . ." Eagle slung his carbine around to his back and turned down an alley. He hoisted himself up onto a wall and reached for a rooftop ledge.

"Cover him," Dean said.

Titanis and Harrier took up positions as Eagle climbed.

A teen rounded the corner, not six feet from Hawk. The teen's eyes widened and he sucked in a breath. Spun. And sprinted.

"He's running," Hawk growled. He glanced to Dean. "Why's he running?" With that, Hawk lurched into a sprint.

To warn someone!

Dean joined the chase. "Stop him!" Behind him, he heard the pounding boots of Falcon, who darted past him despite the seventy-five-pound gear strapped to his back.

"Eagle, you got eyes on our boy?" Dean keyed his mic, rushing forward, eyes and brain processing every shadow and movement.

"Roger that."

"Where's he headed?"

Seconds pounded off the clock. Dean took a corner. Down the main alley that led to the "community center," which was simply a cement-block building erected by the team. One more turn and he'd have it in view. "Eagle!"

"Taking fire! Taking fire!" Falcon shouted through the coms.

A heartbeat too late.

Dean rounded a corner. The world blurred into slow motion. He saw it—a dozen or more fighters had taken position around the truck. M16s, AK-47s, handguns spewing bullets. Hawk and Falcon on the ground, returning fire at a cluster of three trucks parked in front of the building they'd used for a clinic.

Dean skidded to a stop. His boot slid on the dirt. Out from under him. He landed. Hard. Pain jolted through his backside. Shots pelted the wall. The small structure to his right seemed to spit dirt and cement at him. He palmed it, trying to gain traction and backpedal.

Dean rolled out of sight and pressed his spine against the cement brick wall. "Eagle, I need me some eyes in the sky."

"Roger. Two dozen men. Loading up. In a hurry. Armed."

No joke. "Locations!"

Hawk scrambled for cover with him. Lifting his arm that exposed a gleam of red on his sleeve, he glowered.

"Can we take them?" Dean asked.

Falcon dove into them. Together with Hawk, Dean dragged him the rest of the way to safety.

Hawk slammed a grenade into the tube. "Yeah." Now Hawk's grin seemed greedy.

Gears ground. Axles groaned.

"They're leaving." The tight, controlled voice betrayed nothing to the uninitiated. To the initiated—like Dean—Eagle was ticked.

Trucks lurched.

"Not on my watch," Hawk ground out.

Dean peeked around the corner.

Cement smacked him back.

He nodded to Hawk. "Do it!"

Angling his M4 around, Hawk took a bead on the first truck. Fired a grenade through the launcher.

It struck the engine. A fireball erupted. Men poured out like ants from a doused anthill. Dean watched, confused. But just as quick, the men climbed into the other trucks that sped away. He started forward.

Bullets ate up the ground.

He threw himself against another building, one closer. Keyed his mic to ask Eagle to level the playing field. As if a blanket had dropped over the village, quiet reigned. Dean cautiously waited. He circled a finger in the air, giving the signal for the team to group up.

They treaded the road, hugging buildings so they didn't get turned into Swiss cheese approaching the truck.

Sidling up, Dean waited for the others. Falcon angled out in the open, ready to neutralize any threat. Hawk took a knee, watching their six. Sweeping around, Falcon came to the side. Nodded to Dean then yanked back the flap.

Heart in his throat, Dean snapped his sights into the back. A breath whooshed out. Nothing. No one. "Clear." He moved with purpose and precision toward the cab of the truck.

The door hung open.

Falcon shook his head, anger fueling in his dark eyes. "Clear."

Dean turned back to where the street funneled down the hill. He looked in the direction of their team sniper. "Eagle, you got anything?"

"Negative."

"What the heck was that about?" Hawk might as well stomp his feet. "I got shot for. . .what?"

"Raptor, someone's in the building."

The words were a swift kick in the chest. Dean flanked the door with Falcon and Hawk, who lost his mouthy objections in the heat of another potential conflict. Falcon took point kneeling at the door, gloved hand on the rusted knob.

Adrenaline rushes never got old. Dean gave a nod.

Falcon flicked the knob and threw back the door.

Dean hurried over the threshold and went left, pieing out with his carbine as he moved. The room sat open and empty, save the bank of tables used by the team to line up those in need. A curtained-off area served as examination rooms and surgical area, though only outpatient surgeries took place here. As he swept back toward the door, cheek pressed to his weapon, he waited till his line of sight struck Falcon's on the right.

Hawk streamed through them, making a line straight for the curtained area.

As he trailed his coms guy, Dean noted the stacks of papers on the table. Kept moving. Expecting. Ready.

"Get down! Get down!" Hawk shouted, his weapon trained on someone.

Dean hurried forward. A man—no, the teen who'd sprinted away from the team—went to his knees, hands up. "Please. . .I not bad." Tears spilled down the youth's dirty cheeks.

"Why'd you run?' Hawk demanded in Pashto.

"They pay me to watch." The teen ducked, shame ringing his dark, dusty features.

Hawk cursed.

"Get him up and find out what he knows." Dean pivoted and returned to the table. Boxes of papers. . .wait. . .no. There were spiral-bound documents on the table, but the box. . . He tugged back the flap.

"Oh God, help us."

CHAPTER 5

Mazar-e-Sharif
27 May—1245 Hours

Mockingbird, this is Raptor Six Actual." Swiping a hand over his beard did nothing to stave off the doom planting itself on Dean's shoulders as he held the secure sat phone to his ear.

"Go ahead, Raptor Six." General Burnett's voice boomed through his coms. It meant one thing that he answered and not Hastings: Burnett *expected* trouble.

"Your warning paid off. There were armed Taliban here. They had trucks and men."

"No surprise."

Frustration strangled Dean. "No, sir. But what I found is." He stared at the box again.

"Go on."

"A SCIF-in-a-box, sir."

Burnett huffed. A loud thud carried through the connection. "How in the name of all that's holy did they get one of our secure computers?"

"No idea, sir. But it's here." Dean flipped open one of the spirals. "And they have manuals." He thumbed through it. "Pages are missing, but it's pretty close."

"Get it back to the base. Wait for me there. Show nobody—and I mean *no one*. Am I clear, Captain?"

"Yessir." Dean stuffed the phone into his pocket and velcroed it. "Move out."

"Hold up," Hawk said as thumbed over his shoulder. "The clinic."

"Not this week."

Lips tight, Hawk cocked his head. "Hey, man. These people can't control when terrorists get stupid. The villagers need medical attention."

"Harrier will have to play Florence Nightingale's brother next week. General ordered us back to Bagram."

Hawk held up his hands. "Give us an hour."

Dean let out a huff. Noticed the people gathering at the clinic. "Eagle, Falcon, bring the MRAP." He slapped Harrier's chest. "One hour."

Kohistani School, Mazar-e Sharif
27 May—1345 Hours

Clouds broke away from the sun, throwing sunbeams across the hard floor. In silence, the young girls worked on their handwriting, heads bowed over their papers. Three to a desk seemed cramped by American standards, but the Afghan girls in her class were so happy to attend school without fear of reprisal that the proximity to their classmates didn't bother them.

Zahrah walked the room, fingers threaded in front of her as she made her rounds. She touched a paper and admonished one student to watch her spacing. Writing English was as important as speaking it.

Back at the front, she folded her arms and glanced at the clock. "Thank you, children. Pass your papers to the front. Remember your reports on your favorite person are due tomorrow." She accepted the papers from the students on the end and then smiled. Her heart thumped in heady pleasure. Teaching these girls, assuring they could communicate effectively—her dream had come true! "Thank you. Have a good evening, and may God bless you." She'd gotten away with the blessing because *God* could be interpreted many ways. In her heart, she knew whom she meant.

The girls thanked her in unison then filed from the room. Zahrah turned to her satchel and slipped the stack of papers in, alongside math worksheets. When she turned, she stilled. And smiled inwardly. She would not let the little girl know she was on to her. "Ready for tutoring, Ara?"

The doe-eyed child sighed. "Yes, Miss Zarrick."

Zahrah moved to the bench seat in front of Ara's desk. "Okay, let's go over the lesson one more time." She shifted to sit beside the girl, being sure her voice carried well enough to the door and hallway where she knew the girl's older brother listened—learned. He'd been too proud to accept teaching and instruction from a woman, let alone an American woman. Yet he was here. Hungry to learn.

As they reviewed the lesson, Ara hooked a hand around Zahrah's arm and rested her temple on her shoulder.

The comfort and the warmth of her touch sailed through Zahrah. With the strict rules about touching and the pressure to maintain propriety here, she ached for the strong, bosomy embrace of her mother. But for now, Ara's light sign of affection would do.

As Ara finished reading the short story on the page—without complication—she smiled up at Zahrah. "He is too afraid to ask for your help."

"I am not!"

Zahrah tucked her chin to hide her smile as Ara's older brother stepped into view. Finally straight-faced, she acknowledged him. "Ah, Rashid. Ara is ready for home now. *Bia*." She stood as she motioned him to come to her. She went to her satchel and tugged out a small folder then walked to the eight-year-old boy. "Could you be sure Ara practices this?" She nodded at the seven-year-old girl, buying Ara's cooperation. "Apparently she needs the help."

Rashid's shoulders straightened. "Of course."

"Oh, such fine manners, Rashid—and such good English. I'm very proud of your progress."

Ara strutted to the doorway. "Madar said I'm doing better."

"Quiet!" Rashid said, his face betraying the hurt.

"You're both learning so quickly." Pride thrummed through Zahrah at the young boy's hidden attempts to become proficient in English. "Good-bye. I'll see you tomorrow." If she did not know better, she believed Rashid held American soldiers in very high regard, too. Though his father was in the ANA, it still was taboo here for Rashid to take instruction from a female.

As she watched the two slip down the hall and into the foyer, Zahrah spotted her cousin coming toward her.

"Ready?" Fekiria said as she smiled at the two youngsters. "Secret lessons again?"

Zahrah laughed as she retrieved her satchel. "He is so anxious to learn, to speak and write English. It just makes my heart break that his father won't allow it."

"It is true for most men."

"I understand their fears, but they're unfounded."

Fekiria groaned. "We've been over this a thousand times."

As they passed under the iron walk-through gate and onto the city streets toward the home they shared with Fekiria's parents, Zahrah smiled. At times, it was hard to remember Fekiria with her wild ways and desperation for liberation was also profoundly protective of her heritage.

"You're right." In an easy lope, Zahrah linked arms with her cousin. "Have you told your parents that you do not want to marry Yakta?"

Suspicious eyes skidded into Zahrah, then focused ahead. "No."

"Why?" Zahrah straightened and tugged a small bag of figs from her satchel. "And this isn't me making comment against your home or life. This is me caring about my cousin-sister."

"They will be so angry."

"But they love you. And I believe that is more important to them than marrying you off."

"Ha! My father is ready to marry me off. He says so every day and is so worried about his *nang*."

Honor. It was tantamount to every decision here. But Fekiria's own willfulness was as much a problem.

"If you would stop pushing him with your rebellion," she said with a giggle. Kaka Jahandar had shouted that so many times at Fekiria when she spoke up or expressed her disapproval for something. "Look, honestly, it is possible to hold your parents and culture in respect and yet disagree with them."

"Easy for you to say. You aren't the one being married to a grandfather!"

Shouts startled them both and yanked their attention to the small market. Two children bolted out from among a throng of adults. Faces wrung with fear and dirt, they darted toward them.

Zahrah's blood went cold. "Rashid! Ara!"

The boy locked on to her. His face paled. He thrashed a hand at her. "No, go back. Run!"

No sooner had she set eyes on the strange man standing in the middle of the street than a loud noise cracked the afternoon. A white Toyota pickup barreled through the crowd, toppling some who were not fast enough to get out of the way.

Taliban!

"Hurry!" Zahrah waved the children to her. Ara leapt into her arms and Zahrah whipped around. Tucked her head and hurried. Her cousin had Rashid by the hand. "Just keep your head down and walk fast," Fekiria said as she relinked arms.

A bitter taste glanced off her tongue. She'd been so careful. . .all these months. . .

She felt her cousin turn by the slight pressure on her shoulder as she looked back. A strangled yelp stabbed her with fear.

"Run," Fekiria gasped.

The sound of a whiny car chased them down the street. The school gate loomed at the far end of the narrow stretch.

"They're close," Ara wailed.

The heartrending sound shoved Zahrah ahead. Her sandaled feet slapped the ground, twisting and slipping as they ran down the pothole-laden road.

"Open the gate," Fekiria shouted. "Open the gate!"

Panic clutched at Zahrah as she felt a hot trail sear along her arm. Her sleeve shifted. The gate erupted with tiny explosions, wood bursting out and up. More bullets!

Ara shrieked and clutched her leg.

Panic morphed to terror, and Zahrah threw herself at the still-closed gate. She banged. "Open up, please!" she shouted in Farsi.

Clanking on the other side warned her of the lock being unbolted. "Hurry!" She made the mistake of looking back.

The Toyota careened around the corner. Dumping two Talib. The men remained unfazed and lifted their weapons toward her.

The gate gave way against her weight. She shoved through with Ara, Fekiria, and Rashid behind her. "Taliban," she breathed and hurried into the building.

As she passed beneath the tiled doorway, a thunderous crack detonated. She dared not look back. It would slow her. Expose her. The children.

An explosion rent the night. Its concussive blast of heat scalding her back as she threw herself and Ara toward the stair shelter. Something hit her head—snapped it forward, right into the cement blocks. Warmth slid down her face. Fire lit through her side.

Amid screams her world darkened.

CHAPTER 6

Balkh Province
27 May—1420 Hours

They are some kind of stupid."

Dean looked up from the military-grade iPad as their MRAP trounced down from the village back toward Mazar-e. He frowned at Falcon, who aimed the armored vehicle onto the main road. "How's that?"

"Way I figure it," Falcon said, speaking louder than normal without yelling so he could be heard over the engine and road noise, "they had that kid watching for us, which means they knew we'd be there."

"The clinic," Dean said, nodding.

"Right. But. . .why?" Falcon held up a hand. "Why would they be there on the same day as us?"

"Don't need brains to be a terrorist." Hawk hollered from the rear compartment, his green eyes lit with amusement. "I been out here enough times to see that played out."

"Exactly," Falcon said. "Stupid is one thing, but to be *right there. . .*"

"Hey." Hawk lunged forward, thrusting a pointed finger between Falcon and Dean. "Check it out. What's that?"

Dean ducked to see out the window. A klick out, maybe two, a fireball streaked into the sky. Black smoke chased the flames.

"That's—dude!" Hawk growled. "The blue dome—it's the school!"

"What school?" Dean watched the plumes of smoke lighten. Black indicated a fuel source—oil, most likely. But gray meant a natural fuel source, wood or plaster.

"When you were stateside, Command wanted feelers about that place, so we did a one-day clinic." Falcon shrugged, already slowing and taking a route that led them closer. "There's got to be thirty or forty kids there. Teachers."

"Oh, man. That American-Afghan teacher." Hawk struck Dean's shoulder with the back of his hand. "Dude—this chick could be the woman of your dreams. I know she's mine!"

"Down boy." Dean motioned in that direction with a nod. "Let's check it." He keyed the mic on his headset, eying the flames and smoke. Still burning. "Command, this is Raptor Six Actual."

"Go ahead, Raptor Six Actual."

"Signs of an explosion and fire. Possible location is a school. We're going to check it out."

"Copy that, Raptor Six. What do you need?"

Again, Dean eyed the black ball. The location—tight cluster of buildings. "We'll need medevac and air assist."

"Roger that. Dispatching now."

"Raptor Six out." Dean looked over his shoulder to the well of the MRAP. The black seats that lined the hull weren't comfortable but they beat sitting on steel. "Harrier, get your gear. Probably got some wounded."

Dean's gaze hit Titanis. Behind the black Oakley ballistic M Frames, the man stared back. Quiet and formidable. Which made him fit right in with the Green Berets since they were known as the Quiet Professionals.

A curse hit the hot air as Falcon whipped the MRAP onto the street where a structure burned. The blue-domed mosque stood silent as it watched a neighbor building spewing smoke into the sky like an angry dragon. Charred, a gate hunched to the side. Afghans dressed in their *perahan tunban* huddled on the opposite side of the street. A man carried a child across the dirt road to safety.

"There," Dean said, pointing to the large, open courtyard.

Dazed and in shock, people littered the area. Some walking around with mouths gaping and eyes glazed. Too much to take in. Mental overload. Others, sitting on the side, holding crooked limbs or bloody children. The L-shaped building had lost most of its shorter leg, which sat in ruins. A direct hit. Behind it, draped in smoke and chaos, a warehouse-type building looked like the triage point.

After Falcon eased into the area, Dean swung open the door and leapt down from the MRAP before the engine died.

"Oh, thank you," an older man with a graying beard said, rushing them. "Help us! Children are missing!"

"Are you in charge?" Dean swept the courtyard with an experienced eye. A dozen or more adult males stood around, staring. Shell-shocked. Faces and clothing smudged with ashes.

"Yes, yes. I am Doctor Kohistani."

"Oh, good. A doctor."

His brown eyes widened. "No no." Dirty, blood-smeared hands waved at him. "Not that kind. I am a school doctor, the director."

Dean considered the man who stood about five-five. His long, tan kaftan bore black marks and blood. "Are there wounded?"

"Yes, yes. Please hurry." He shuffled toward the large building at the back of the compound, away from the fire that forced the school to surrender its fight despite the volunteers sloshing buckets of water against its fury.

"Harrier." Dean waved the field medic with him.

"What happened, Doctor?" Dean asked as they hustled across the paved courtyard and into the relative shade of the other building.

"I do not know. One minute all is calm. Next—boom!" The small man raised his arms in emphasis. "Here, here." He scurried out another door and into a smaller building. At least twenty men, women, and children were laid out on concrete with varying wounds. Some sat along the wall, waiting, bleeding.

Someone behind Dean cursed, knocking Dean out of his own shock and assessment. "Hawk, call in backup and medical support." Dean removed his Oakleys and set them atop his helmet. "Rest of you, let's get to work." Since every American soldier had field-medic training, they'd be able to stabilize most of the patients.

"Help! Please help," a woman's shout drew Dean's attention back to the courtyard. "*Komak! Komak!*"

He shifted and jogged toward the voice screaming for help.

Dressed in a red kaftan, a woman stumbled from an alley between the two buildings with a boy in her arms. Tripping beneath the limp weight, she cried out. "Please, help him!"

That's when it hit him—she wasn't wearing a *red* kaftan. It was covered in blood! "Harrier!" Dean sprinted toward her and heard the pounding of boots behind him.

"Easy, easy," Harrier said as he lifted the boy from her arms.

"He...he...breathing," she said, a trembling, bloody hand going to her forehead. Distress creased her brows. Lost, stricken eyes followed Harrier, who laid the boy on the ground and went to work. "Then... he..." She shook her head.

"We've got him." Dean touched the woman's shoulder. Assessing her, he noted the glazed expression sliding over her face. Shock. "Ma'am?"

"We were. . .the Talib. . .they—Fekiria! Ara!" She spun around toward the building, as if looking for someone. Her feet tangled. She stumbled.

Dean caught her. "Ma'am." He held her shoulders. Had to get her—

"Fekiria!"

Resisting the urge to put her into a tight hold to help control her, Dean reminded himself of the protocols here. Of the propriety. "Ma'am, please."

"Zahrah!" Another woman rushed out of the makeshift hospital. "Here, I'm here!"

The woman next to him stilled. Her gaze fixed on the newcomer. Relief bottomed out her fight and her limbs went weak.

Dean stepped back, aware that men should not touch women. He and Raptor team had worked hard to gain the respect of the Afghans. He wouldn't screw that up.

"Fekiria!" She sighed and sagged, her hijab sliding down the back of her head, revealing glistening black hair.

No. Not glistening black hair. Glistening *blood*. His mind registered the crimson rivulet escaping her hairline and streaking down her temple. Registered the rubbery movement of her legs. The way she wavered. The angle her head went.

"Zahrah!" the other woman shrieked, her face wrought.

Dean lunged. Caught the woman. Her head thumped against his vest. Limp in his arms, she let out a soft moan. He lifted her as the thunder of choppers drowned the compound. Rotor wash fanned smoke across the chaotic scene as Dean lowered the woman to the ground.

"What happened, Captain?" Hawk asked.

"Head injury," Dean said. He held the sides of her face as Hawk secured an inflatable brace around her neck. "Medic!" he shouted over his shoulder then checked Hawk's work.

Rich brown eyes opened. Fastened on him. Then rolled back.

—∞—

German Military Hospital, Camp Marmal, Afghanistan
28 May—0900 Hours

White light blinded. Streaked through her eye socket like an electric shock.

Zahrah cringed and ducked, squeezing her eyelids tight. She shook her head and forced her gaze back to the military doctor wielding his penlight.

"Sorry."

She curled her fists around the blanket as he continued his checkup.

He flashed the light from the side, above, even below, but each beam stabbed her cornea. "Are you experiencing pain?"

"Only when you do that," she said with a soft laugh.

He gave a sniff as he stuffed the penlight into his breast pocket and stepped back. He jotted some notes on her chart. "You have good reflexes and your vitals are stable. The stitches will take time to heal, but tests reveal no intracranial bleeding or worrisome swelling. All in all, very good, considering."

"Then, I can go home?" Or back to her kaka's house. She'd left home eighteen months ago.

"Yes, I'll have the nurse get your discharge papers started. We'll send you home with some anti-inflammatories and painkillers."

"Doctor," she said, braving his gaze and the question. "What of the children from the school?"

"I'm sorry." He shot her a sympathetic look. "I can't talk about the other patients. I'm just glad you came out with only a few stitches and a mild concussion. I'd hate to try to explain to your father anything worse."

Zahrah studied the gray blanket. She'd prefer her father not be dragged into this. He'd retired for a reason. Told her not to come to Afghanistan for the same one. Never would he believe this was a very unlucky coincidence.

A female in ACUs entered, handed the doctor a file as he left, then presented Zahrah with a stack of papers to sign. "Your escape papers." She smiled.

As Zahrah penned her John Hancock to the documents, the nurse set a bag on the portable wheeled tray. "Your cousin brought these clean clothes for you. She's waiting in the hall."

Zahrah finished the papers and returned them to the nurse, who went through them verifying. While she did that, Zahrah went behind the curtain and slipped into her long tunic and pants. She stuffed her toes through the thong of the sandals and emerged, running a brush gently—so very gently considering the stitches—through her hair.

The nurse handed her a printed sheet. "Your discharge instructions. Stitches will need to be cleaned with antiseptic daily. Keep it covered for the first couple of days. The prescriptions include an anti-inflammatory." She handed her a bottle. "Take that twice a day until you return in two weeks to have the stitches removed. The painkillers"—she handed her another bottle—"you can take as needed. You probably aren't feeling any pain right now because of the morphine IV you had, so I'd advise you take the first one about two hours from now, and then every four to six hours for the next forty-eight hours. Then as needed."

Zahrah nodded, her head already thumping when she looked down.

"Any questions?"

Overwhelmed, she took in the soiled clothes, the bottles, the instructions, and shook her head.

"Good. Captain Watters has asked to speak with you, so I'll notify him."

"Who? Why. . . ?"

"He's captain of the team first on scene. He needs to get your statement for his review."

Though her pulse sped, Zahrah told herself she had nothing to be afraid of, that she'd done nothing wrong. "Did I—?" She gulped. "Am I in trouble? Does he think I had something to do with the explosion?"

"He does not," came a deep, firm voice.

Zahrah glanced to her left as a soldier entered, removing his dark ball cap.

"Miss Zarrick." Very tanned and very athletic, the soldier eased into the room. "I'm Captain Watters, the commander of the team onsite shortly after the explosion. I have some questions about the incident." He thumbed toward the female soldier. "Specialist Bramlett will stay with us while we talk. Do you remember what happened last night at the school?"

"I remember. . ." Not him. But the relief that pulsed through her veins when the uniforms spilled into the compound. "Honestly, it was a blur. I remember seeing smoke, then soldiers—you, I guess. Really, I was just so worried about finding help for Rashid. . ." As the pressure in her head increased, she leaned more heavily against the mattress, wishing to be pain-free.

His camo-clad arms were held in a V, large hands clasping a manila folder flat against his pants. Corded muscles strained against the sleeves that bore no rank or name patch. Dark brows framed hazel eyes that had the same effect a drill might, boring right through her. "Are you up to a few questions?"

"I. . ." She wasn't. Not really. Not with him. He made it hard to think straight. But it wasn't like she could escape his questions. "Sure."

He lowered himself into a chair and set the file on his right knee before pinning it with his elbow. "Were you there when the explosion happened?"

"Yes."

"I'm not here for any reason other than to hear what you know. Please tell me what you remember prior to the explosion."

And she did. Zahrah told about leaving the compound, seeing the Talib, running back to the school with Rashid, Ara, and Fekiria. The chaos.

"I came to, covered in debris and choking on smoke. When I realized Rashid lay next to me, unconscious, I was terrified he'd died. Because of me."

"Because of you?" Something sparked in his eyes.

Oh. "No, not like that—I didn't have anything to do with the explosion. I just. . .Rashid and his sister stayed late for tutoring. If they'd left on time, they wouldn't have been there. How are they? Is Rashid okay? And Ara?" Zahrah's stomach squeezed.

Captain Watters darted a look to the nurse. "I just spoke with the doctor about the boy. He's in a coma, serious but good chance of survival."

"He'll live, then?"

"They think so, yes."

Zahrah wanted to breathe her relief, but— "Ara?"

Captain Watters's expression went stone-like. "I haven't heard about a girl. Maybe she wasn't involved."

"No, she was there."

"I'm sure they'll find her."

Zahrah grabbed the tendril of hope he offered. "She stayed at the school for tutoring, but she didn't need it." She managed a smile and a one-shouldered shrug. "Ara knew Rashid wanted to learn, but he was too afraid to ask their father. So on certain days, when he would come to walk her home, she would stay late with me, repeating the lessons so Rashid could overhear. Learn, we hoped." Zahrah squelched the tidal pull of grief. "She's such an amazing child—they have to find her."

"Zahrah?" Fekiria stepped inside, her gaze questioning.

Captain Watters rose, a respectful, courteous gesture.

"Captain," Zahrah said, smiling at him. "This is my cousin Fekiria Haidary."

"What. . .what is going on?" Fekiria asked, a scowl digging into her olive skin.

Why did she suddenly feel nervous with her cousin here? "Captain Watters asked me to tell him what I saw at the school, what I remembered."

"You saw nothing," Fekiria spat out.

Zahrah stilled, confusion rippling through her. "What are you—?"

"You should leave," Fekiria snipped at the captain. "It's not right for you to be here with her."

He looked at Zahrah, gauging.

Something in Zahrah squirmed under his scrutiny. She took her cousin's arm and tugged her aside. "What has happened?"

"How could you be so stupid talking to them? Do you want those men to come after you?" Fekiria's green eyes were a mixture of terror and rage. "Because they will. I promise those men will not care that you were born in America."

Captain Watters demanded, "What men?"

CHAPTER 7

German Military Hospital, Camp Marmal
28 May—1000 Hours

Hands planted on his belt, Dean gritted his teeth as the two women hurried toward the main gate's security checkpoint. He wanted to detain them, question them, but that would work back the hours he'd put into gaining the trust of the locals. The small ground he'd made with Zahrah Zarrick. She trusted him. Liked him—he could see it in her eyes. And that benefitted his need to gain information.

Until her cousin had entered.

Anger pulsed through him. They were hiding something. When the younger woman—the cousin—had hissed something about "those men," Miss Zarrick's face paled. Then neither of them would talk. Or speak against their people.

Wait.

"Those men will not care that you were born in America."

Dean pivoted and started for SOCOM's sub-base, the walk letting him work off the anger and think through the questions. The possibilities. He didn't want to believe those young women were embroiled in something against coalition forces, but out here in the heat of combat, he couldn't afford to rule out anything. He stepped inside, smacked by the stale, quasi-chilled, air-conditioned smell. A wheezing AC unit crowded out the whine of computers lining the walls.

Seated at his desk, Falcon looked up from a file—probably his AAR—and stilled. "What's wrong?"

Had to admit—felt good that his first knew him that well. A bit scary, too. "What do we have on the female teachers from the school?"

A swiveling chair squeaked as Hawk rotated to face them from a table. "Dude. You mean the hot chicks?"

Dean ignored the comment. "Who are they?"

"That's where it gets interesting," Hawk said, green eyes pinched with amusement as he held up a file. "The hottie who got the head wound and passed out in your arms? She's the daughter of the indomitable General Peter Zarrick."

"General 'Z-Day' himself?" The man known for cleaning house when he assumed command of the coalition forces in a single day. Those in the know called it Z-Day. The day General Peter Zarrick revamped a flagging Army.

"So she's American." Falcon's voice pitched.

"Half." Hawk smirked. "Seems the good general met an Afghan woman and married her. What's even more interesting is that her mother is the sister of one Jahandar Haidary."

"Either tell us what that means or give up the file." Falcon had a short fuse when it came to Hawk, the two sparking off each other like static electricity.

"The hottie's maternal uncle is cousin to the physicist who went missing two years ago. Remember that? Dead of night tracking and"— he flashed his hand open—"*poof*! SEALs lose him." Hawk grunted with a smart-aleck grin. "Should've let some real soldiers handle that mission."

Dean took the file and scanned the information. Twenty-six-year-old Zahrah Zarrick had come to Afghanistan eighteen months ago with—*Oh great*. "Tss." The weight of what he read pushed him into a chair.

"What?"

"Christian nonprofit literacy organization."

Falcon gave a loud, clipped laugh. "Might as well paint a target on her back. Think that's why the school got hit?"

"The cousin"—Dean flipped the pages looking for the other girl's profile—"mentioned something about men coming after Zarrick if she talked to me."

Easing forward, Falcon frowned. "What men?"

"That's what I want to find out. Both of them looked like scared rabbits when Haidary mentioned them. After that, I couldn't get Zarrick to talk."

"Yeah, that's not a good thing. Because she's a hottie, and we need conversation." Hawk winked.

Dean glared. "We need *information*. Whoever set that bomb is out there. We have to avoid unrest when we're trying to scale things back in the region. Don't need innocents dying and us getting blamed." Even as the last words left his mouth, he realized how terse they sounded. How much like his father he sounded. He twitched away the thought.

"I need to talk to Zarrick. Without her cousin." But with the rules of society here, Zarrick couldn't be alone with him—so maybe he'd find common ground. "How bad is the school?"

"Half gone," Falcon mumbled.

"Structurally sound, usable?"

His second in command eyed him without turning his head. "What're you thinking?" Falcon set aside his AAR and straightened.

"That if they don't have to leave, they won't. We need information, and if the school has to be relocated, we lose a possible lead. That school was targeted for a reason. I want to know why and by whom, because once Z-Day finds out, he'll be eating us for lunch." Dean stabbed a finger at the file. "These women saw men who didn't belong. What if the men were at the school?"

"Dude." Hawk sputtered a laugh. "They could've seen the men walking to the school, walking to the market—anywhere in the city."

"Maybe, but I have a feeling Miss Zarrick doesn't loiter around the city—she knows the dangers here. She abides by the customs, wears local clothes, and even looks the part, but her speech gives her away." Dean nodded, thinking through the facts. "As an American, she knows she's an easy, soft target."

"You know this isn't our problem," Falcon said. "We aren't CID. Let them handle it. Besides, nothing's happening at the school—a kid's missing."

"Our responsibility is securing the area, and since we were first on the scene and there's a missing child, we own this. Finding out how that SCIF got into the village on the outskirts is priority one, but this upheaval—it's mighty interesting that a stolen military computer is found the same time as this school is blown and mysterious men are reported in the city."

Hawk smirked again. "No, that just sounds like a day in Mazar-e."

Irritation clawed its way up his spine and pushed Dean from the chair. "I'm going to talk to Burnett."

"And say what?" Falcon asked.

"That I want to follow up."

"With who?"

"Zarrick. I have a feeling she'll be forthcoming if I can get her alone."

Hawk let out a catcall.

Dean balled a fist. "Without her cousin."

Hawk hooted more.

—⚉—

Haidary Residence, Mazar-e Sharif
28 May—1020 Hours

The ride home had been made in stiff silence that strained Zahrah's nerves. By the time they reached the compound of her uncle's home, she withered beneath the thunder of another headache. She lifted the bottle of pills she'd been given and remembered the nurse saying she'd feel the pain soon enough. But it was not just the physical injury. The pain of Fekiria's admonishment, the undulating disapproval from her uncle, who kept glaring at her in the rearview mirror. . . Zahrah drew in a breath and looked out as the car pulled up to the blue painted plaster wall. He honked twice and the gate swung open. Her half-dozen cousins, all younger than Fekiria, swarmed the car. Laughing, waving at Zahrah, running alongside as her kaka threaded the sedan through the gates to the compound.

He hopped out and stormed inside the house.

Car doors swung open and in flooded the children. Laily dropped across Zahrah and hugged her. "We were scared you weren't coming back," the five-year-old announced.

Arms around her little cousin, Zahrah savored the welcome home the others gave her as she climbed out. They clamored around her. All save thirteen-year-old Daoud, who wore the same severe expression of his father and older brother, Adeeb. Zahrah worried over her uncle's temper.

"He is angry with you," Fekiria said as they moved inside the two-story home.

"Why is Daoud angry?"

"Because Baba is angry."

Zahrah set down Laily and turned. Her khala Hafizah scurried toward her, arms raised for a hug. "*Salaam, bachem,*" she said, tears pooling in her dark eyes.

"Salaam, Khala," Zahrah greeted her aunt in return, grateful for the warm embrace and concern flowing out of her expression and words.

"Your father has called so many times." She pressed a kiss to each side of Zahrah's face then handed her a phone. "You must call him so he will stop acting like an old woman!"

Zahrah laughed then winced as a pang stabbed through her skull. At the same time, she spied her uncle glowering at her from the other side of the room. She lowered her head, a sign of submission, but it also allowed her to break his gaze.

Her aunt didn't miss it. "Go. Call Peter then rest. I will bring up food for you later."

"I don't want to be any trouble."

"No, no trouble. You are family. It is my joy."

"Thank you." Zahrah started for the stairs. At her elbow, she felt Fekiria following her.

"Fekiria," her aunt called. "Come help me."

Though her cousin groaned, Zahrah was secretly glad to be alone. She let herself into the room she shared with Fekiria, Laily, and Camila. On the mattress of the lower bunk, she took a moment to compose herself. To sort herself from the chaos of the last twenty-four hours. The explosion. Seeing Rashid so bloodied...wondering if Ara had died. Grief strangled her anew. Zahrah lowered her head. Closed her eyes.

Father, I know You wanted me to come here, but I'm struggling to understand why. There is so much death here. No happiness.

With a slow breath for courage, she dialed her father.

"Zahrah!" The way he said her name radiated his relief, which flooded through the connection and soaked her.

"Hi, Daddy," she said, feeling unusually American using that term.

"Are you okay? They said you were hurt. What happened? Why did they keep you? Speak to me!"

She couldn't help the laugh as she pushed back across the mattress and rested against the plastered wall, knees up. "If you'd stop talking," she teased. Then sighed. "I'm okay, Daddy. I am. Really. They took good care of me at the base."

"It's German run, you know. But American personnel are there, too. You shouldn't have had any problems." He made a clicking noise. "Then again, it's German run. If you had problems, I want to know. I can make some calls. Run a few butts up the flagpole."

Another laugh. Ever the general. "No problems." She thought of the handsome captain who'd put Fekiria on edge. "I need your advice though, Daddy."

"Shoot."

She smiled. Now he sounded in control of himself. "One of the soldiers was asking me about what happened, what I saw."

"Good. They'd better find out who did this."

"Your protective side is kicking in."

"It never kicked *out*."

Her father's protective side unleashed something in her that she'd held close, tight. Her vision blurred. It was the headache. The exhaustion. That's why she wanted to cry. But what she wouldn't do for one of his thick-chested, strong-armed hugs right now. "I miss you, Daddy."

"I miss you too, Z-baby." His voice cracked. "I. . ."

"Please, don't." She didn't need his "I told you so" lecture. Not now. He hadn't wanted her to come to Afghanistan. It was unsafe. . .it was dangerous. *There's a reason your grandfather left that place.*

"Fair enough. But what I wouldn't do to get you out of there, to change your mind," he said. "But you come by that stubborn streak honestly. In fact, you got a double-barrel dose of it."

Laughter was good medicine. The Word said so. And she believed it because the cloud that had hovered over her heart and life parted.

"You said you needed advice."

"Right." She cleared her mind and throat. "The captain wanted to ask me questions, but Fekiria wouldn't let me answer him. She was afraid of the men at the school."

"What men?"

"I. . .I don't know who they were." She rubbed the middle of her forehead, trying to think. "Fekiria and I noticed them before, but yesterday one of them all but threatened me." She told her dad of the way he'd held Rashid and what he said. How they'd been in the lower basement. "He's one of those men who makes my skin crawl."

"Okay, you listen to me," he said, General Zarrick front and center. Strange comfort always embraced her when he shifted into this role. "I want you to find a way back to that base. Do you remember the name of the soldier talking to you?"

"Watters, Captain Watters."

"Okay, good. You get to that base and tell him everything you've told me."

Her heart skipped a beat. "So, you think it's serious?"

"Z-baby, they blew up the school. This is beyond serious." He grunted. "In fact, I don't want you going back to the school."

Zahrah swallowed, thinking about the children. This is how suppression prevailed. What was it they said? All it takes for evil to prevail is for good men—or women in her case—to do nothing. "Daddy, I can't let the bullies stop me from teaching. They'll win, but more important, the children will lose. They'll lose so much."

"Baby, if you're dead, who's going to fight that battle for you?"

Why did he always have to make sense? "I can't just give up."

"I'm not asking you to. I'm asking you to arm our troops with information needed to put insurgents away, to give them time to rout this enemy. That's what this captain needs to do. You need to stay low. You hearing me?"

"Yes, sir."

"That's my girl. Now, I'm going to make some calls to a few friends. Make sure they look out for you."

"Daddy." Her heart climbed into her throat. "Please. Don't. It will draw attention."

"Attention's already been drawn. We're beyond that."

"But. . .the children—"

"Need protection. That's why our troops are there, and to help souls of gold like you to stay safe. To make sure innocents stay living and breathing so they can see what freedom is really like." The clacking of a keyboard carried through the line. "I'm sending an e-mail to an old friend. Now, how do you plan to get back to the base?"

"I. . ." She searched for a plausible excuse.

"I know your mother's brother. He won't let you out of his sight if he can help it."

"I'll talk—"

"Hafizah will be your best option."

"Yes," Zahrah said with a smile, as if he'd read her thoughts. "I'll. . . Rashid." She smiled bigger. "I'll try to see him tomorrow. They wouldn't let anyone see him today. I just have to find a way to keep Fekiria from going with me."

"Good. Good. Work on it. Hafizah will believe that about visiting the boy. Check in with the family, too. That'll buy charity points with locals."

"Daddy," she hissed. "I'm not buying points. I love these people. They were Mom's people."

"I know. I'm just—"

"Thinking like a general again."

"Yes, ma'am." He chuckled. "You can take the dog out of the fight, but you can't take the fight out of the dog. Even one as old as me."

"That's because you're a sheepdog."

"Hooah."

"I love you, Daddy."

"Love you too, Z-Baby. Take care. Talk to Captain Watters. Give him all you got."

CHAPTER 8

Sub-base Schwarzburg, Camp Marmal
Mazar-e Sharif, Balkh Province
28 May—1845 Hours

Fresh from a workout and shower, Dean sat on one of the leather sofas before the flat-screen TV on the wall at the USO center. Images moved across the display, but his mind had already vanished into the past. He should e-mail Desi.

And say what?

Didn't matter. It'd been too long since they talked.

Way too long. She'd lecture him about dropping off the face of the earth.

Like he needed more guilt.

A shout snapped his attention to the partially walled-in area beneath the rec deck, where two tables offered a friendly game of pool. Emphasis on *friendly.* Which was the opposite of Hawk's angry, twisted face.

Dean came out of his seat.

Hawk shoved a specialist. "Get off. If you can't play without cheating—"

"I ain't cheating!"

Closing the distance in a half-dozen long strides, Dean noted Falcon moving in, too. "Hey." Dean pressed a hand to Hawk's chest. "Stand down."

"Sorry, sir," the specialist muttered. "He said I was cheating, and I can't take that sitting down."

Dean pointed the young kid, who couldn't be more than nineteen, away from the tables. "Grab a soda or something."

"But sir, this is my game. I signed up for this hour."

"Hey, didn't you hear the captain?" Hawk growled.

Dean rounded on Hawk. "*Sergeant.* A talk. Outside."

Fury lit Hawk's eyes and rippled through the guy's entire body.

"I think it'd be wise to listen to our commander," Falcon said, using his presence to push Hawk out of the situation. "Now, Sergeant Bledsoe."

Hawk thrust a finger at the Spec-4. "Don't let me see you—"

As Dean turned away, Hawk's entire demeanor shifted. And Dean knew the Spec-4 had given Hawk a one-fingered salute. Hawk lunged.

Dean did, too. He rammed his shoulder into Hawk's pec. "No!"

Falcon hooked an arm up and over Hawk's shoulder, dragging him backward. Boots squeaked against the floor as they herded him out of the room. Something about crowds and competitive sports brought out the worst in the top-notch operator.

The door to the USO building flung open. Hit the wall. Flapped back.

Hawk kicked it. Spun around. "You see what he did to me? And you're going to treat me—"

Dean stepped into Bledsoe's personal space. "One more incident, Bledsoe, and I'm writing you up myself."

"You gotta be—"

"So help me."

"But—"

"You're one of the best soldiers I know, but you walk into a place and pick a fight."

"Me?"

Nostrils flaring, Dean took a step back. "One more time and I'm yanking you."

"I don't understand."

"I know. God help me, I know." Dean hauled in a steadying breath. "I don't get it. You run around with some chip on your shoulder, looking for a fight. Looking for someone to glance at you crossways. What is this? Ego?"

"I want respect!"

"Then earn it! Those guys in there, they're nineteen. You're twenty-eight and a freakin' hero. Special Forces." He slapped Hawk's arm with their unit patch on it. "Raptor team. And so help me, if you don't soldier up and act like you earned that, I'll rip it off you."

Hawk's smirk vanished. "You're kidding, right?"

"You have to be above the fray, better than the best!"

"It was just a scuffle."

"Yeah, but you have those scuffles every time you enter the USO or a bar. I'm not sure what's happening with you, but you need to get it together." Dean's secure sat phone rang. He nailed Hawk with a look he hoped warned him not to press his luck then turned as he lifted the phone. "Watters." He stomped away before he said or did something he regretted.

"Captain Watters, Pete Zarrick."

Dean slowed, turning away from the congestion of foot traffic back toward the air-conditioned tent that had been his home for the last few months. It took a split second for him to get his bearings on the caller. Which was why his heart rapid-fired for another second before he could answer. "Yes, sir."

"Do you know who I am, Captain?"

His heart beat a little harder as he stepped off the path and turned a circle. "I do, sir." *What on earth?* His number was secure. Only Burnett, SOCOM, and his team had it.

"Then I need you to listen very carefully. I have two concerns right now, son. Do you know what they are?"

Confusion peppered Dean, but the biggest question was *why*. Why was he having this conversation with one of the fiercest, toughest generals to serve as commander of the coalition forces? A general now retired. "I'd imagine one of them is your daughter. Sir."

"You would be right, Captain."

"With all due respect, sir, I'm not sure I understand. . ."

"Zahrah said you tried to talk to her when she was in the hospital."

"Sir. You know I cannot discuss this."

"Bull! I wouldn't have this number if I wasn't cleared to talk to you."

Dean didn't like being bullied. And he didn't like being cornered. As ticked as he was, he knew chain of command. Knew this guy could string him up with a flick of his little finger. "I'm listening, sir."

"Zahrah is coming back to talk to you."

Lifting his hand in question—why would the man's daughter need her father to inform him of this?—Dean turned another circle. Met Falcon's curious gaze. Shot him a wicked scowl that drew the Italian closer. "Very good, sir."

"My daughter is a brilliant young woman with a good heart."

And your point is? "Good to know, sir."

"Don't you get on your high horse with me, you piece of—" A huff. Another huff. A clank in the background. "Zahrah might need protection she doesn't know she needs."

Falcon gave him a questioning look.

Dean shrugged. "Sir?"

"Read her file, son."

"Already have, sir. Twice."

"And how many times have you stared at her picture?"

Heat spread down Dean's neck. "What you are insinuating, sir?"

"You know very well because if you'd paid attention to her file and not her pretty face, you'd know why I'm calling."

—∽—

Haidary Residence, Mazar-e Sharif
29 May—0700 Hours

Mission impossible. Small white cup in hand, Zahrah paused and muttered, "Whether or not I choose to accept it." When the general spoke, the general *spoke*.

Voices skittered through the narrow hall and drew closer.

She dumped back the last of her tea, washed her cup, then lifted her messenger bag. She swallowed the thick knot of emotion—it was the same bag in which she'd carried her students' assignments home to grade. She slung it over her shoulder, wrapped a burgundy hijab around her head, and hurried to the rear door on said mission.

She pushed it open and bright Afghan sunlight stabbed her. Ducking, she took a second to let her eyes adjust.

"You are out already then, Zahrah jan?"

Zahrah closed her eyes. Hesitation kills every time, her father would say. If courtesy and respect did not demand she answer, Zahrah would pretend she hadn't heard her aunt. But she did. She stepped backward. "Yes, I'm. . ." She would not lie. Not to the only family she had out here. "I. . .I must hurry."

"Fekiria went to see Rashid's family. You will see her?"

Fekiria had left already? So early? Zahrah's mind blitzed, preventing her from answering. Odd that she'd gone to see Rashid. Her cousin had never shown as much fondness toward the children as Zahrah had.

"She was in such a hurry. Tell her to bring home eggs."

"I can get some on my way back," Zahrah said, deftly avoiding a lie and guilty conscience. Besides, she wouldn't be lying—she was headed to Rashid's home to visit with his mom, see if she could convince her to go to the base. "Must hurry. Bye!"

And with that, she was out the door and tapping a note into her phone to remember the eggs. Warmth kneaded Zahrah's muscles, still tense from the explosion and the stress of the entire episode. But somehow, some way, she still felt the peace that had drawn her to Afghanistan, to her mother's people.

A song about God's beauty filling the sky drifted through her mind and sailed across the battered edges of her nerves. God had watched out for her in that explosion. Kept her from further injury. Kept her alive so she could find Rashid and get him help in time. And yet. . .all those things did not give her the sense that she had completed the reason God had drawn her here.

She rounded the corner and nearly collided with another woman. "So sorry," Zahrah said with a laugh, then realized—"Razia!"

"Zahrah," Rashid's mother breathed then kissed her three times, alternating cheeks. *"Assalaam alaikum."*

"Wa 'alaikum assalaam, Razia. *Sanga ye?"*

"Not well," she said with a deep frown.

"Why? What is ?"

"They cannot find Ara."

Zahrah's stomach squeezed. "She didn't come home?"

"She was at the school, yes?" Razia teared up.

Mutely, Zahrah nodded as the knot of dread grew. She'd been *right there* with her when she and Rashid were knocked to the ground.

"They believe she was. . .that she is buried. . . ."

Zahrah shook her head, as much to ward off the tears as the possibility of that sweet girl trapped beneath the building.

The woman's tawny face went pale. "They say it is too dangerous to search for her."

"And Rashid?"

Razia lowered her head. "Atash. . ." She swallowed.

Ah. Razia's husband did not want her going to the American base. Very well. Zahrah had an option for her. "I'm on my way there now. Would you like to go with me?"

Razia brightened. "You would do this for me? Atash refuses to go.

He says bad things will happen to me. And he's very angry with the American soldiers."

"But—this wasn't done by the Americans. They are the ones who came and helped—*after* the blast."

"I know. He is just angry because there is still no word of Ara."Tears slipped free. Her long lashes dusted her cheeks as she looked down then back up to Zahrah with a smile. "I need to see Rashid. To touch him."

"Then let's not waste any more time." She hooked arms with the woman who could not be much older than Zahrah.

It took them longer to make the trek on foot than she'd expected, leaving Zahrah sweaty and longing for a glass of water. As they walked the road that led to the main gate and checkpoint, one of the guards at the foot gate signaled someone from inside.

Razia clutched Zahrah's hand. Squeezed tight.

"It's okay. Probably just getting a woman to help us." At least, that's what Zahrah hoped was happening. Hoped they didn't suspect them of being suicide bombers.

A female soldier emerged in her desert camo and waited as they approached, hands at her side. "Assalaam alaikum."

Appreciating the efforts the soldier took to greet them appropriately, Zahrah smiled, gave Rashid's mom a reassuring squeeze, and returned the greeting to the soldier. "Wa alaikum assalaam."

Face tanned, the female soldier smiled at them—a friendly one that did little to counter the fully automatic weapon slung across her chest or the handgun strapped to her leg. Her name patch read HOMEWOOD. Her rank marked her a specialist—yes, sometimes it benefitted Zahrah, being raised by a general. "How can I help you this morning, ladies?"

Zahrah motioned to Razia. "Her son is the little boy injured in the school explosion the day before yesterday. She would like to see him again."

"Very good. If you'll come with me," Homewood said as she turned, "I will need identification, and we can get an escort assigned."

Zahrah hustled after the soldier, her father's mission at the front of her mind. "I wonder. . .I. . .there was a captain I spoke to yesterday after I was released from the hospital. He is familiar with the incident and the boy—could he help us perhaps?" She needed a plausible explanation since it wasn't proper for a woman to ask after a man.

"You were here, too?" Homewood stepped through a small door

into a receiving area where Zahrah knew they'd be checked for threats they might possess.

"I was knocked unconscious in the explosion."

"She is my daughter's teacher." Razia sucked in a hard breath. "*Ara*." Tears welled in her eyes.

As the image of Ara popped into her mind, Zahrah drew the woman into her arms and held her, noticing the soldier watching. "Her daughter has been missing since the explosion."

Another female soldier joined them, and the two conferred as Zahrah comforted Razia.

Specialist Homewood nodded. "I'm sorry, ma'am." The woman bunched her shoulders. "I just can't imagine. I will pray that they find your little girl. I have two children, and I miss them like crazy."

Razia, made of tougher stuff than her initial tears bespoke, lifted her head. "Thank you."

The other soldier asked for permission to do a pat down, and Razia consented.

"What was the name of that captain you mentioned?" Specialist Homewood asked.

"Captain Watters," Zahrah said.

"First name?"

Zahrah stilled. "I . . . I don't know." Had he ever said his first name? "He was Special Forces, I believe."

Specialist Homewood lifted a phone and dialed.

The other soldier patted her down, too, verifying they weren't carrying weapons or bombs or anything else that could cause injury to the personnel on the base. Cleared, they were instructed to wait by the door.

"I'm sorry," Specialist Homewood said. "Couldn't track down Captain Watters. But I'll escort you to the hospital."

"Thank you." Disappointment lurked behind her civil answer. She couldn't give up on the mission. Her daddy would grill her for surrendering so soon. When they stepped outside, Zahrah was surprised when Specialist Homewood led them to a golf cart.

"No." Razia gripped Zahrah's arm and drew back. "I walk."

Zahrah looked to the specialist for direction, concerned they were already creating tension.

"No problem." Homewood set out on foot. "If you don't mind getting more sweaty."

Razia frowned, and Zahrah gave her the translation, eliciting laughter from the woman, who explained it wasn't *hot* yet. This was *cool* to her.

"How have you come to speak English so well?" Homewood asked as they made their way across the base.

"I'm American," Zahrah said. "My father is American." No need to mention he commanded coalition forces. "My mother was from here." Might as well explain why she was here, or they'd drill her, just like every other visit she'd had. "I came with a relief organization to teach girls, really to teach any child eager to learn."

Homewood motioned to the right. When they rounded the corner, the hospital loomed ahead. "I've been in country twice, and I'm not sure I'd come here willingly ever again."

Zahrah didn't miss a beat. "That would be because your calling is different."

The soldier eyed her from beneath the brim of her cap. "If you say so." She tugged open the front door.

Broad shouldered and tall, another soldier stumbled out, apparently opening the door at the same time. "Excuse me," he said in a deep voice.

And eyes. . .those brownish-green eyes hit hers for a split second. To her, time stopped. *The heat is really getting to you, Z!*

A second soldier followed, talking nonstop. The two looked at a folder.

Then the eyes snapped back to Zahrah.

CHAPTER 9

Camp Marmal, Mazar-e Sharif
29 May—0800 Hours

Dean stopped cold. His heart sliding into his throat as General Zarrick's threat loomed in the back of his mind. From the corner of his eye, he caught the salute the female specialist offered and gave a curt nod with a return salute before turning his full attention to Z-Day's daughter.

A smile teetered on her lips as she lowered her gaze in the customary fashion. "Good morning, Captain."

Dean closed the folder and tucked it under his arm. "Miss Zarrick." He acknowledged the other woman, careful to maintain appropriate distance with the Muslim. "Ma'am." He caught the curious gaze of the specialist who'd escorted them in and knew he'd need to shed her if he intended to get information from Miss Zarrick. "Thank you, Specialist Homewood. Sergeant Russo and I can take it from here."

"Yes, sir." She headed back to her MP duties at the gate.

Hands clenched before him, Dean tried to muster as much friendliness as he could manage into his face and tone. "Russo said you were on base and looking for me. Is everything okay?"

Face encircled by a dark red hijab, she indicated with her head to the older woman. "This is Rashid's mom, Razia Mustafa. She hoped to see him again today." She then turned to the mother and spoke to her in Pashto.

Dean tucked his surprise in the same folder under his arm. The woman before him was an enigma. And there was something about her he was supposed to crack, or he had a feeling her father would be breathing down his neck, if not breaking it.

Mrs. Mustafa bent quickly, saying, "*Manana, manana.*"

He had no idea what she was thanking him for, but he needed these women in his court and the gates of communication open. So he put his limited Pashto to use and offered, "*Har kala rasha,*" which wasn't just the quick, shortcut American "you're welcome," but a full commitment in Pashtun fashion of "you're welcome at any time."

Thin eyebrows arched as Miss Zarrick met his gaze. If he wasn't mistaken, admiration sparked in her brown eyes.

Good. One more ball in his court.

"If you'll come in, I was just visiting with Rashid." Dean tugged the handle and held the door open for the women. "He's awake."

"Rashid?" Mrs. Mustafa repeated, obviously hearing her son's name in his English. Miss Zarrick translated, taking the woman's hand and leading her inside. Her gaze flicked to his for a second as they entered.

Russo gave him a nod, a silent "this is working" indication. And it was. They just had to keep the dialogue open. He guided them to the ICU and to the private room. Dean faced them, noting they both kept a proper distance. "Don't let his appearance worry you. The doctor said he's doing good."

Zahrah again gave the translation. When Dean nudged open the door, she entered behind Mrs. Mustafa, but not before sending him an appreciative smile. "Thank you."

That smile only did one thing: remind him he hadn't figured out what General Zarrick referred to in her file. He'd gone over it several times.

A stream of joyful, yet worried words flew as the mother and son were reunited.

Dean leaned back against the wall, watching through the partially closed blinds in the window. *What am I missing?* At twenty-six, she had a killer résumé. Graduated high school at sixteen as valedictorian. College was mastered just as fast and impressively, earning her master's degree shortly before she left the States to work here. Spoke multiple languages. Father the feared and famed coalition forces commander. Limited information on the mother, other than being an Afghan national and giving birth to a son and a daughter.

"Going well," Falcon said.

"I'm flying blind." Dean folded his arms and leaned his head against the wall. "It's like if I blink, this whole mission will tank."

"You'll get it figured out."

"I'd better. My butt is on the line."

Falcon grinned.

"What?"

With a sniff, he shook his head and looked down. "Nothing."

Dean wasn't in the mood to drag thoughts out of his men. Not even Falcon, who'd served with him the longest. Though Dean had to admit he missed Candyman. Missed the way that guy seemed to read his mind and do what he needed to be done without asking or attitude. He roughed a hand over his jaw. "Speaks English, Pashto, Dari, and French. Lived here eighteen months. Family here."

"Relax," Falcon said. "It'll come."

Relax. Right. Easy for him to say. His name wasn't on the radar of a man everyone feared and respected. Who Dean considered a true hero.

A creaking snapped his attention to the door. Miss Zarrick stepped out, fingertips to the door so it'd close quietly. She looked at him. A smile that spoke of trust, relief.

And he felt punched in the gut.

What. Am. I. Missing? He wouldn't let this woman get hurt because he came up short. . .again. Involuntarily, he came off the wall. Straightened. Even he was aware of his own posturing.

"I think they needed time alone." Zarrick didn't join Falcon and him, her actions clearly dictated by Muslim customs. Men weren't to be alone with women. Weren't to touch. She'd need to keep her distance to maintain her "purity."

"It's rough," he said, his throat dry. "I think I'd lose it if my kid died like that."

"Died?"

Dean frowned. "Her daughter—"

"Hasn't been found yet."

If the kid was beneath all that rubble. . . "My apologies."

Her thin brows seemed to ripple before her gaze slid to his left hand then back to his eyes. Why was she checking him out? "You have children?" Voice soft, she considered him.

Her question unplugged the false hope he'd caged twenty years ago when he decided having kids must be too hard. "No. But not having them doesn't mean I don't relate or that any of this violence makes sense."

Zarrick eyed him. "True." Her wide brown eyes shifted to the mother and son. "But they have lived this their whole lives. Their world is not safe, padded from reality the way it is in our country or the way it was before the Taliban."

Dean noted Falcon slip back a few paces, making a call. More like giving Dean room to open the line of questioning with Zarrick again. *To the mission.* "If you have a minute, I need to continue our conversation from yesterday."

Her lips twisted in a sardonic smile that, even though it was fake, brightened her face. "Let me guess—you got a call."

No way would he admit that. Too many confidentiality breaches.

"A certain cranky general?"

Definitely not answering in the affirmative. Wouldn't that be great—for her to tell the general that Dean said he was cranky. Yeah. He'd get slapped with an Other Than Honorable discharge so fast, he wouldn't see it coming.

Rubbing the side of her face where a scab had formed, she sighed. "I talked to my father last night. He told me to come back and tell you what I know."

Okay. Good. This he could address. "About the men your cousin didn't want you mentioning."

"Yeah. My dad thought it might be important, and now that I've had time to think about it, I believe he's right." Her gaze slid again to the room, but something in her expression—the narrowed eyes, thinned lips—told him she wasn't thinking about the boy and his mom. "We noticed these men at the school. One day they weren't there, the next they were."

"When'd they first show up?"

"I can't remember exactly." Nose scrunched, Zarrick bobbed her head from side to side. "About a week ago, maybe two."

Dean nodded.

"They were unsavory, left me feeling"—what looked like an involuntary shudder twitched through her torso—"unsafe."

"Did you talk to them?"

"Not if I could help it. They stayed in the lower room, a place Director Kohistani forbid anyone from entering, which was what drew my attention to their presence the most."

"What's down there?"

She rubbed her left arm. "We weren't allowed in there, so I can't say what is down there or how big it is."

"Fair enough." Raptor would need to recon that place, see if anything remained after the explosion. Dean checked Falcon, who was probably recording the conversation on his phone. "What else—did they talk to you, did you hear or see anything?"

She swallowed, touched a hand to her throat. "The day of the explosion, the men left in a truck together. Then returned—one was bloody. Shot, cut"—she bunched her shoulders—"I don't know. Later, one of them bumped into me. He grew very angry, threatening. Not with words, but with the way he towered over me. Glared at me." Arms around her middle, Zarrick seemed to be holding herself together. "It was the first time I've felt unsafe since coming here."

Bloodied men. . .could they be the same men who'd been in the village, the ones who tried to snipe heads off his team? Cowards like this man who harassed Zarrick made Dean want to be Allah's personal messenger, delivering the wicked into the arms of the seventy-two virgins. "Did you mention this man to your father?"

"And have him send the four horsemen of the apocalypse here?" She laughed, but there was no humor in her voice. "No, I have to stand on my own two feet. I'm aware of this man, and I'll stay smart by avoiding any further dealings with him."

Dean shifted on his feet, watching Zarrick. She possessed a strength but also a vulnerability. Which was more dominant? Her eyes, the color of amber like that necklace his mom had, were looking past him, past the here and now. . .straight into the *past*.

Recollection tweaked her left eye. "That day—the day of the explosion," she said, her voice quieter, "he held Rashid by the shoulder. Very roughly. It scared both of us. The man asked Rashid who I was." She sniffed. "He would not even speak to me directly."

Interesting. The man had taken note of Zarrick. Was it because she was pretty? An American? A teacher? All of the above? "Do you know why he was interested in you?"

Was this connected to what her father wanted him to figure out? The pressure gauge rose.

Zahrah nodded. "Rashid said I was his sister's teacher then the man told Rashid to tell me to keep to my books and teaching if I valued those I taught." She hauled in a shaky breath. "The whole time, he talked as if he was not right there in front of me, staring at me with those hateful, cruel eyes."

Dean clenched his jaw. Sent a look to Falcon, who nodded and left. He'd get the team together so they could head out and track down something on those men and that lower room.

Zarrick looked at him. "Do you. . . ?" She swallowed. "It doesn't make sense that those men would bomb the school since it's where they were staying."

Straightened to his full height, he planted his hands on his belt. She was right, of course. But it meant another complication—it meant someone else didn't like that those men were at the school. So, who had been the target? The women or the men?

"But," Zarrick said softly. "I also don't think the school would've been hit if it weren't for those men."

Jumping to conclusions only removed his feet from safe ground. Another possibility presented itself as he studied her creamy olive complexion. But with her dark hair and eyes, she didn't especially stand out as a foreigner. Yet Americans were Americans. Hated by many. "There are a lot of Afghans who don't agree with girls being educated. Especially by female American missionary teachers."

—⁂—

Zahrah refused to take offense. But still, he'd basically just diminished what she did to something controversial rather than the mission field that brought her. And all the same, he had a point. "True, but that trouble is more common in the south—Kandahar and Helmand provinces."

His eyebrow quirked. "Only 5 percent of children receive a primary education in Afghanistan."

She smiled. "True, but again—the vicious attitude toward girls getting an education is more prevalent in the south. Far from here. It's not so surprising that I would know and love my mother's country so well, is it?"

"Most who come over don't care. They get in, do the job, and get out." How did he look casual yet powerfully intense? *Just like Daddy.*

"Ah, that's the difference." She smiled.

"What?"

"You said 'job,' but I don't see what I'm doing as a job."

"Then what is it?"

"Passion. I grew up with a mother who performed during my father's military balls, entertaining officers' wives, doing her duty, but she would then be in bed for days afterward. She never felt like she measured up to the American woman because she struggled with the language. She felt isolated and so very alone. My brother—I think it embarrassed him that she could not speak better. But rather than help her, he rebelled. It drove her depression deeper till she could not take it anymore."

His silence warned her that he probably already knew.

"It's been almost three years since her death, and I can still remember coming home from school and finding her sitting in the living room. No lights on. The curtain parted the way she always did. My dad was deployed, my brother gone. . . ."

"You found her?"

Zahrah gave a slow nod. "No, I lost her." The twist of words was unfair but opened the wound she had struggled with for so long. "I lost my brother then, too. Guilt, I think, consumed him. He hasn't spoken to us since. He got a job as a consultant with the CIA because he is bilingual. It was as close to government work as Jay was willing to go."

"Jay?"

She nodded, squinting against the sun as she remembered Jay, five years her senior and so unlike her in every way. He embraced neither their mom's culture nor their father's. "Jahandar Peter. My mother named him after the brother she left behind—Kaka Jahandar."

"So, your brother is at Langley?"

Another nod. A fire that had fueled her heart and forbidden her mind from taking any other path. "So this passion drives me to be here. To teach. To make sure no girl faces what my mother faced. Which is why I want your help."

His eyebrows shot up. "My help?"

"You and your team. The school—they can't get the site cleared, and Ara is still missing. I know you can talk to some higher-ups and get a team together."

He seemed to consider the request.

And she knew where his thoughts would go. Or should. "You can gather more intel on the school." She stretched her chin toward the door Russo had left through. "Your man there, you sent him off when I mentioned the men. This would give you the chance to look over the school, possibly figure out who the men were. Right?"

He just watched her.

"Will you help us clear the school so we can resume classes?"

"No promises. I have to clear it with Command."

Zahrah breathed sweet relief. "Thank you. I'm going straight there after Razia is done visiting."

"I'll do this, on one condition."

Now it was Zahrah's turn to raise her eyebrows.

"We escort you in."

"I . . ." It wouldn't be so bad to be with him more, but she feared the fallout. The castigation for being seen alone with the American soldiers. And Razia certainly wouldn't be willing to ride with them. Atash would beat her. "I'm not sure that's a good idea."

"Sorry. It wasn't a suggestion." He was resolute. Immovable.

"Normally, I wouldn't object, but in light of the bomb, I think it could be risky." She did not want him to think her defiant or ungrateful for his gestures. "If whoever did this sees me enter with American soldiers, they might be more inclined to strike out again, and personally."

He angled a little closer. "My team knows the people of this town. They know us. The show of force will go a long way in protecting you."

Her pulse did this crazy dance as she held his brownish-green eyes, so pure against his heavily tanned face. It tapped a line direct to her heart and knotted her stomach.

"I'm going to make sure," he said, his voice deep and husky, "nobody hurts you again."

Stirred, she struggled to think beyond his declaration.

But then he shifted. "Me—my team, it's what we do."

She touched his arm, a breach of protocol, but something in his vehemence tugged at her heart. "Captain Watters, that's not your job."

"Beg to differ."

"I appreciate the gesture, but whatever happens to me, you can't control that. Neither can I." An insane peace surged through her again, one that had been with her since she set foot here. A peace that said she had a purpose driving her. She had to pull herself from his gaze and turned toward the door. "God wants me here, and I'm surrendered to Him. He will protect me."

He grinned. "That's why *I'm* here."

Surprise tugged her around, forced her to face him as she smiled back. "Are you saying you're God's guardian angel?" The words swirled through her like a branding iron, unnerving her.

Captain Watters laughed. "I've been called worse." He folded his arms. "Listen, a compromise."

Oh she liked this guy. Daddy would go ballistic. "Go on."

"We'll get a civvie driver to take you to the school, but Raptor team is coming in right behind you."

CHAPTER 10

Undisclosed Location

Twizzlers. Fun to eat. Makes mouths happy.

Or something like that. Whatever—they keep me happy and my mouth busy. Sitting up in this cave 24/7 would drive normal men crazy. But then, I've never been normal.

Wow. Is that a lame line or what? Like something you'd see in a bad Hollywood movie or read in a clichéd psycho-thriller.

But seriously. I defy the norms.

Voted most likely to succeed.

Check. When one sits on a multimillion-dollar contract like this—*hello? Success!*

My mom said I'd never hold down a desk job.

I'm dying laughing over this one. Desk job? I think she meant some stock broker or something on Wall Street. But yeah, I'm at a desk. And yep, this is my job.

Loner. That's another thing you always hear about people like me.

Hmm, maybe not like me. I'm not a loner. Okay—yes. I'm in this hole night and day, but it's pretty much driving me crazy. Thus the PS Vita, online gaming subscriptions, chat rooms. No animals. Just don't get what the attraction is to having some flea-bitten four-legged animal crawling around your feet or lap.

The feed brightens, light from an open door blasting through the command center. And who walks in but our own Raptor Six, along with his right-hand guy, Falcon. Sure makes it easier taking notes.

"Welcome to the main event," I boom in my best announcer voice and again check the dials. After stuffing another red licorice between my teeth, I grab my notebook and make a log. There are any one of a dozen spec ops teams basing out of this center, so I gotta make sure I record everything. Detailed notes make nice with the boss.

But hold up. Who's the beauty?

Craning my neck, I stare at the feed. Wearing a hijab? In the SOCOM sub-base command center? "What the. . . ?" With a few clicks, I snap her picture. "So," I mutter as I transfer the image to another computer. "Who are you, and what are you doing in my feed, your hotness?" Transferred, the image runs through the codex, trying to get a facial-recognition match. Get her name, rank, and serial number, if you catch what I'm saying.

Right. Like Raptor Six would give me an inch when it came to this babe.

I'm not digging how attentive Raptor Six is to this woman. And by the looks of things, what with Hawk and Falcon eyeing the two. . .they notice the difference, too.

And just as quick, they walk right back out.

CHAPTER 11

Sub-base Schwarzburg, Camp Marmal
Mazar-e Sharif, Balkh Province
29 May—1315 Hours

That girl is going to be the death of me.

Outside the sub-base, Dean watched Zahrah Zarrick vanish with Specialist Homewood, who'd secured native dress to act as escort for Zarrick. Pushing a thick breath through puffed cheeks, Dean pivoted and entered the sub-base. He punched in the AHOD code. Texted the guys to meet up ASAP at the motor pool while he updated Burnett.

"Augh!"

Crack!

Dean stopped short, reaching for his weapon, as his gaze hit Todd Archer, the man he'd once dubbed Pops. Now known as Eagle on official reports where his real name had been blacked out.

Face red, palms flat on either side of the hole he'd just punched in the Sheetrock, Archer kicked the wall. His hands fisted.

"Archer." Dean approached slowly. "What's up?"

His buddy turned, slumped against the wall as he slid a pained expression toward Dean. He banged his head back and groaned.

At the guy's side, Dean waited. Assessed. This reaction, the tears. . . "What happened?" He had a sinking feeling. A very bad one.

"It's Amy," he said and ducked. Jaw muscles danced. "Cancer's back."

Words proved inadequate. But he had to say something. "Aw man. I'm sorry." *Is that the best you can come up with?* "What're they saying?"

Archer pursed his lips tight. "Not good. They"—he bit down on his words—"they don't—" He swiped a hand over his mouth and nose. His gaze pierced Dean. "I've got to go home."

"Agreed." Even as he said it, Dean wondered how things would fare with the team. Archer was a top-notch sniper. Raptor's sniper. While everyone had qualified sniper, nobody held a bead to this guy. Integral part of the team beyond sniping. Wisdom, experience, sage advice. "I'll do whatever you need, Todd. We're here for you."

Archer peeled himself off the wall and started around Dean.

"Keep me posted." He gave his shoulder a reassuring pat. "I'll. . . pray."

Shouldering out the door, Archer winged up an eyebrow with a crooked grin. Light haloed around his reddish-blond head and beard. "I'd like to see that."

"Hey." Dean spread his arms. "Don't knock it. The Big Guy and I talk. . .on occasion."

Smiling, Archer nodded before sunlight swallowed him. He then vanished behind the closed door.

Alone with the grief of his buddy and the nagging sense that the shift of the tide had only begun, Dean headed into his office and powered up his computer, haunted by his own words about prayer. While he couldn't pretend to be as close to God as Archer, Dean had had a few too many deadly encounters to doubt God was up there watching over him.

"God," he whispered, feeling woefully inadequate. "Help Archer. Help Amy." Okay, so he wouldn't win a scholarship to a Bible school with that prayer, but he meant it. He hoped it made it to God's ears.

Dean logged in and lifted the phone from its cradle. He dialed and waited.

"Make it good, Watters."

Dean smiled at Burnett's gruff tone. "Team and I are heading to the school. Zarrick said some men were there—"

"You talked to General Zarrick again?"

Dean hesitated, confused. "Uh, no. I meant Zahrah Zarrick."

"Go on."

"I've got a hunch they might be the Taliban who hit us in the village. We'll help them clear the debris and search for a missing girl, but that will also give us good reason to be there and gather intel."

"Agreed. Keep me posted."

Dean stuck a hand on his knee. "Todd Archer's wife's cancer is back. Doesn't look good. I want him to go home to be with her."

"We need him here."

"Not if his head is back home."

Burnett grunted. "I'll get Hastings on it."

Dean nodded. Then his mind drifted to Zahrah. Once again, it nagged at him that he hadn't figured out what General Zarrick had meant about her. "Sir, is there something I should be aware of about Zarrick?"

Burnett chuckled.

Unease slithered through Dean. He checked his watch. "Gotta go. We head out in ten."

More laughter. "Let me know what you find."

"Yessir." Dean ended the call, too ready to remove the cackle bouncing off his eardrum. Burnett knew what was going on, and he wasn't going to help Dean figure it out. He hurried across the base and met up with the guys.

Titanis looked up from his gear. "Got something out there?" The burly Australian tossed his pack into the back of the MRAP.

"Heading back to the school. Officially, we're just there to help and hopefully locate the missing girl."

"Unofficially?" Sal Russo asked.

"Gathering intel on a group of men who turned up bloodied the day of the explosion. We need to ascertain why that school was hit and who hit it."

"Well." Hawk sauntered toward them. "That's one mighty big coincidence, don't you think? Them showing up all bloody the same day we bloodied some terrorists in that village." He held out his hands. "And we're just there to help, right? It's the mission of the Special Forces, isn't it? Training others, looking out for the locals, teaching them to take care of themselves." He grinned and winked. "And killing the bad guys."

Across the motor pool, Dean saw the reddish-blond hair of Archer bobbing among the cars. "One of our parameters," Dean said. "Listen." He roughed his hands together. "Archer's heading home soon. His wife's sick again. Doesn't look good. We're going to support and cover for him."

The somber message shriveled the cocky attitudes, forcing a dose of brutal realism down their throats. It was part of life. Men got married or had girlfriends. Someone to go home to. But often, those loved ones ended up *not* being there, one way or another. Just like Mom. And Desi.

Shift gears. "One of the teachers we picked up from the explosion is going to be at the school, too. We don't want to tip off anyone that she's in collusion with us."

"Terrorists wouldn't bat an eye at stringing her up," Falcon said.

Archer strolled up, looking as if he hadn't slept in weeks.

"Mate." Titanis offered his hand. "I'm sorry to hear the news."

Archer hesitated then accepted the sentiments. "Thanks."

"Do what you need to do, Eagle," Falcon said from the driver's seat. "We got your six."

"Thanks, guys. It means a lot. I . . ." He shook his head. "I need to be there. This might be the last time I . . ."

Quiet punched through the metal building. Nobody wanted to finish that sentence. Jinx the mission or the team. Or Archer.

Dean nodded. "Okay, let's check it out."

—∞—

"Did he figure it out?"

Lance laughed. "Not yet, and it's eating him alive."

"Then he doesn't understand the danger."

Easing forward in his high-backed leather chair, Lance propped his elbows on the desk. "Watters might not have the specific threat nailed down, but he knows something isn't right. That boy is one of the best, Pete."

"I don't give a rat's behind. If my daughter dies—"

"She won't." Lance shifted and sighed. "Listen, you told me to keep her expertise under wraps, and that's what I'm doing. And quite frankly, I don't appreciate you trying to lead one of my guys down a path that could get him—and your daughter—killed." He dragged the Dr Pepper can across the desk and slurped. "Now, get off our backs and let my men do their job."

Pete grunted. "If they find out. . .if someone knows. . ."

"If you want that secret kept, stop talking."

His friend released a heavy sigh. "She's all I've got left of Izzah. I can't—*won't* lose her."

"Understood. Now, give us some breathing room. I'll keep you posted."

—∞—

Kohistani School, Mazar-e Sharif, Afghanistan
29 May—1400 Hours

Charred and blackened, the building looked somber. Wounded. As the car waited outside the gate, which had gone remarkably unscathed, Zahrah traced the roof of the section that seemed undamaged. Her gaze shifted to the outer building missing an entire wall and another leaning outward, as if reaching for help.

What would the children think? Could they return here and study without distraction? Zahrah felt a niggling. Never mind the children—she would never feel safe here again.

But then...*I'm not here for my comfort.*

She was here with a purpose.

"What made you come here?"

The voice almost startled her. The female soldier hadn't spoken during their twenty-minute trip away from the base. "To teach them." It was the obvious answer. But something in Zahrah made her resistant to open up to this woman. Maybe because of the way the woman had eyed Captain Watters. Or maybe because this woman was probably the type of woman the captain would like—tough, willing to step into danger.

How silly. Jealous over a soldier she wasn't even on a first-name basis with. Just that she admired the captain would be enough to earn her father's ire. That Captain Watters was a soldier wouldn't matter; that he wanted to date his daughter would. It'd be amusing to see those two in the same room.

"Looks like there's a crowd."

Zahrah snapped out of her musings and looked through the front windshield. Her nerves hiccupped when she spotted Fekiria standing with Director Kohistani and a group of men. "That's my cousin," she muttered. Then looked at Specialist Homewood. They needed a story to cover the woman's presence. "You're a missionary...looking...for a school for your children while you're here."

The specialist held up her hand and wiggled her ring finger. "Not married."

"You're widowed." Zahrah stepped out of the car. She strode up to her cousin and kissed her warmly on each cheek. "Just play along," she whispered as the specialist joined them. "You remember Rachel Phelps. She finally made it over."

Fekiria's wide green-brown eyes slowly shifted to the other woman as she smiled.

At the palpable tension, Zahrah's stomach knotted. She turned to Director Kohistani. "This is Mrs. Phelps. She's visiting, looking into schools for her children. Her husband died recently, and she wants to take up his work here." It was a miracle her nose hadn't grown for all the lies she just told. She had to believe, though, that God would forgive her, the way He had with the Germans hiding Jews. Considering what some Muslims did to Christians. . . "I hope you don't mind me bringing her."

"No. Of course not." Director Kohistani's lips were tight. His posture stiff. "Mrs. Phelps."

Zahrah turned a circle, eyeing the school. "It has a lot of damage."

"Yes," the director said with a long sigh. "I'm afraid it's too dangerous for the children to stay here." He pointed to the roof. "There is structural damage there, and it might cave in."

"But where would we go? The children. . ."

He tossed up his hands. "We have nowhere else."

"Over there," Zahrah said, going to the section of the building where her classroom stood. "It does not seem damaged. What if we had someone block off the left side and—"

"We can't stay," Fekiria said, her tone sharp.

Zahrah eyed her cousin. "But we have to resume school. The children will need to know that some things cannot be stolen from them. That life goes on."

"But for some, it does not. And putting the lives of the children in danger is foolish!" Fekiria's tone bordered on hysteria.

"What—?"

A form coalesced from the shadows of the heavily damaged building. Zahrah recognized it—him. The man. The same one. Involuntarily, she took a step back.

Director Kohistani lowered his gaze.

Fekiria, back to the man, pleaded with Zahrah. "Let's go, we should—"

"You have been at the American base," the tall, strong man said in Pashto, his voice loud and forceful.

Zahrah would not be bullied. But she also knew better than to engage in a confrontation with this man, with *any* man. She averted her gaze. "Of course I went to the base." She kept her voice light. "I was injured. They kept me overnight to make sure I wasn't hurt more."

"Then you went back this morning."

Zahrah felt a gush of warmth across her abdomen. Fear. This man had her followed. She must retain control. Not show how much he scared her. "Yes, I went to see Rashid, a little boy who was hurt in the explosion. I—I took his mom there." When she saw Specialist

Homewood step forward, Zahrah flashed her a warning to stay back. "He was badly injured in the explosion, and she wanted to see her son."

When he lurched toward her, she drew her arms up to protect herself.

He grabbed her wrists. "Who do you think you are lying to?" His crushing grip forced her to cry out. "You've drawn the anger and attention of the Taliban, you stupid, lying woman!"

"Please! I am not lying." Zahrah wrestled the panic writhing in her chest. Pulled away from the man. "Release me!"

"It's true," Fekiria said. "She took Rashid's mom."

The man reared back and rammed his elbow into Fekiria's face.

Her cousin yelped and covered her nose with her hands, drawing the sympathy of Director Kohistani. Would no one help her? No, of course not. This land was plagued with fear of those who wore hatred and vengeance like a mantle.

"Release me," Zahrah said. "It's improper!"

His hand came down hard on her cheek, clattering her teeth. "Do not speak to me, wh—"

"Americans coming!"

CHAPTER 12

Kohistani School, Mazar-e-Sharif
29 May—1405 Hours

D'you see that?"

Two Afghan males darted out of sight as Raptor's MRAP rolled through the gated entry. "Titanis, Hawk, Harrier, walk the perimeter. See if you can figure out who they were and where they went—and eyes out. There could be more than those two hiding." Dean shoved open the armored door. "Falcon and Eagle on me."

Helmet on, Dean climbed down and adjusted his M4A1 slung around his chest. "Nice and easy," he muttered into his mic, taking in any place insurgents could hide. Once he'd noted the layout and possible hot spots, he turned to the man in gray. "Director Kohistani?" He briefly met gazes with Homewood.

The man gave a bow with his capped head then smiled—*fake*—at them. "To what do we owe this pleasure?"

Pleasure. Right. "Captain Watters, U.S. military. We are doing a routine patrol and thought we'd follow up on your school after the explosion. We'll take a quick look around. Be out of your hair soon."

"You have no right—"

"Innocent lives were taken and others injured, including an American. It's our responsibility to ensure safety." Dean came around the civvie vehicle that had delivered Zarrick here. His gaze fell on her now, and he stopped. Something squirreled through his chest as he noted the red, swelling spot on her cheek that glistened.

She reached for her bright hijab that had slid back, leaving long, dark strands of hair in full view. He noticed her beauty, but more than that—the red marks on her wrist. She'd been manhandled.

She looked down, then her gaze flicked to the other woman— her cousin, if he remembered right—who adjusted her silk scarf, not meeting his eyes. Blood spotted the front of her hijab and orange kaftan.

Zarrick wouldn't look at him now, and that bothered him. She wasn't a hider. Heat poured across his shoulders. "You okay?" he finally asked.

With a furtive nod, she moved to her cousin's side. "Just a rough. . . afternoon. Thank you for your kind concern." Her wide brown gaze hit Kohistani's back and her eyebrows raised with meaning.

Right. Dean shifted to the director. "Have you found the little girl yet? My team and I are here to help."

"Oh, that's not necessary. They say it is not safe yet to dig." He motioned to a crane and large equipment.

"I appreciate that, but I have orders to look around since Americans were involved. We're looking for some men, possibly Taliban, who assaulted my team in a village a few klicks north of the city. They escaped before we could intercept." Dean watched the director's face to see if any glint of recognition flickered through his eyes. "We thought they might have been the ones who hit the school, too."

"Was anyone hurt?"

What Dean didn't like was the implication behind this question. Nobody was shot or killed, so he could hear the ill-placed logic that there was nothing to worry about because nobody got hurt. A common stance among locals who didn't want to face the wrath of Taliban leaders. Which was part of the reason Dean wasn't climbing down someone's throat for the marks on Zarrick. His gaze collided with hers. His promise to make sure she didn't get hurt again churned in his mind.

"Check it out," he said, finally releasing the men hovering nearby.

"I do not—"

Dean shot a fierce look at the director.

The man cowered. "Forgive me, I just. . .I am not sure your presence here is such a good idea."

"Don't blame us for this," Dean said, his chest rising and falling faster with each breath. "You were bombed before we showed up, remember?" He squinted at Zarrick again. Then pointed at her. "Besides, if that's how you protect the innocents under your charge. . ." He balled his fists, realizing how much he wanted to punch someone.

"Captain, please." Zarrick eased forward. "Without the director, this school would not exist."

"No," Director Kohistani said, skirting a gaze to Dean then back to Zarrick. "He's right. I should've stopped them from harming you."

Fierce and defiant, he glared at Dean. "But I did not have anything to do with the horrible things. And that you accuse me—"

"Whoa, chief," Falcon said, his voice slick and smooth as he stepped closer. "Nobody's blaming you."

Kohistani turned, challenging. "Then why are you here?"

Dean stepped forward. Not in a threatening way. Just to let him know they weren't backing down. "It's our job. And no matter whose side you're on, it's wrong to beat women and bomb schools. I'm sure we all want to make sure that doesn't happen again."

The man wilted. "Of course, of course. You are right." He touched a hand to his chest. "Forgive me. I am so. . .there is so much stress. The school"—he waved to Zarrick and her cousin—"the teachers. So much hurt and fear. I am tired from it all."

Dean clapped a hand on his shoulder. "You and me both." He skirted around the slick-talking guy, careful not to put his back to him—that would be rude. An insult. And the last thing they needed was more bad PR. Standing almost perpendicular to Zarrick, he craned his neck and eyed her. Over his shoulder, he tossed, "Harrier—med kit."

Zarrick's hand went to her cheek.

"Director." Falcon motioned the guy toward the vehicle. "Ca'I have a word, sir?"

Now able to face her full on, Dean didn't like the way her cheek was still dribbling blood—not a lot. But maybe deeper than he'd first realized. He reached toward it. Surprise knifed his bravado when her lips parted and her shoulders drew up at his touch. "Easy." He hesitated for a fraction, thankful the Oakleys hid his gaze as he probed those large brown eyes that slowly came up. Then back down.

"Stitches?" At their side, Harrier dropped his med pack and dug into it.

Dean stepped back. "Maybe."

"It's just a scratch," Zarrick said.

Again, he secretly probed her eyes. Was she embarrassed, or was this to defuse tension that would register on a Richter scale? Dean turned to the other woman tended by Harrier, who'd just tossed bloody gauze into a contamination bag. "How's she?"

"I'm fine," the woman hissed. Then stabbed a finger at Dean. "You leave her alone, hear me?" Her ultra-green eyes surfed the courtyard then locked on him again. "They find out, and they will kill her!"

Dean gave a quick shake of his head from the whiplash-style tongue lashing she'd just issued. "Excuse me?" But even as he said it, General Zarrick's warning blazed across his mind. The cousin knew? She knew and he didn't? Dean closed in on her. "If they find out what?"

Her head snapped straight and she avoided his gaze.

"Find out *what*?" How on earth. . . ? If it was so dangerous to her existence, *why* wouldn't anyone give him a clue? He invaded her personal space. "Tell me. If you value her life—"

"The way she looks at you. The way you look at her."

Seriously? That. . .she was worried about *that*? "Lady, don't sweat it. That's not a problem. Not for me."

But she was right. The only way Zahrah Zarrick's life could get worse was if the American—*strike one*—Christian—*strike two*—woman—*strike three*—was involved with an American—*strike four*—soldier—*strike twenty*.

In his way of counting, that equaled dead. Capital D.

—∞—

Sub-base Schwarzburg, Camp Marmal
Mazar-e Sharif, Balkh Province

There was not enough Dr Pepper in the universe to heal the wound that gaped in Lance Burnett's chest today.

"Get your nose back where it belongs, Burnett."

"I'm just asking questions. Mighty suspicious that my team finds a secure computer—"

"*Your* team?" General Ramsey shouted. "You're military intelligence, DIA. Operatives. Spooks. What the heck are you doing with an exclusive SF team?"

"Diverting the conversation. Nice try."

"I'm warning you, Burnett."

"Threats now?" He chuckled. "I must've hit a nerve."

"I don't care who you think you are. You get your nose out of this, and stay out."

"We just want the authorization to explore options."

"You have no options, Burnett! And if you don't get that through your thick head, you'll find yourself picking those stars out of the trash!"

Lance tossed the phone on his desk and pushed back in his squeaky leather chair with a heavy expel of breath. Roughing both hands over his face, he fought off the drowning and suffocation.

"He said no?"

With another heavy sigh, he glared at Lieutenant Brie Hastings. "That along with a half-dozen expletives attached."

"But, sir—"

"There isn't a butt big enough, Hastings." He shoved out his chair and stalked to the minifridge. He grabbed a burgundy can and popped the top, letting the *tssss* settle his nerves. Guzzling, he reminded himself that he'd been sure many times before that there was no other scenario. That the situation was hopeless.

"Raptor needs to ferret the source of that SCIF. All facilities need to be on alert."

"Good. Because if whoever is behind this overruns a facility and gains more, then the ability to compromise the network goes up at least tenfold, perhaps one hundred fold. That cannot happen."

"Agreed. CID is working on it." Head tilted, she expressed her disapproval with a seething look. "Our men are there. They know what to look for."

"And our troops are pulling out soon. We're powering down. Can't afford any incidents."

"You mean like ANA soldiers turning against the very heroes who trained them? You mean like—"

"Stand down, Lieutenant."

She recoiled as if he'd struck her.

"I'm with you." Holding the can, he pointed two fingers at her. "Hear me, okay? But we have a fine line to walk."

"Sir, with all due respect, that fine line may just be a walk down a plank."

"Don't be dramatic."

She gave a half smile-grunt. "Sir. . ."

Tenacious had a new name: Brie Hastings. But why? She'd gone all guppy over their operatives before, but she'd never shown interest in any of the Raptor guys since Cardinal flew the coop. No, this wasn't her distraction with one of his men. "Do you know something?"

Hesitation answered for her.

He waited. But nothing came. He chuckled. "I couldn't shut you up two minutes ago. Now I give you the floor and you go dark."

Trapped in her hesitation, Brie sat there, eyes darting back and forth over the carpet. Thinking. Considering. "I came upon something using. . .less-than-conventional methods."

"Most of what we start with happens that way."

She gave an acknowledging nod. "Yes, sir. But this could cost me my bars."

Lance drew up. Tensed. "Go on."

She slid a photo onto his desk. "In my. . .trolling, I found this."

The eight-and-a-half-by-eleven photo was divided into four sections, each holding a different image. "Same building?" he asked, sliding on his reading glasses.

"Yes, sir."

The upper-right image provided an aerial image of the building, intact. Undamaged. The other shots were from various angles, capturing varying degrees of damage. Black marks scorched several doors. The bottom right revealed a sizeable hole in one section of the roof. "Where is this?"

"It's one of our secure data facilities."

Without lifting his head, Lance peered up at her over the rim of his readers.

"It was attacked last night. The only reason I know about it is because of an inordinate amount of chatter in and around the facility. We have a couple of officers there, and it snagged my attention."

"Attacked? By whom?"

"Insurgents, as far as I can decipher. They overran the facility. Reports have six dead. No official report of this."

"You gotta be—"

Hastings handed him another file. "Just before I came in, SATINT picked up a caravan traveling far north of the villages." Brie nodded to his monitor. "I sent the image."

He opened the file. Took a cursory glance. "Bedouins."

"No, sir." She came around his desk. "I believe it's the same group that hit Raptor." She pressed her finger to a grainy image of a large white truck then laid out another image over it. "Bullet holes in the side."

Lance laughed. Loud. Hard. "Get out of my face if that's all you have. Half the vehicles in that country are like that."

"Sir." Brie sounded ticked now. "Think about it. If I'm right, if that's who hit Raptor, the same ones who had the stolen computer. . .what if they went back for more?"

"Then who are the men at the school?" Lance asked.

"Maybe opposing forces. Maybe forces competing for the same prize—breaching our systems."

"You're reaching, Lieutenant," Lance warned, but his mind churned the very scenarios she mentioned. What a nightmare that'd be!

"You're considering that I might be right, so let's talk it through." Dag-blame it if she didn't know him well enough to seize on his internal hesitation. Brie pointed to the monitor again. "That's a lot of trucks heading north. I know you don't need a geography lesson to know what that could mean."

"Besides one brutal trip over a rugged terrain?"

"What if they have our secure computers—?"

Lance dragged the first quad-photo sheet closer. "Ramsey would've told me." Even as he muttered the words, he knew they weren't true.

"Right, because he's been so open and honest already."

Lance felt his blood pressure pop like a sonic boom. He ground his molars.

"Sir, what if they hit that location and Ramsey is covering his six? The bad guys get over that mountain with our computers, and. . .what happens to our *secure* network?" She looked stricken. "The name of every operative, soldier, troop movement, strategy, code names. . ."

"Okay, okay!" Lance waved her away from his desk. "Get out!"

She was right. He knew it. She knew it. But that didn't mean it wouldn't cause one massive headache if he went with their gut instinct on this. Agitation ticked its impatient fingers along his spine, like a big hairy spider. If he made this call, he could end up busted down to private. If he didn't. . .

Lance grabbed the phone. Coded in. "Gear up. Raptor's going in."

TODD & AMY

She had a way about her, one that made a guy lose his good mind. And maybe that's what put him here now, dressed in a monkey suit. Death by bow tie. Great. Try explainin' that to the guys. Todd jabbed his arms through the tux jacket and headed out of the bedroom, avoiding the mirror. One thing to attend a formal event, another to have to see it for himself.

Hustling down the stairs, he fought with the gold links at the cuffs. Darn things—who needed something this fancy on *sleeves*? Probably just end up dipping it into his food. His foot hit the bottom step and movement from the corner of his eyes stopped him. Heart in his throat, he grinned. The light from the Tiffany lamp stroked her brown hair and made her complexion look finer than any China she had in that cabinet that cost as much as his truck had. Amy stood in a little black number. Emphasis on little. Emphasis on, "Sexy Mama."

She laughed and shook her head. "You've always known how to charm a girl."

Todd swooped up to her and wrapped his arms around her waist. "Not just any girl." He kissed her bare neck, inhaling that flowery perfume she liked so much. "*My* girl." As he kissed and pulled her closer, he felt her boniness, felt how the cancer had already stolen so much of the woman he'd married. *Fragile* came to mind.

She adjusted his bow tie, her eyes misty like an early spring dawn. "You wouldn't even wear a tux for our wedding."

"Yeah, well. . .I was more worried about what your dad would do if he found out." Todd shrugged. " 'Sides, I wanna do this right." He cleared his throat. "Just don't tell the guys."

Hand around the back of his neck, she drew him down for a kiss. Todd dove in, savoring the taste of his wife, knowing their kisses were numbered. Her days were numbered.

Amy gave him a coy smile. "I suppose we should go before you chicken out."

"Or you could distract me with more of those kisses."

"Nice try, cowboy."

He glanced down at the black tux. "No cowboy here. This fella's all city slicker." He let her take his hand and pull him out of the house to the dualie. "My lady. . ." Todd opened the door and helped her up into the cab.

Tugging the seat belt across her, she smiled down at him. And he saw it—saw in her eyes the grief that came with the diagnosis. The grief that came in knowing she wouldn't be with him much longer. He wanted to freeze the moment. Capture it. Memorize it—her. Amy.

Throat raw, Todd hopped behind the steering wheel and cranked the engine. He shifted into DRIVE and eased the truck away from the house.

Cool and delicate, her fingers rested on his thigh as they made their way into town. "You don't like the opera." She leaned against the headrest. "In fact, I do believe my hunky cowboy called it the place where they strangle cats."

Todd lifted her hand and kissed it. "Maybe I can put my operator skills to use and save some of those tortured felines. Sure could use them in the barn."

She playfully nudged his shoulder. Laughing, she rolled her gaze out the window. Only the sound of the engine and road noise filled the gaping silence.

"Thank you," she said in a whisper. "I'm sorry—"

"No. Don't." He ripped the truck to the side of the road then angled toward her and held her face. "No regrets. Not here. Not now. Not ever. We're all"—his throat constricted, making it hard to talk and breathe—"we're all dying. God just gave us a cheat sheet with your timing." Grief swam to the surface. "So, we do this. No apologies. No regrets. We live these next few weeks to the fullest. No holds barred."

CHAPTER 13

Hindu Kush, Afghanistan

Ddrake got a hit!"

Heart in his throat, Dean held up a fist. He eyed the spot where the black-and-tan German shepherd sat then the path beyond. The choke point before going down into the walled-off village. Son-of-a-guns had booby-trapped the only path in. Those who knew about the IED would sidestep the spot where a few large rocks marked the location. A pattern he and his team wouldn't have recognized.

Which could've translated into a few missing body parts or team members.

Dean glanced back at the team, spaced evenly out across the tangled mountain path toward the designated location. The others took a knee, waiting for the outcome. His gaze swung back to Titanis, who stood with the military working dog, Ddrake, and his handler, Sergeant Grant Knight, who had been assigned to Raptor for this mission.

Ddrake's tactical explosive device detection training already proved invaluable. After Dean's experiences with the MWDs on previous missions, he tried to request an MWD team as often as he could. Which wasn't often enough. But Burnett seemed willing to give him whatever he needed to get the job done.

"Eyes out!" Dean went down on a knee and scanned the sloping hillside for insurgents with a trigger. Common tactic—lure the Americans to an IED then while they inspect it. . .

Dean's gaze instinctively flicked to Titanis.

Designated engineering—had to make the Aussie useful—Titanis knelt beside the location. Sergeant Knight petted the dog and affirmed him for doing his job then lured the TEDD away with the promise of Kong time.

Titanis shifted his weapon to his back and bent his large form toward the earth.

Face to face with death.

Dean shook off the thought and returned to watching their surroundings, protecting Titanis and themselves as the minutes fell off the clock like thousand-pound weights.

"Found it," Titanis said.

"Need to give that dog some Scooby snacks when we get back," Falcon said, cheek to his weapon as he stared down the sights monitoring.

"Steak. That dog earned a steak for saving my parts," Hawk muttered.

Less than three klicks from the last location the caravan had been spotted. Even from this elevation, they hadn't seen anything resembling that down on the road, hundreds of feet below. They'd chosen to hoof it along a footpath, hopefully get a line of sight. Be able to see what was happening without having to engage. Recon, in and out if necessary, but nothing more. Just report back. Tell them why these men were all secrecy and rushing.

"Clear!" Titanis held up a soda can, the name written in Arabic script. "Haven't you mates heard?" The guy grinned through his beard. "Fizzy can kill you."

"Fizzy?" Hawk chuckled. "That like your head?"

Collective snickers flickered through the narrow footpath.

"Let's move," Dean said. "Not give them a chance to pick us off."

TEDD Ddrake and Knight took point, canvassing the path. Quiet rose with the clear and present threat of danger. Dean kept his weapon ready, eyeing the slopes above them, the rocks below, the path. . .

"Ddrake, heel!"

Dean hesitated.

Knight looked back. "Stairs."

"What?" Dean asked, incredulous. He eased up to the guy and peered around the sheer wall that formed a barrier. He tensed—not only was the earth gouged into a crude stair-path down the sloping hill into the mountain, but there was also nothing to hide behind anymore. Wide open.

Waving the dog team back, he lifted his binoculars, suddenly wishing Eagle hadn't already hopped on that flight back to the States. Dean sure could use him here, his keen eye. His keen sniping. While he wanted his man back on the team, Dean feared the way that could happen—with Amy dead.

"Are they still there?" Falcon asked as he squatted beside him.

Dean scanned the twenty-plus crumbling structures that had slums beat hands down. All connected. All plastered. Fabric covering entrances and lone windows. And circled around the largest building. . . "Ayup." He swept the lens over each vehicle peppering the small village. "Seven, maybe eight." Behind him, he heard frantic lapping and knew Knight was refreshing Ddrake.

"Okay, let's dig in," Dean said to the team. "Ferret out their secrets."

The team settled into position, watching, waiting. For dark. For insertion. A few hours of recon should net info on how many had holed up down there. Raptor would be the eyes in the sky, so to speak, and know which structure had their objective. They'd go in, check it out, tag a truck or two, get their evidence, and get out. Burnett made it absolutely clear they could not be compromised. Nobody could know they were there.

Titanis slid down, his back against the small canyon's wall, weapon ready as he took up patrol.

Appreciating the way the guy operated without yielding to the general resistance of the team to accept him as one of their own, Dean nodded to the burly soldier. "Did good back there with the IED."

Titanis nodded.

"That there was a compliment, my friend," Hawk said as he set up his position. "Not many cross the captain's lips. I'd take pride in that, if I were you."

Straider's intense gaze hit Hawk.

Dean watched. Amused with the men who sat on two ends of the spectrum. Hawk with his smart mouth, straight-forward shooting. And Titanis, who hadn't spoken much but his presence said plenty. Small on talk, big on action.

The way it should be.

—∞—

Mazar-e Sharif

"Hideous!"

Zahrah shook her head as she stood in the makeshift classroom, eying the benches. Her cousin was more worried about her nose, now permanently bent. Makeup had done little to hide the yellowing of the skin around her eyes. For Zahrah, the students, the classroom, resuming the lessons took a higher precedence.

"You can roll your eyes," Fekiria said, "but your cut has almost healed. Mine will forever be disfigured!"

"Don't be absurd. You are still one of the most beautiful women in this country. Your new look only adds to the intrigue." She eyed the clock again. Almost half past nine. They were supposed to start at nine. But the children hadn't shown. Which she found odd since most of the families were used to the constant threats. One should not stop living because wicked men worked their evil.

"Intrigue? Who wants intrigue? There is enough of that here," Fekiria said as she walked around the cramped room. The room she had used before had structural damage.

"Good news," Director Kohistani said as he fluttered into the room. "We are in talks with the university to have access to three of their classrooms."

Zahrah moved away from the wall. A half-dozen questions peppered her mind at once. "Would the children still go? It can be as dangerous—"

"We have little choice. We must move."

"Why? The children we serve are here," Fekiria said. "Not near the university. They won't go there. Many feel it's too Westernized."

"We must!" the director barked, silencing further objections.

Zahrah recoiled at the flood of his anger. "Forgive me," she said, her voice trembling. "I...only..." Her thoughts tangled amid his swift shift.

Like a tidal wave that rose, fierce and threatening, he crashed and receded. "So." His smile swept in and out just as fast. "I will keep you posted."

"Are the children coming?" Zahrah braved the question.

"No." That flickering smile again. "I turned them away." Sweat beaded his brow.

"You what?" Fekiria's eyes blazed. "You have no right—"

"He has every right," another voice boomed.

Instinct shoved Zahrah backward. Her heart raced as the man who'd struck them loomed in the shadowed hall. Hand to her hijab, she verified she'd covered her head. The tunic hung long and plain. Nothing too flowery to draw attention. She did not want any from him. Ever again.

Perhaps Captain Watters would come.

Don't be a goose. He wouldn't show up every time there was trouble. Though he'd come twice now, that was coincidence.

"There is no school today," Director Kohistani said, shifting on his feet. "Go home to your family. I will call when we have worked things out."

Outrage coursed through Zahrah, but now was not the time to voice her objections. They would not be heard. Not by the director, especially not as long as the other man sat on Kohistani's shoulder, whispering, controlling his strings like a puppet master.

That—*that*—was what Zahrah hated about Taliban. Not so much their violence, though it was egregious, but their smothering of people's minds, hearts, and souls. They lived in fear, captive by thought alone at what could happen. Captive in actions, afraid they'd do the wrong thing. Anger the wrong person.

And though she had railed against that type of life, the one her mother had lived, Zahrah experienced a tingling when she realized that bondage had infiltrated her own existence. Hands trembling, not out of fear but out of anger, she turned and gathered her things. She would find a way to talk to Director Kohistani outside this facility, away from the puppet master.

Books clutched to her chest, she turned.

A wall of flesh towered over her.

Zahrah drew in a breath, gaze locked on the man's chest. She blinked and redirected her attention to his feet. Heat blasted through her body. "Excuse me," she muttered in Pashto, noting by the dusty shoes that more had joined them. Her pulse whooshed in her ears.

"You are very friendly with the Americans," the big one intoned.

The accusation stung. Perhaps he did not know she was American by birth. Perhaps it'd be best not to educate him on that detail. "It is said, 'There is less goodness in the one who is not friendly or likeable.'" The words were bold.

"Then you consider yourself good?"

"I am only a servant," she muttered then tried to move around him.

He inched to the side, blocking her path. Touched her face.

Zahrah sucked in a breath and jerked away. "Sir, it is not right that you touch me."

"Kamran, do not defile her," the director said. "Her kaka is a generous donor to the school."

A crooked smile snaked into the man's mouth.

Heart thundering, Zahrah barreled around him, chased by a wretched fear and his taunting laugh.

"Remember, Zahrah Zarrick, I am watching you. Would be a shame to rid the world of your pretty face."

Zahrah hooked her arm through Fekiria's, and together they hurried from the building. "What does he want?" she hissed.

"If you do not know, we are in more trouble than I thought." Fekiria's breathless laugh hinted at her nerves.

Her cousin's bad attempt at humor only tightened her agitation. "Why is he still here? *What* are they doing?"

"Did your American boyfriend find anything when he was here?"

"He's not my boyfriend, and how would I know what they found?" Zahrah felt enmeshed in warmth even as the face of Captain Watters filled her mind. They made their way around the gate, which had been strung together with wire and cord after the explosion, and headed back to the house. "I would suspect they didn't find anything, or we wouldn't be here."

"Or better, he would be here."

Zahrah stopped a few blocks away and scowled at her cousin. "I do not understand you. One minute you hate them, you're yelling—"

"No, not here." Fekiria took her arm, her gaze locked on something behind Zahrah. "Wait." They hustled a few feet before Fekiria added, "They're following us."

Arms linked, they walked with heads tucked and voices low. "Why? What have we done?"

"It's your American soldiers."

"They're *not* mine."

"But they show up wherever you are."

"Not true. They showed up at the explosion because the fire drew them. That had nothing to do with me," Zahrah said.

"What of the day Kamran hit us? Will you tell me that had nothing to do with you?"

Zahrah swallowed.

Fekiria started to turn then glanced back. "Later. In the house."

"I have a phone number. . . ."

Her cousin's bright eyes flashed.

"For if I remembered anything else. I could call. . . ."

"No. He is too far anyway. And it would mean trouble if he came to your rescue again. Let me call Adeeb." She fished her phone out of her bag. Dialed. "Adeeb, men are following us. . . Yes, almost."

They turned onto the narrow road and spotted their bright, coral-colored home. Such a stark contrast in the city to the drabby outlying villages. The wide gate swung out and Adeeb stepped into the open. Zahrah quickened her pace. Though he didn't display a weapon, the bulk beneath his vest made it obvious he was armed.

A surge of giddy relief rushed through Zahrah as he welcomed them as if nothing were wrong then ushered them into the courtyard. "Go!" He urged them to the safety of the house.

They darted up the stairs and into their room. Zahrah dropped against the bed, panting hard, aching to shed the memory of that disgusting man towering over her, touching her—

"You're holding that like it's sacred."

Zahrah blinked at her cousin leaning against the door. "What?"

"Your phone." A knowing smile sifted the fear from Fekiria's expression.

Zahrah glanced at the silver device clutched to her chest with both hands. Like a lifeline. "I. . .I. . ." When had she taken it out of her bag?

"You must give up the idea of him, cousin."

Zahrah tossed her phone on the bed, right along with her cousin's advice. "Why?"

"Because he is American! And a soldier. Fighting *our people*."

"He isn't fighting our people—he's fighting terrorists. And I am also American like him. Or have you forgotten?"

"You certainly should, especially with the attention of those men on you. They would as soon cut your throat if they thought you'd been corrupted."

"You are double minded!"

"Me?"

"Yes, one minute you are chiding me about Captain Watters and the next you're taunting me about him. I cannot make sense of what you're doing, why you do this."

Fekiria bristled. "I only want—"

"I know what you want." Zahrah recognized her anger and frustration. She scaled it back. "You want your country back."

Fekiria slumped on the thin mattress. She toyed with her gold necklace. "Is it too much to ask?"

"It's understandable." She joined her cousin. "But there is a restlessness about you that I do not understand. You love it here, yet you rail against it." She brushed a black strand away from Fekiria's brow.

"The same could be said of you."

"I. . ." Zahrah checked herself before she went on. "I do not think I rail against it."

"You came here to help girls learn, but did you not also come to change it?"

"No—"

"Do you not wish me to become a Christian?"

Zahrah felt the wind knocked out of her with the direct question. "I. . .yes, I would like that—"

"Then you do rail against it."

"No, not rail. I love Afghanistan's people, her heart. A cloud of evil shrouds the land, strangling freedom, and I do not like that."

"But you believe we're wrong to believe in Allah."

Toeing a treacherous line, Zahrah prayed for inspiration. She had not expected this conversation. And she could do serious damage to her relationship with Fekiria. And yet she could not deny a conviction she held dearer and truer than life itself. "Does it not make you wonder why even the Qur'an mentions Isa as *the* Messiah, and all others are mentioned as *a* messiah?"

Her cousin studied her.

A thought lashed through Zahrah and she sighed, shaking her head. "You've done it again." Just when she thought her cousin sincerely wanted to engage in reasonable dialogue about their lone difference. . .

Fekiria frowned.

"You've turned this on me when I asked about you. What are you hiding, Fekiria?"

Silence held them in a tight grip, her cousin's grim expression deepened then flashed into a smile. "Nothing." She punched to her feet. "I'm hungry. You?"

If only Zahrah could figure out what was going on in that pretty head. But she'd been here long enough to know there was no prying out of Fekiria Haidary things she was unwilling to discuss.

"No. The last thing I want right now is food." She rubbed her thumb over the phone.

Fekiria slipped out without another word.

Heart heavy, Zahrah sat with her back against one wall, her shoulder against the side wall. Knees pulled to her chest, she wished she had a friend to talk with. Someone to help her sort what was happening at the school, someone to reassure her she wasn't alone, to figure out what on earth was going on with Fekiria. *A friend. I just need a friend.*

She flipped open the phone and scrolled down. . .down. . . Heart pumping a little faster than it should, she hesitated for a second, thumb poised over the TALK button, then pressed.

A woman answered, her words so rapid and riddled with acronyms that Zahrah couldn't process them.

Zahrah sat up, gathering her thoughts. "Uh. . ." *What am I doing?* "May I speak with Captain Watters, please?"

CHAPTER 14

Hindu Kush, Afghanistan
02 June—0230 Hours

Temperatures had dropped to a biting forty degrees. Enough to chill a guy but not kill him. But Dean chose to appreciate the cold elements. Keep his focus. Remind him he was alive.

"Oy," Titanis grunted, tapping Dean as he nodded toward their objective. "Lights out."

On his knees, Dean traced the darkened compound. Just as the Aussie had said—no more lights in the large building, their focus considering the security and the number of ins/outs.

"Hawk, Harrier, and Knight, on me," Dean said, nodding to the handler. "Falcon, Titanis, you have overwatch." The three nodded as Dean went through a gear check, his mind replaying the facts: at least a dozen unfriendlies, two leaders, possibly more. The large building at the back had a lot of foot traffic, along with more than average security measures. That was his focus. Get in there, find out what was drawing the terrorists like flies to a carcass.

On his haunches, he pivoted to face Hawk, Harrier, and Knight. "Quick sneak-peek. Keep it tight and clean. Do not engage. Again, *do not* engage." He met their eyes, all but glowing—whereas Ddrake's *did* glow beneath the bright moon—to make sure they got the point. "Take a look-see then hoof it out."

"We'll cover, be your eyes and ears," Falcon said.

"If we get separated, rendezvous two klicks south of our present location."

"At the well?"

Dean gave a quick assent, remembering the stone well with the wood planks over it. Like something right out of biblical times. "Stay sharp." With a hand signal, he pivoted and pushed up into a crouch-walk. Weapon trained on the surroundings, Dean slid his NVGs down.

The dark blue night washed green.

A double-pat to his shoulder stopped him. He glanced over his shoulder.

Knight stood. "Ddrake and I should take lead."

Considering the soldier's comment forced Dean to also weigh what could happen. Another IED. A bomb. Getting limbs blown off, if not his entire body, blown past the pearly gates.

Dean relinquished point but not control. "Stay close."

Step by step, gut cinched inch by inch, Dean made his way forward. The pant of the dog went almost unnoticed. Rocks slipped and crunched beneath his boots. Each sound like the report of a weapon in the still, dark night. The incline worked against him, forbidding him from making a 100-percent-stealthy approach. He counted on the enemy's belief that they were here unnoticed. That the UAV they shot down two klicks west didn't get the skinny on their compound.

As the path wound out to the north, Dean stepped off the beaten earth and headed south. More treacherous but it'd deliver them down the backs of the terrorists. They sidled up to a rock and knelt, eying the compound. The dark alley straddled the gap between the long line of huts built together.

Dean tapped Knight.

The handler nodded. "Ddrake, heel."

Dean scouted the compound, made sure they hadn't been spotted, as Knight moved into position. "Go."

Knight hopped down the three-foot drop, landing with a soft thud. He crouch-ran into the shadows of the building. Dean swept up the east and west end with the muzzle of his weapon. "Clear."

"Ddrake, hup."

The dog sailed silently through the night to the ground.

"Hawk," Dean said, but the Raptor team member was already in motion. As soon as he made solid footing, Dean followed. Hustled up to the building and pressed his shoulder against the plaster. "Bravo, we're in."

"Copy that. You're clear," Falcon said.

Dean turned on his helmet cam and eased around the wall, clearing the corner and holding it while Knight and Ddrake hustled across the open to the first large truck. Dean signaled for Harrier to follow. Then Hawk. Bound and cover. Until they established a secure perimeter.

With Hawk as his cover, Dean eased aside the tarp on the first truck's cargo area. His NVGs revealed nothing. "Empty," he whispered.

They moved to another. Using as little motion as possible in case someone waited inside one of the trucks, Dean peeked inside. Nothing but an empty bed. "Same." And the next.

The mission just escalated. They'd have to breach the buildings. That shot up their chances of getting seen, of being engaged. He keyed his mic. "Going in."

"Copy, going in."

Dean moved to their primary target—the larger building. To get to it, they had to pass through three smaller buildings, all attached and with only one entrance. The one right in front of him. He blew out a thick breath. Nothing like a bottleneck to get good men killed.

He moved into position. Hand on the door, he waited for the others to group up. He tested the handle, relieved when it twisted without objection or noise. Kicking in a door didn't make for a quiet entrance. They slipped into the dark hall, grateful for the darkness.

With stealthy movements, he and his team snaked into the building. Moving quickly. Quietly. Farther into the building. Farther away from the exit. Farther from safety.

Safety doesn't exist.

They navigated past a series of closed doors. Dean noted the doors, knew the possibility that armed Taliban were in each and every room. Like walking into a veritable lion's den. Bound and cover delivered them to a door.

With Hawk, they breached.

Two conference tables stretched the length of the room. Parts strewn over the surface raised the hair on the back of his neck. He walked the length, staring down at what he, at first glance, thought had been a mess. Now, standing over the pieces, he saw a deliberate pattern. His gut tensed.

"SCIF," Hawk whispered, eyes wide.

Dean nodded, his gaze on another door. He pointed to the table. "Photos." He signaled to Knight to follow him as he moved to the next door. Angling toward it, he listened. A strange thrum oozed from the space beyond.

He sent Harrier to secure the first door, then once it was closed, Dean and Hawk breached the second. Hustling right, he pied out to ensure there was no threat. The night vision's green illumination marked squares atop dozens of tables.

Hawk's curse, though a whisper, carried like a rocket and echoed the tightening in Dean's gut. A dozen or more SCIFs-in-a-box stared back. Dean hurried toward the closest one, traced its outline. Verified it. Then... His gloved finger found a hole. Heart thundering, he rushed to the next. Another hole in the side of the box.

Hawk caught on. Saw the same thing.

Drill holes.

Ticked, Dean stared at the room. At the representation of a lethal, imminent threat against the American military. Those drills holes meant someone was hacking. But it also meant that amateurs weren't doing this. Drill holes meant someone knew the DOD's largest network for transmission of classified information was tamperproof. If they tried to remove the outer casing, the box would pretty much render it useless. Self-destruct.

Hawk hissed more curses. "Do you know what this means?"

This...this...if they broke the code, so to speak, the entire American military could be taken down. Every mission compromised. Every operative endangered.

Get out. Get out. Now!

"D'you get pictures?"

Hawk nodded.

"Clear out."

"We can't leave these!"

"No choice," Dean ground out. He keyed his mic again. "Mockingbird, this is Raptor Six."

Static crackled in his ear. "You are not cleared for chatter."

"Copy that. We need Glory One and three packages at our location in ten."

"Negative, Raptor Six," the response finally came. "You are ordered *not* to engage and clear out."

Rapid footsteps silenced Dean as he turned toward the noise. Hawk and Knight slipped up alongside the door. Dean joined them. They couldn't engage. Knock the guy out then run like crazy. The steps were getting louder. In the seconds before the man would appear, Dean darted through options: killing the guy would raise alarms. So would knocking him out.

Again—no choice. Optimal success would include escaping without the man knowing they'd been here. Second runner-up would be exiting without the man being able to raise an alarm, though when he came to or was found unconscious, they'd know someone had been there.

"Psst!"

He shot a glance to his three. Hawk stood by an open window, waving him that way.

Dean sprinted and, with more stealth and grace than he'd ever thought he possessed, threw himself through the window. He rolled through the landing. Came up, hearing the slight scrape of the window as it closed. On a knee and shielded, he covered Hawk, Harrier, and Knight as they bolted out of the compound.

CHAPTER 15

Camp Marmal, Mazar-e Sharif
02 June—1023 Hours

Armed with information and a really ticked-off attitude, General Lance Burnett stalked into the command office of General Ramsey.

Peering over his glasses, the sixty-something man continued scribbling on a stack of papers. "How d'you like life in the desert, General?"

"Hate it," Lance admitted. "But I like being where my men are and where intelligence isn't lost in translation." He let the insinuation hang in the air. Ramsey hadn't gotten to this station by missing innuendos.

Ramsey tossed his pen down and leaned back in his chair. "I'm still trying to figure out how you ended up with a black-ops team."

Lance shrugged. "Why not? You have spooks."

The man's face was a wall of granite—but a dark shade that colored his expression. "What do you want, Lance?"

"You know what I want to know."

"Maybe there's a reason you don't know."

"I deserve an explanation on this, since I have more clearance than you."

Leaning forward, Ramsey, a man who stood no more than five-eight and had a mound of grayish-white hair, folded his hands. "Clearance doesn't fight wars. Soldiers, sailors, airmen—"

"I don't need a lecture."

"You need something. You've sent your men into hostile territory without being fully informed."

"Ah, there again is that information I'm missing. The reason I haven't been informed—care to enlighten me?"

"All you had to do was ask."

"Ask what? Your permission to send my men where they needed to go?" Lance's blood pressure boiled. "You're messing with lives, thousands of them."

Ramsey said nothing. Did nothing.

"There are a dozen SCIFs out there—"

"I'm late for a meeting." Standing, Ramsey lifted his head cover. "Good day, General Burnett."

Lance shoved to his feet. "Son of a biscuit box!" He stormed out of the command office and stalked down the hall after the general. "If one more man gets hurt, I swear on my mother's grave, you'll answer for this."

Ramsey stilled. Turned. "There is *no* danger." His gaze slid around the open room where a half-dozen desks cluttered the space. Wide-eyed grunts pretended not to hear the exchange. "There are things you don't know. Never will." His lips tightened. "And let's remember that *I* am in command of efforts in this country. Go back to the Potomac and push some paper."

Lance drew up beside the general. "A dozen secure computers with drill holes and you're going to sit there and say there's no danger?"

Ramsey hesitated, uncertainty lurking in his muddy eyes. "They saw them?"

Could strangulation under duress be expunged from his record?

"Actually set eyes on the boxes?"

"Haven't you been listening?"

Pivoting, Ramsey said, "Come with me."

—⁂—

Sub-base Schwarzburg, Camp Marmal
Mazar-e Sharif, Balkh Province Afghanistan
03 June—1408 Hours

Arms folded, Dean stood with his legs shoulder-width apart, watching the interrogation in the middle of the warehouse. The fully bearded Afghan sat with his hands cuffed to the chair and legs secured. A cut on the man's cheek looked fresh. "Where'd he come from?"

The prisoner's muscles and whimpers trembled.

Sal glanced at him, dark eyes ripe with conviction. "The village we visited."

Dean snapped his gaze to his friend.

"Apparently, the boxes were more lost than originally thought. They sent in a team, extracted him, and blew the place sky high."

With a snort, Dean shook his head. *So much for "do not engage."*

Dampness thickened the air, left over from the early morning rain. A bright light shone in the man's face, glinting off the sweat from the humidity.

"Where did the boxes come from?" an interrogation agent asked.

"I know nothing," the man muttered, not lifting his head. Bloody spittle dribbled down his chin.

Dean sighed. They'd been at it for an hour. The interviewer clearly planned to wear the guy down through exhaustion and redundancy.

"I know you were there, know you saw things—"

"No. They kept me outside. Would not allow me in the building."

"What building?"

Skittish eyes bounced to the questioner.

The interrogator chuckled. "See? Guilt shows in your eyes. You do know what I want." He leaned forward. "There were what, fifty men in that compound?"

"Seventy," the suspect countered.

Game over. He'd given information without realizing it, which meant the beginning of the end. They'd worn him down. If the guy would cooperate that easily, this shouldn't take much longer. Though Dean could think of a thousand other things more entertaining, he stayed. And though this setting smothered him with some seriously bad memories, he wanted to know everything this man knew. He was the enemy. Playing ball with an even greater, shrewder enemy. Secretly, Dean wanted to be the one to hunt down whoever had done this. Whoever was trying to dismantle the military and kill his brothers in arms.

"Seventy," the questioner said nodding. "And you do not think I can snatch your family just as easily?"

"We will kill your family!"

Dean could still hear the words they shouted at him as they drove a burning iron into his shoulder again. The pain had been so great, he went numb. The thing of it was, the threat they tried against his family didn't work. He didn't have family. They'd left him, every last one of them. One way or another.

This line of dialogue always made Dean's gut knot. They had to get information and time was short, but the threat against innocents didn't sit well with him. Then again, some family members were more notorious and dangerous than the men being interrogated.

"Please." The man shook his head. "I don't know what you want."

"You do." The interrogator lifted a small instrument.

Dean tensed. Lowered his arms, hands balling. Fiery pain sliced through his back. Nausea roiled.

Wide, frantic eyes bounced around the room, searching for a sympathetic soul. "I don't know him. I haven't seen him."

"A name then."

The man whimpered.

"A name!"

"They will kill me!"

Sadly, the man was already a dead man no matter what he did or didn't say. Nobody would trust him again. Especially not the kind of people involved in an intricate plan like this.

"You are already a dead man to them." The interviewer's words bounced off Dean's thoughts. "If you help us, we will get you and your family to safety."

The man's head came up. "My family? America?"

"It depends on your information."

"Zmaray. That is all I know."

Dean straightened. *Zmaray.* That was one of their months, right?

"The fifth month of the Afghan calendar," the questioner said. "Is something going to happen then?"

"I do not know." Wild, black, stringy hair trembled as the man shook his head. "I tell you everything. I only work as guard to make sure it stay safe in compound."

"You're lying to us!" The questioner had to apply pressure. Zmaray was a cheat word. As ineffective as saying "a black-bearded man" in this region. And with that pressure came ugly things.

Dean wasn't going to watch. He'd been in that chair once before. He'd been the captive. Been tortured. Beaten. Left for dead. Had the scars to prove it. He wasn't going to relive it through this man.

He punched open the door and stepped into the light drizzle. With a long exhale, he stood, regaining his bearings as he slid on his head cover. Stretching his neck, he shoved off the memories of captivity. The smothering pain. Felt the fire fresh on his back that melted his flesh, scarred his back.

Rolling his shoulders, Dean stepped onto the gravel path and headed to the USO building. He sat at one of the telephone terminals, phone in hand, before he realized what he was doing. *It won't do any good. She won't talk to you.*

The number connected. Rang. Rang again. Three times. Four.

"Hello?" a masculine voice barked.

Dean hesitated.

"Hello? Who is this? Do you know what time it is?"

Everything primal in Dean rose up. "This is Desi's phone, so why don't you tell me who you are."

The man cursed him.

"Where's Desi? I'm her brother."

"She ain't got no brother!"

The line went dead. Dean considered calling back. He hadn't been a part of her life since they were split up and put into foster care. He'd tracked her down just before entering Basic. Young and stupid, with a head full of idealistic familial passion, he thought she'd be elated to see him. Cry and hug him or something. He didn't know what he expected, but finding her with more track marks than the subway and aiming a gun at him wasn't it. That and the way she flipped him off and drove away.

Roughing a hand over his stubble, he sighed. Why did he even try?

He knew why. It didn't make sense, but he'd wanted a connection. To prove the "no-family" thing wrong.

But it wasn't. Never would be. He'd be alone. Always.

Dean exited the building and headed to his tent. As he crossed the paved street, he heard laughter and looked in that direction. He stopped short. There, thirty yards away, moving toward the hospital. . .

Zahrah.

CHAPTER 16

Camp Marmal, Mazar-e Sharif
03 June—1439 Hours

All business with a weapon strapped to his leg and his ball cap pulled low, Captain Watters stalked toward them. Zahrah spotted him the moment he'd stepped from the tentlike structure and into the sunshine. But he hadn't seen her. Not yet.

"Hey, Captain," the soldier escort called.

Zahrah twinged, feeling as if she'd been caught staring.

Captain Watters lifted his head and met her escort's gaze. "Falcon, did you—?" His gaze hit hers. He slowed—or had he? Was it just her imagination that the hard, tense lines of his face suddenly didn't seem as hard? "Miss Zarrick," he said with a curt nod.

"Captain." At least she didn't stutter the way her heart did.

He eyed something behind her then frowned down on her, those rich eyes assessing. "You okay?"

"What?" She looked back. Only the hosp— "Oh! No, I'm fine. It's not me. I mean, nobody's hurt. We just. . .I just. . ." So much for not stuttering. "I'm here for Rashid, the little boy who was injured. He's coming home today."

The captain frowned again. "Where's his mother—did they find his sister yet?"

"Hey," the other soldier said. "Can you take over? I have an AAR to get filed."

This time, Captain Watters scowled. But nodded.

"Uh, no. Ara hasn't been found." She felt punched, but whether from the guilt of Ara's missing status or the way Captain Watters seemed disappointed at her being pawned off on him, she couldn't be sure. Was that how he saw it—being pawned off? "Rashid's father is traveling for work and his mom. . .well. . ." How could she say this without offending him?

"I get it." He pointed to the main doors and started walking. "Most around here appreciate our help, but when you get some whacked Talib with a thirst for blood, suddenly, nobody's our friend." He tugged open the door and held it.

Zahrah slipped in, hesitating just inside as she waited for her eyes to adjust. "I'm sorry you had to get pulled aside to escort me. I'll make this as quick as possible so I don't interrupt your day."

"Please!" Laughing, he tugged off his cap and smoothed a hand over his almost-shorn brown hair as they moved down the hall. "Interrupt me. The boredom is killer."

"Boredom?" She appraised him as they turned a corner toward the pediatric ward. "You do not have the look of boredom on you."

He raised an eyebrow. "Yeah, what does a bored person look like?"

Zahrah peeked into the area where Rashid had been yesterday. She clapped a hand over her mouth as she watched him balance a spoon on his nose, a male nurse doing the same. Beside her, she felt the warming presence of Captain Watters. She quirked an eyebrow and looked up at him. "How about that?" she asked with a giggle.

"Definitely bored."

The two goofing off jolted at their laughter. The male nurse stood straight. "Captain, ma'am."

"Learning secret techniques of the American military?" Captain Watters grinned at Rashid as he trailed her into the curtained-off area. "I might have to insist we keep you here, young man."

Rashid's eyes widened.

With more laughter, Zahrah smoothed the boy's hair, hoping to ease Rashid's fear.

"Will you?" Rashid asked breathlessly. "I want to be a soldier, too!"

She blinked. And laughed again—mostly from nerves. "Okay, Rashid. You've had too much fun. Your mom is waiting at home." She reached for the crutches and smiled when Captain Watters handed them to her. "Massoud is waiting for us."

The boy's countenance shifted. Humor gone, he stuffed the supports beneath his arms and stood. Wobbled a bit.

Captain Watters stepped forward. "Use your hands to absorb the weight, and keep the crutches close to your body." He seemed to talk out of experience.

Rashid gave a nod and tried again, and on his face shone the enormous desire to make this American soldier proud. To prove he could do it. Zahrah stepped back, affording Rashid's pride and his tutor some room.

"We were working on that before you caught us...with the spoons," the nurse said as he tucked his chin. "I'm going to get his discharge papers."

Captain Watters straightened, folded his arms over his chest, and walked, a half smile stuck to his deeply tanned features. " 'Ere you go. You've got it."

Rashid moved quicker.

"That's it—nice and easy though."

The boy wonder hopped around till he faced them again. "Did you have to use crutches?" Rashid asked Captain Watters.

His answer came slow, almost unwillingly as he nodded. "I did." He rubbed his stubbled chin. "About ten years ago, my leg got busted up like yours."

Rashid had far too much amazement in his features. "You did?" Awe spread through his voice like molasses.

"Yeah, and I think you're doing better than I ever did on those sticks."

"Okay, folks." The nurse returned with a clipboard and pen. "Just a few John Hancocks and you're outta here."

It took only a few minutes to write in the family's contact information on the medical forms for Rashid before they were officially released. The nurse pointed to a small camo duffel. "That's his stuff."

"Stuff?" Zahrah looked to Rashid. "You came here in just your clothes."

"The soldiers brought me a few gifts," he said with a toothy grin.

Captain Watters lifted the bag. "A few? Feels heavier than my footlocker."

"What can I say?" The nurse shrugged. "He became our own little hero around here, fighting hard to survive and recover."

The captain nodded. "That's the mark of a true soldier." He slung the pack over his shoulder. "Ready, recruit?"

Bright brown eyes beamed at the captain. "Yes, sir!" He gave a mock salute then started hobbling down the hall.

Zahrah had to work to control the tears. Watching the way these two American soldiers treated Rashid with such respect, as if he were any normal boy... She could not stop from stealing glances again as she walked beside the captain. "You've kept his spirits high. I can't thank you enough."

He gave a one-shouldered shrug. "I was a kid his age once."

She laughed. "I cannot imagine."

He eyed her. "It's true—I remember having heroes." Another shrug. "You know, Batman, Superman. . . ."

He made her giggle. A lot. It was a nice change from the stress and restrictions necessary to integrate among her mother's people.

"So, you mentioned a Massoud earlier."

Right. Just his job. And right now, that included escorting her off base. Zahrah nodded. "Rashid's uncle. He's a fierce man, and there has been little love between the two. Massoud feels their parents are too soft on Rashid."

Captain Watters's jaw muscle popped as he eyed Rashid at the end of the hall, waiting by the door. "Don't like to see a kid wear fear like that."

"You and I have that in common." Zahrah watched as he punched open the door and held it for them. There was so much she admired about him—strong, handsome, focused. Yet there was so much she didn't know about him—like his first name. Would they ever get to that point? She secretly hoped so. But how? What would that be like?

Futile. If she entertained these notions any longer, her father would find a way to have him reassigned to Timbuktu. But she was a grown woman, and she'd never found a soldier, sailor, airman, or Coootie worth pursuing.

Until now.

Pursuing. Gah! That sounded like a hunt.

With Rashid's rubber-tipped crutches grinding against the pebbled path, their progress was slow. But it gave her more time with Captain Watters. What could she ask him—about his family maybe?

"So, this Massoud," he said as he fell in step beside her, this time on her right. His shoulder angled toward her. "You said he's waiting."

"A couple of blocks beyond the gate." Which was far too close.

They approached the security checkpoint, and Captain Watters turned to her. Caught her elbow, his gaze sparking in the sunlight as he scanned the area beyond the checkpoint. "So, Massoud. . ." He finally looked down at her. Right into her soul, it felt like. He was close. Much more than he'd ever been. Made it hard to think.

Zahrah felt a flicker of confusion. "You seem concerned about Massoud."

"You'll be safe with him?"

Her thoughts and pulse ping-ponged from one thought—did he know something she didn't?—to another: Was he concerned for her safety? More than a soldier just doing his duty—until she was left with a blush he couldn't miss. "Y–yes. I believe so."

Once more, his jaw muscle popped. He nodded as he looked around again. A smile quirked one side of his mouth. "Wouldn't want your dad coming after me if something happened to you." He moved to Rashid and went to a knee. "Okay, recruit." Captain Watters removed his navy-blue cap. "I have a mission for you."

Rashid straightened.

"You're brave, I've seen that already. But now I need you to protect someone."

"Who?"

"Miss Zarrick."

Zahrah's stomach churned at the way he peered up at her, intense and focused.

"Think you can do that, recruit?"

"Yes, sir!"

Captain Watters slid the hat onto Rashid's head. "Now it's official. You're my Top."

"Top?"

"Yeah, my first sergeant. You report to me. Now, to protect Miss Zarrick, you have to protect yourself." He adjusted the rim of the hat and tugged it down more. "You can't protect her if you let yourself get hurt."

"No, sir—I mean, yes, sir!"

Captain Watters stood, hands at his sides.

Rashid was grinning like a wild dog.

The handsome soldier leaned forward, almost conspiratorially. "You have to salute me to make it official."

"Oh!" Chest puffed out, Rashid snapped his hand up to his forehead—and nearly lost his balance when the crutch slipped. Laughter rumbled through them as he steadied himself.

Zahrah shook her head, trying to dislodge the tears blurring her vision. She did not imagine Captain Watters could fathom what a great gift he'd bestowed on the young boy. He'd been through a horrific event, and yet he was leaving the base with a smile, a commission, and a new hero.

So am I. She shook her head again. He cared. He truly cared. It wasn't just a thirst for violence as some liberals back home had insisted. Men like Captain Watters made the difference. It touched her deep. Deeper than she could understand. Overwhelmed with gratitude—the experience for Rashid could've been terrifying—she fought back tears.

"Hey." Captain Watters caught her elbow and bent toward her. "You okay?"

Zahrah nodded quickly. "You're amazing. Thank you." She tiptoed and planted a kiss on his cheek. Stunned at her own actions, she scurried through the checkpoint with Rashid, never looking back. They made their way off the base and headed down the street.

"Do you like him, Miss Zarrick?" Rashid hopped along, really getting the swing of walking on crutches.

"Who?" If her burning cheeks hadn't answered for her, she sure wouldn't.

"Captain Watters! You kissed him."

"I *thanked* him."

"With a kiss," he said.

Mercy! That would be frowned upon by his family and definitely by her uncle, cousins, and aunt if Rashid shared. "Rashid, listen." She squatted before him, holding on to his waist as she sought the right words. "I'm your protector. I have to know these things."

"I shouldn't have kissed him. It was. . .I was so. . ." Oh for the mercy of heaven! How did she get out of this without lying or making Rashid feel bad?

His face was thoughtful and serious. "It is okay, Miss Zarrick. This is our secret. I won't tell anyone."

Sweet relief smoothed out the anxiety that had knotted her shoulders. She managed a small smile. "Thank you. I'm afraid most people would not be very understanding."

"I know." He beamed. "That is why *I* am your protector."

Tussling his hair, she straightened. "Captain Watters picked the best recruit! Now, we should hurry." As she pivoted and started down the street, she saw them. Men hovering around a black BMW—Massoud's car. Her stomach churned. She wanted to flee back to the base. To Captain Watters.

Though she didn't know the men with Massoud, she knew one thing with absolute certainty now. *I am no longer safe here.*

TODD & AMY

I'll be tied to you, right?" Amy's gaze skidded from the harness to Todd.

He tucked in the extra length and grinned. "Have been for six years, darlin'. Or d'you forget?"

The plane's propellers fluttered to life.

He patted her shoulder. "All set." Handing her the helmet, he noticed the brief flash of fear in those blue eyes that had brought him to his knees many times. "You don't have to do this."

Breathing in—as if inhaling courage—she lifted her chin and placed both hands around the helmet. "Yes, I do." She strapped on the helmet. "If you can listen to strangled cats for me, I can jump out of a perfectly good plane." Amy smiled and shook her head. "Still can't believe you got qualified to tandem so we could do this together."

She'd always been strong inside, many times more than she even realized. He loved the moments where that courage crested her need for safety.

She smiled. "No holds barred."

Todd hesitated. Parachuting was nothin' to him. To her. . . "There's no holds barred—"

"You calling me weak, Todd Archer?"

Hands up, he surrendered, lowered his gaze, and eased back. "No, ma'am."

"Then quit wasting oxygen." She turned and walked toward the plane.

And yes, the girl still had it. Even in a jumpsuit—*especially* in a jumpsuit. She was stepping into his territory a bit with this stunt. His heart clenched. *God, help me. . .help me make these final weeks unforgettable.*

He climbed up into the plane and sat beside her, intertwining his fingers with hers immediately. Pilot-friend Jeremy aimed the prop plane down the runway. Soon, the plane climbed through the clear-blue sky. Todd couldn't help but think he didn't like this for more reasons than one—she was closer to God here in the plane and in life. It wasn't fair. Then again, Bobby Ray said the same thing when Amy chose Todd for homecoming.

A few minutes later, the plane leveled off and Todd stood. He hooked up with Amy, seeing the terror in her eyes.

"Amy," he shouted.

She kissed him. "No. Holds. Barred!"

And with that, they jumped. The exhilaration of wind ripping at him was nothing to the thrill of experiencing it with Amy. Todd willed the descent to drop into some time warp. To never end. For them to never hit the ground and reality again. Up here in the sky, almost floating above the world. . .yeah. Just like that. They seemed above all their problems.

They landed feet up in a butt slide. The best six minutes of his life.

They unhooked and secured the chute. Todd turned—

Amy threw herself into his arms. Hooked her arms tight around his neck. Buried her face in him. He felt her sobs before he heard them. Todd closed his arms around her, holding her close and safe. Her adrenaline was probably crashing.

Wished like he did with Raptor, he could get a bead on the threat to his wife and kill it with one shot. A trained warrior and he could do nothing but *adventures* that only reminded him he'd never do them with her again.

"I don't want to leave you," she cried. Then sniffled. "There has been nothing better in my life than being your wife!"

CHAPTER 17

Kohistani School, Mazar-e-Sharif
04 June—0900 Hours

*T*hud. Thud.

As Raptor team climbed out of the armored transport, each door closure pounded against Dean's conscience and heart. This hadn't been their doing—the collapsed building, the missing girl, the death tolls. But he couldn't shake the sense of guilt that clung to him like the heat and dirt. *If I'd just been here. . .*

That wasn't a logical thought, but it plagued him all the same as Dean stood at the front of the MRAP in a pair of tactical pants and his combat shirt. No vest. No weapon. Surveying the scene, he felt the presence of his team. They'd agreed to do this, agreed to help however they could. It was what Raptor did. Winning hearts of the locals, one person at a time. But here, winning hearts wasn't the goal. It was an end product of their mission to show the people here that they cared.

The mud bricks that towered two levels up surrounded a cloud-shaped hole. Debris puddled at the bottom of the gaping structure that leaned heavily to the right. A dying sentry.

Strapping on his gloves and jamming the fingers down for a snug fit, Titanis leaned toward him but eyed the same structure. "We need to stabilize that before we start."

"Looks like they attempted stabilization." Falcon nodded to a piece of timber propped diagonally from the ground to the arching wall.

"Won't hold. I'll get on it." Titanis waved two soldiers from the engineering corps over with him.

Dean took in the massive rubble pile that filled the gap between the two buildings that once served as a breezeway. That's the same area Zahrah had stumbled out of. The same one he'd found Rashid in.

A group of men withdrew from their digging and stood, eyeing them warily.

"Eyes sharp," Dean said, waiting for one to approach him.

Director Kohistani emerged from a crowd of men working the large pile of rubble. Hands scratched and bleeding, he lumbered toward them, the weight of the job pushing down his shoulders. "Assalaam alaikum."

With a slight, respectful nod and hands clasped in front of him, Dean replied, "Wa 'alaikum assalaam."

"How are you and your men doing?" Kohistani asked, his smile held in place only by societal rules.

"Well, thank you." Dean glanced at the team gathered. "We heard from Miss Zarrick that you still have people missing. We're here to help in whatever way we can."

The director gave a somber nod. "Your offer is appreciated."

Shouts rose from the men at the site. Kohistani turned and watched. Thirty seconds later, the men passed a body from the rubble to a sheet spread on the ground. "Wafa. . ." The director watched, his face ashen, his lips moving slowly.

"You knew him?"

Kohistani flinched, as if he'd been hit. Sorrow kneaded his thick, bushy brows. "I knew them all, Captain." Lines scratched into his aged face as he nodded. "This was my school—I met them all, their families, their friends. Wafa was twelve. Anxious to be twenty." A smile wobbled on his thick beard.

"I'm sorry."

He touched his forehead. "*Inna lillahi wa inna ilayhi rajiun.*"

Dean hesitated, unsure what the man said. If Zahrah had been here, she would've translated for him. But maybe it was better that she wasn't—he didn't want her seeing bodies of children being pulled from the rubble.

"Forgive me—it means 'To Allah we belong and to Him we return.'" He drew in a ragged breath. "It just seems more are *returning* than I could've imagined."

"Would you like to take a break?" Dean asked. "My men and I are ready to help."

Kohistani, his head partially bald and his face worn with grief, gave a half nod. "No." He touched Dean's upper arm. "You are here and have revived my will. If you, who have no relation here, can dig, so must I."

Tugging his gloves on and tightening them, Dean followed the older man to the heap. They were introduced to the others, who were coated in sweat and dust, hands bloodied from the digging. A few moved into the shade as Raptor joined the work.

Dean made his way to the epicenter and started passing off debris to Hawk, who passed it to Falcon and so on until they had formed a human chain. The labor proved mindless as they worked through the mound that must've been five feet high. Locals had made a good dent in the removal, but this would take hours. Dean wouldn't let his mind go to where it wanted—to the possibility of where Ara might be found. If she'd been with Zahrah. . .

A flicker of movement to the far side snagged his attention. Dean glanced up as he lifted a rod with clumps of mud brick dangling from it. He handed it to Hawk, hesitating as his mind caught up with his vision. Zahrah. She stood with a satchel, one hand reaching in as she delivered bread and water to the men slumped in the shadows.

"Need me to do the heavy work?" Hawk teased.

Dean glanced at the coms specialist and refocused on the job. Where had she come from? *Please don't let me find Ara while Zahrah's here.*

"Hey, Double Z's looking your way, Cap'." Hawk snickered. "Maybe I should take my shirt off. Show her what a real man looks like."

"Shut up," Falcon growled. "This is a cemetery. Be respectful."

Even Dean felt chided. He'd taken a bit of pleasure in seeing Zahrah with her teal hijab and gray tunic. It'd felt like the sun had broken through a storm cloud called death. Besides, everyone knew it was Hawk's way when times got tense to crack a joke. Lighten things up. And Dean had to admit—he liked that the guys had given her a nickname. Double Z. Nice.

"Meant no disrespect," Hawk muttered as Dean removed a piece of vinyl that had once probably been part of the upper floor.

"Idiot. Laughing when we're digging out bodies." Falcon's tone bordered on dark. Angry.

Dean shot the team sergeant a glance. Where had the venom come from? One thing to be respectful, another to end up disgusted by an innocent mistake. And Dean couldn't help but track Zahrah's movements around the area as she showed her compassion and care for the people.

As she inched her way closer to them, Dean wanted to tell her to go home. She didn't need to see what they'd find. Not bodies. Not of children she'd taught and cared about.

Nah. You're just worried about seeing that wound in her eyes. Don't want the guilt. He'd had enough of that when he'd served at Ellen's funeral. Stood at his own parents' gravesite, the dirt still mounded and wet beneath the pelting May rain.

Stretching his neck did little to shake off the memories.

"Water, Captain Watters?"

Dean started. Looked to the side where Zahrah held a sweating bottle. He glanced at his watch, surprised to find they'd been working more than an hour. Not taking it would be rude. Taking it would keep her close to the rubble. "Thanks." He accepted it and downed it in three huge gulps.

"I didn't expect to see you here," Zahrah said as she handed bottles to the team, who downed them and went back to work.

"I could say the same."

Her face glowed beneath the sun's bright touch. A strand of dark brown hair peeked from beneath her hijab, accenting her amber eyes. Smiling eyes. Always smiling. She bobbed her head a bit and bunched her shoulders. "I am here to serve."

But there was more to her being here right now, wasn't there? A shimmer of trouble skittered through her olive complexion. She chewed the inside of her lip as she traced the worn-out men. Her gaze dropped several times. Guilt.

Yeah. That made sense. She'd rushed the children back to the school right as the explosion happened. "It's not your fault."

Her chin dimpled in and out with a wave of grief.

"You know that, right?" Dean shifted to the side and stood before her.

"She would've been home had they not stayed behind, had they not walked home with Fekiria and me." A tear slipped down her cheek. With a knuckle, she brushed it aside.

"Hey. Crap happens. Things we can't control. What happened here was out of your control. You did your best to protect those kids. Got it?"

She breathed a smile and nodded. "Just. . .just find her." She looked at him and Dean felt the world tilt. "Please."

He felt the strings of propriety tying his hands and stopping him from giving her a reassuring touch. "We'll find her." With that, he returned to the laborious task. Zahrah faded out of view but never far from his thoughts. He dug his fingers around a brick, the cracked and hard material scratching at his fingertips. The way she'd asked him to find the girl, the way she looked at him. . .

He passed the brick to Hawk.

Shouts broke out. Dean paused and looked up.

Hands held up at chest height, Titanis backed up, apologizing. Dean frowned as the Aussie walked around the pile till he stood beside Dean.

"What happened?" Dean muttered, lifting more rebar and chicken wire.

"There's an area they won't let anyone enter."

"Unstable?"

"Only politically."

Dean frowned as he handed off another chunk of mud and looked at the big guy, waiting for an explanation.

"Same area Zahrah said the men had been holed up in."

Dean reached for another brick. "Think something's there?" His fingers grazed something. Something *not* hard. He froze, eyes sorting the debris. A dash of blue. A rock, rebar—

Time powered down to an excruciating speed. One where his pulse thumped against his conscience. One where he saw the tiny gray fingers, slightly curled and bloodied. In the next heartbeat, his pulse spasmed. A tiny boom of his heart shot adrenaline through his body.

He swiped away the dirt from the palm. The blue—it was beads on a bracelet. A little girl. Ara. He lowered his head and clenched his eyes.

"He's got something!" Hawk shouted.

Dean shifted aside, assessing, figuring out which way her body lay. And in what felt like three heartbeats, he uncovered her. Hurrying so he could save her. Illogical, he knew. But maybe. . . *God, You do miracles, right?*

He yanked off the bricks. Threw them aside. Beside him, the men did the same.

Dean went to all fours, cement and mud digging into his knees and palms. Empty eyes stared back at him. Blood covered the left side of her head. Slumped with his head down and between his shoulders, he tried to hold it together. With a hitch of breath, he straightened. Cupped his hands beneath her broken, cold body. Lifted her from the rubble. Stared at the innocent face, hair matted with blood and dirt. He curled his arms, tugging her closer to his chest. Wanting desperately to protect her. From what, he didn't know. She didn't deserve this.

Grief-riddled shouts and moans drenched the afternoon. A man rushed toward him. Dean stepped off the mound and stood before the man, who beat his chest. Cried out and took Ara from his arms.

And suddenly, Dean felt empty. So very empty.

—⁘—

Camp Marmal, Mazar-e Sharif
04 June—1310 Hours

Right cross. *Thump!* Uppercut. *Thump.* He threw another right. It landed squarely, the impact carrying through his arm and shoulder. The telltale ache in his back haunted him, even after ten years. He toed the mat, bouncing and moving. Energy trained on the black bag. On shedding the frustration. The confusion.

The truth was staring him in face.

Had to be. *"If you weren't distracted by her pretty face, you'd know why I'm calling."*

Pretty face.

Dean threw a hard right. Connected. The impact rippled through his muscles. Felt good. Burned.

The memory of her flowery scent and soft lips spiraled up and spiked his adrenaline. He aimed with a left cross.

"Saw the boy went home yesterday."

Dean didn't break line of sight on the punching bag as Sal came up beside him, removing his wraps.

"That school teacher sure takes good care of those kids. Saw how it ate her up over that little girl."

An uppercut. He knew what was happening. Knew where Falcon was headed.

"Have a nice chat with her?"

Dean leaned back and drove his foot into the bag. Came up with a hard right. "D'you run the IDs?"

"Nothing yet."

After toweling off his face, Dean moved to the speed bag.

"Any closer to your mystery puzzle?"

With a quick shake of his head, he tapped the bag. Right. . left. . . right.

"Oy, word is that the schoolteacher is one of your top general's daughter." Titanis morphed from the shadows, gym bag in hand. "I'd be chuffed with that news."

"Not if her daddy was breathing down your neck like he is with the captain here," Falcon said.

Right. . .left. . .right, left, right, left.

"That right? She's a missionary, right?"

Rightleftrightleftrightleftleft.

"A bit crazy, mate. Coming into a war-torn country for religious reasons."

Rightleftrightleftrightleftrightleftrightleftrightleftrightleftrightleft.

"That won't egg him on. See the wings on his back?" Falcon smirked—he could hear it in the guy's voice. "He's here for religious reasons, too."

"The wings are raptor wings, I thought," Titanis said.

"For us they are, but for Dean, the wings are also angel wings. Or so he says. That's why he's here."

"Wrong." Dean stopped the bag. Held on, his breath heaving, his mind trampling the wrong assumption about the wing and sword tattoo covering his back, covering his scars. "I'm here because I wasn't going to let them win."

Titanis eyed him. Then with a toss of his chin said, "Let who win?"

Dean rounded on the men, startled to find the entire team huddled. Breath leveling, he used that as an excuse for more time. "The ones who tried to break me." He ripped off his gloves and tossed them to the side. "Look, we have things to figure out. I'm not the mystery."

Titanis smirked. "Aren't you though?"

Dean eyed the Aussie.

"That's some artwork on your back. And I don't mean the ink."

"It's not relevant to our mission." Dean grabbed his bag.

"Isn't it?"

Dean slowed. Gritted his teeth. Hung his head.

"I've been wondering why this mission has your brilliant tactical mind so clouded you can't see the obvious."

He turned. Slowly. Met the guy's pale gray gaze. "Obvious?"

"Yeah." Titanis seemed a brute of a guy, with a voice that wasn't deep but contained a depth with what he said. "This girl—why is she here?"

Hawk snickered. "Dude, she's a missionary. They got religious fervor, need to proselytize everyone."

"Nah." Titanis's lips pursed. "See, I'm not buying that."

Though his heart beat a mean cadence, Dean waited. Listened. He'd wondered this, too. Beyond the normal stuff in the file.

"There's something behind her being here. What is that?"

"Her mom," Dean said. Now it felt more like bouncing off ideas with a like-minded soldier. Falcon used to do that. Till something made him withdraw. Their friendship hadn't been the same.

The guys looked at Dean.

He shrugged. "Her mom was an Afghan."

"Maybe." Titanis jutted his strong, bearded jaw. "But there's more to it than that," he said again. "See, you—you're here because you want to beat what your captors tried to do to you, the lies they tried to beat into you. You're here amid insane circumstances facing down death. That girl—she's doing the same thing every day. And I just have to ask—why? What compels her to be in danger, day in and day out?" He shook his head. "I don't know many women, or men for that fact, who would. So what's behind it?"

Dean nodded. This was good.

"She's here because of our captain." Hawk chuckled. "She's sweet on him."

"I think the captain's sweet on her, too." Falcon sounded ticked.

"If he's not, he should be. Or sign me up." Hawk. Ever the gentleman.

"You're stating the obvious." Titanis sounded like an instructor now. "Get past those rudimentary elements and dig a little deeper, eh, mates? This girl might be sweet, but we'd be foolish to mistake that for soft or schoolgirl behavior."

"What are you getting at, Titanis?" Falcon folded his arms over his chest, intent.

"That girl has steel for bones to be here, to face Taliban who'd as soon kill her as let her teach. So why? What is here? She's got this mind-blowing degree. What is she doing in a dusty school with children and death blowing up her front door?"

Dean froze. Gaze darting as he mentally reviewed the data from her file. He grunted. "That's it. Her degree. The SCIFs." He slapped Titanis on the shoulder then looked at the others. "Shower up. Meet at the command center in twenty."

Scrubbed and changed into fresh duds, Dean sat at his computer in the command center. He logged in and pulled up Zahrah's profile.

Scrolled to her education. Eyed her internship. Dropped back against the rickety office chair. He steepled his fingers and breathed against his hands. He lunged out of his seat and stomped down the hall. He rapped twice on the door.

"Enter."

"General Burnett," Dean said, his heart thudding against the question he was about to ask. "Neither I nor my team has any room for games. We are engaged in a deadly scenario."

"Yeah, it's called war."

"I need to know one thing." Dean didn't want to give voice to this. But he had no choice. "Is Zahrah Zarrick an enemy combatant?"

CHAPTER 18

Sub-base Schwarzburg, Camp Marmal
Mazar-e Sharif, Balkh Province

You don't really believe that, do you?" Lance Burnett leaned forward, feeling his temper in the bulging veins along his neck. "I thought you had more brains than that."

"Sir." Tight lips, tense shoulders, the guy was ticked. "That is the last thing I want to believe about Miss Zarrick, but the dots are leading me there."

"Then get off the leash! Start walking this dog, Watters. That girl is no trouble to you or your mission. She has aided us countless times as translator and advisor."

"I understand, sir. But her area of specialty—"

"I don't think you do understand, Captain." Lance didn't want to tear into the guy, but it'd taken him too long to figure things out. "That girl holds incredible information in her head, but she's got a heart of gold."

"Agreed, sir. That knowledge she possesses is rare—invaluable. I imagine she's helped SOCOM."

"Many times." He slammed down his pen. "She's an asset, not a target."

"For us, but it sure would be dangerous if someone with criminal intent found out about her area of specialty."

"That's right."

"And I'm sure General Zarrick would breathe fire if anything happened to her."

"It was bad enough when she was involved in the explosion."

"Which is why she should leave the country. ASAP."

Lance stilled. Son of a gun. "You walked me right into that one."

Watters lowered his head. Probably to hide the smirk he wore. "I believe it's in her best interest that she be removed from the area until we get this thing figured out and stopped."

The captain might be right, especially if the guy wanting to send her back was part of the problem. "You don't trust yourself."

Pulling straight, Watters scowled. "Sir, I'm not on babysitting detail. I can't be with her 24/7. There's no way with her active life—one that has already drawn the scrutiny of men under investigation—and mine as a member of SOCOM that I can maintain OPSEC and keep her alive, too."

Lance could not argue. Especially not after the dialogue with Ramsey. "Agreed." He sighed. "But leave off about that. I'll talk to Pete and see what he says. Right now, we have bigger fights to pick."

"What's happening, General?"

"Intel came down from Ramsey about a connection to the SCIFs."

—⁓—

Mazar-e Sharif
05 June—0930 Hours

Raptor team kept its distance, not standing with the family but also not significantly distinct from the friends. The somber atmosphere kept them in check. With war ravaging the lives of those he knew, Dean held an intimate knowledge with death and funerals. He'd buried too many friends. Those took their toll but nothing like the funeral when he was eight years old. His gaze strayed to the little boy held close by his mother. Dean knew what it was like to be that young, to bury someone you loved. . . .

He rolled his shoulders and stretched his neck. Trained his eyes on the tiny, frail body wrapped in white and being lowered into the hole. His gaze tracked on their own to the lithe figure of Zahrah Zarrick, who stood behind the little girl's mom. Arms linked with her cousin, she blended in with the other Afghan women in the gathering. Dark brown hair, brown eyes, black hijab and tunic. Sunlight captured a tear as it slid along her cheek, a hostage of her grief. She swept away the drop. Her shoulders lifted as she drew in a breath and raised her chin.

In the moment that their gazes connected and she managed a small smile, she suddenly seemed worlds apart from those gathered. How could he protect her when she stood out like that? It seemed a desert stood between them, her vulnerable and open. Him too far away to do any good. He wanted to move closer so he could react quicker.

What possessed a beautiful woman like her to give up the relative security and safety of life back in the States? He had to hand it to her, though. She fit right in. Nothing unusual about her—until she spoke. That American "accent" got her every time. And yet. . .it didn't. She could speak fluent Pashto.

A nudge against his right elbow pulled his gaze to the ground.

"Two o'clock," Falcon muttered without moving a muscle. "Hundred yards."

Dean skated his gaze in that direction, not wanting to draw attention to himself. A line of clay and mud homes built into a hillside tried to hide from the sun in the desertlike setting. A glint from one of the rooftops tightened his gut. Was he staring down the wrong end of a sniper's scope? As he took in the dwellings, he spotted the front of a white truck.

Heat flared across his shoulders. Threat? He eyeballed Hawk, standing to his left with Titanis and Harrier. Hawk must've heard Falcon's whispered words because as soon as Dean's gaze struck him, he gave an almost imperceptible nod and slowly shifted away. In minutes, he'd navigated around the crowd and slipped behind a building.

When Zarrick looked at him again, her eyebrows knotted in question. Had she seen what just happened?

A loud voice boomed over the crowd, a prayer he guessed, because the thirty-plus family and friends went to their knees again. Dean and his team took a knee out of respect to the family but not to their god. When the others rose, Raptor rose.

A quiet yet strong presence loomed to his left. Hawk had returned. "Same guys from the village."

The gathering started breaking up to make the passage back to the house, where they'd sit with the family for a while, share in a meal and in grief.

As Dean turned away from the burial site, he nodded to Falcon.

"All the more reason she leaves." Falcon started out of the graveyard.

"Roger that." As they drifted from the family, Dean locked on to Zarrick.

"Cousin's going to be a problem," Falcon hinted as he headed up the hill.

"Got it." Hawk shot him a grin.

Though he wanted to warn Hawk to keep it respectable, the warning wasn't needed. Raptor team knew what was important here. Knew a slipup could cost them.

Protected from view of their unwanted visitors watching from afar, Dean kept tabs on Zarrick's position without being obvious by staying to the side. Trailing behind as they walked the two klicks to the family's home, Dean steadily moved himself up into position. Falcon stayed beside him to maintain propriety. Together, they fell into step with Zarrick and her cousin.

Had she noticed him? He wouldn't believe she didn't—she seemed too aware of her surroundings to miss that, so Dean kept pace. Waited.

"It was kind of you to come," Zahrah said quietly.

"Mr. Mustafa extended an invitation."

Her large brown eyes struck his. "You were wise to accept. It's a miracle he did—he has been one of the most vocal opponents of your presence here."

By "your," she meant the American military. The narrow flight of stairs prohibited conversation and forced him to walk behind her. Less than two klicks left to convince her. At the top, she shifted aside and paused. Waiting for him? Something about that simple gesture slipped a noose of guilt around his neck.

"I noticed," she began, a little quieter as she came into step with him, "one of your men leave during the funeral. Is everything okay?"

As he'd noted earlier—she didn't miss much. Impressive.

Her gaze came to him when he didn't answer. "Okay, you're worrying me." Though there was a laugh to her words, she clearly didn't find it funny. Neither did he. She wouldn't like this conversation. In fact, it felt over before it even began.

Zahrah turned to him. "Did my grumpy father call you again?"

He almost smiled.

"He wants me to go back, right?" She nodded to where Hawk walked with Fekiria a few paces ahead, but close enough to chaperone, and smiled. "Can't believe she hasn't hit him or something yet."

"Hawk can play nice when he needs to. And no, sorry." As Dean made his way down the road, he watched the hard-packed earth. Habit. Kept him alive. "I haven't talked to your dad again."

"Well, that's a surprise." She sounded relieved. "He hasn't let up since I arrived. He's afraid something's going to happen to me. He thinks I'd be safer back in Virginia, working at a lab or something."

"I agree with your dad."

She stopped. Didn't look at him. Just stopped. "Why does that not surprise me?"

Dean took a step before being bungeed back by her hand. He moved aside when an older couple eyed them as they passed. To keep things proper, he didn't face her. Just stared out over the road. "That's probably not what you wanted to hear."

Cocking her head slightly, she stretched her jaw and gave an airy snort. "Talk about an understatement."

"It's smart. And for your own safety."

"Captain, I belong here." She thrust an arm back and pointed to the graveyard. "That little girl they just buried is why I'm here. Children like her."

He leaned in. "Miss Zarrick—"

"No."

"Please hear me out, Miss—"

"Stop it!" She stilled, closed her eyes for a second, then opened them again. In them he saw pain. From what? She looked past him. As if the wound was too much for her to accept. "I'm sorry, but I'm not having this conversation with rank and formality. My father tried that as an overbearing general-father. And you see where it got him." A smile wobbled at the edges of her lips. "If you can't use my given name the way a friend would, if all I am to you is a liability, then go back to my father and get the briefing."

Stunned, Dean stared at her as his mind snagged on one word: *friend.*

"No, wait." Her eyes held precision targeting as she shot him a piercing glare. "I'll give you the condensed briefing: *Mission to talk Zarrick's daughter into going back failed. Zahrah refused.* There. That's exact enough even for my father." She started forward.

Dean moved into her path. "Please, Miss"—he cringed—"Zahrah. Hear me out, *please.*"

She drew up, lifting her chin. Then cut him another fierce look. "Not fair. I don't even know your name."

"It's better that way," he said, feeling his heart ricochet off his ribs. *Keep it light, Watters. Keep it light.* "Operational security. . ." He was losing her fast. Had to crank up the charm or something. "Also, if you end up hating me, it's no loss."

She rolled her eyes—

"Dean."

His name came from the side, from Hawk. Dean rounded on him, furious, but the guy pretended as if he'd never spoken, as if he wasn't listening.

Zahrah's fire hadn't waned. "You expect me to listen to your advice, but you're unwilling to even tell me your name. Clearly, it's my mistake for thinking we were friends." Her nostrils flared. "Do you understand that I'm not under your command, *Captain*?"

He never thought he'd hate hearing his rank spoken, especially not from her. But this felt like a samurai sword through his heart, lungs, and gut. "Do *you* understand, Zahrah,"—man, that felt weird—"that I'm trying to protect you? Keep you safe?"

"I do." Softening around her eyes and mouth made a profound difference. "But I also know that I'm here for a purpose"—doubt sparked in her eyes for a second—"or a few reasons." She hesitated. Met his gaze.

"It's not safe for you here."

"I'm well aware of the danger I'm in. It surrounds us here. This isn't like living in the States where an isolated incident like the Boston Marathon garners worldwide attention. These people, my mother's people, live with violence every day. I've been living it for eighteen months."

"But you've never had the crosshairs of a sniper's scope trained on you."

—〰—

Heart thundering, Zahrah turned toward him. "What're you saying?"

He looked down, then away, his hazel eyes fighting the sunlight. The kindness in his expression that had always drawn her to him lay hidden behind some. . .she wasn't sure what. "Can you just trust me on this? I can't say more. But I would not be here if I did not believe you—not just any Afghan woman, but you, Zahrah Zarrick—are in imminent danger."

She swallowed. Took a step back. "Wh–why would I be in danger?"

He shook his head, his gaze dropping once more. After a deep breath, he looked at her. In him, she saw that he wanted to tell her, but those regulations. . .

Figure it out on your own. Just like always. Like with her father. He'd go all spec-ops quiet and she'd have to piece together the puzzles. What had happened? The bombing. She considered Dean—was that it? The bombing? But wouldn't he have said something sooner?

Then. . .the confrontation in the school yard.

But that seemed more like testosterone fighting.

Then. . .the funeral. "Whoever was watching the funeral—that's the danger?"

His jaw muscle flexed. But he didn't answer.

"Did you find anything out about the men?" She searched his face. Traced the stubbled jaw to the small indent in his chin that wasn't quite a dimple. Studied his eyes, a mixture of green and brown, only the brown was more goldish-orange. But the intensity. The anger roiling through his irises. "You ask me to give up everything and yet you will not tell me a single thing that will convince me."

He rounded on her, his brow knotted. "Will anything I say at this point convince you to go back?"

He's angry. The thought pulled her up. Scared her. She wasn't sure why, but just as swift, her own anger crested her frustration and coiled around her. She wanted so much for this man to open up to her. To just shoot straight and treat her like an equal. "I understand you have mission parameters, but do *not* put this back on me."

"I've tried, Zahrah. I've tried to convince you that the danger is real. A bombing, the confrontation, and now snipers, but you insist on staying." He planted his hands on his hips. "I thought you had more sense than this."

Lord, have mercy, he sounds just like Daddy!

No doubt existed that he was right—she *was* in danger. From whom or what, she didn't know, but she could feel it breathing down the back of her neck like a hot wind. Yet if she surrendered her conviction over the hint of danger, then it wasn't a conviction. Just an excuse. If at the first sign of trouble, or in the face of a fierce Special Forces operator, she surrendered her belief that she should come to Afghanistan and serve her people, then she was no friend of God.

It took every ounce of her courage, her strength, her conviction to hold her ground. "I appreciate your concern"—Dean or Captain, which should she use? Neither.—"but I'm staying."

"Why are you being so stubborn about this?"

"It's not stubbornness, not in a bad way. I just have this deep conviction that it's not time to leave." She considered him for a moment. "I'm not ignoring the facts, Dean. They scare me, but I can't walk away from a mission. You wouldn't, right?" She pointed to his men. "You wouldn't let them either."

Hands up, he splayed his fingers. Touched them to his forehead for a second, and she could see the way he worked to restrain his frustration. That startled her. Worried her. She didn't like him angry. "I don't think—"

"Miss Zarrick! Miss Zarrick!"

Zahrah stepped out into the road again and spotted Rashid hobbling along on his crutches. He hopped up to her, leaned on the crutches for balance, and then extended an arm. "Madar said to give this to you." His bright, beautiful smile warmed her heart.

In her hand, he set a three-strand turquoise bracelet. In a flash, she recalled the countless hours of writing instruction and leaning over Ara's work to guide her, the bracelet clacking against the table or jangling as she played games in the courtyard. "Oh, Rashid. I cannot take this."

He closed her fingers over the bracelet. "Yes, you must. *Baba* said you should have it."

Zahrah searched the road ahead for the sign of Atash Mustafa. But then. . .she realized, no. Mr. Mustafa was strident in his views about Americans in his country. He'd only allowed Ara to come to the school because she was a girl, and he saw no loss in it. That Zahrah's mother was born not far from Mazar-e helped, too.

"Rashid, hurry," someone called.

He hobbled around and scurried off as quickly as he could with the extra set of wooden legs.

"That. . ." Dean's voice croaked. "That bracelet. . .it's the first thing I saw when I discovered her."

Zahrah turned to him, her heart a mixture of grief and fear but also a flood of resolution. "Dean, *this*—what this stands for—is why I can't leave. It stands for Ara. It stands for all the little girls and boys who need and want an education. It stands for my purpose here, and until God tells me to leave, I'm not going anywhere. Just like you, as a soldier, would not abandon your post without orders, I cannot abandon what I'm doing here."

"What is that, Zahrah? I don't see you being a missionary and preaching to them. Why can't you do this in some inner city back in Virginia?"

"God didn't ask me to." For the umpteenth time, she felt the conviction electrify her bones. And the stirring within her that there was yet another reason she had come sizzled along the edges of her nerves. "I don't want to make you angry. I really don't. If I didn't feel so strongly, I'd listen to you. I trust you—you're a good, wise man. But I can't leave, Dean. Not now. I love these children, and I belong here."

"What if you die?"

Sorrow burned the back of her eyes. "If I truly belong to God, then I have no rights, which means it is not my place to put demands on how or what He does with my life."

Those vibrant hazel eyes watched her with no little amount of frustration. She could tell his hands were fisted, though she didn't look at them.

Seeing him like this twisted her stomach into nauseating knots. "I'm sorry. But please"—why was it so important to her?—"*please* don't be angry with me."

"I can't change your mind, can I." It wasn't a question and had so much agitation behind it. His lips went flat and he started away. Then jerked back. "You realize this is stupid. You're putting yourself and everyone you know at risk. Is *that* what God wants?"

Zahrah blinked.

He ran a hand over his head and the back of his neck. "Sorry." Seeing him contain his anger, reel it in, poured more respect for him into her soul. "I can't protect you if you stay. You realize that, right?"

His broken words wilted something inside her. "That's not your job, Dean. It belongs to God."

He hopped a step closer, shoulder angling in again. "What if *I* am God's protection—what if *He* sent *me* to warn you?"

Zahrah tilted her head, surprised at the direction he'd taken. "Well, if it is..." He had a point. Was she wrong? Should she leave? He had the experience and intel to know when things were dangerous.

A strange rush of hope filled her. Should she leave? Be safe, back in Virginia, with Daddy? It'd be so nice. She felt a pang of guilt for the small longing that lurked deep in her stomach.

Should I leave, Lord?

No. The word was simple but strong.

"If God had sent you to warn me, then I'd leave." And she meant it. She trusted Dean Watters like few others.

Some of the tension seemed to drain out of his shoulders. Just a little. "Then you'll go?"

Frustration began to nudge aside her soft answers. But she tamed that urge, knowing Dean would feed off that. "I'm supposed to stay, for the children, and for"—some other reason she couldn't yet name. Was she staring at that reason? Was it *him?*—"for now. I'm sorry if it makes you angry." She'd do almost anything to make that expression on his face go away. The one that rejected her answer, rejected *her*. In her need to smooth the rippled waters, she offered, "Call me to make sure I'm still alive." She meant it as a lighthearted commented. But his eyes darkened.

"Even if you die? Even if staying means your death?" It was meant as a challenge. Maybe even a threat.

There were many horrible deaths a woman could die here. The thought made her shudder. "Yes."

Jaw muscle popping, he gave a shrug-nod. "Fine." He took a step back. "We tried." A quick nod again. "Good-bye." Dean pivoted and stalked off, his broad shoulders taut as the rest of his team clustered to him like a magnet before climbing into a black truck a half mile away.

She'd lost one of the most precious children today, possibly her job as a teacher since there was no school, and now. . .perhaps the only man she might have been able to love.

CHAPTER 19

*Camp Marmal, Mazar-e Sharif
05 June—1140 Hours*

This couldn't happen. Not again. First his sister, then Ellen. Screams pierced his thoughts. He clenched his eyes tight against the memory. Against the grief. Dean ran both hands over his head, down the back of his neck. Not again. Not again. Just can't.

He'd be hanged if he was supposed to send another body home because he came up short and innocents paid.

How—*how*—was he supposed to fight against God and divine purpose in an argument? There was no fighting conviction like that. No fighting radical faith. Why did it anger him so much that she rejected his solution that maybe God sent him?

He punched the dash. Felt the eyes of Falcon on him, but he had enough sense not to comment. Instead, he accelerated.

Dean's sat phone rang. "Go ahead."

"Watters, where are you?" General Burnett demanded.

"En route to the base, sir."

"Good. Call me up when you get there. Raptor's on the next plane out."

He straightened in the seat. Had he heard correctly? "Yes, sir." It angered him that she'd been right—God hadn't sent him to protect her. He couldn't do that if the CIC wanted them in another country. "General wants us in the command center ASAP."

"Aw man, I had a date," Hawk muttered.

Falcon chuckled. "You mean with the girl who couldn't stand talking to you?"

"She was dumbstruck by my wiles," Hawk said.

"Dumbstruck by your *dumb*ness!"

Falcon returned the truck to the motor pool and the team piled out. As he made his way back to the sub-base, Dean couldn't shake a dread that had a fist hold on his throat. Zahrah wouldn't have anyone to contact if something happened. She'd be alone.

Why did she believe in God more than Dean? So willing to put herself in the hands of an intangible God than a man with an M4.

Same reason you tattooed those wings on your back.

He couldn't fight her logic, but he wanted to. With both hands, feet, his Beretta M9 and M4. *God. . .You did it for me. Do it for her. Keep her alive. Please.*

"She say no?" The quiet, firm voice of Titanis punched a breathing hole through Dean's thoughts.

He slumped back against the chair. Shook his head, still unable to understand her bullheadedness. "She won't go. Says she'll trust God."

"Can't argue that, mate."

"Can't I?" Dean held out his hands and shrugged. "Look, I get faith. I believe in God. I know He works miracles and all that, but. . .isn't there a line between faith and"—he hated to say it—"stupidity?" Straightening in the metal folding chair, he placed a hand over his chest. "God has me here, a part of elite security forces. To protect people just like her. But she won't let me do my job."

"Tough call that one, but theology later," Straider said, clapping a hand on his shoulder then pointing toward the sub-base command center.

Rolling up his frustration, his anger at Zarrick, and the unshakeable fear that stalked him down the narrow hall lined with pictures of home, pictures of dignitaries who'd visited, Dean vowed to try once more to convince her to leave. Then if she still refused, her safety was in her own hands.

—⚬—

Undisclosed Location

Someone really should clue the six stooges into the fact that their secure location isn't quite so secure. Then again, if someone did that, I'd be out of a job.

Huh. More like out of a life.

So far, they haven't provided quite enough to bring down hail-fire rain on themselves. But it will happen. Eventually. I just have to log a few more hours. Maybe a few more months. Who cares with the eight-digit paycheck sitting in my accounts?

"So, what'd she say? She's leaving, right?"

Hawk always makes me pay attention. Never know what's going to come out of the guy's mouth. He's not stupid. Just straightforward. I like that.

Annnd. . .of course, Raptor Six doesn't answer. Man of few words. But he sits at his computer and starts banging on the keyboard. In seconds, the team gathers around him.

"Guess she said no," Hawk mutters.

Really, did anyone besides me see that coming? The girl might be sweet and might not have nerves of steel, but she doesn't strike me as one to whimper and lie down at the first sign of opposition. For cryin' out loud, she's a general's daughter.

The team closes in as Raptor Six ignores the question Hawk posed. Closes in—and perfectly closes *off* my view via the hidden camera. Dunces.

"C'mon, c'mon." Seeing what he accesses goes a long way in my filing a full report. Incomplete report equals angry evil overlord. But they still aren't yielding. I drum my fingers. Growl.

"Move!" Shouting at them doesn't do any good, but I feel better. Or not. "Your lazy carcasses are blocking my view." Really, not a bad problem. Unless they stay there the whole time and go silent on me.

"Ah, Raptor. . .*team*."

Angry they're still blocking my view of the monitor, I hit the voice analyzer and wait as it drums up the information.

"Good. I need you all there anyway." Hold up—is this the big cheese, Burnett? Sounds like him. But I'm waiting for the computer to verify it.

"Sorry, sir. I just wanted to code in and let you know Zarrick refused to leave."

Sir. That means a superior, and by my estimation—a noise blips to my right and confirms my suspicions: Burnett, Lance, General.

Alrighty then. Time to listen a little more carefully.

"Yeah, well, we got bigger problems. I've got intel from Ramsey that demands you head to Majorca."

Silence drops on the command center like a concussive boom. Only. . . quieter.

"Majorca," Raptor Six repeats. He sounds a little stunned.

Same here. *Dude, can I go, too?*

Falcon leans one hand on the desk. "Want to explain this very big diversion from our current mission, sir?"

"No."

I laugh. Nothing like the general's dour attitude to lighten conversation.

"Ramsey gave me some credible leads on those SCIFs you stumbled upon. The containers have been traced back to Majorca."

This is when I wish I had taken a course in shorthand. But I'm scribbling as fast as I can. Boss Man will need to know about this.

"That doesn't make sense."

"Tell me what does, Bledsoe." Burnett never tolerated anyone giving him lip. At least, not while I was listening in. "But we've got a lead, and we're not letting this rest till we've stripped away every secret and found out who's behind it."

"When do we leave?" Raptor Six runs a hand over his short, dark hair.

"Next flight departs at fifteen hundred."

"Tomorrow." Russo huffs.

"Sir, I don't believe it's wise to leave Zarrick here unprotected. She's. . .she's in danger, sir."

"Well, let's just hope her secret doesn't make it past this room."

Oh man. Laughing here is so wrong, but I can't resist. "Trust me, General," I say, calling up the boss man on my secure phone. "It does. It goes *way* beyond."

—⚬—

Sub-base Schwarzburg, Camp Marmal
Mazar-e Sharif, Balkh Province
05 June—1750 Hours

"Captain!" Hawk, a wad of food in his left cheek, grinned as he leaned back in a chair around the conference table. "You were so ticked out there, I knew she said no." His grin was enough that Dean saw pearly whites he'd willingly knock out. "What'd I tell you? She's staying."

Dean glared at him. At Falcon and Harrier and Knight with Ddrake snoozing at his handler's feet.

After swallowing whatever he'd been eating, Bledsoe punched to his feet with a *"Hooah!"* Laughing, he held out his palm to the others. "Time to pay up, brothers." The others handed over fives to Hawk, who made no apologies for his enthusiasm or being right. He pocketed the money and moved back to his seat. As he went to sit, Dean strode past and gave him a little shove.

He toppled back, caught himself as his face went wide with shock, then righted himself. "Sir, pardon my saying so, but you've got some serious attitude going on. She mean that much to you?"

Falcon said, "Unless you want us to pin you down and ink your back like we've been promising—"

"Hey." Hawk pointed toward the Italian he could take any day of the year. "Leave the body alone. It's mine. A sacred temple."

"Well, sit your sacred temple down and shut it," Dean said as he logged into the terminal.

"What do we do about the girl while we're gone? About both of them?"

"Nothing," Titanis replied.

"You have to do something." Knight grunted.

"How many tours you done?" Falcon asked.

Silence drenched the encounter, then, "This is my first."

Hawk chuckled.

"Let's remember," Knight said, "Ddrake saved your butts out there."

"Easy, chief." Falcon unwrapped a protein bar. "It's all in the family."

"We have a much bigger fish to fry. I'm talking great white."

At his back, the team leaned in—Dean could feel the cumulative clogging of the air with the five of them gathered tightly. But that was good because they were a tight team. Dean folded his arms and leaned back, staring at the monitor.

Burnett continued, "The intel connects the SCIFs with a cyberse-curity group there in Majorca."

"So the trip to Majorca is legit?" Hawk hooted. "Beaches...babes... bring it!"

Titanis eyed Hawk. "They have tattoo artists there."

"Brother from another country"—no laughter in Hawk's voice now—"leave the temple alone."

Dean fisted a hand, giving the hold signal.

"I won't kid you," General Burnett said. "This could get messy quick. I want you to get in, find out who is connected to this."

Something weird thrummed in the general's words. "You have concerns about the intel, sir?"

"It came from Ramsey. Need I say more?"

CHAPTER 20

Mazar-e Sharif
12 June—1515 Hours

Doubt crept along the edges of her confidence. A shiver traced her spine. *You are my hope and refuge, an ever-present help in times of trouble.*

"It is for the best," Khala Hafizah had said as Kaka Jahandar stood behind her.

Zahrah glanced around the small flat she and Fekiria would now share—"prudent," her aunt had called it, "a smart, independent move"— until the school building had been repaired and they could return to holding classes there.

Two weeks ago, she would've loved the freedom of living alone with her cousin. Freedom! But now? *"Imminent danger. . ."* Dean's words pummeled her courage.

Dean—his name still made her pause—had been so angry when he left. Or should she say, *stormed* off? While his warning hadn't convinced her to leave, it compelled her to be a bit more cautious.

Oh, who was she kidding? Flat-out scared was more like it. "Thank you, Captain Watters." The severity of his expression and his harsh words were like watching a horror movie late at night during a storm. Just added more anxiety where it wasn't needed.

She placed a hand to her throat. Disappointment tugged at her composure. She slumped onto the chair in the living area and stared at the phone. An ache bloomed in her chest, one that longed to have the tenacious captain treat her more like the friend she wanted him to be.

Friend? No, she had to admit, she'd hoped for— Well, it didn't matter. It wouldn't happen. She hadn't just burned that bridge. She'd blown it with C-4.

A shout outside made her heart skip several beats. Slowly, she rose and moved to the sliding glass door that led onto a small balcony. She looked over the edge, down three floors, and saw a rowdy bunch of college students in the parking lot. As she turned, a glint caught her eye. A silver Mercedes parked in the far corner of the main lot. Window down, the man smoked—

Zahrah shoved back several steps, her heart in her throat. The man from the school. The one who'd threatened her.

"Imminent danger. . ."

Dean's words haunted her as a heavy blanket of dread draped her shoulders. She held her elbows and considered the danger. What was Kamran doing here? Watching her apartment? Why? Was he the danger Dean had detected at the funeral?

"You're leaping without facts, Z," she whispered to herself. But she couldn't shake the question—was he somehow connected to whatever Captain Watters *wouldn't* name in their conversation? She rushed to the couch and fished her phone out. Who. . .who would she call? Dean?

You trust God, remember?

The taunt smacked some sense into her. She did trust God. And she did *not* believe it right to leave Afghanistan. But should she have stayed at the base for a while? Or. . . ? She shoved her fingers through her long hair. Doubts bred like maggots in her confusion.

Keys jangled at the lock.

Zahrah shoved off the couch. Keys. Fekiria. Only she had keys.

The lock turned and the door opened, sucking Zahrah's breath from her chest.

Fekiria slipped in and released the key from the lock. She pivoted, cheeks flushed from the warm afternoon, and smiled. "Ah, you're home."

"Where have you been?"

Fekiria scowled. "You know where I was."

Fingertips to her brow, Zahrah took a steadying breath. "Forgive me." She shifted to the curtain. "He's here, Fekiria. The man from the school, Kamran."

Dropping her purse, Fekiria frowned as her face drained of color. "Where?"

"The parking lot—silver Mercedes."

Her cousin eased up to the balcony and peeked. She returned quickly. "What is he doing here? Back to break another bone? Make sure we obey the Qur'an?"

"Shh!" Zahrah looked around the apartment. The couch and coffee table. Kitchenette tucked in the far corner. To the right, the bedroom where twin beds meant she no longer had to share a bed with a cousin—or two. But nothing to serve as a weapon if he tried to come in.

Ha! Right. With his bulk and her size, he'd overpower her easily. She had to do something.

"Okay, enough." Zahrah went for the door.

"What are you doing?" Her cousin caught her wrist, eyes bulging. "You can't go to him!"

"Of course not." She smiled. "I have a better idea." She slipped into the hall and went down to the lobby where a phone hung on the wall. She punched in the emergency number. "Yes, I'm scared. There is a man sitting in a silver Mercedes in the parking lot. I—I think I saw him before at the bombing where the children were killed. He's just. . .waiting. Do you think he. . .? Oh, I just can't say it." Making her voice weak, her words frantic added the dose of fear she wanted the dispatcher to believe.

"Stay in a safe place," the dispatcher said. "We will send someone over."

"Thank you." Zahrah hurried back up to her apartment, knowing the ploy would work this time. But next time. . .he might not wait. "You should go out, stay away for a while," she said to Fekiria.

"Where are you going?"

"A bit of shopping."

"Are you crazy? Shopping—when he's stalking us?"

Zahrah smiled. "Yes, I'm crazy. You've told me that since I arrived." When she heard the sirens shrieking through the city toward them, she lifted her purse. "Go home with your parents."

"No. I'll go to Khaled's." Fekiria's face paled, but then she faked a smile. "He invited me to eat with his family."

"A boyfriend?"

Fekiria wrapped her favorite pink silk hijab around her hair and neck. "It's better than grandfathers!" They wound down the stairs to the main level then parted at the back door.

A few blocks later, Zahrah entered a small shop. Three men wandered the cramped aisles while a couple of women chatted with the employee. Nerves skittered around her belly as she gathered the items and headed to the counter. This purchase would halve her savings, but if Captain Watters was right. . .

As she hurried back, she scanned the parking lot then watched for ten minutes before darting back into her building. In her apartment, she locked the door, slid the chain over, and then went to the two-person kitchenette.

She worked quickly and put her experience, the same one Captain Watters insinuated placed her in jeopardy, to work for her. God had given her a keen mind, and He'd put the captain in her path to warn her of danger. Now. . .now, she'd make sure to protect herself in the only way she knew how.

Palma de Mallorca, Balearic Sea, Spain
12 June—1730 Hours

A cool breeze wafted off the Balearic Sea, smelling of salt and fish. Dean tugged down his black, nondescript ball cap and shouldered his pack a little higher. Sparkling water nearly blinded him as the Majorca coastline chugged closer. Still weighted over the unsatisfactory ending to his conversation with Zarrick, Dean tried to push aside the anger that she wouldn't listen. He didn't want to face losing someone else while he was gone.

Just didn't make sense. She was smart. She had to know things were escalating.

Powerless to stop her, to force her stateside, he feared she'd end up just like Ellen Green. He and God would have some serious words if that happened.

So many things about Zahrah confounded him. Her faith. Her comment that she had no rights. What was she? A slave? He didn't get that. Sure, Christians talked about being servants of God. And he was okay with serving God. That's what he felt he did in the field as a warrior. But he'd never met someone who took that to a literal level like Zahrah Zarrick. It was foolish. Idiotic to intentionally put one's life in danger. If she died, how could she fulfill her calling?

How can you?

And yet he did it every day. Walked out into the desert with the team, aware that it might be the day he didn't come back alive. Faced Talib and other terrorists.

But that was different. *I'm a soldier.* She's not. She's. . . He hated himself for wanting to say *a woman.* It wasn't just that. He didn't have any of those idiotic prejudices. He just didn't want her to get hurt. Didn't want that guilt on his shoulders. Not again.

Walk away from it. Had to. He'd done his job to warn her. She made her choice to stay. Now he had to focus on the mission. And that had taken him and the team to Majorca. After much shouting at Burnett for leaving Zarrick vulnerable, Dean knew he'd lost again.

The boat bumped against the dock and the crew set up the walkway. Dean stalked down it and waded through the thick crowd of tourists. He sighted Hawk in a bright Hawaiian shirt chatting up a blond. Dean shook his head and aimed for the rendezvous. At one of the tourist traps, he picked up a prepaid cell phone, a bottle of water, and a bag of nuts. He paid cash then headed down away from the crowds. Down a street and past the church to the condo that served as the safe house to host the team.

At the door, he rapped three times.

"Hold up," a voice called from deep within. The locks clicked and the door opened. At about six-three, the guy almost looked Dean in the eye. "Can I help you?"

"Yeah. I'm here about the Lotus you advertised."

"You got the cash?"

Dean held out a stack of bills he'd been given.

The man eyed the money. "C'mon in. We can talk."

Dean stepped inside. The door slammed shut.

A blow to his back sent him into the wall. Eating peeling wallpaper off a dank-smelling wall, he tensed—ready to fight. But stopped. Knew he was in their territory and if he fought, he could go home free of charge with an extra bullet in his head.

A forearm braced his shoulders as the guy patted him down. The pressure released.

Dean turned, irritated.

Hands braced on his hip, the guy stared at him. "You're early."

"Blame it on the boat captain—I hear they're not reliable."

A meaty hand thrust out. "Name's Jaxon."

Peeling his pride and self off the wall, Dean returned the gesture. "Dean. My team will show up over the course of the next few hours."

"As scheduled. C'mon back."

Drowning in the guy's shadow from a lone window at the back of the anemic hall that led to the rear of the condo, Dean tried to take in the layout. But there wasn't much to take in. Two closed doors.

"Door on your left," Jaxon said, "is the latrine. To the right, a closet. And in here, we've got everything set up."

"We?" Dean rounded the corner to find a small kitchen barely navigable. But Jaxon strode onward and palmed a panel. A three-by-four section of the wall popped back, revealing a control box. Jaxon punched in a code and a door whooshed back from the dark cherry wood paneling. Stairs offered an escape from the cramped kitchen.

Taking the steps two at a time, Dean detected a murmur of conversation and hum of devices above him. He stepped onto the next level and stopped. Cables strewn over the floor made crossing it hazardous. A woman looked up from a computer.

"The scrawny guy is Kilgore," Jaxon said as he moved around him. "That's my wife, Shiloh."

"Welcome to the Cave, Captain Watters," she said, then turned to Jaxon. "Brutus, we got two more on approach."

"Got it." He slapped Dean's shoulder. "Make yourself at home. I'll be back."

The sixty-by-twenty room stretched to his right and left, walls blocking the stairs in what seemed to serve as additional rooms. Exposed beams and pipes left the space drafty but open. Dirty, grimy windows blocked anyone from seeing in but allowed natural light to fill the room. Tables and desks littered with computers, monitors, cameras, and a lot of other high-tech gadgetry Dean could only dream of having in the field made the place feel cluttered and unkempt.

A wheeled chair rolled over the wood floor, hopping one set of cables before another tripped it up. Dean caught it, his gaze snapping to the booted leg that kicked it over. Then to its owner.

With a baseball cap on, she spun around, her reddish-brown hair protruding from the cap. "Have a seat. Lot of info, not a lot of time."

Rolling the seat toward her, Dean eyed her setup, which consisted of multiple monitors. One held a map, one provided a quad-split screen with grainy images that all looked like various angles of the house—which would explain how she knew someone else had shown up—and one held streaming data that hurt his eyes to even glance at. The last held a smattering of images layered on top of each other.

"Kilgore, send me the latest."

"On it," the techie said.

"Shouldn't we wait for my team?"

"We are here, O great one!" Hawk trudged up the steps, arms held wide and exposing his thick muscles in a T-shirt that held a skull with crosshairs, the Hawaiian shirt balled in his hand. Behind him came Falcon and Harrier. "Dude's giving Knight and his dog a hassle."

"Kilgore has allergies."

With amusement rippling through his face, Hawk eyed the geek. "Ddrake can take care of those for you."

The tech looked up through his eyebrows. "My fingertips hold your lifelines. Seriously want to mess with that?"

Hawk clapped and laughed then his gaze hit the female operative. "Well—"

"She's taken," Kilgore said without looking up from his bank of monitors that splashed a weird hue across the pocked face. "And her guy knows how to rip your throat out before you know he's there. Not worth it." Now he looked at Hawk. "Please? Will you try to flirt with her so I can watch it happen? I might even video it and put it on YouTube. It'd go viral."

Hawk cocked a challenging look. Arms went out.

"Hey." Nodding toward him, Dean tried to intercept. "We have a mission."

Hawk glared at the tech as he came toward Dean then shifted his attention to the operative in his typical straightforward way. "Whoever your guy is, he's lucky. If you get tired of him," he said, eyeing her computers, "I imagine you know where to find me."

"Especially when you're unconscious and within range of a Remington 700." She had an expression that almost dared Hawk to flirt with her.

This time Hawk laughed. "Lady, you are my speed."

A hand clamped onto Hawk's shoulder and his knees went out before anyone knew what happened.

"Wanna try that again?" Jaxon pressed his thumb into Hawk's soft spot.

"Dude," Hawk said, his face reddening as he struggled back to his feet. "*You're* her guy?"

"You got a problem with that?"

"Yes, a very big one," Hawk grunted. "One weighing"—his gaze traced Jaxon's frame—"250."

Jaxon laughed. Released Hawk.

Dean eyed the couple, wondering how that worked. Both covert operatives, both constantly in harm's way. His mind slung back to Zahrah. Walking away mad. Guilt nagged him as he took the seat Shiloh had offered earlier.

"He has a lethal a sense of humor," she said. "Prior Navy SEAL." Pride soaked those words and a hefty dose of awareness that she was poking the ego of every member of his team, including him. Well, maybe not Titanis, who hadn't shown up yet.

Behind him, Dean heard Harrier and Falcon sniggering.

Rubbing his shoulder, Hawk ignored the proffered help and came to his feet. "No wonder you're messed up. Navy." He grunted. "If you need help on how to take down your opponent, I can give you some lessons."

Jaxon's eyebrows winged up. "You think I need lessons? Come here, grunt. I'll show you—"

"Boys, boys," she said with a wry smile. "Enough with the biggest toys contest."

"No harm done," Jaxon said, extending his hand to Hawk.

Glaring, Hawk said, "Tell that to my shoulder," then shook his hand.

"Okay, so here's what we've got." She pointed to the topmost image. "It's blurred because we captured it from a speedboat at about a mile away."

Dean squinted, though it did no good. A tall man stood with his face blurred below a slick of black hair. He had two women with him. "Who is that?"

"We aren't sure," she said. "He showed up about two weeks ago, right about the time your computers started disappearing. He's Iranian and powerful." She used her pinky to point out a half dozen other blurs. "His henchmen, sporting some serious firepower. They're with him 24/7."

"Nah, he's not Iranian." Dean leaned forward, his forearms on his knees.

Falcon turned his hat backward and folded his arms. "Unless he isn't holding to the tenets of Islam."

"You're assuming that because of the half-naked women." A wicked intelligence lurked behind her blue-gray eyes. "We backtracked the boat to Bandar Taheri."

"Port doesn't guarantee nationality," Dean countered.

"That's the only picture we've been able to capture of him to date, so we're going to try to get in closer," Jaxon said.

Dean considered that. Risky. His Special Forces training taught him how to sluice through water undetected, but out in the middle of nowhere, when eyes are on the water constantly and they probably had radars, too? "How?"

Jaxon smirked. "Doing what I do best."

"What *I* do best," she said. "Dive." She popped up another screen. "This is your target, Ashgar Asad. He's been glued to Sadri Ali, a known opium supplier who uses the ports here for running his drugs."

"We don't care about drugs," Dean said. "We need Asad."

"Ya know," Jaxon said quietly, "I'm really wondering about this mission."

Confusion pushed Dean's attention to the former Navy SEAL. "Why's that?"

Narrowing his eyes, Jaxon locked on to Dean. "Exactly—*why?* I've been tracking these guys for weeks." He shrugged. "They deal drugs. Party. Live the high life. Nothing else."

"Two peas in a drug pod," Hawk said.

"Until Mr. Yacht showed up."

"That's where it got weird." Jaxon eased back and propped against the surface where his wife worked. "The yacht is registered to an Iranian official *high* up the ladder, but he's not on board."

Dean pointed to the blurry-faced man. "That's not him?"

With a shake of her head, Jaxon's wife hammered on the keyboard. "This is our rich Iranian. Short, bald, and overweight."

"I've run all the back channels and nothing unusual comes up with Asad or Ali, except that they've been ferried out to the boat twice." With a shrug, Jaxon sighed and rubbed his jaw. "I've seen stranger things happen than discovering drug dealers went tech for higher profits." He nodded to Kilgore. "That's why I brought him in. That's his field."

Tech. Anti-tamper computers. It'd make sense that these things were connected, but how? "What'd you find?" Dean asked.

With a snort, Kilgore looked up from his bank of monitors. "Nothing. A whole lotta nothin'." A wiry mess of dirty blond curls framed the guy's face.

They were throwing a lot at him, and none of it sounded good. "Which means. . . ?" Dean wasn't sure he wanted to know.

Jaxon, a brute of a guy, stared at him long and hard. "To be frank," he said then heaved a sigh. "We're not sure why you're here."

"Which means?" Falcon asked, a bit intense.

"Which means things like this that on the surface are quiet and innocuous"—Jaxon looked at Shiloh then back to Dean—"they blow up in your face. So I recommend you have a very quick, very foolproof exit strategy. Or be prepared to die."

CHAPTER 21

Palma de Mallorca, Balearic Sea, Spain
13 June—0115 Hours

This mission leaked hazards like a nuclear reactor. One of those leaks could ignite and blow the whole thing sky high, just like Jaxon said.

Midnight rolled around with Titanis a no-show. Dean and Jaxon checked local scanners while Shiloh watched computer logs at the airports and police stations. Nothing. The guy had vanished somewhere between Afghanistan and Majorca. He never made port. Not on a boat, plane, or foot.

Dean flopped on his back and stared at the rafters. Couldn't sleep. Not with a man missing and a mission promising to fail or get him killed. It left Dean's mind wide open. Drifting to places he shouldn't go. To people he couldn't protect if he died—his men, innocents. . .

Zahrah Zarrick.

He'd never forget the way her hurt carried so clear on her face. Screamed her feelings. Young, attractive, and so naive.

No, she wasn't naive. She'd seen too much, both as a general's daughter and as a missionary, to be naive. Sweet Ara Mustafa was a prime example. Ugh. He'd never get the first glimpse of the little girl's hand out of his mind. Lifting that cement block, seeing her tiny fingers. . . the dusty turquoise bracelet. . .

Dean rolled over, more to turn his back on the deep wound that he'd inflicted on Zahrah than to get comfortable.

Sleep crowded his thoughts and dragged him into its depths. Ara's hand became larger. Coiled around his grubby fingers. Squeezed. The bracelet, still caked with dirt and blood, now clung to an adult's wrist. A scream echoed in his mind. The eyes he'd closed became Zahrah's. She stared at him, blankly, and yet. . .she fell. . .farther. . .farther. . . .

Thud! He looked down, where he felt the impact. Found her lying at his feet. Dead. Panic pounded his chest.

Something hit his leg.

Dean snapped awake, his hand thrusting upward.

"Hey!" The person over him deflected. "Blue! Blue!"

Dean blinked, his heart pinging, as the face coalesced into a recognizable, friendly—*blue*—form. "Titanis."

"Listen, mate, we got trouble."

Coming off his cot, mind alive with the threat of danger, Dean swiped the cobwebs from his mind. "What? Wait—" Dean checked his timepiece: 0300. "You just got here?"

Titanis looked over his shoulder, and that's when Dean saw Jaxon standing there.

"What's going on?"

"I had a tail," Titanis said. "As soon as I got off the plane. Wouldn't have made it but for the kindness of a stranger." Again, he glanced back.

"I have contacts in town. They watch out for me and vice versa." Jaxon let out a heavy sigh. "The board's been lit up since your team hit town."

Shaking his head, his mind struggling with the news, Dean scowled. This only meant one thing. "They know we're here."

—⚋—

Undisclosed Location

It's just my luck that these guys believe their area is secure. Really, just one sweep by security teams would figure out how wrong they are in that belief. But for now, my secret is safe. And even if they are enlightened, I'll just send in another device, a different one that will be harder to detect. That's more expensive, which is why it's not there now. That and their arrogant assumption of their invincibility.

But Boss Man already knows of their trip to the exotic location.

My phone rings and I glance at the caller ID. "Speak of the devil," I mutter as I hit jamming frequencies. No way does he need to know my location. Headset on, I hit the ANSWER button. "You rang?"

"Let me inside."

My heart does this crazy do-si-do. My hick mother would be proud. My elitist father disgusted. In fact, so am I. Pushing to my feet, I wonder how he's managed to find me. "L–let you in where?" No, this just can't happen. "We agreed. No face-to-face. No compromising identities."

"We are beyond that, aren't we? Do you think I would wire that much money to an account when I do not know the name of the person receiving it?"

My breath catches in my throat, forcing me to cough.

"Open it."

My eyes slide to the gray walls that have protected my location—me—from discovery. Lent me some anonymity. Or so I thought. "This is a major breach of contract."

"Do I need to have it blown?"

"N–no." That could damage the millions of dollars of equipment. That could attract more attention. The hatch-style door to my hovel is locked. Secured. With triple redundancies as well as other security measures, including the bracelet that resembles a POW memorial bracelet.

But still. . .my heart trembles.

"Do not make me say it again."

Not sure if my heart or shoes thud louder as I cross the steel floor, punch in the codes—*snap*! I race back to the computer and enter my passcode for the disable function on the primary security. Ya know, the ones that will kill everyone if I don't disable. I also protect my computers. They're my babies. Mothers would strap bombs to their chests to protect their children. So would I.

"My patience is wearing thin."

"Right. Just one more. . ." I hit ENTER and the lights around me turn blue. Glancing up and confirming their neutral status, I hurry to the door. Swing the wheel and release the locking mechanism.

Light explodes through my steel cave, and I blink. And freeze as the business end of a gun presses between my eyes.

"Step back," Goon One says.

Hands up, I'm moving. "Easy there, turbo. I'm the good guy, remember?" Okay, that's almost hysterical. "Well, not really the *good* guy since I'm spying on the real good guys with a wad of your cash."

"And what," a slick-suited lanky man glides into the hovel, a hand in his right pant pocket, "are you doing with"—he sneers down his flat nose as me, those slanted eyes filled with more heat than the Afghan desert in summer—"my 'wad of cash,' Scythe."

A laugh-grunt thumps from my chest. I can't believe I actually got him to use that nickname. It's kind of twisted, really, but— "Okay, okay!" I wince as the gun presses hard into my temple. "I'm working. Day and night."

"It would seem so." His lip curls as he takes in the portable cave as Goon Two enters and closes the door, standing in front of it like a mafia thug. Seriously? "No housekeeper either." Really, it's amazing the way Boss Man sounds British and Chinese at the same time.

"L–look, we agreed." I swipe my tongue across my lips. It's obvious that I'm scared, but. . . "This is massively uncool. Remember, we agreed: You do your thing, I do mine, and"—I take a deep, shuddering breath of nerves and let them out—"we're both happy."

He turns around, both hands in his slacks pockets now, and slumps against one of my supercomputers. "I am not." Arms folded, he looks like he might work out. I wish I hadn't noticed that. "Not anymore."

"Wh–why? What changed?" I scowl at Goon One and lean away from the weapon. "Seriously? Is that necessary?"

Boss man gives a nod and Goon One backs up to the door, standing just like the other. Thing One and Thing Two?

I take a step forward, hands out. No way I want to tick off this guy. He's got the guns—literally—to take me out. "Why are you here? I've provided all the transcripts, all the information you need—"

"You do not determine what I need."

Dude. The world had totally shifted, and I'm not even sure I'm still on the same planet anymore. "I don't understand. We had a contract. We agreed. I gave you everything you asked for. I had   "

"It is not enough." The calm on the guy's face is just. . .sick. And not the cool *sick* either. He's in complete control and knows it. What's worse—so do I.

"I want to see the video you have secured. I want their faces. I want to see it for myself."

"Why?" This makes no sense. I gave him everything needed to take them down. But then it dawns on me. And suddenly there's a warm surge at the back of my throat, and I swallow the bile. The words sneak past my lips before my brain can engage. "The girl."

CHAPTER 22

Palma de Mallorca, Balearic Sea, Spain
14 June—1845 Hours

Three massive cranes towered over the docks like steel scorpions waiting to inject their poison. Between the second and third, a black sedan waited. It sat ominous and predatory, out of place in the dingy surroundings mucked by the seawater and years of use.

Concealed, Dean verified his team's location. Jaxon and his wife waited a half mile out in a nondescript boat. Titanis and Harrier kept their distance, set up on a rooftop with a bead on the car and its occupants. Five feet behind and stuffed in one of the rubber bumpers shielding the cement dock from ship hulls, Hawk waited.

"Ready?" Falcon asked.

Dean nodded. Rolled his shoulders then started walking down the dock toward the waiting car. Anything and everything could go wrong here. Especially with the warning Titanis brought that the "they" knew Raptor team was here. Nerves tingling, he felt himself again reach for that tendril of faith that seemed to be growing since his first encounter with Zahrah.

God, keep her safe. Help me make it back to ensure that.

Doors swung open as they approached.

"Welcome party," Falcon muttered.

Two men who could easily compete in the WWE or against some of Dean's SF brothers emerged. Arms out, awkwardly.

"And armed." Falcon grunted.

"Just messengers." Dean resisted the urge to run his hand over his short crop. They needed Ashgar in the open and he hadn't even shown his face yet. Dean had no weapon, no coms piece, nothing. Just him, Falcon, the terrorists, and. . .God. He hoped.

"You're late."

Jaxon's warning slammed to the front of his mind. *"They will try to take control, put you on the defensive. Don't let them."*

"Not true." Dean slowed to a stop, six feet from the man. "We're right on time." He put his hands on his hips, trying to visibly show he wasn't armed, unlike the men facing him. And unlike the team surrounding the area. "But we do have a problem." He squinted against the sun glaring off the water.

"What would that be?" Distinctive Arabic accent. Curly hair. Arrogant.

Dean brought his gaze from their surroundings, acting like he wasn't comfortable. "You're not the man we need."

Challenge lurked in the man's eyes. He looked to the other guard then grinned. "Who do you think you need?"

Dean glanced at Falcon, shook his head, then started to walk away. "This meeting's over."

The thunk of a door handle hit his ears, but Dean kept moving. He'd dealt with enough terrorists not to show fear. Or weakness. Make them want it. Make them show the weakness.

"One cannot be too sure," a slow, menacing voice said, "in this business who is a friend and who is not. You would agree, would you not, Mr. Michaels?"

Dean slowed, turned. His heart thumped a little harder as he met the steely gaze of Ashgar Asad. Behind him, Sadi Ali. "I would." He purposefully met Falcon's gaze. They'd need to divide up the two men. It just got complicated. "But I'd also say we're wasting time playing games."

"Games?" The man slid a stick of gum into his mouth.

Dean tensed. Was that a signal?

Chewing loudly, Ashgar eyed him. "You think being safe is a game?"

"I think we both went through a lot to set up this meeting. If we can't trust our contacts, we're in the wrong business."

"History is filled with traitors, Mr. Michaels. Benedict Arnold, Julius and Ethel Rosenberg, Aldrich Ames. . ." His gaze surfed the waters, then came back. Almost smiling. Deliberate. "Wang Jingwei."

Dean waited. Didn't know the man's point. Or the significance of the traitors mentioned. "Forget it, man," Falcon said. "I'm over this."

"Your friend is impatient." Ashgar smiled.

Dean took the cue. Paced to the edge of the dock. Huffed. Out of the corner of his eye, he noted Hawk hunched in the rubber tire-like bumper. Rubbing his jaw, Dean looked out across the waters. Acted perturbed. He pivoted, stayed close to the edge. "My friend is right. It's over. You should've checked us out. The longer we're here, the more risk of exposure." He shrugged. "You don't want our money"—another shrug—"fine."

Ashgar held up a hand, chuckling. "Be at peace, my friend." He ambled toward him.

Yes. A little closer.

Angling sideways, Dean glared at Sadi Ali. Tried to keep up appearances.

"My friend, you are too jumpy." Standing a head shorter than Dean, Ashgar patted him on the shoulder. "You need some time on a boat with some beautiful women to relax."

Sadi Ali laughed. "Does wonders for the soul."

"Are you ready to do this?" Dean asked. But not to Sadi or Ashgar. He gave a signal. Threw himself into Ashgar. A shout collided with the movement. His body jarred against Asghar's rigid frame. And they were falling...

Dean crashed into the murky water, Ashgar in his grip. He pushed downward. Water rushed around him. Devoured his hearing. Blinded him. Movements took on a warbling sound.

Ashgar writhed against him. Fought him. Railed.

Dean held tight. Felt a pat against his shoulder. Released Ashgar as something slid into his hand. He slid on the air bladder and the rebreather into his mouth. But with Ashgar's panicked flailing, if Falcon didn't get him rigged, the guy would drown. Once more, Dean dove into the guy, propelling them down into the depths, but also away from the docks. Toward the boat that should be waiting a few blocks away beneath a pier.

A tap on his shoulder alerted him to Falcon, who slid a rebreather toward Ashgar. The man stilled, his wild, frantic eyes connecting with theirs. With Falcon's help, the Arab accepted the breathing apparatus. As he calmed, Dean noticed a dark plume around the guy's left shoulder.

Shot!

No time to assess the wound. Impossible to dress it underwater. He hooked arms with Ashgar, and Falcon did the same. Together, they swam to the rendezvous point, his only thought the consequences if the man died. No answers on what was happening back in Afghanistan.

The entire military community could be in jeopardy. Zahrah— He squeezed off the thought. They had to make it. Time pounded against his every breath, warning him of the imminent failure.

It grew harder to swim. He must be more tired than he realized. While the swim was strenuous, it wasn't anything he couldn't handle.

But they were sliding. . .down. Not forward.

Only as he glanced to the side, did he notice Ashgar's head hanging limp. He shot a look to Falcon, who nodded. Then checked his compass.

Dean pushed himself to swim harder and faster. They could *not* lose this guy. He was their only hope of making headway with whatever was happening back in Afghanistan.

Finally, he saw the hull of the boat bobbing. They slowly broke the surface. The *Brutus* lurked five feet in front of them.

Jaxon stared down at them. "About time—"

Dean whipped the water out of his face and removed the rebreather then swam to the edge of the boat. "He's shot," Dean said, panting. "Left shoulder."

Jaxon and another man hauled Ashgar out of the water. Dean and Falcon clambered aboard and slumped on the deck. The burn in his lungs had nothing on the burn in his mind as the two men performed CPR on the Arab.

"We need him alive," Falcon said.

But even as his first said the words, Dean eyeballed the wound then the quickly growing pool of blood beneath him. Ashgar hadn't been shot by accident. It was a sniper shot.

Ashgar coughed, gagged, then slumped, hauling in several long breaths.

Dean did the same. Relief. Sweet, painful relief that the man was alive and breathing.

Then. . .chuckling.

Frowning, Dean went to his knees and stared down at the man.

Ashgar snorted. "You thought you had me. . . ."

"We do have you," Falcon said. "Your men shot you."

With a shake of his head, he closed his eyes. "My. . .orders. . .never taken. . .alive."

"Why? What are you protecting?"

The man's eyes seemed to focus on Dean. Then on the sky. "Ever'. . . thing." The left side of his lip, a rivulet of blood sliding down his jaw, lifted in a smirk. "You won't. . .win. Won't stop. . .him."

"Who?" Dean grabbed the man's sodden clothes and jerked him up. "Who's behind what's happening?"

Ashgar's head jerked. A gurgling sound replaced a laugh. He slumped, limp.

Dean released him. Dropped back against the boat. Defeat clung to him heavier than the water that sucked his clothes against his frame. He shoved dripping seawater from his face. Kicked the boat. Punched the seat.

Thudding his head against the back of the boat, he fought off the despair. Where? Where would they go from here?

"We've got company!"

Dean lifted his head, glanced to the side.

Jaxon and his guy raced to the front, to the steering well. The boat's engine revved and they ripped away. Dean glanced over his shoulder and saw a large speedboat roaring up their six.

Falcon cursed.

"Hey," Jaxon shouted, bringing their attention back to him. He tossed an M4A1 at Dean. Then an M16 to Falcon.

Dean verified a round was in the chamber, the safety off, then went to a knee. The boat bounced over several waves, tossing him against its fiberglass hull. He gritted his teeth and pushed back into position. Sighted the speedboat driver. Eased back the trigger.

The *Brutus* went airborne. Dean grabbed the rail and held on.

Fire lit across his arm, leaving a trail of blood. He hissed against the graze but refocused on the target. He couldn't hear them firing, but the graze told him they were. He'd return the favor. Dean again targeted the black speedboat driver. Fired. The man flipped sideways.

Falcon kept a bead on the boat. Fired. Again and again.

A spark. A ball of fire. Black smoke shot into the sky.

"Hooah," Falcon shouted. "One speedboat down."

"One to go." Dean pointed to the slick boat whipping up alongside them.

"Over, over," Jaxon shouted.

Falcon cursed, snatched up his rebreather, and dove over the side of the boat. Doing the same, Dean dropped into the depths of the water. It'd been Plan B if they came under attack. They couldn't be found together, the American military with the spies.

Exhausted and defeated, he swam. Pushed himself to the ends of his strength and mental abilities. When he crawled up on the beach, the sun had set. Darkness loomed. He hiked down to the pier, retrieved a pack planted there earlier, and changed in the shadows. He was alive. His men were alive, as far as he knew. Good things. But that's where the good stopped.

This failure, this defeat felt as if he'd taken a bullet straight to the heart. Though he couldn't explain why, he knew today would prove to be a *catastrophic* failure.

In the pack, he felt a buzzing. He rifled through the contents and dug out the throwaway flip phone. He opened it. His heart vaulted into his throat at the message:

COMPROMISED. GET OUT OF COUNTRY.

TODD & AMY

How ya doing, son?"

Todd looked at his father. Then at the beautiful brunette sitting in a rocker on the back porch with his mom and good friends while he stood here by the hot grill. How was he doing? Besides having his heart ripped? Going to bed every night wondering if she'd be there in the morning? Afraid their adventures would end badly, either in an accident that cut their little time together short or if she collapsed. . . .

He turned back to the sausages and turned them.

"I'm proud of you. The leave you took from the Army, the way you've been here 100 percent for her—"

"Should've done this years ago."

"Nah, don't do that to yourself. You had a job, so did she."

"Maybe." Todd trained his attention on the grill, on the heat plumes, on the smoke, on anything other than this conversation. "But my job took me away from her." He closed the lid so the smoke would seep into the meat. "She wanted to start trying for a baby last year." Now there'd be no baby. No Amy. His life would be empty.

His fingers closed around the handle—tight.

Something splatted his face. Todd twitched and swiped it away. Water?

Another splat.

He turned. Amy stood there with a bazooka soaker. She laughed.

"Ha. Ha. That's enough—I'm grilling."

She didn't stop.

"Amy. . ."

Pumping that thing at him for all she was worth.

Todd set down his grill tongs and launched himself at her.

Dropping the water machine gun, Amy squealed. Sprinted around their guests. Todd navigated the table of food and the lawn chairs, sailing clear over one that held a friend's four-year-old son.

Amy zigzagged and raced around toward the barn. Into the waist-high grass. Laughing hysterically, Amy slowed. A lot. He caught her shoulders.

She tripped. Went down.

Todd cringed, frantic she'd get hurt. He dropped beside her but quickly realized, with her laughing gasps, that she was fine. He crumpled beside her. "All right, Rambette."

Laughter bounced her chest against his.

The wave of grief came stronger than ever before. He didn't want to miss her laughter. Didn't want to miss chasing her through the fields. Didn't want to miss her feistiness.

"I am your prisoner, Mr. Special Forces."

He couldn't help the grin. This was their private joke. "I guess I'm going to have to torture you."

A twinkle glittered in her blue eyes, just the same as on the night of their honeymoon.

Todd leaned against her and kissed her. "I love you Amelia Celine Archer."

"Hey," someone shouted. "You still have guests over here, you know."

"Reminds me of our wedding night. The guests just wouldn't go home." Amy ran a hand over his short hair. "I've always loved your reddish-blond hair. Your beautiful gray-blue eyes."

"I'll tell my parents they did good."

She laughed again.

He smoothed her hair from her face. "I'm sorry I didn't—"

"Hey." She held his face. "No." She kissed him. "Regrets." Another kiss. "Todd."

"Amelia?"

At the sound of her mother's voice calling uncertainly, Amy groaned and rolled her eyes. "You'd think I was still living at home."

Todd pushed to feet and held his hand out. "C'mon. Meat's probably burning."

As they walked, he dusted off his pants. Seeing the amused and yet thoroughly pleased looks their friends shot them, he announced, "The aggressor is subdued, ladies and gentlemen. No regrets!"

A collective gasp and widened eyes followed.

Todd glanced to the side. Amy lay on the ground. Unconscious.

CHAPTER 23

Palma de Mallorca, Balearic Sea, Spain
14 June—2010 Hours

Legs trembling, he made his way into the dark alleys. Toward the empty warehouse that had been their "last resort" option. Their only way out. Jaxon promised to have a van and driver there to ferry them to a private airstrip that would give them a hop to U.S. Naval Air Station Rota in Spain. From there, he and the team would get back to Mazar-e. Their cooperation with Jaxon and his wife was over. They wouldn't see them again. Had to be that way.

Compromised. How? What happened? They'd had nothing identifying. They'd been brutally meticulous and careful. How could so much go wrong so fast? Had they been betrayed? But by whom? And why?

The musty stench of rotting food and sewage, that sour, pungent smell that makes eyes water, swarmed him. Choked him. Much like his failure, it wouldn't leave him alone. He couldn't escape it.

No weapon. No passport. Life hanging on the lone thread of hope that Jaxon would make good on his word. *You're trained for this.* One way or another, they'd get home. But there was a piece of him that wanted to lie down and give up.

Until an oval face and brown eyes swam into his mind's eye. Was she alive? If he gave up, who would protect her?

Who's protecting her now? No one.

He pushed on, refusing to surrender to the gloom.

"Hey."

His feet tangled. He shifted and leaned against a wall, not moving. Hoping whoever saw him would ignore him.

"Raptor," the voice hissed. "Inside. Quick."

It took seconds to register the voice—Falcon. Dean flopped around, strained to see in the dark alley. Slowly, his vision adjusted and he spotted his buddy. He shoved off the wall and hustled toward him.

Falcon hauled him in. "Van's here. Waiting on Hawk then we're good."

Dean nodded and climbed into the van. He dropped against the vinyl seat and slouched. Rested his head against the window.

"How long do we wait?" the driver asked.

"Till he comes," Dean growled.

It took fifteen minutes for Hawk to show up, his shirt plastered to his bodybuilder frame with sweat. He sprinted into the van. "Go, go! They're following me."

The van lurched out of the warehouse and careened down the alley without lights.

Ping! Tink! Crack!

"Shooter," Dean said.

But they couldn't do anything. No weapons. No identities. Their only option—escape!

Dean gripped the driver's seat as they whipped around a corner. Barreled down a crooked road. The van screeched right then launched onto a busy street.

Searching the road behind them, Dean sought their pursuers. Nothing but more of the same—cars, lights, and the normal congestion of tourist nightlife.

"We need to get out of here," Falcon snarled.

"We're fine. No more tails," the driver said as he wove in and out of traffic, zipping through the crowded streets.

Fifteen minutes of running red lights and avoiding pedestrians delivered them to a private airstrip and to the droning noise of a prop plane. They crowded in and were airborne almost before the door could be secured. A half-hour flight had them touching down on another airstrip where a Seahawk waited.

"It's good to be home," Hawk shouted as he jogged toward the helicopter that had a small contingent of armed operators protecting them.

Dean could almost breathe easy as he slid onto one of the canvas seats. They were ferried to Rota air station. There, they were immediately put on a C-17 Globemaster III back to Afghanistan.

Head back, he closed his eyes. Forced himself to walk through what happened rather than fall asleep. He hadn't just failed. They'd floundered, lost a man, and two were wounded. Technically, Dean didn't qualify his scratch as a wound, but it'd get logged in his AAR, and that didn't sit well with him. Guilt plagued him. What could he have done differently? Could he have stopped Ashgar from the suicide mission?

"Sir," someone shouted.

Dean flinched and opened his eyes.

A private stood over him with a sat phone and shouted over the din of the engines. "You're ordered to code in ASAP, sir."

Right. Because yelling into a secure line on a troop transport made sense. But if he didn't, he'd never hear the end of it. Phone in hand, Dean freed himself of the crowded row and made his way to the comfort pallet, where he stepped into the walled-off latrine closet. Shoulders practically rubbing the walls, he leaned back against the door and coded in. Dean wasn't small, but he knew someone like Hawk would probably get stuck.

"What in Sam Hill happened down there?" Burnett's voice ricocheted through the receiver.

"That's what I'd like to know, sir."

"Two people got shot, our target is dead, and all of Majorca is screaming."

Dean gritted his teeth.

"Well?" Burnett barked.

"They were on us from the second we set down. It was like they knew we'd be there."

"And how in this sick planet would they know that?"

"Again, that's what I'd like to know."

"Are you blaming me, Watters?"

"Negative, sir."

"You sound ticked."

"Yes, sir." Dean's pulse amped up. "We were ambushed. My men were put in danger. Lives were lost. Operatives were compromised. The target ate a bullet so he couldn't be forced to talk." He held his forehead. "It was a waste of time. Sir."

"Well, get back here. We need to sort this thing out."

"Roger that."

"I'll start with Ramsey."

"Good enough, sir."

"Anything else?"

"How—?" Dean clamped his mouth shut, startled at what was about to escape his lips. Would not go there. The general already had a noose around Dean's neck. He didn't need to give him ammo, too.

"What?"

"Nothing, sir. I'll code in when we're boots on ground."

"Good." Burnett's huff carried through the line. "By the way, she's fine."

Dean's eyes slid closed. He gave a nod but said nothing. Couldn't voice how big that weight had been that lifted from his shoulders.

"Get some rest. Full debrief at 0800."

"Yes, sir."

"She's fine. . . ."

Breathing in deeply, he rested his head against the wall. His prayer had worked. God kept her safe. Roughing a hand over his face, he thought of the dream. The one where little Ara Mustafa morphed into Zahrah Zarrick. The images, the possibility of that happening, punched a hole in his gut. No way he could live with that. Why wouldn't she just trust him and go back?

He saw it in her eyes that day of Ara's funeral. The conviction that told him she wouldn't leave because she believed in something. And Someone. It'd angered him. Frustrated him. Scared him.

He snorted. He'd been scared a lot. But not like this.

Why? She wasn't anyone to him except a missionary teacher.

But she was the only missionary teacher he'd wanted to spend time with. Learn about. Get to know better.

"Call me to make sure I'm still alive." The sarcasm of her words had annoyed him. It wasn't a joke. She could end up dead. Even now, though Burnett gave reassurance that she was fine, that information was old. It'd take just a split second for that to change. And still. . .he wasn't close enough.

He considered the phone in hand. What if something *did* change? What if Burnett hadn't been right? Thirty-four thousand feet above the earth, Dean couldn't do a thing to keep her safe. The walls closed in on him. Reminded him of another time when he'd been powerless. Scared. Unable to fight back.

Shots banged through the house. Shouts. Screams.

"Donny, no!"

Bang! Bang-bang!

Even from his darkened closet in the bedroom, Dean heard the screams. Heard the howl of death. Felt the sting of betrayal.

Feet pattered to his room.

He drew his legs closer. Tighter. Curled against the wall, the phone clutched in his hand. Prayed against all odds his brother wouldn't find him.

The door swung open.

He sucked in a breath.

"Dean—"

A rap against the door startled him. Dean straightened, his thoughts slamming shut with the weight of a steel vault. He drew in a breath and exited. Nodded to the specialist waiting then waded through the sea of bodies and wedged in between Hawk and Falcon, the two snoring loud and long.

Dean thumbed the keypad again.

—⁓—

Mazar-e Sharif

They wouldn't have desks after all. Only tables and benches. And just half the children would return. Zahrah spent the better part of the day trying to reach the families by phone, mostly to no avail, and then visited the ones she couldn't reach. If she didn't have children to teach, what good was she here?

Her mother had taught her not to question the bad things. But to embrace them—because God was there regardless. God wasn't taken by surprise when things went wrong. His plan hadn't changed.

Yet. . .what if the plan she thought was God's ended up vanishing before her eyes? Did it mean she had misunderstood? Or maybe—the niggling she'd had the last six months—there was a bigger plan shielded behind the smaller one that had flopped?

Either way, she would thank God the few children who would return could sit in chairs and not on a dirty floor or mats. They'd have electricity and running water. The children should be safe here among collegiate students on a large campus. But it was a false sense of security. If someone was determined enough, no security protocols would stop them.

With her purse and books in hand, Zahrah started for the door. As she flicked off the light of her first-floor classroom, her phone buzzed. She fished it out, saw Fekiria's name on the display as she pushed through the door. "Ah, just in time. Where do you want to meet for dinner?"

"I, uh. . ."

Dusk wrapped her in its embrace as Zahrah stomped her foot on the path. Then she felt foolish. "You can't tell me you're having dinner with him *again*."

"I think he really likes me!"

Never had she seen her cousin so. . . "This isn't like you, Fekiria."

"What would you know about that?"

Zahrah frowned and slowed. "I've lived with you for the last eighteen months. We've been like sisters!"

"You're American. You'll never understand what it's like to be a real Afghan woman."

Shocked and numbed, Zahrah tried to fight the stinging tears. "How can you say that?"

"I have to go."

"Fekiria, please." She wandered to a quiet spot. "Talk to—"

The call ended with a loud, droning noise. Grief weighted Zahrah as she stumbled the rest of the way to her dorm apartment she was supposed to share with her cousin, who had been more absent than present since the move four days ago. It was as if she'd found her wings and flown the sanity coop. Her cousin had a deep passion for teaching, for helping others, but she'd also been irritable for the last several months. Zahrah prayed her cousin wasn't getting into something that would shatter her, something that would shame the family. While Kaka Jahandar had been reserved in his behavior, a fierce loyalty to Islam hovered beneath his facade.

As she crossed the parking lot, she scanned it for signs of the white pickup or the man from the school. Skirting the perimeter, she saw no threat. Zahrah hurried up the steps, into the apartment, and secured the locks. She eyed the small green light peeking out of the hanging ivy plant in a corner. Fekiria hated the thing, but Zahrah told her to leave it alone. She made her way to a cabinet, opened the door, nudged aside a couple of cans, and eyed the black box. She slid the cans back into place and headed to the bathroom. A long, hot shower would work the knots in her shoulders, the sense of defeat over the classroom, and she had to admit, the lingering frustration over her conversation with Dean Watters. As the water warmed, she sat on the edge of the tub with her forehead propped on the heel of her hand.

"God," she whispered, bone weary, tears right on the verge of spilling over. "I know I'm supposed to be here, but everything—*everything*—is going wrong." It wasn't that she expected things to go perfectly, to be easy, but could just *one* thing be good? She'd thought she found that with Dean.

"And he said unto me, My grace is sufficient for thee: for my strength is made perfect in weakness."

Zahrah groaned. "Then you must be very strong, but I am very weak right now." She undressed and slipped into the shower. She scrubbed her hair clean. "I should've gone home like Dean asked."

Shampoo slid into her eye.

"Augh!" She rinsed out the stinging soap. "Okay, okay, I get the point. No more complaining." After she was clean and refreshed, she wrapped her hair in a towel. "Would it hurt, Lord, to help me know I'm on the right path?" Her mother had called them kisses from God, moments when something happened that left no doubt God had orchestrated it. A bread crumb along a hard path.

Tummy growling, she made her way to the fridge. It sat almost empty. She grimaced. Nothing really edible. They hadn't really had time to do much shopping, and Fekiria loved takeout. "Which. . .looks like that's what I will have to do." The campus cafeteria had okay *halal*, but it wasn't like homemade. She really missed Khala Hafizah's cooking.

Guess it's takeout.

Dressed, she retrieved a scarf and returned to the small living area. Her phone buzzed. Had Fekiria changed her mind? "Oh!" She hurried to the phone. Maybe Fekiria would grab something on the way home for dinner. She eyed the caller ID. Hm, weird number. The message read: THOUGHT I'D CHECK—STILL ALIVE?

Warmth flooded Zahrah as she slumped onto the small cushion with a smile. "Dean," she breathed.

Thumbs poised over the keypad, she hesitated over how to respond.

A noise outside her door drew her attention. Kids again. Had she really been so foolish at twenty?

She typed, QUITE ALIVE, TH—

Crack!

The door flew inward.

Zahrah jolted. Dropped the phone.

A half-dozen men flooded in. In the split seconds of their entry, her mind registered several factors: With their faces hooded, they didn't want to be recognized; they were heavily armed; they said nothing, though her ears rang with the intrusion.

Terror replaced her calm. She spun around—not to search for a place to escape, but to stare at the plant. Her only hope. *Please, God, let them find it!*

A weight plowed into her back.

Her cheek collided with the short table as she went down. On all fours, she took a second to collect herself. To not panic. Daddy said panic and stupid reactions got people killed.

"Who are you really, Zahrah Zarrick?" a man demanded.

She started to look up, only to see a fist flying. It connected with her upper cheekbone. Pain exploded across her face and neck. Snapped her head back. She crumpled beneath the weight of the blow.

"I asked who you are," the man—not the one who attacked her, but one behind him—demanded again, removing a glove. The black-and-white keffiyeh made his chest appear broad and thick. He waved and two men hoisted her onto her feet.

"I'm Zahrah Zarrick, a missionary teacher with the—" Something smacked across her face and jaw, spinning her vision. Warmth slid down her mouth.

"No!" he roared. "You are not a missionary. You are not this innocent little teacher."

"I am!"

"I will ask one more time: who are you, and why are you in my country?"

"I told you—"

He jutted his jaw toward one of the men.

Zahrah saw the man rear back with the butt of his weapon. "No! You don't have to kill me!"

They lunged at her. Something sharp pricked her neck.

"No. . ." The word gargled in her throat against a paralyzing body.

"You are the daughter of General Peter Zarrick and the niece of Jahandar Haidary. A teacher? Perhaps," he gloated. "But of what? What secrets are you stealing from us, Miss Zarrick?"

Zahrah shook her head. "No secrets! No secrets."

The rifle butt flew at her face. A flurry of fists hit her. Zahrah felt an oppressive dark cloud blanketing her.

O God—help!

"See? The truth is much easier when you don't fight."

CHAPTER 24

Camp Marmal, Mazar-e Sharif
15 June—0945 Hours

Lights out. Thirty-two hours without sleep made him hit the rack like an M1 Abrams. Dean closed his eyes. Welcomed the greedy claws of sleep with an audible groan. He just wanted to sleep. An hour. Two, if God felt generous. Trembling muscles caved to the powerful force. Surrendered the nagging irritation that Zahrah hadn't replied to his text. Wasn't hard to say, I'M ALIVE. Then again, maybe it was hard—she could still be mad at him. Whatever. He had to rest. Sort it out later.

"Watters!"

Dean jerked. Eyes open, he stared at the tent ceiling, digging through his foul mood to find a modicum of civility. "What?"

"All hands," Hawk said bending to retrieve the tac vest. He tossed it across his legs. "Might need this."

Groaning, Dean peeled himself off the cot. He hadn't even removed his boots. "Where are we going?" On his feet, he threaded his arms through the vest. Strapped on his belt.

"Don't know." Hawk shot him a fierce look. "But we won't be alone."

Securing his gun clip, he eyed the communications specialist. They were pairing Raptor with another team? Why? "Who?"

Hawk shrugged, his anger scratching long lines into his tanned face. "If I knew, I'd tell you."

They stalked across the base and entered the subcommand center for SOC. Once inside the building, Dean's nerves buzzed. Loud and fierce. First because Titanis stood outside the room like a tornado ready to rip. Beside him, Falcon simmered. Though few Italian jokes had been cracked, Dean knew this guy had the classic Italian temper. And it was brewing a big one. If his men were ticked. . .

Dean acknowledged them and returned their irritation. Whatever had upset them did the same to him. He gave a nod to the briefing room and headed in, trailed by his men. The door swung open, and an odor of betrayal drenched him. Crossing the threshold felt like he'd walked into a trap.

Around the table sat a half-dozen SOC operators, bearded and grungy. Lieutenant Brie Hastings sat between one of the hairier operators and none other than General Burnett. The searing glare shooting lava out of Burnett made the back of Dean's neck tingle, especially as he glanced at the other four-star seated with his team. What irked Dean most was the lack of chairs. Only two. His team had six men.

Hands at his side, Dean stood at attention, awaiting instruction. He felt his team fall in beside him, doing more of the same.

"Captain Watters," Ramsey barked. "Good of you and your team to join us."

Baiting me.

Burnett's reddened face and flared nostrils coiled a knot in Dean's gut. Whatever was happening, it wasn't good. "I want it known," Burnett said, his voice a low growl, as he stabbed the table, "here and now, that I had no knowledge until an hour ago of what will be said in this meeting."

Dean's pulse jammed. His gaze slid to Falcon then back to the general.

"Relax, Lance." Ramsey slumped back in the chair and stared up at Raptor team. Assessing. Analzying. Picking them apart with his gaze. "You're a darn good team," he finally said. "But I couldn't let you screw up an above top-secret operation."

Hawk shifted. So did Dean.

"Which is why we sent you to Majorca." Ramsey leaned forward, threaded his hands, without breaking Dean's gaze. "I needed you out of the way."

Dean felt the scowl and confusion ripple through his face. "Sir?"

"Don't get all sanctimonious, Watters." He flipped his hand at him. "At ease, soldier. Or have a seat. This could take a while."

"Thank you, sir, I'll stand with my team." Dean slid his hands behind him, spread his feet, and remained in position.

"Suit yourself." Ramsey opened a folder. "I needed you out of the way because you were too close to the truth."

Dean gritted his teeth. "Sir?"

"SCI, Captain Watters. You jeopardized other intelligence operations." He shot them a fierce glare. "It couldn't happen."

Sensitive Compartmented Information—information that needed

extra protection above a top-secret security clearance level. "Majorca was a diversion." Though he understood the meaning, Dean didn't understand putting lives in danger to get Raptor out of the way. "Raptor has handled sensitive situations before. We could've—"

"Negative." General Ramsey rapped his knuckles on the table. "Son, you are so far in over your head, you can't see straight. And I'm not giving you the glasses to do it."

Ramsey hadn't been a fan of Raptor's formation, and now he was doing everything he could to snip its wings. Dean could deal with SCI missions being kept from him, but knowingly and deliberately sending the team on a wild drug-lord chase. . .

"What. . .what are you saying?" Falcon asked, then added, "Sir."

"I'm saying, I need you boys out of this SEAL team's way. I need you to shift your priorities. Track down drug dealers. Patrol some villages."

Fury singed Dean's spine. "Sir, we have tracked SCIFs. We're close—"

"I know full well what you've done." The general's lips stretched taut. "And I don't give a donkey's behind how close you are to anything. What I care about is that you stay out of this."

"Lives are in jeopardy." Dean's fingers curled into fists. He talked himself down—at least, he tried to.

"You aren't the only heroes on the planet, Captain Watters." Ramsey stood and shoved back his chair, knuckles on the table as he stared at them.

Dean flipped his gaze to General Burnett. "What about Zarrick? Does he know—"

"Zarrick? Peter Zarrick?" Ramsey chortled. "He's retired. He has no say. You think you can get past me, Watters?"

"Negative, sir. I have concerns."

"Who doesn't?"

In his tac pant pocket, Dean felt the secure phone buzz. Ignored it. "Innocent American lives are in danger—right here. We can't just walk away or pretend—"

"Don't lecture me, Captain!" Gray eyes blazed with wounded pride and anger. "I know more than you could pretend to!" He faced off against Dean, who went rigid.

The heat pouring through Dean's back and gut warned him to step off—he was ticked. Beyond ticked. His respect for the rank forbid him from unleashing the fury roiling through his veins.

With a huff, Ramsey slid his gaze back and forth along the line of Raptor team. "You men look tired. Get some rest." He pushed past Dean and headed for the door. "That's an order!"

Chairs squawked as the SEAL team stood and started for the door.

Dean met the gaze of one of the operators. A shorter guy. Black hair and just as black eyes. Teeth grinding, he forbid himself from saying anything stupid. Or smart. Anything he said would probably erupt in a fight.

Thud!

The SEAL's shoulder bumped Dean's.

Dean reacted.

A hand clamped on his shoulder. Spun him around.

"Easy, easy." Falcon pressed him in against the grease board.

Hands on the wall, Dean worked his anger out through calculated breathing.

"Let the real men take care of this," a SEAL said with a snigger.

Dean jerked.

Another hand clamped around his shoulder. Titanis huddled in with him and Falcon. "Not worth it, mate."

Inhale. Exhale. Inhale.

Behind him, he heard shoes squeak. Chairs squawked.

"C'mon, you piece of—"

"Hey!"

He glanced over as Harrier and Knight held back a writhing Hawk. The door thumped closed, and in the hall came the telltale laughter and high fives of the SEALs. Dean spun toward Burnett.

The graying general raised his hands. "You're not going to say or feel anything I haven't already felt."

Dean took a step forward, pointing to the door Ramsey had just escaped through. "Are you telling me. . .did he imply what I think he did? We're sidelined?"

"Officially?" Burnett nodded. "Yes."

Hawk flung up his arms. "Son of a—"

"Check your language." Dean thrust a hand at the guy. "There's a lady present."

Lieutenant Brie Hastings stood and arched an eyebrow. "Who could write the manual on foul language." She smiled at Dean. "But I appreciate the sentiment."

Dean's phone buzzed again. "Sir—"

"I said *officially*." Burnett stared up through his bushy eyebrows at the team.

Thick tension hung suspended, each breath begging the general for release. "If you gentleman will excuse me. I need a Dr Pepper." Burnett glanced at Hastings then thumbed at Raptor team as if to say, "Tell 'em." He left the room.

Anticipation thrummed through Dean. The two were playing coy about something. He waited for the thump of the door then eyeballed Hastings.

She closed up the briefcase, walked around the table, and stood directly in front of Dean. From somewhere, she produced a piece of paper. "You do all look tired. It's a disgrace that you'd let yourselves get so worn down. That's how mistakes happen. That's how bad judgment calls are made." The little actress wrinkled her nose as she tucked the paper into Dean's hand. He curled it into a ball without breaking eye contact. Did she think someone was watching?

"Good night, gentlemen." She almost pulled off the demure thing. "You've got what, a week? Maybe more?" At the door, she smiled. "Oh. And stay out of Ramsey's way. He and his team are heading out first thing."

Dean waited until after she left.

"What in a gypsy's uncle was that all about?" Hawk frowned. Then saw Dean's hand. "What—?"

"No." Dean stalked out, his stupid phone buzzing again. He tugged it out and glanced at the number. Didn't recognize it. Stuffed it back in his pocket. At his bunk, he stepped under a lantern. Uncrumpled the paper as the team crowded him.

ACTIVITY AT BOMBED SCHOOL. EQUIPMENT OFF-LOADED.

Dean's pulse kick-started at the news. They needed to move. Now.

Falcon slapped him on the shoulder. "Think it's time for Hawk to get inked?" His grin was wicked. "Don't you?"

"Hey." Hawk scowled, his face the epitome of challenge as he pointed at the team sergeant. "Don't touch the temple."

"Seems someone needs a little graffiti on their pristine, self-absorbed shrine," Falcon said. "Bet there's great artists near the Blue Mosque."

Tattoo artist. Outside the wire.

Dean nodded, following the ruse. " 'Bout time you committed to the team." He shot a mean warning to Hawk. "Seal your deal with wings."

"No." Hawk started backing up. "No way. I don't need poison in my body to prove I'm all-in."

"Afraid of a little ink?" Titanis smirked.

Hawk's nostrils flared. "You have wings, boy from Oz?"

Titanis grinned then tugged up his shirt, revealing the Victoria Cross over his heart. He'd earned two of those before being attached to Raptor for a mission involving MWDs and WMDs.

"*Wings*, Oz." Hawk looked triumphant. "No wings." He raised his hands. "If he doesn't have them—"

"We'll do it together." Titanis's bearded jaw jutted. "Take one for the team."

Hawk's eyes blazed. "Not happening."

"You're looking a little green there, runt." Titanis gripped Hawk's shoulder. "What do you say?" He patted Hawk's chest. Though Hawk was about six inches shorter, the two were well matched in muscles. "Tell you what—I'll hold your hand."

Raptor tightened up on Hawk.

With a shout, Hawk crashed through the team and raced out of the tent.

"Get him!"

—◊◊◊—

Mazar-e-Sharif
15 June—2115 Hours

A half mile out, they lay prostrate on a building, peering through scopes. The old school compound stood somber and broken in the dark night. Gate fixed and now guarded by two armed men in keffiyehs, the courtyard glowed beneath the halo of light the generator lamps cast across the crowded area where Dean first met Zahrah.

"Grand freakin' Central Station," Hawk muttered.

Two large canvas-topped trucks huddled against the back area, being disemboweled of large crates. Firearms. RPGs. Who knew what they were delivering.

"Recognize anyone?" Dean asked Falcon, who lay to his right, snapping pictures.

"Negative." As Raptor's expert in ops/intel, Falcon had a broader knowledge than most. "Hold up." The soft shutter of a lens snapped a dozen times. "Kohistani just emerged. He's got the ear of someone."

Dean scanned the scene and located the bearded director walking with a man in a long tan tunic and even longer beard. Head and neck wrapped, he had the classic imam look. "Recognize his friend?"

"Hold up, hold up," Hawk said, having temporarily avoided an inked back. Their ruse to escape the base had worked, especially with the extent to which Hawk had howled at the security point. They'd taken their time secreting into this position unnoticed. "Check the gate. Check the gate."

Dean slid his binoculars down to where a dark van pulled up to the gate, which was already opening. *What am I missing?*

"Dude in the passenger seat is the guy who hit Double Z and her cousin."

Sliding the nocs along the moving van, Dean caught a blurred glimpse before the van swung around on the other side of the large canvassed trucks.

"D'you see him?" Hawk asked.

"Negative." The mechanical whir of the long-range zoom gave Dean hope that Falcon would capture something.

"They've got someone." Falcon's words held warning. "Hooded, hands tied."

"Male? Female?"

"Unknown."

Dean scratched his jaw. Whatever Kohistani was running, it couldn't be legal. Not with a night operation and blindfolded hostages.

"Do we go in?" Harrier asked.

"Negative." Dean shook his head, not as an answer but to ward off the knot in his gut. Hated leaving anyone in the clutches of these men. But there were too many unknowns. Not enough information. "Not our mission."

"Technically," Hawk muttered as he adjusted and continued staring through the nocs. "Neither is—oh crap!"

Cement exploded in Dean's face. He buried his face in his forearm and covered his helmet. "Exposed! Exposed!" he shouted as he scrambled backward.

He rolled to the left. Swung his body down over the lip of the rooftop, reached for the open window and caught it. Then dropped.

His boots crunched and hit the ground running. Behind him, he heard a half-dozen others pounding the dirt. Hoofing it without the ruck helped, but his tac vest and weapon added to the weight.

Cracks of gunfire robbed him of the hope they'd avoid an encounter. M9 out, he stuffed himself into an alcove, braced himself, and aimed down the dark alley and beyond the team as they sprinted for the vehicle.

A figure whipped around the corner. Weapon up and firing.

Dean eased back the trigger and neutralized the target.

Another skidded, probably seeing his friend go down, and slid straight into the body. Dean fired again.

"Go, go!" Hawk shouted as he slammed up against Dean.

He darted to the other side of the alley. Took up position, halfway down the alley. Dean searched but saw nothing. Traced the shadows with his muzzle. What he wouldn't do for NVGs. "Clear!"

Hawk lunged toward him.

A tiny explosion in a shadow revealed the shooter.

Dean calculated—the spark had been a bit low. . .probably kneeling—and fired. A grunt preceded a tinge of cream slumping out of the shadows.

"Augh!" Hawk released an angry growl. "Crap. That freakin' Talib clipped me." Disbelief colored his words. A breathy grunt knocked out of Hawk as he dropped against the wall to Dean's left.

Even in the dark shadows, the faint moonlight glinted off the blood seeping through Hawk's shoulder. "How bad?"

"It's bad—I'm shot!"

"Harrier—"

"No," Hawk said. "Let's get out of here. I can make it."

"You sure?"

"Not if you keep wasting breath."

"Falcon, cover us. We're coming in—Hawk's hit."

"Roger!"

Dean threaded an arm under Hawk's and grabbed his far drag strap. Together, they hurried to the armored vehicle and dove in.

They were in motion before the door closed. Dean unvelcroed Hawk's tac vest as Harrier crowded in, anxious to do his medic thing.

Hawk leaned back against the seat, hissing. "Son. . .of a. . .*biscuit*." His face screwed tight.

"Calm down."

"It burns like—"

"Need me to hold your hand?" Titanis asked.

Hawk's gaze locked on to the Aussie.

"Dope him," the Aussie said. "He'll never know how many needles hit him."

Hawk glowered. "You touch me"—he grimaced as Harrier worked on him—"and the last thing you'll see is my fuzzy kangaroo fists in your face."

Dean snickered. Did Hawk realize Titanis was getting his mind off the pain?

"We'll give it a go when you have your strength back." Titanis cocked his head. "Or have you ever had it?"

With another powerful glare at Titanis, Hawk shook his head. Groaning, his face red and veins bulging as Harrier slid a needle into the meaty part of his shoulder, Hawk steeled himself. Then let out a breath. Focused on Dean. "How'd they see us? Two blocks away? Dark?"

He shook his head again.

"That's what I'm wondering," Falcon said.

Harrier pressed bandages to the wound and taped it. "Bullet's deep. We'll need to wait till we get back."

"Beginning to think we have a traitor or spy," Hawk said. "I'd start checking with foreigners on the base. Those assigned to SOC teams." His gaze slid to Titanis.

The man took the half-tease, half-accusation hard. "You think—"

"Easy," Dean said. "He's just giving back what you dished."

Face coated in a sheen of sweat, Hawk held his ground and expression. "Am I?"

When the lights of the base beamed into the vehicle, Dean leaned forward. "Falcon, take us to the motor pool. Harrier, you can fix this, right?"

"Yeah."

If Ramsey got wind that Hawk needed surgery to remove the bullet, he'd climb down their throats. Dean would fill out the AAR with complete details, but he'd delay submitting it till things calmed down.

In the motor pool, they curtained off an area and Harrier went to work. Dean waited outside, watching. Analyzing. The others headed to the showers. How. . .how had the guards noticed them? No way they should've been seen. Not for some little operation like that stuff at the school. And who was their captive?

Dean coded in.

Behind the curtain, Hawk's words slurred. Not using morphine, but something to dull the pain and keep him from fighting the surgery.

"Burnett."

Dean focused on the general. Explained what happened. About Hawk. Told him about the hostage.

"How's Bledsoe?"

"A little loopy." He glanced toward the curtain.

"What's new?"

Dean chuckled. "Sir, any chatter about a missing VIP?"

"Nothing. And we're not going to get involved until I get more answers. Whatever Ramsey's doing, it's gotta come out eventually. And I'm going to make sure that's sooner."

"Roger that."

The far door opened and Titanis strode in with another man. An Arab. Who was this?

"I'll do some digging, see what I can find. You and Raptor stay low. Get some rest."

"Roger that, sir." Dean stood as the two men joined him.

Looking far too pleased with himself, Titanis held a hand to the man with him. "This is Osman. He's a local friend."

With a nod, Dean acknowledged the man.

"He's the best," Titanis added.

Dean frowned. "At what?"

"Tattoos."

CHAPTER 25

Somewhere in Afghanistan
17 June—0800 Hours

Twenty-four hours and nobody is talking about your disappearance."

Zahrah tried to peer between the fibers of the hood where light shone through, but she could not see anything but shapes and blurs.

"Perhaps you are not as important as you thought."

"I'm *not* important. I'm a teacher."

Thud!

Her head knocked sideways. The world tilted. She felt herself falling. Hands tied behind her, she could not break her fall. Her shoulder thudded against the ground. Warmth slid down her lip. Since they'd removed her from her apartment, she remembered little. A pinch in her arm—probably a drug. Then traveling in a vehicle. And now this. It could've been days for all she knew.

And with Fekiria shutting her out. . .it was possible her cousin would not miss her right away.

Footsteps approached. Zahrah braced herself for another hit. Or kick. Instead, hands gripped her arms and shoulders, righting her.

"Please," she whispered, "I don't know what you—"

Shouts and thuds garbled her words.

Through the fibers, a vague shape burst into the room. He rattled in Arabic, "We need to leave. Americans are coming—they're searching the buildings."

Zahrah's heart thudded. *Thank You, God!* Her father or Captain Watters had found out. They were looking for her!

"Get her ready."

Someone approached and reached toward her.

Zahrah cringed. *Get her ready.* That meant they wouldn't kill her yet. Right?

The person grabbed at the hood and yanked—along with a fistful of her hair. Fiery darts tingled along her scalp. Before she could do anything, someone grabbed her head. Jerked it so she looked to the ceiling. The other wrapped silver tape around her mouth—around her neck and head, too! Then he dropped a blue mound of material around her. The suffocating silk covered her, head to toe. She blinked. A small rectangular opening had a netlike barrier. A burqa?

Still tied and now robed in anonymity, two of her captors herded her down a hall. Pulling and pushing her. The material coiled around her legs. She stumbled.

They yanked her onward. Into a dark room then another. Right into—

She gasped. The old gym. They were back at the old school?

They shoved her into the backseat of a van, and someone, also draped in blue, moved in next to her. Another captive? Her heart surged at the thought of an ally.

The person jabbed something into her ribs. "Say nothing and do nothing, and you will live," came a man's voice.

Only then did Zahrah identify what was poking her—a gun!

—⁓—

Camp Marmal, Mazar-e Sharif
17 June—0815 Hours

In the mess hall, Dean sat with his lunch. Since budget cuts and no hot breakfast, lunch had suddenly become important. Falcon and Titanis joined him.

"Give any more thought to what happened last night?" Falcon lifted his burger and bit into it.

Dean nodded. "A lot." He munched on some potato chips. "Either we've gotten sloppy or they were tipped off."

"How?" Titanis shrugged his big shoulders. "Nobody but us knew we were going."

"Except Hastings," Falcon noted. The guy tipped back his head and guzzled water. He had strong facial features that made words unnecessary. With that hooked nose and longer-than-normal black hair, Falcon had his own style and attitude.

Arms folded, Dean leaned on the table. "Not convinced she's trouble, but it's something to consider."

"We need to consider all facts," Falcon said. "Something stinks. We go to Majorca. Yeah, it's a diversion, but they knew our every move. They anticipated us. Pinned us. Had we not gone to water"—he shrugged—"we might not be sitting here."

"Heads up," Titanis said, eyebrows winging toward the door.

Hawk ambled in, stiff and looking wrecked. Dark circles under his eyes, he kept his right arm close.

"Think he figured it out?" Titanis asked, head low, eyes on his food.

"Has he punched you yet?" Falcon sniggered.

A few minutes later, Hawk slid his tray on the table. "Man," he said as he hooked his legs over the bench and dropped down. "I've taken a bullet before, but this one. . ." He stretched his neck. Rubbed his shoulder and hissed. "Must've hit a weird muscle or something. My back is *killing* me."

Dean stretched his jaw, fighting the smile. He hunched closer to the table. Shoulder shielding him from Hawk.

"Hey, what'd you find out about last night?"

"Nothing yet," Falcon said, not missing a beat. "You get some acetaminophen from Harrier?"

Hawk nodded. "It's not even touching it." He dug into his slop. "Says eating a good meal will help."

"Good thing we're off the grid for a few, huh?"

"Amen. I slept till ten-hundred then hit the showers." Another grunt. "My back felt like it was on fire." He downed a sport drink. Dug two pills out of his pocket, tossed them in his mouth, and took a swig from a second bottle.

"Nice tat," someone called.

Dean pushed to his feet and grabbed his tray. "Got some work to do."

"Me, too," Titanis said.

"Hey. Bledsoe." A sergeant made his way over. "D'you hear me?"

Dean made a beeline to return his tray, rushing ahead of the oncoming storm.

"Saw that sweet tat when you were putting your shirt on. Where'd you get those wings?"

"What are you—?" The fleshy clap of a slap on the back sounded. Then a howl. "No!" Metal scraped against cement. *"Titanis!"*

Dean and Titanis sprinted down the hall, dodging soldiers. Behind them, the telltale *thwack* of the mess hall doors flying open pushed them. "If he catches us. . ." Dean shoved against the security bar. Broke into the sunlight.

A meaty roar chased them.

Dean couldn't stop laughing. "He's going to kill us!"

"He had it coming," Titanis said with a laugh and shook his head.

"You sorry pieces of work!" Hawk yelled as he burst into the sun. Flexing his biceps, he fisted his hands. "C'm—"

Sirens blazed. The warning howl pierced the afternoon. Dean spun, searching his surroundings, weapon out, ready to take on a target. His nerves jangled, shifting from a joke to a life-and-death scenario. Troops getting hit by the locals they trained had become all too common. He felt Titanis at his back as they turned, searching for the threat.

"Stop him!"

Dean pivoted toward the chaos, toward the voice. Lined up his sights. Let the sight blur as he focused on the crowd at the business end of his weapon. A cluster of MPs rushed toward them. Thirty yards and closing.

Dean's pulse knocked up a notch. *What. . . ?* He searched for the target.

His gaze slid down a fraction. To the slight frame of a boy. Pumping with his arms. Leg still tangled in a cast, he hobbled. Terror gouged his face. His long tunic flapped hard, as if trying to take off.

Rashid!

"No!" He rammed his gun back into the holster and rushed forward, his goal stopping the guns aiming for the kid. "Stand down! Stand down!" he shouted to the MPs. "Blue—friendly! Don't shoot!"

The boy flew the last twenty feet to him. Threw himself against Dean, screaming.

Hand out to stay the police, Dean held the boy close. Verified they weren't going to fire. He peered down. "Rashid." His lungs burned. "What—?"

"I'm sorry! I'm sorry! I failed!" Rashid clung tighter. When Dean tried to pry him off, the boy clenched. "No, please! You must help."

After wresting free, Dean went to a knee. Held the boy's trembling shoulders as tears formed dark rivulets down Rashid's dirty face. "Hey." He gave him a light squeeze. "Rashid, slow down. What's wrong?"

"I failed!" The eight-year-old boy threw his head back and struck his chest with another cry. "You gave me a mission and I dishonored you."

Mission? What miss—? Dean's breath jammed in the back of his throat. *Zahrah.* He gripped the boy's shoulders. Stared into his eyes. "Miss Zarrick?"

A frantic nod. Dirty black hair fringed red-rimmed eyes as tears streaked down his face. "She's gone! They can't find her."

"What do you mean, they can't find her?"

"She's gone! Just gone."

"Rashid—"

The boy lunged into Dean's arms and hooked his arms around his neck. "Please do not hurt me. I am sorry. I tried—"

Dean pulled the boy close. A hand cupped the back of the boy's head as Dean glanced up at Hawk and Titanis, who stood there. Their faces bore the shock Dean felt. And the anger. *Get it in gear! She's missing!*

Someone meant to harm her. Kill her. And. . .that meant Rashid could be in danger, too. All of them, for that fact.

He lifted Rashid into his arms, thankful the boy was on the small side. To Titanis he said, "Get Burnett. And the team."

CHAPTER 26

Camp Marmal, Mazar-e Sharif
17 June—0900 Hours

Holy Mother of God, help me!

Lance stormed into the sub-base, the narrow hall clogged with a dozen or more soldiers. Titanis led the way, the man a mountain of muscle, so when he barked, "Make a hole!" the sea of uniforms parted as if God Himself had ordered it. They stepped into the briefing room.

Watters, who'd been sitting in front of the Afghan boy, stood. "Sir."

"What do you know?"

"Not much," Watters said. "They aren't sure when she was taken or by whom. Just that she's gone. She'd been staying in the dorms with her cousin."

"When did the cousin last see her?"

"Unknown. The boy just heard his parents talking to one of the Haidary cousins."

"But she was just taken this morning?"

"Unknown."

Lance considered the boy. Short but stout in heart, the kid had lost his sister in the same explosion that ripped his leg up. Fear and sincerity marked the boy's wide brown eyes. "You're sure he doesn't know anything else?"

Watters hesitated, eyed the kid, then nodded. "He's a good kid. I'd made him an unofficial first sergeant after the explosion."

Lance grunted. Were they too late already? Nothing had hit the wires. No ransom demand. No videos showing a beaten or otherwise harmed Zahrah. "Well, get over to the dorm and find some answers. I'll send CID over, too."

"Yes, sir." Watters turned to the boy. "Ready?"

"What are you doing?"

"Taking him. He knows where she was living. We don't."

"You gone soft?"

"Too thickheaded for that, sir."

Lance tried to laugh. But this was a butt-ugly situation. "You realize I have to make a phone call. And that someone is going to be climbing down your throat."

Watters hesitated then nodded. "You can tell him to blame a certain general who got us out of the way so he could play war games." His nostrils flared. "So help me—if I. . ." Dean's jaw muscle popped. He shook his head, looking down.

"Take it easy with that anger, son."

"No." Dean cocked his head. "He put lives in jeopardy and now she's gone. Had we been here—"

"You couldn't have done anything."

Watters drew up straight.

Lance held up his hands. "I hear you—I know you're ticked. So am I. But we aren't going to fly off half-cocked. Get the facts. Figure out our strategy. Then. . .then we'll see." Ramsey would be through the roof to have something like this happen as the American presence wound down. This wouldn't go over well in the media. He'd fight like the dickens to make sure Zahrah Zarrick came home alive and in one piece. "We'll see."

"Just make sure I don't *see* him because I make no promises."

He'd chosen this man for a reason, and this was part of it. But if Watters lost control. . . "Just remember, if you do something to soothe that beast inside you, she may be lost."

The man lifted his chin. The lines between his eyebrows knotted.

Good. Lance had made his point. "Her life depends on you keeping your head on straight." He nodded. "I'm depending on you, her father is, and so is your team."

"Hey, Cap'?"

Watters looked to the side where the communications expert waited, rubbing his shoulder.

Bledsoe stood. Surveyed the surroundings. "Had a thought."

"Go on," Watters said.

"Remember a certain school and late-night deliveries? A hooded captive?"

"Let's move!" Watters launched out of the room.

CHAPTER 27

Mazar-e Sharif

The weight of his uniform, M4, tactical vest, M9 holstered at his hip, and helmet with live cam had nothing on the one sitting on his chest. A thousand-pound cement block called guilt. Dean jogged toward the waiting vehicles that would ferry them out to the airstrip. There, two Black Hawks waited, engines whining in anticipation of the flight.

Dean hustled toward the birds. His gaze hit a team waiting, and he slowed. The very SEAL team that had gotten them kicked off the mission, diverted from doing their job. The same guys, Dean felt, who'd sacrificed Zahrah's safety and life for a bit of brass ego.

"No," Hawk said with a growl over the din of the rotor wash. "No way are they coming."

The SEAL who'd bumped Dean's shoulder with his own two days ago offered his hand. "Lieutenant Commander Chris Riordan." Ferocity defined his features. "Heard what happened." Greased up and bearded, he held his M4 over his chest. "We want to offer our help."

Dean considered the other half-dozen men. Six men he didn't know. But they were six men interested in protecting and preserving lives, especially American lives. If they were doing an extraction, if this got ugly, more manpower never hurt. He stuffed his hand against the SEAL's. "Thank you."

"You're kidding me!" Hawk threw his hands up then headed for the chopper. On board, he pointed to Commander Riordan. "After this— watch your back."

One of Riordan's men snickered as he passed Hawk. "You should take your own advice. Surprised that vest doesn't hurt." He slapped Hawk's shoulder. Hard.

Hawk about came out of his uniform.

The tattoo. The SEAL knew about the tattoo Hawk now bore. As

Dean climbed in, he leaned in and pressed Hawk down. "Later." He patted his friend's shoulder.

The ten-minute ride to the compound was made in virtual silence. They had their objective: secure Zahrah Zarrick at all costs. The SEALs didn't know Dean's connection to her. While they might know she was General Z's daughter, he guessed they had no knowledge of her area of expertise.

Or maybe they did. Maybe he was the slow one. The one to blame for her disappearance. The numbing vibration of the chopper needled its way into his brain. If he'd figured out sooner what they wouldn't openly tell him, he could've spent more effort on convincing her to leave.

"It is not my place to put demands on how or what He does with my life."

Maybe she wouldn't take that liberty, but Dean sure would. *God. . . You gotta keep her safe. This can't happen. Not again. I can't do it again.*

Twisting his hand around the grip of his M4, he felt the Oakley gloves twist. Tighten. Constrict. Much like the agony of knowing how this could end.

Screams shrieked through the passages of time. Pierced the steel box where he'd stowed his heart. Stowed his ability to care ever again. He stared down at the steel hull where boots touched and felt as if he'd died in that cell ten years ago.

Dean Watters, the kid fresh out of Basic and still wet behind the ears, had died. In his place, the sole survivor emerged. Hardened. Focused. Maybe even a bit jaded. A screwed-up life and torture did that to a guy.

Blond, blue eyed, and so sweet, Ellen screamed into his present.

No. Gritting his teeth, he pushed her visage back. Refused her voice.

Descent pulled his thoughts out of the quagmire. He lifted his chin and found Commander Riordan watching him. Dean checked his NVGs and shifted to the edge of the seat, eyeing the city as it blurred beneath them. Almost there.

The Black Hawk hovered over the compound. Harrier went first, fast-roping down. Dean followed, the wind ripping at his duds as if telling him to hurry. Dirt peppered the little flesh exposed.

His boots touched ground and he rushed out of the way and went to a knee. The shelled-out building that once housed a large gym-like area gaped at them in shock that it'd lost a fight. Cinder blocks tumbled out like broken teeth. Stock pressed into his shoulder, Dean used the M4 for a line of sight, scoping the windows. Doors. Searching for combatants, expecting opposition like they'd encountered unexpectedly. Why hadn't they come out fighting? Last night, they'd kept a safe distance but ended up eating bullets. Now, they were on top of them and. . .

Too quiet.

Pulse hammering, he again eyed the doors and windows as the team disembarked from the bird and took cover against the building. As soon as Falcon patted his shoulder, giving the all-clear, Dean sprinted to the building. Slammed up against the wall, back to the plaster, gaze down and to the side, waiting. Any moment it could open. . .or fly apart. His team with it.

Hawk knelt beside the door on the other side, his muzzle trained on it. Weeks back, Zahrah had said the men hid in the structure. With the condition it was in, it didn't surprise Dean that terrorists were using it for a bunker. Smart. Nobody would think to check here, not after the explosion. Not after his own team had cleared it. They hadn't—until Hastings gave them a heads-up on the activity.

A pat on Dean's shoulder kick-started the adrenaline and signaled the team's readiness to breach the building.

Dean stepped out, leaned back, and thrust the heel of his boot toward the door handle. It cracked but didn't give. He caught his balance. Gritted his teeth. Rammed his boot into it again. The door flung back. *Crack!* Chunks of wood splintered. Even as his foot came down, Dean brought up his weapon. Even with the wash of green illuminating the setting, gloom spiraled up a short flight of stairs.

Falcon pivoted around the opening and rushed in, sweeping left and right as he descended into the darkness. Dean rushed in behind him. As he made the third step, he spotted a hall off to the left. At the corner, he pressed his shoulder to the wood and waited. Soon as he got the signal from behind that they were ready, he stepped out. He hurried down the long, narrow corridor. His breath puffed in his ears, every crunch of his boots feeling like an RPG. Gripping his M4, he forced himself to stay focused. Stay calm. Something bugged him, tugged at his conscience.

Too quiet. Holding up a fist, he blew out a breath through his mouth. Scoped the hall. Three doors right. One left. Threat of death at every step. Over his shoulder, he made eye contact with Riordan. Sent the

SEALs left while he and Raptor would clear right. Hawk put his hand on the first knob and waited.

Dean gave a nod.

Hawk flicked the door open.

Scuttling inside, Dean went right, using the wall to guide him as he rushed along the L-shape and pied toward the center, trusting Falcon had done the same on the left. The room sat empty. No dust. Dirt. Not even a gum wrapper.

After walking the wall, he angled back to the center. "Clear."

In the hall he heard two more clears. He motioned Harrier and Titanis to the next room and rushed to the end of the hall, where he and Falcon cleared a left turn. Times like this made him appreciate the team, the way they moved without hesitation. Their skills. No need to give directions beyond the game plan. The men knew what they were doing and were the best at it. They might have disagreements or talk crap, but here, in the thick of combat, they knew who to count on.

Within a dozen paces, a corner seemed to lure them into another trap. Blind to what might be waiting—more of the same or an entire band of fighters—he once again attuned himself to the team, to the movements. Clears, swish of tac pants, crunch of boots. Mutters. Behind him, he felt Falcon close up. They hurried, moving quickly, giving the enemy less time to sight and shout.

He banked left.

Clear.

Another turn—he nearly cursed. Another corner. What was this? A maze? He stalked, back arched a little, weapon stabbing the darkness before he reached it. Two more "clears" behind. How many rooms did this hole in the ground have? Moving faster but not with less caution, he approached a door. No Arabic lettering or signs to tell him what lay behind, what to expect. Just like the Taliban—ambush seemed the method of choice. Dean checked Falcon, who nodded his readiness. At the corner, Dean did his quick look-see.

A tiny spark threw him back for cover. "Taking fire!"

On a knee, Dean leaned out and fired. Tight, controlled bursts where he'd seen the black blur against the dingy wall. No spraying and praying. As he made the shots, he watched the guy disappear through a door on the right. A commotion ensued not unlike a door flapping and hitting something.

Think I got him.

With a signal, he sent Falcon and Hawk down the hall. The two moved swiftly, confidently. Fear—heck yeah. But this was where the boys were separated from the men. As they moved without incident, Dean pushed from his position. He walked backward, covering their six.

"Tango down. Going in," Falcon radioed as he vanished into the room.

Weapon up, heart hammering, Dean moved forward. Noticed a slight break in the wall plaster on his right. But he trained his attention on the left, where Falcon vanished. Harrier and Titanis were on him. Dean made a wide arc around the door, prepared to take more fire. Each second without contact gave him hope that Falcon had either neutralized threats or there weren't any more.

A body lay almost across the threshold. The fighter who'd shot at Dean.

"Cap', we got something," Hawk's husky voice served as a towline on Dean's movements.

In the room, row upon row of shelves greeted him. Empty. He'd guess only recently since no dust had collected. Through at least a half-dozen racks, he detected movement at the back. Sweeping left and right, his gaze tracking the team and the SEALs, Dean headed along the length of a shelving unit that reached almost to the eight-foot ceiling and spanned almost the entire length of the room.

"Here," Falcon said as he stepped out and waved them on.

Dean slipped around the corner and slowed. Curses behind him echoed his feelings. Bounced off the hiccup in his heart rate. A dozen or more men—dead. Shot.

"Freakin' bloodbath." Hawk squatted next to the mound of bodies.

Riordan joined them, hunching down, his weapon cradled across his arms. "Blood's coagulated, but there's no bloating. Little discoloration."

In other words, they hadn't been dead long. Maybe even the fighter he'd just taken down had done the deed. But one against eight or ten fighters? Hands weren't tied. No blindfolds. These men had been killed so they couldn't talk. About what?

Falcon stood, rubbing his beard. "Eliminating witnesses."

Did that include Zahrah? Dean grimaced. Didn't want to look, but he had to know—was she here? "Is she. . . ?" The words jammed at the back of his throat.

Straightening, Hawk waved a hand toward the feet. "All males."

Swallowing the shot of adrenaline at the thought of her being on the bottom of that pile, Dean shook his head. "Record it, call it in." She wasn't here. She wasn't dead. For her sake, he almost wished the latter for her. But not for him. He'd never be able to live with himself if he didn't bring her back alive. But where? Where were they supposed to begin? Where and why had they taken her? He just wouldn't let himself believe they'd found out about her quantum crypto skills. He started for the door, more defeated than ever.

"Commander," a SEAL called from where he stood in the hall, wreathed in shadows, squatting at the same place where Dean had earlier noticed the break in plaster. Tracing a gloved hand down the joint, the SEAL looked over his shoulder.

"What've you got?" Riordan's boots scritched against the dirt as he came up behind Dean, who shifted aside as the commander exited the room.

His guy grinned as he pointed to distinct track marks and boot prints, half hidden beneath the wall. As if someone walked through walls. "Think we have a secret room."

Riordan nodded. "Get it open."

Weapon at the ready, Dean eyed the commander, whose eyes possessed the same fierce determination Dean felt. Was Zahrah behind this panel?

Or would they find more bodies?

Or just one?

"Hawk, Falcon," Dean called. "Group up."

The SEALs breached the panel. Dean followed the commander in—who stopped. Cursed.

Dean wove around him. Ice dumped down his spine. He stilled. Held his breath at the sight of a female captive bound to a chair, head down and covered in a filthy hood. One with a gaping hole and dark stain. A lone bulb served as a mocking spotlight. What yanked the breath out of Dean was the teal blue hijab peeking out from under the hood. A soft moan issued from the woman. She went limp.

Dean threw himself forward. "Zahrah!"

"Don't move—don't move!" Riordan thrust an arm at him. Nailed him with a forearm across the chest. *"Bomb!"*

CHAPTER 28

Camp Marmal, Mazar-e Sharif
17 June—1005 Hours

Though his heart shoved him forward, his head slowed him. "Zahrah!" Made him nod when the SEAL punched his shoulder, making sure the threat was understood. "Got it." Dean drew up straight. Swallowed—hard.

The SEAL eased over the trip wire, and Harrier moved forward. With the guy's medic skills, she had a chance. As long as they weren't too late. Harrier placed a finger gently against the woman's wrist bound to the chair.

The heartbeats it took for Harrier to assess her situation defied Dean's anxious plea to hurry up. "No good. She's gone."

"Is it her?" Hawk's quiet question plagued Dean as the SEALs worked to defuse the bomb that booby-trapped the room.

Every second felt like an RPG hitting him. She was dead. Unmoving. Death by terrorist.

God, please. . .

"Okay," Riordan said. "Clear."

Dean couldn't move. Couldn't bring himself to remove the hood and find out it was Zahrah. *Never hear her laugh. Never hear her thoughts on things.* Somehow, his body moved forward. A step closer. Then another.

"You're sure. . ." Hawk looked to the SEALs. "Sure you didn't miss any wires?"

"She's clear. I checked."

Slowly, Hawk drew off the hood.

Black curly hair slipped from the hood and bloody hijab. The head lolled to the side, revealing a round face.

"It's not her." The realization knocked the breath loose Dean had been holding. Bending forward and catching his knees, he gulped air.

Tried to breathe. *It's not her.* Though he wanted to laugh, he didn't. Instead he turned a circle. Rubbed his forehead. He closed his eyes, tortured by the incredible relief that it wasn't Zahrah yet grieved for the young woman who'd died.

"She can't be but fifteen," Falcon growled.

Dean shook his head as he turned away, aware of how he'd just acted. Aware of his weakness. Aware the vault around his heart had a crack in it.

"Teams are en route to inventory," Hawk said.

Fresh air. Need fresh air. Still drunk on the relief that Zahrah hadn't been among the dead, Dean made his way aboveground. They had one colossal problem—Zahrah was still missing. He didn't dare remove his helmet though he wanted to shed every weight clinging to him. But even he knew the real weight bothering him was Zahrah. She was gone. He'd had a hope that he could get her back before it was too late. Before anything happened to her. Now, now they had nothing. Not a single clue to her whereabouts.

He stalked to the MRAP and climbed in. Dropped against the bench. Punched the seat beside him. Gripped his head in his hands. *How do I get her back?*

"I think whoever took your girl," Riordan said as he joined him, "wanted you dead."

Startled at the company and the words, Dean stiffened. Ground his teeth together. But nodded. Yeah, it made sense. The explosives. The lone sentry to lure them deeper into the hole. His gaze scraped the structure. If the bomb detonated, the whole thing would collapse. Nobody would find them for days. By then, it'd be too late. "They assumed we'd find her, be enraged, and not notice the bomb."

"Good thing I was here then, right?"

He eyed the SEAL.

Riordan shrugged, broad shoulders bunching against his thick neck. "Hey, no skin off my back." A smile lingered in Riordan's eyes. "And if you need help finding your girl, we've got your six."

"She's not my girl. She's Zarrick's daughter."

He straightened. "You mean *Z-Day Zarrick*?"

Dean nodded.

"GeeBee, you picked the wrong chick to go soft over."

"I'm not—"

Riordan held up a hand. "I saw your face when you thought that girl was her. I expected to have to medevac you out." He laughed too loud for Dean to voice the objection on his tongue.

Fists balled, Dean jerked his gaze down. Harnessed the anger spiraling out of control.

"Don't worry," Riordan said. "We'll get her back."

Come hell or high water.

"Cap!" Hawk jogged toward them. "General wants us at her apartment. They found something."

—⁓—

Somewhere in Afghanistan
17 June—1130 Hours

Jammed between two large men posing as women, Zahrah clung to hope. To a frantic, desperate hope that she would be found. Noticed. The van lumbered out of the courtyard, away from the place of death that had stolen Ara. Even now, Zahrah felt the bracelet cutting into her wrists, but she savored that feeling. She was alive.

Yet terror seized her as the van sped out of Mazar-e Sharif and headed south. The landscape raced by without remorse, pushing her farther from American forces. Farther from Captain Watters. Farther from discernible hope.

All too aware that most Americans taken by Taliban ended up on videos getting their heads chopped off, or being found strung up dead and naked for all to see, Zahrah struggled against the panic.

Do something!

But what? They were all armed. She was now in the middle of the desert. Alone with four men. It was not a matter of *if* they would violate her, but *when*.

She clenched her eyes. Fought the tears.

God, help me. . .please help me.

And yet, she knew praying didn't guarantee that things would turn out the way she wanted. It just guaranteed God would hear. Insufferable heat drenched her in sweat beneath the full-body burqa. Hands behind her back, she felt the tingling in her wrists and hands as her circulation slowly cut off. She leaned to the right, toward the open window and off the nerves in her arms, desperate for a breath of air and to stop the tingling needles.

The man rammed her shoulder. "Get off me, you whore!"

Zahrah drew into herself.

"Don't worry," Kamran spoke over his shoulder, leering. "There will be time for that later."

His insinuation hung as rank and thick as the body odor around her. Zahrah searched Scripture for solace. *You are a shield about me, a refuge, an ever-present help in time of trouble.* And hello? She was definitely in trouble!

The car slowed. "Americans," the driver hissed.

A mile ahead and between the shoulders of Kamran and the driver, a military roadblock gave her hope. Dogs circled cars that passed through the checkpoint.

"Act normal," Kamran said. "We have nothing to hide. If they dare touch our women. . ."

Sick laughter bellowed around her as the car eased up to the checkpoint. Though she was the only real woman in the vehicle, the two men on either side in hijabs would be off-putting to the military. Arab men often shouted at American soldiers for improper conduct toward their women. It'd worked. Suicide bombers used the same ruse—dress up in a hijab and approach a checkpoint.

Kamran sneered at her, his strong features cruel and chilling. "Say nothing, or you will die."

How she was supposed to talk with tape over her mouth, she didn't know, but he made his point with the gun pointed at her. And if that wasn't enough, the man on her right jabbed his weapon into her ribs.

Zahrah sucked in a breath and grunted.

"Quiet," he hissed.

If they killed her now, she wouldn't be able to serve their purpose—whatever it was. They must have one because they could've murdered her in the apartment rather than going through all this. But she wasn't willing to find out if her theory was right. She didn't want to die. *Lord—why did You have me stay?* She wrestled against what she'd felt when talking to Dean. Telling him she couldn't leave, that a conviction kept her here.

And where was that conviction now?

Back in Mazar-e with Dean Watters.

"I can't protect you. . . ."

The car in front of them pulled into the checkpoint area. A soldier and a German shepherd circled the car, the dog sniffing, going up on his hind legs to check inside then dropping back to all fours as he trotted around, whiffing the bumper and then easing up off his front paws to sniff where the trunk and bumper met.

The dog would know, right? They were trained to ferret out trouble—weren't they? Wasn't it said that dogs smelled fear? She was oozing enough of it to attract an entire pack.

"Be ready," Kamran spoke quietly into a small radio.

Where had that come from?

"Muhammad will create a diversion if anything comes up," Kamran muttered. "Stay calm. It will be okay."

Okay for whom? Certainly not Zahrah.

Dark eyes rose in the mirror. Looked right at her then past her—over her shoulder. Zahrah could not resist the curiosity. She tried to look back.

A sharp stab in her side froze her.

"Turn around," the man growled in her ear.

Trembling, she obeyed. Sat stiff and awkward as the sedan eased up to the checkpoint.

The soldier, a fully automatic rifle in hand, greeted them with the traditional greeting. "Sorry to interrupt your day."

"It is well," Kamran said, his smile convincing. "You have kept our country safe. For that, we are grateful."

Smooth talker just bought a lot of political capital with his lie.

The soldier couldn't be more than nineteen or twenty. Praise was more scarce than shade out here, so it did not surprise her that he seemed to relax. "Just doing my job."

Zahrah could hear the dog sniffing. She flinched when its nails scratched the door as he went up on his hind legs. A black, dust-encrusted nose poked in through the window. Brown eyes considered them. Another couple of sniffs. She stared right into his brown eyes. Every heartbeat thudded against her breast like an anvil. *Please—help!*

Pressure increased against her side. Her eyes clenched. When she opened them, the dog was gone. So was her fleeting hope.

She heard the dog at the trunk. Then to her left. The window wasn't open as much, and again the dog rose up and leaned in.

C'mon. You have to notice something is wrong. You have to!

"What are you searching for?" Kamran asked.

"Drugs, weapons," the soldier said. "That sort of thing." He stepped back and raised his hand. "Clear!" To Kamran he said, "Sorry for the interruption. Have a good day."

No!

The barrier ahead dropped. The driver pulled out of the corral.

No no no! They couldn't—she had to warn them. Zahrah whimpered. The gun poked against her ribs.

She didn't care. She bucked. Wiggled. Tried to shout around the tape. A futile effort, but she couldn't just sit here. Couldn't just—

"Shut her up," Kamran hissed.

Through the tape, she shrieked.

Music, loud and clanking, blasted from the radio, deafening her scream for help. Tears streaming down her face, she banged her head back. Writhed.

A fist slammed into her face. The world slid away with momentum that dragged her beneath its gloom.

CHAPTER 29

Residence Somewhere in Afghanistan

Ah, Tahir!" Hands extended, a short, round man glided toward them with a welcoming smile beaming past his thick beard. "Assalaam alaikum, my friend."

The tall, broad-shouldered man holding her leash gave a slight nod. "Wa 'alaikum assalaam, Kamran."

Dark eyes flicked to Zahrah, who waited in a courtyard amid trees, shrubs, a water fountain that made her parched tongue ache for water, and a tiled mosaic that rivaled anything seen in a museum or palace. Two men, their meaty hands clutching her upper arms tightly, lowered their heads as the short man considered them.

Zahrah did not. She kept her head up. Her father long taught her that showing your enemy weakness was handing them the victory. Though with the burqa, the man could see nothing, definitely not the fear in her eyes. Or the determination not to give up that she undoubtedly wore on her face.

"That's her?" he asked, almost breathless.

Kamran's eyes slowly skidded toward Zahrah before he gave a slow nod.

"*Ya Allah.*" The older man touched both sides of his head. "I told you *not* to bring her here."

"I have need of your home for a day or two."

"No!" He waved his hands frantically. "No, you cannot do this. I told you, I will help you with money and supplies, but not. . .not this. You cannot bring her to my home. What would they say if someone saw?" A servant approached with a silver tray, but the man dismissed her with a wave.

"We must." Kamran led them farther into the house.

No doubt away from my ears and eyes.

"I have guests. Preparations for the event in two weeks."

"You want this as much as I do."

"Take her there now. It's too dangerous to leave her here when I have guests. I must not be tangled in this, Kamran. My position is tenable!"

"It is impossible to move her until tonight." Kamran strode back into view.

"I forbid—"

"It *must* be done!" Kamran's ferocity moved in like a storm cloud. "It must," he said, much quieter. He motioned to her captors. "Bring her."

The older man threw his arms up and spun around, hurrying out of sight. "Do not let her be seen!"

Kamran stalked down a wide hall decorated with murals and adorned with live plants. The men hauling her after their leader gave little care for the treatment, how they wielded her. They dragged her onward, her feet slipping on the slick marble floor. Such extravagance! Whoever he was, Kamran's friend had wealth. And probably a good deal of power, with the servants and the way even Kamran, who yielded to no one, had responded to him. In the time since she'd encountered the giant of a man, she'd not seen him yield to one person.

If they were that powerful, if they were revered, hope was trickling through her fingers as she grasped for a lifeline.

Through the kitchen and around a massive room that resembled a small store rather than one family's food pantry, Kamran continued. Moving without concern that his henchmen would haul her through the house. Moving with such confidence that said no one would dare interrupt or question him.

With her mouth still taped, her hands still bound, there was little for Zahrah to do but make sure the men did not rip her arms from their sockets. If that happened, she could not escape. Could not fight back.

Down they went. One flight. Another. Right into the pit. Past large barrels of wine and other items that needed to be kept cool. A chill scampered across her shoulders as they turned a corner. Kamran stopped before a door, produced a key, and unlocked it.

Something in her recoiled. The room wasn't just a room. It was a dungeon. She'd never emerge from here. This is where they'd kill her. Where she'd vanish forever and never be seen again. She tugged back, her feet scraping against the dirt floor as two men wrestled her through the doorway. From behind, she was lifted off her feet.

Zahrah kicked and writhed, screaming against the gag and tape. She went sailing through the air. Braced herself. *Thud!* She dropped hard onto the ground. Her teeth clattered. Ears ringing from the jolt, she struggled onto her knees.

But again, hands pawed at her. Pulled her to her feet.

Hair pinched as they grabbed at her head. The burqa headdress yanked off. She found herself staring into eyes of hate and fury. Kamran. He produced a knife and held it to her cheek. Pressed it against her bone.

Zahrah drew up straight, hissing as a fire lit through her flesh.

Lip curled and nostril flared, he leered. "I will not hesitate to give you a lasting reminder of what will happen if you try that again." He stepped back and spun her around. Pinned her to the wall.

Zahrah pushed back, revolted at his proximity. Feeling his body against hers.

He shoved her forward. Her cheek collided with the wall. He leaned on her, tugging at her arms, straining ligaments and tendons in their sockets. The pain plied out a whimper.

With a rip, her hands went free.

Zahrah clutched her hands to her chest, leaning against the wall. Cowering. Even as she noticed them moving away in her periphery, she kept her chin down. She watched as they stepped into the semidark-ened passage. Kamran stood with his arms over his chest as the two men pulled the door closed, and with that, darkness swung victorious over the cell. Pushed Zahrah against the wall, where the vestiges of her strength seemed to leak out and puddle on the floor.

Father, have I not been obedient? Did I not stay as You prompted me? Why. . .why are You letting this happen?

She slumped to the floor and curled in on herself, hot tears slipping down her cheeks as she buried her face in her knees.

—⁂—

Zahrah's Flat, Mazar-e Sharif, Afghansitan

"Wondered if you were going to show."

Ignoring Lieutenant Hastings's jibe, Dean stepped into the one-bedroom apartment. A small sofa and even smaller table served as the living room. A plant dangling from a three-pronged hanger seemed to be the only soft touch happening in the Spartan decorating. Four steps in and he could see every corner of the apartment—kitchen, living room, and straight into the bedroom with two beds pushed up against opposite walls.

"They said you found something." Dean didn't belong here. Not in her private place. Though he considered the fabrics, the spotless kitchen, and he saw nothing of Zahrah in this apartment. "How long did they live here?"

"Less than a week." Hastings walked to the kitchen counter, retrieved something, then returned and handed it to him. "We found this under the couch."

Her phone. Dean shrugged.

"Last two calls."

Dean tore his gaze from Burnett's aide to the dark gray phone. He flipped it open, took a minute to figure out the device, then accessed the last calls. His heart thumped against his chest. "Wait. . ."

Brie's blue eyes brightened as she grinned at him. "Thought you might recognize that, Romeo."

"I didn't get any calls from her though." Dean dug his secure phone from his tac belt holster. Checked. "Huh." Two calls. One a voice mail. One a text. A smile wormed into his face at her text. It'd been stupid, their banter about being alive, but he could tell she appreciated it. He accessed the voice mail and put the phone to his ear.

Finely arched brows rose as Hastings said, "You have a voice mail from her?"

Dean shifted around her and moved to the window with a sheer curtain and blind. The static of the voice mail carried. He hit the speaker button. Nothing but—

"Who are you?"

Dean stilled, staring at the phone. Feeling a surge of adrenaline and anger.

"I'm a teacher."

"No! Do not think I am stupid!"

A clatter of noises. . .probably the phone dropping.

"Why did she have your phone number, Captain Watters?"

He considered the lieutenant. "Need to know."

"We'll *need* that message."

Dean wanted to laugh. "You already have it." He knew they could access his phone at any time, that all calls were recorded and monitored. He checked the other call. It was made. . .*while I was in Majorca*. He clamped his jaw tight and returned the phone. "Anything else?"

"Nothing." She motioned around the room. "CID and DIA are sending agents out, but I've found nothing else."

"Mind if I take a look around?" He moved into the kitchen, not waiting for her permission.

"I think you should."

Her comment surprised him and drew his gaze back to the petite brunette.

"Hey, come on. Everyone knows you had a soft spot for her."

Dean ground his teeth as he opened the fridge.

"And she called *you* when she was in trouble."

Saying anything at this point would only feed the frenzy, strengthen the erroneous belief that he had a soft spot for Zahrah Zarrick. "Has her cousin been back?"

"She said she returned yesterday morning."

"And she didn't find it unusual that Zahrah wasn't here?" A small corkboard bulletin area hung over a desk unit. Pinned to it, a photograph of General Zarrick and Zahrah. But not just everyday Zahrah. Zahrah was on the arm of her father at a military ball. A stunning, dolled-up adult Zahrah in a sparkling navy gown that hugged curves he hadn't noticed before.

Not true. They were noted. But not *noticeable* like they were in that dress.

Behind him, someone whistled at the picture.

Dean glowered at Hawk. "Be respectful." Titanis turned, his back to the kitchen, took two steps, and walked right into the—

"Titanis, watch—"

Too late. The big guy thwacked his head against the hanging plant. A green light winked through the leaves.

"Hold up!" Dean rushed across the room and nudged aside Titanis. He used his lamplight to trace the plastic prongs of the plant hanger.

"What the. . . ?"

"Bingo!" An electrical cord snaked up out of the plant and ran along a small ledge. Around the corner. Dean hopped over a half bar as he followed the cord into a cabinet above the microwave. He opened the door. Stacks of canned goods stared back. But he tracked the wire. Shoved aside the cans. And felt a punch of relief as his beam struck a silver laptop.

"Atta girl," he muttered as he lifted the computer out and handed it off to Hawk.

"Sweet," Hawk said. "The only loaded program is a security program—it'll crack easy under my skills—and the video software." Grinning, the guy seemed giddy. "That girl is wicked smart—her own personal security system?" Now he laughed. "I'm impressed!"

When Hawk opened the video program, a dozen or more videos filled the icon list. "It's on an auto-feed loop. The girl's a genius. Here." Within seconds, he had a video up and running. He stood back as the team and SEALs grouped up. He set it to fast-forward and played an entire twenty-four-hour period in a few minutes.

"This is a little creepy," Hawk said. "It's like stalking them."

It was. Dean had to admit. But it was nice, too. To see her alive, walking around. Being normal. She couldn't do that now that she'd been taken. And she looked so comfortable, but several times her gaze hit the hidden camera. Though she *looked* comfortable, she was aware her every move was being recorded. What would she be like without knowing? Was she always laid back? Always so confident and. . .*beautiful?*

Hawk queued up the third vid. Thirty seconds in, things went berserk.

"That's it," Falcon said.

Hawk hit the PAUSE button. "The dude from the school, the big one who'd hit them."

Dean nodded. Eyed Hastings. "Get on that. We need to know who he is and, more important, *where*."

Dean watched as they made copies. But that's not what he watched. He studied the way the guy moved. The way they beat Zahrah and put her in a burqa. "Put a call out to all checkpoints."

"You crazy?" Riordan laughed. "We try to search women in burqas, we'll have the fury of every conservative Muslim on us, the UN climbing down our throats, and the CIC decrying our actions. We'll end up at Leavenworth!"

"And if we don't," Dean said, blood rushing through his ears, "she dies."

CHAPTER 30

Somewhere in Afghanistan

Time alone gave her entirely too much time to think, to wonder, to fear. And that fear, the paralyzing, haunting fear, kept her wake. Forbid her from sleeping. Though it was June, the cool earth bled coldness into her bones and veins as she sat on the hard-packed ground. Head against a barrel, she kept her eyes closed. The storage room, chilled and black as a moonless night, became her enemy, holding her hostage. Preventing escape.

And yet. She was a general's daughter. One who'd taught her to never give up. That there was always hope as long as one breathed. That...that was what pushed her once more to her feet. Stomach rumbling, she paused. How many meals had she missed? No matter. If she remained a captive, she would miss a lot more. Though her captors had mentioned moving her at night, it'd been much longer. Days? She wasn't sure.

Zahrah trudged across the room, blindly stumbling around the stacked crates and barrels. Her fingers slid along the wood surfaces as she made her way to the door. It'd be the sixth time she'd checked it for some fault. Some cooperation in aiding her escape. Her fingers traced the earthen wall. Cool and a bit damp. Smooth in a grainy sort of way. Along the wall to where the softness gave away to the knotty texture of wood. And steel braces. She dug her fingers into the arrow-like hinges that strapped the door in a firm hold. Pulled. Tugged. The uppermost one had no give.

She traced down to the middle one. About a hand span from where it stopped, a hole—no knob to grip or tug—gaped for a key. Cramming her fingernails between the steel support and the wood, she felt the familiar prick of a splinter slide beneath her nail.

She hissed but didn't stop. There had to be a way out. Had to be.

But still, just as the previous five times, she found no leverage with which to pull the brace off. She went to her knees, thinking how much like defeat it seemed to do this. But one more brace waited for her testing. Maybe to mock her. Laugh at her vain attempts to pry it from its position.

Warm stickiness against her fingertips warned her the splinters were aggravated. "Yeah, well me too." She stuck the tip of her finger in her mouth and sucked the blood off. *I am not defeated. I am not defeated.*

Her hand slid back up to the keyhole. She tried to jiggle it away. Tried to stick her fingers in—maybe the slick blood would make it easier for her to jam in and nudge the lock back.

Right. Like trying to cram a camel through the eye of the needle. She sighed. Dropped her forehead against the door. Slapped the wood.

Panic swirled around her. *I don't want to die.* She pounded her fist against it. Her father. . .she'd never see him again. He'd be disappointed. His little soldier wasn't so brave and strong after all.

And Dean. Fierce, handsome Captain Watters, who couldn't see beyond his mission. Never saw that she admired him. So very much. Yes, she'd been attracted to the intense soldier. He'd been so much like her father. So strong, in a quiet but powerful way. He wasn't a mound of muscles, but he was well built. It'd been so silly to even entertain thoughts that he might notice her. He had missions. The most important thing to him was the military. He wouldn't leave that for her. And she wouldn't leave her mission—teaching children.

But there'd always been more than that to her purpose in being back in Afghanistan after her mother's death. She'd come with conviction to teach children, but something else, something she'd never been able to pinpoint, kept her here.

A pair of greenish-brown eyes?

She turned, her cheek against the wood, quiet tears slipping free. "God," she whispered raggedly. "Please. . .let me see him again." Selfish and maybe a bit schoolgirlish, but if she got to see him, then it'd mean she wasn't dead.

The odds were not in her favor. She knew the history of terrorists. Back home, hope existed that those held captive would be found alive.

Not here. Not when held by Taliban.

The Taliban took captives to make examples. Dead examples.

Voices skidded into her awareness, breaking through her grief and depression. Zahrah stilled, listening as thuds of boots approached. She scuttled back to her spot and tucked herself against the barrels.

A beam of light shot through the keyhole.

Metal jangled against the lock.

Light shattered the darkness. Zahrah shielded her eyes as the beams of light hit her.

"Get up!" Kamran's voice boomed against the silence that had cocooned her.

Hand in front of her eyes, she climbed to her feet.

Someone grabbed her wrist and yanked.

"No," Kamran said. "She'll need her hands."

The words surprised Zahrah.

"B–but. . ." The heftier of the two men shifted. "She'll escape."

"She won't." Gaze steadfast, Kamran stared at her. Hard. "Not where we are going."

They hauled her out of the cellar and half pushed, half dragged her back toward the main house. Up five steps. Across the kitchen with an enormous stove and many refrigerators. Glossy counters glinting in. . . *moonlight*!

A thud against her back made her stumble. She struck out a hand to break her fall. Even as Kamran shouted, Zahrah heard a tink-tink. Saw one of the turquoise beads from the bracelet skitter across the floor.

Rough hands threw her forward. She stumbled again but didn't fall as they shoved her out a rear door. Into the night. Thick mist clung to the grass.

Mist? Dew—predawn.

They guided her toward a shedlike structure, no bigger than a normal American garage. Inside, lights blossomed and dispersed the shadows. Lawn mowers, trimmers, leaf blowers, gas containers cluttered the space, making it feel much smaller. And trickier to navigate.

They nudged her toward a door.

"Where are we going?"

The door swung open. A tunnel, burrowing through the shed and apparently into the back of the hill behind the house, yawned at them. Ready to devour them. Two of the guards went before her. Strange. What was it? An underground crypt? Somewhere they hid the bodies of their enemies? A foul odor trickled out.

If I go in there, I'm not coming back. At least not alive.

"Go!"

Another thrust against her back. But she stomped her foot, refusing to budge. "No."

Kamran pointed a weapon at her. "In. Now."

With a quick shake of her head, she said, "No. I'm not going in there." When one of the grunts inside the tunnel grabbed her hand, she wrestled against them. "No!"

Without a word, Kamran turned. Produced a hand grenade, pulled the pin, and lobbed it at the entrance.

Zahrah's gaze flicked to the half-dozen bags of fertilizer. . .just feet away. Kamran leapt past her. Zahrah threw herself into the tunnel.

BooooOOOOOOOooooom!

—⁂—

Sub-base Schwarzburg, Camp Marmal
Mazar-e Sharif, Balkh Province
20 June

The sub-base command center buzzed. Burnett and Hastings focused on sending the feeds to CID and DIA in the hope they could pin down the identity of the man who'd taken Zahrah. Raptor worked feverishly, printing stills of the kidnappers. Nearing four days, best they could tell, since she'd been taken. Yet, they had nothing. No certainty as to why she'd been taken or where.

Arms folded, Dean watched the video again. Something. . .something nagged at him, but he couldn't tell what. Not yet at least. It'd come. *God. . .sooner is better. For Zahrah's sake.* Interesting how the more she'd been in his life, though in an indirect way, the more he talked to God. Was that a good or bad thing? He'd tried it for years as a kid. Then his brother took things into his own hands. Later as a teen, he'd begged God to save Sergeant Elliott, a man who believed in Him, heart and soul. Yet. . .He hadn't. God took him, just like he took Dean from his family. Which wasn't a terrible thing. It'd have been a greater loss if he had a good family.

"Find anything new?"

At Falcon's question, Dean plucked his mind from the past and sighed. "Just four armed thugs and their leader."

"It's a precise strike."

He nodded. "They knew what they wanted. Knew where and when, and wasted no time taking what they were after."

"Double Z." Holding a bag of chips, Falcon pointed to the screen. "And that's *three* armed thugs."

Dean stilled. Scanned the image from the video he'd frozen. Sure enough, the guy behind the broad-shouldered leader just stood there. Dean felt a scowl sift through his face. "That's it." He hit the fast-forward and watched the men move around. "He's not armed, and he does nothing."

"So, why's he there?" Falcon muttered.

"Cap," Hawk said as he tapped his computer screen. "I think I have something."

Pivoting, Dean pried himself from the haunting images. At Hawk's desk, he leaned forward, a hand on the desk and one on the back of his chair.

"I've been tracking video feeds—you know, doing CID's work for them." The grin mocked. "Look what I found on YouTube." He hit the PLAY icon.

The video bounced. Images blurred—green. Grass? Road with pot-holes. Buildings. Then more grass till it honed in on a teen hopping around on the lawn with a soccer ball bouncing off his knee and ankles as the kid showed his skills.

Like Dean had time for this. "What is this?"

"Some kid filming his friend or brother or something." Hawk's eyes scanned the screen.

"Why do I care?"

Hawk grinned. "Check out the background." He maximized the screen and pointed to a car.

Leaning in, Dean squinted against the hopelessly grainy video. Until he saw a silver Mercedes jerk up in front of the building. "That looks a lot like the dorm parking lot."

"Score one for the captain," Hawk said with bravado. "There's a reason I'm on your team."

"Yeah," Falcon said, "because nobody else would have you."

"All right, be like that. I still owe you jerks for the tattoo," Hawk said. "But keep watching. It gets better. . .well, sort of." He bobbed his head toward the monitor. "Right—there!"

The men from the car vanished into the building. Anticipation of their return leapt through Dean's veins. He leaned farther in. Just as their shapes reemerged, the video swung away from the kidnappers to the laughing soccer player. "No!"

"Easy." Hawk sipped his coffee. "It'll come back around."

Twenty seconds later, it did.

Just as the big guy tossed Zahrah into the Mercedes. Two men conferred. Big guy—"Isn't that the guy from the school? The one that punched Zahrah's cousin?"

"Kamran Khan," someone said. "We've been watching him for a few months. Showed up out of the blue. Trouble wasn't far behind."

On the video, Kamran looked away. The other man, lean and tall, poked his chest. Several times. Kamran's arms went out, in an "I'm ready to punch your lights out, but I won't" way.

"Kamran's not the boss," Dean said, his voice a whisper.

"And Big Guy's not wearing a mask now—I'll have to tighten it up to get a good visual on his face, but he's looking pretty Asian." Hawk smiled. "I love stupid terrorists. They make my job fun. And easy."

Dean pointed to the screen. "Send that to Hastings. Find out who that guy is."

"As usual," Hawk said with a laugh. "I'm one step ahead of you, el capitan. Sent it her way as I called you over."

"That was easy," Hastings's voice carried loud and clear through the base as she stalked their way. "The man in the soccer video is Lee Nianzu."

Burnett appeared behind her, his weathered face worn. "And that's really bad news for you."

Chin up, shoulders back, Dean waited for the explanation.

"He's a known assassin and associate of Zhang Longwei, son of General Zhang Guiern, a political envoy who gave hope to a U.S.-China peace accord."

Dean shrugged. "That sounds like something we could work to our favor."

"Except Guiern was found dead two years ago. Nobody was charged, but many believed Lee"—Burnett stabbed a finger at the image—"was the guilty party. Impossible to prove." He rubbed his chin, eyeing the frozen video. "What I can't figure is why Nianzu would be here, what he'd want with Zahrah Zarrick."

"A soft target?"

Burnett laughed. "There are a lot softer targets than her." He clicked his tongue. "No, I'm afraid we're entering some pretty dangerous scenarios with this revelation."

The only obvious one that existed, considering the twisted, tangled paths they'd been on the last few months. "SIPRNet."

"Is there another explanation?" Burnett started for the door, glancing at his phone. "I'll be right back."

Dean turned away, looking for something to punch. To hit. To kill. Because that meant. . .somehow, in some way, their interaction with these guys was what put Zahrah on the enemy's radar. "How did they know what she could do? It never made it past my lips."

"Didn't have to," Hawk said with a snort. "It's on her Facebook page."

With a scowl, Dean pivoted. Glared. "Her *what*?"

Hawk hammered a few keys and pointed to a wall, where a monitor held the Facebook profile of Zahrah Zarrick, sans hijab. Sunlight shone against her dark hair, which hung in waves around her face. "It's all right there. May graduation with advanced degree in quantum cryptology. Scroll down and she even mentions the job offer. Then at the top—she announces she's leaving the next morning for her mom's homeland." He then whistled. "Check out this picture from her birthday party at the lake."

When the images of her in a swimsuit with friends splashed over the screen, Dean jerked to Hawk with a piercing look.

Head tucked, smile gone, Hawk changed it back.

"I hope, Sergeant Bledsoe," came a deep, gravelly voice, "that you are staring at those pictures for research, not to exploit my daughter's body."

Dean stiffened.

Hawk punched to his feet. "General Z-Day. I mean, Zeneral." He coughed, face redder than a gushing wound. "Gen—"

"General Zarrick." Dean intercepted the bigger-than-life man who only stood about five-nine. No taller than Zahrah. About a half-dozen inches shorter than Dean. "Thank you for coming, sir."

"You're thanking me, son?" The general ignored the offered hand and stalked the sub-base, eyes roving data and images and personnel. "I'm about to climb down your throat and rip your kidney up your esophagus—and you're *thanking me*?"

CHAPTER 31

Sub-base Schwarzburg, Camp Marmal
Mazar-e Sharif, Balkh Province
20 June—1420 Hours

Chairs scraped. Soldiers stood. Grouped up around Dean as he stared down General Peter Zarrick, most likely feeling like the kid who stepped on a fire-ant mound. A storm raged in the man's face.

Dean gritted his teeth. "I have done *everything* in my power to protect your daughter."

"Except protect her!"

"Out of my control," Dean countered. "I asked her to leave the country—"

"So it's *her* fault, now?"

"Yeah," Hawk snapped at the same time Dean said, "No, sir."

Nostrils flaring, Zarrick didn't remove his seething glare from Dean. "Then whose is it?"

The man's daughter is missing. He's overreacting. Dean also reminded himself the man before him, the one whose chest rose and fell in a quick cadence of fury, was one of his heroes. A man with a dozen commendations and as many medals. A general with a stunning leadership record. Heck, Dean would've followed him to hell and back if asked.

Until now.

How quickly the hero tumbled from his marble pedestal. Though he still respected the guy, Dean wouldn't let him decimate his team like this. "Sir, I understand you're upset—"

"Son, you don't have the first clue about me and what I'm feeling."

"I think it's pretty plain with your disrespect of my team and me, sir."

"You challenging me, son?"

"I'm questioning your presence on the command floor and your disruption of efforts to locate and retrieve an American citizen," Dean said, his pulse simmering.

"That American citizen is my daughter, and I have every right to be here!"

"No, sir." It felt like a bass drum beat against his ribs. He'd never dreamed he'd do this to General Peter Zarrick, a man who had more years serving than Dean had breathing. "You are a retired general and civilian consultant, invited most likely at the behest of my commanding officer, General Burnett. And as such, you may *consult* with us, but you are not in command, as much as I would have respected and appreciated that."

"How on earth do you expect to find my daughter when you're standing around ogling her body on giant monitors?"

"Sir." Brie Hastings stepped forward.

"Stay out of this, Lieutenant," Zarrick shouted.

Dean frowned, angry at the way he'd stormed in and rampaged over the team working so hard to find Zahrah.

"And you"—he stabbed a finger at Dean—"if you hadn't been so lovesick and trying to steal my daughter out from under me, you'd have seen this possibility before it was too late."

Dean flinched forward.

Falcon cleared his throat, enough of a signal to haul Dean back.

Draw it down. Rein in control. "If you'll excuse us, *sir*, we are in the middle of an investigation. And every second you spend here shouting accusations and insinuations"—he moved forward a step—"and demeaning my team is another minute, possibly another day, your daughter is in danger."

"Don't you dare blame me."

"Have you seen a woman *tortured*?"

"Don't lecture me—"

"*Raped* right in front of your eyes while you're pinned down, eyes forced open by a half-dozen men."

"I—"

"*I've lived it!*" The muscles in his neck strained against the force of his words. "Watched it—*them* as they brutally murdered her!" His voice bounced off the insulated ceiling tiles. "And I won't go there. Not again," he said, his voice deathly low. "I promise you, *sir*, I won't sleep until Zahrah is back on this base, but so help me God, if you don't get out of our way, I will have you removed—"

"General Zarrick!" Burnett's voice cracked the tension.

Only as the general stomped toward them did Dean realize he stood less than a foot from the shorter, stockier Zarrick. Surprised at how his anger had taken over, how he'd lost focus, threatened the man, Dean eased backward.

—m—

Undisclosed Location

"Yes. *Yes!*" On my feet, I grab a Butterfinger bar and hold it up like a microphone. "Welcome to the Special Operations Command Center *Smack down!* In the right corner, you have Captain Dean Watters."

Excitement thrums through my veins as I watch the two face off. I mean, like one more step and Watters's fist is going through the general's thick head. It's like two guys fighting over the same love interest, only the love is different.

Okay, yeah. So maybe that analogy doesn't work. Never was any good at English crap. Give me numbers and computers, and we're good.

I doubt Watters even knows he's slipping closer to the general and right up to the edge of a slippery slope of disrespect and an Other Than Honorable discharge. Even tossing out the nut jobs, Americans succumb to political correctness.

Still, I practically drool at the thought. Love seeing guys like him, drunk on their own power, brought down by their pride and stupidity. I've seen Watters's type before. And let me say it—this guy will fall. Hard.

Some of those jerks have some magical shield around them. They walk through life, obstacles crumbling in their wake, disaster knocking down everything in a two-mile radius *except* them, girls groveling at their feet. . .nothing fazes or affects them.

That's Dean Watters. He walks tall with the arrogance of those superheroes.

But every hero has weakness. Superman his kryptonite.

Every hero has his nemesis. Batman his Joker. Spider-Man his Green Goblin.

I am kryptonite. I am Joker. I am Green Goblin.

Dean Watters will fail. I'll make sure of it. Somehow. Some way. If I have to stay in this godforsaken trailer for another year, I will. Because it's guys like him that have me sitting in tin cans like this. Boss Man might've invaded my space, but he knows I'm indispensible. I have access to mission briefing rooms of the most powerful armed force in the world. And he'll need to remember how easily *I* can shift the tide.

Just let him try to find me where I've parked the tin beast this time. He'll find out what I'm made of, what my mad skills can do. The havoc. . .

———

Sub-base Schwarzburg, Camp Marmal
Mazar-e Sharif, Balkh Province

Lance had seen a lot of intensity rolling off Watters, but this looked as if he'd stepped from a thermal bath.

Holy Mother of— "Pete!"

Fists balled, the retired general didn't move or respond. One more inch and the two would go to blows.

"Dean," Russo said, his voice low, shouldering closer to Watters, who shifted back a step, right into the cozy nest of brothers in arms surrounding him.

Didn't Pete see he was outgunned? Maybe he didn't care. His daughter was missing. Lance could only imagine the carnage if Hastings hadn't retrieved him when she had. He might've been making a trip to the infirmary.

"Pete," Lance said as he eyed the man, shoulders and lips pulled taut. "Glad you could make it. Can I have a word with you?"

"Lance. Good to see you again." Peter's snarl hadn't lost any of its bite, though he'd been out of the fight for three years. "Since your men can't do it, let's put together a plan to get my girl back."

Lance followed Pete down the hall and into his temporary office. He shut the door. "You always did like unbeatable odds."

Peter Zarrick, built like a tank still—a short one—pivoted. "You didn't think I could take him?"

Lance barked a laugh. "I'd pay to see you try. Didn't you see his team tighten up on Watters?"

Peter eyed him.

"I'd give you an A for effort. . .right after I checked you into the infirmary." He pointed to the door. "Those men are some of the finest warriors I've ever encountered."

"And yet, she's gone." Pete dropped into a chair and ran a hand over his face. "Lance, you and I both know how this can end. And how it often does." Pain pinched his features. "I can't lose her. She's all I got left. I can't lose her the way I did Izzah."

"Then don't climb on the back of the one person—"

"Don't you dare say 'the one person who wants to find her as much as me.'"

"Never crossed my mind." But that helped Lance understand a few things. "Watters is one of the best. I handpicked him and his team for black ops. They're good. They get it done. He's invested and has been on this since it started."

Pete grunted. "You mean that kid I just bawled out?"

"Eight years SOC makes him more than a kid."

"Not when you're standing where I am."

"And where is that?"

Another long glare.

Lance retrieved a Dr Pepper from his personal fridge and offered it to Peter, who waved it off. After popping the top, Lance moved to his desk and sat. He knew what this was about, what scared Peter almost as much as the thought of his daughter dying. "What did she say about him?"

Surprise skittered across Pete's face, his eyebrows winging up and lips parting. "Who?" He rubbed his bushy eyebrows, something that had always given his friend's nerves away.

Lance snorted. "She likes him that much, huh?"

Pete frowned, and for a second Lance thought he'd deny the truth. "She said he was like me."

A laugh seeped up through his chest and took over. Lance couldn't stop. Why hadn't he seen that? "She nailed it." He wiped the corner of his eye. "Seeing the two of you about to eat each other's throats was like watching two pit bulls."

Pete pushed out of the chair and paced behind it. He drew in a breath, maybe two, then turned and gripped the back of the seat. Blue eyes bored into his, laced with the ferocity that came with commanding coalition forces, facing untold terrors and horror. "Can he do it, Lance? Can this kid figure out how to get her back?" His lips flattened. "Or do I need to order another oak box?"

"If we knew where to go, he'd have her back already. But we don't. We aren't even sure why they took her."

"Don't give me that. You know full well they took her because of the cryptology stuff, what with those SCIFs that went missing." He scruffed the back of his head. "Her and that brain of hers..."

Lance set aside his soda. "Pete, sit down."

Peter Zarrick stuffed his hands on his hips.

Phone in hand, Lance punched in a number. "Better yet." He set the device back down "Come with me."

His longtime friend eyed him warily. "What is this, kiss and make up?"

"Quit your grumbling and come on." They strode back to the command room. He pushed past the door into the area thick with tension. Conversations clapped shut. Lance expected the silence. It happened a lot. He didn't expect the seething glares from the team. "Hastings." He met her gaze. "Put that invitation up on the board."

"Yes, sir."

Huddled with Bledsoe, Straider, and Russo, Watters straightened and folded his arms over his chest.

"Captain." Lance pointed to the board. "I need to show you something." With that, he lifted a laser pointer. "Hastings dug out this information about a gala about an hour ago at the house of President Tahir, so I've been making some calls."

"A benefit?"

"Party." Lance beamed the red stream of light onto the paper. "Look at the name of the honoree."

"Jeffrey Bain," Watters said as eased closer, his posture stiff but his curiosity worse. "That's the journalist we rescued a few months back."

"One May. We executed with solid efficiency," Falcon said.

"And crazy opposition," Hawk muttered. "But we won. Got the journo out, intact and alive."

"Correct." Lance meandered around the room, positioning himself at the back, behind the men. Watching. Assessing.

"What the heck is Bain doing back in country after that nightmare?" Hawk asked, munching a protein bar.

"Never left." Lance rubbed his chin, noticed the thickness around his neck and reminded himself the doc ordered him on a diet. But that was just *die* with *t* on the end. And he wasn't going down easy. Just like the man of the hour. "Bain stayed in country and has been quietly reconnecting with his sources. This invitation is said to be a goodwill gesture, an apology."

"Apology my big hairy butt," Peter barked. "They're going to make an example of him."

"Exactly," Dean said. "Lure him in, string him up, drag him through the streets." When Burnett shot him a look, Dean lifted a shoulder. "Wouldn't be the first time."

"Or the last."

Good. Good. The two were finding common ground. Not good that the alignment was against his plan, but he'd turn that. "What you don't know is that Jeff Bain's mother married some Arab prince who has demanded a full apology for Bain's imprisonment and treatment."

Pete laughed. "He's out of his mind."

"Well, he's not, in fact. This prince, we believe, has been funding. . . *expeditions* of late. We don't have hard proof, but his fingerprints are all over the place. He's influential, powerful, and *very* rich. Bain was held for ransom—a message to his stepfather, who had not been playing nice with the Taliban, that they could reach his family. Without his deep pockets, the bad guys would be hurting."

"Which means without this guy, we'd be better off," Hawk said. "Right? Please tell me he's our next mission."

"So, it's legit, the big party?" Dean didn't look or sound convinced.

"It is." Lance hesitated. This was the part that would take some convincing.

"What's your point?" Pete slid the paper back onto Lance's desk. "What's this rich prince got to do with Zahrah or getting her back? If it's on the up-and-up, why bore us with it?"

"Bain's going to the gala."

Hooting, Hawk clapped. "Brothers, we're going in! Slip this rich prince a permanent Mickey." He held out this hands. "Please, General. Tell me I'm right. Nothing I like better than killing these—"

"You want Raptor to run security." Watters nodded. "I like it." Another more assured nod. "This could work."

"Negative."

Both men scowled. "No?"

"Bain's going all right. But not with Raptor." He looked up at them through a furrowed brow. "He's going with me."

"Sir." Watters straightened, arms sliding free of the knot he'd formed around his chest. "That's not tactically or strategically sound. If they discovered your—"

"I'm well aware of the risks, Captain, but there's two reasons this is going to happen."

Watters folded his arms again, his disagreement shouting through his tough posture.

"One: Bain is high risk—"

"All the more reason to have us there," Bledsoe said.

"*All the more reason* we need to be shrewd but intelligent." Lance had practiced this dialogue for the last several hours. "We put too many men onsite, and we might as well go in full dress, guns blazing."

"Sounds like my kind of fight." Bledsoe remained unrepentant.

"Lance, I gotta agree with the men," Pete said. "This smells of stupid, sending you in."

"I understand how you might see it that way, but this is how it has to be. Sadra Ali will be there, so it's imperative that none of you are visible. He gets a whiff of you, and I'm dead." He didn't need to mention what that meant for Zahrah. The men knew, so did Pete. "Bain agreed to bring me as a favor for extracting him." When Watters opened his mouth, Lance held up his hand. "Two"—he nodded to Hastings, who popped up a picture of a gray-haired and bearded Pashtun—"Behrooz Nemazi will be there."

"Nemazi?" Watters scowled. "How do you know him?" The question came out as a snarl.

"Remember that '04 bombing outside Kabul? The one that cost us a SEAL platoon and a couple of Black Hawks?"

"And some sensitive intel," Straider said with a nod.

Bledsoe and Russo eyeballed the Aussie with scowls.

"You're not the only ones who have news, mates."

"Nemazi and I were there," Lance said. "We worked together to get things settled down. He was very grateful."

"So, he owes you a favor?" Bledsoe grunted.

Watters watched Lance, keen intelligence lurking behind his eyes. He'd fallen out of the conversation. Gone pensive.

"So that's why I'm going alone. With Nemazi, I'm confident I'll be safe, and I can almost guarantee he'll know what's happening. Maybe even give us a map to her location."

"Then why haven't we bagged this guy before now?" Pete demanded.

"Because he's not easy to get to these days. Finding him is about as easy as finding your daughter right now."

"Not what I want to hear."

"Not what anyone wants to hear, but it's the truth. However, with Bain's invitation, I can get in and talk to Nemazi." Lance started for the door.

"Sir." Watters almost seemed pale. "With all due respect, I have to voice my objection to this. Once anyone there discovers you are DIA, the intel you know, we are screwed.

"We go in full black, You'll never know—"

"I will know," Lance said. "And so will Nemazi. If he knows, then his minions know."

"Sir, there has to be another way. Nothing is worth losing you." Watters glanced at Zarrick. "No offense meant, sir. But Burnett is key."

"Plenty taken." Pete was as ticked as Watters.

"No. It's decided. I go alone." Lance shook his head. "Sometimes, gentlemen, you have to take great risks that you know are likely to fail. But if we don't try, the fallout is too high: Zahrah is lost, right along with the entire safety of the U.S. We all know the repercussions if they manage to hack SIPRNet. We'll be dead in the water before we know what hits us."

Merciful God, help me. It took him everything in his own power and a hefty dose of supernatural not to look at Watters before leaving the room. He hated himself for doing it, for baiting that hook, but Dean Watters was the only hope now for Zahrah. But would the captain embrace the mission and the possibility of death?

TODD & AMY

Nothin' harder than watching the one you love deteriorate. As an elite soldier, he'd seen some of the worst violence perpetrated against humanity. It all paled. After she'd passed out two weeks ago at the barbecue, Amy declined. Fast.

"Please, don't cancel the anime convention."

Todd glanced at her as he stood in the bathroom brushing his teeth. He'd canceled the trip to the Grand Canyon. As Friday raced up on them again, Amy grew frustrated with her weakness. He rinsed and wiped his mouth then flicked off the light.

"There's no hurry," Todd said as he climbed into bed.

She laughed, but it never reached her eyes. "You just don't want to put the costume on."

"Busted."

"I want to go."

Though he knew the likelihood of her getting to go was slim, Todd couldn't tell her no. "I won't cancel the tickets."

She traced his face and then his longer-than-normal hair. "I scared you." Eyes rimmed in shadows of her former vitality, Amy sighed. "I'm sorry."

Todd tried to nod. And whether he did or not, he couldn't tell. It hurt to admit he'd been scared that he'd lost her. Right then and there. "I guess I realized how much I don't want you to go."

A tear streaked toward her ear as she lay on the pillow. "I don't want to go either." More tears, her eyes and lids reddening. "I'm glad. . ." She tried to compose herself. "I'm glad you weren't ready. . .for children."

Todd frowned. "I thought—"

"I wouldn't want to leave. . .a child *and* a husband."

"But if we had tried, maybe I'd have a piece of you to help me go on." She gave a weak smile. "Good thing it wasn't in our hands."

He kissed her nose. "Father knows best."

A soft snort as she closed her eyes. "Does it bother you?"

"What?"

"Me dying."

"Bother me?" He snorted. "It's ticking me off."

"Really?"

"Yeah," he said, a disbelieving laugh puffing into the air. "Nothing makes me feel more powerless than watching you suffer."

"You've helped me..." She sighed again, her eyelids heavy. "...fight. Seeing...your...face. Thanks."

"For what?"

"Being here." She seemed to struggle for air. Then, "Loving me. I can...go."

Her words were mixed and slow—was she falling asleep again on him like the last several nights?

"I'm...thirsty. Can you—?"

"Water coming up." Todd threw back the covers. He plodded to the kitchen, where he filled a glass and returned.

Amy lay on the bed. Eyes closed. Hair haloed around her on the pillow. She looked so peaceful. "Here's the—" Todd's stomach plummeted. Her chest wasn't rising. "Amy!" He touched her shoulder. Nudged it.

But he knew. *She left me.*

He dropped to the mattress and pulled her limp frame into his arms. He held her close, tenderly. A sob ripped from his chest. "I love you, baby." Every breath was pinched in grief. "No regrets. Except that you're gone."

CHAPTER 32

Camp Marmal, Mazar-e Sharif
23 June—1400 Hours

Dean took to the heat and pavement to beat out his frustration. Running helped clear his mind and burn up some of the agitation building in his muscles and clogging his thoughts. Being cut out of the efforts to secure Zahrah, to bring down the men who'd taken her. . .

What was the point? Why shut out Raptor when they'd been neck-deep in this thing from the start? Had Burnett been out of the field so long that he'd forgotten the probability of succeeding? Granted, Burnett was DIA, but. . .walking in there alone?

It was a suicide mission.

Burnett had to know that. Had to know the chances of his survival were slim. Or at least, his chances of emerging without leaking vital and sensitive intel.

Burnett. Why Burnett? Why not Dean or one of the spooks?

It. Makes. No. Sense.

After a ten-mile circuit, drenched in sweat and frustration, Dean gave it up. Headed to the showers.

But the bigger mystery was Behrooz Nemazi.

After cleaning up, Dean returned to the command bunker. Trolled intelligence reports hoping for a sign of something unusual that might indicate or hint at Zahrah's location. But it was like everything and everyone had closed up shop and gone underground.

Perhaps they had.

He dropped into his chair and rested his elbows on his knees, scanning the data. Glanced at the paper in his hand. . .Zahrah. Scrolled through the stills taken at her apartment. Printed the photo of Zahrah and her father to pin to the wall, a reminder to him and the team of who they were saving. Not just a beautiful woman, and she was that, but the daughter of one of their own. Almost a week she'd been gone.

He lifted the print from the feed bin at the printer and paused when he realized it'd printed two on the same piece of paper. He ripped it in half and pinned one to the wall. He stood back. He'd never seen her without the hijab. A half-dozen images of the woman who'd pursued a passion to watch out for children. Teach them. Protect them through knowledge and education.

Protect.

Something he hadn't done for her. Something he couldn't seem to do for anyone who mattered. He couldn't protect Eagle from watching his wife go through the unimaginable. Couldn't protect Hawk from getting shot. Couldn't protect Ellen from dying ten years ago.

Or Mom and Dad twenty-two years ago.

He closed his eyes and tucked his chin, hands running over his buzz cut and down the back of his neck. The paper in his hand crinkled, dragging his attention back to it. Swiping a thumb over her image stirred something in him.

"If you can't use my given name the way a friend would, if all I am to you is a liability. . ."

Friend and liability in the same sentence. Strangest part—it was true. Friends were a liability. Not because of a twisted attitude, but because those he cared about seemed to shrivel up and die. As if his presence proved toxic.

It was just the way it was. A curse, he guessed. The only friends he kept were his team. They had a morbid way of living, a violent method, but they stayed alive. Thrived on the camaraderie amid the adrenaline, amid fighting death face-to-face. Zahrah didn't fit in that world with hardheaded, smelly grunts. She was sweet, beautiful, and soft.

And I already failed you.

The kiss she'd planted on his cheek teased his mind. He hadn't expected it. Didn't give it a second thought.

Liar.

Okay, maybe not a third thought. He hauled his brain out of the fog she'd blasted him into. It'd been a simple gesture, a thanks, but—

Her light touch on his arm.

His gaze slid to the spot, where he could almost see her long, thin fingers. The floral smell that wrapped his brain in that fog. . .

I'll find you. I swear on my life.

She might not belong in his world, but she didn't belong or deserve what they'd do to her in captivity.

Which was why he had to sort out Burnett's lies.

Going in alone didn't make sense. They'd figure out who Burnett was and rip the truth right out of his skull. Bleed him—literally—of national secrets.

And Behrooz.

The bombing.

Staring at her oval face, Dean probed possibilities. *What's he doing?* This wasn't like Burnett.

That's the point.

But. . .why? how?

A concussive boom from that explosive revelation heated Dean's chest. *No.* The general couldn't be that stupid. . . .

"Hey."

Dean jerked up and glanced over his shoulder to find Falcon crossing the room. "What're you doing here? Thought you were going to grab some rack time?" He folded and slid the picture into his tactical pant pocket.

"I did. Four hours."

Dean shot a look at the clock. He grunted.

"Been here all night?"

"Yeah. Lot to think through, maps to pore over, intel chatter. . . She's out there, somewhere."

"You haven't slept in thirty hours."

"I'm fine."

Falcon's dark eyes bored into him.

"I'm *fine.*" Dean pushed to his feet and went to the small coffee-maker. Started another pot.

"Got a minute?"

The way Falcon asked that, with tension and gritted out, pulled Dean around. And he saw it. The storm that had been simmering on the horizon had blown in full force. "Sure." Dean fixed his coffee then returned to his station.

"Look, I just need to clear some air."

Cuppa joe halfway to his lips, Dean paused. "A'right."

"I think it's time we ditch the Australian."

Nuke out of left field. "We need him, especially with Eagle gone."

"We *don't* need him. He's duplicating a role."

Dean eyed his friend, the Italian who'd been a wrecking ball when he'd first come into SOC. "Your role."

Falcon's mouth twitched. "He's stepped in on me more than once."

"His advice is solid, tactical experience invaluable, and he's been right there more than once."

Lips tight, jaw muscle popping, Falcon looked at the ground. "He's stirring up trouble—and what's with you letting him bring in that tat artist to ink Hawk?"

Dean couldn't help but laugh. "Hawk had that coming. You and I—"

"That's right. *You and I*. . ." Falcon's face reddened.

"Sal," Dean began as he rose to his feet again. "You're my first, the team daddy. Titanis—"

"Shouldn't be here. And if you can't see that, then—"

"Then what?"

"Have you even realized how long Eagle has been gone? Or checked his Facebook page?"

"I've been a little busy running ops."

"So have I, and it takes exactly one minute to find out his wife died." The words knifed Dean's heart. "Wha. . . ? When?"

"Yesterday."

"Nobody informed me."

Falcon's fury left but not his tenacity. "And Knight."

"What about him?"

"He's been reassigned. We lost him."

Dean shrugged. "He wasn't ours to lose."

"But we need a dog like that. Ddrake saved our sorry backsides out there."

Still scrambling—no, *reeling* that his friend's wife had died. . .that he hadn't been there for him—and frustrated with the line of questions, the thinly veiled accusations, Dean drew in on himself. Coiled up the ball of tension and pitched it behind the vault that held him in check. But Sal had hit a nerve. "What're you saying?"

"I'm saying, you're not all in."

That bass drum thumped against his chest again. "That right?"

"I'm not accusing—"

"Don't play me, Sal. We've been friends long enough, been through enough—"

"Exactly. And the last few weeks, you've been distracted."

Dean blinked. Laughed. "Distracted by what?"

"Ya know, I wasn't sure at first, but now. . ." His steady eyes considered Dean. "I think it's the girl."

"What girl?"

Sal snorted. "You've always been a bad liar, Dean."

"There is *nothing* more important to me than the team, the mission. You know that. I've always held our team in top priority. Show me one time I've been derelict, where I've been *distracted* and compromised a mission."

With a shake of his head, Sal distanced himself. A tactical move to disengage. "I can't."

The satisfaction of the answer didn't touch the insult his friend had thrown, that he'd compromised the team. *Distracted!*

"I think this is about you not liking that SOC put Titanis on the team, that he's a top-rate soldier and can hold his own against you. I'm not going to ask for his removal. He adds too much to the team."

"Yeah." Sal pursed his lips. "Maybe you'll listen to him. . .maybe with him, you don't deflect the truth by pointing the finger back at me." He turned, walked out of the room, and punched open the door.

Crap. Dean lowered himself into the seat and buried his head in hands. Sal was right—he'd deflected the blame. But seriously, he felt ambushed by the accusations. He'd thought he held it together pretty well. Then an RPG soared straight into a concealed area—his heart.

—⁂—

Sub-base Schwarzburg, Camp Marmal
Mazar-e Sharif, Balkh Province
26 June—1040 Hours

"Is that right?"

"Yes, sir."

Lance considered the soldier standing at ease. "That's a serious charge against your commanding officer, Russo."

His Adam's apple bobbed as he swallowed. "I know, sir. I didn't feel I had a choice."

"No, I guess you didn't." Lance folded his hands. "But tell me, how do you plan to go back to the tent, sleep, eat, and operate with Captain Watters now that you've reported him on something based on *suspicions*? How will you look him in the face?"

"Sir." He tensed. "Not suspicions. I've seen it with my own eyes.

He's compromised. Not thinking clearly."

"Russo, do you have a psych degree now?"

"No, sir."

"Then leave it to them to write the diagnosis."

"But, sir. His past—"

"Is as screwed up and ugly as mine." Lance gave him a smile. "Are you going to my bosses now to tell them I'm compromised?" He saw Watters headed this way from down the hall. Well, great. This could get interesting.

"No, sir. But I do believe he is compromised because of his past."

"Your concerns are noted." *In the back of my head.* Put this on Watters's record, and the guy would get passed over for major on his next performance eval. Speaking of—Watters ducked into the briefing room. Time to get rid of Russo. No need to aggravate the situation. "Dismissed, Russo."

Confusion rippled across the guy's brow. He saluted then pivoted and left.

He saw a collision down the hall with Russo and Watters. The two bumped shoulders, apologized, then stiffly went in opposite directions, bringing Watters to him. Dean glanced back at Russo once before knocking on the door.

Lance waved him in.

"Sir, a word?"

"Shut the door."

Watters entered and closed the door behind him.

"Just had a talk with your team daddy." Something in Watters's expression shifted, but something so slight, Lance almost didn't notice. So, Watters knew about Russo's concerns. "D'you have something you wanted to talk about?"

The facade slipped back into place. A granite one. "Sir, I do."Watters hesitated for a second. "Permission to speak freely, sir?"

"Always."

"I'm going to the event with you."

"I told you I'm going alone."

"You also said you'd met Nemazi in Kabul in '04. But I know you didn't."

Lance struck his most menacing pose and leaned forward. "You calling me a liar?"

"Perhaps a bender of the truth, sir."

"Explain yourself."

"Nemazi wasn't in Kabul in '04. He was in Jalalabad." Watters swallowed—hard.

"And what proof do you have?"

Lips tight, Watters fisted his hands. "The scars on my back, sir. Nemazi was my captor, the one who beat and tortured me." The man's chest rose and fell in a run cadence.

"So, you're saying I lied to you and the entire team?"

"I'm saying you altered the truth, sir."

"What reason would I have for doing that, Watters?"

"To bait me, sir."

Lance laughed. "Bait you? Did you forget I'm your superior? Why would I bait you when I can just order you?"

"You needed me to come to this decision on my own, sir. Or I'd have fought you all the way."

"Kicking and screaming," Lance said with a smile.

"Like a little girl."

"Now that you've taken the bait, tell me why you're doing this, son." He pointed to the door Russo had exited a few minutes earlier. "Your team sergeant thinks you're distracted."

"I am, sir. But not in the way he thinks. I can't let go of this mission, of what the end game is for these people. I just know it'll be unlike anything we've seen, sir."

"Agreed. And with Zahrah, the knowledge in her mind. . ." Lance saw a dozen different scenarios with the American military being crippled, with U.S. national security compromised, buildings crumbling, nukes detonating. . . And that young woman—Pete's daughter. "And you're sure about Zahrah?"

"Sir?"

"You're sure this is about just the mission?"

"Sir, it'd be foolish for it to be about anything else."

Lance almost laughed. "A lot worse has been done for love."

The guy looked like someone punched him. "Sir—that's not going to happen. I've known since I signed up that I wouldn't get married. I knew before that. Men like me don't marry. I'm smart enough to recognize that."

"To recognize it, or avoid the effort it'd take to make things work?"

Watters snapped his gaze to the wall, lips tight.

"Made you mad, huh? Over what? You said there wasn't anything there."

Nostrils flared and his jaw flexed.

"I have to be honest with you, Dean." Lance almost felt like a father to this soldier. "I know about your family, what you've been through, and I can't help but wonder if Russo has a point."

The man flinched. Face red, he said nothing.

"You *are* distracted."

"Sir—"

"No." Lance took a moment to gather his thoughts. "You're going to hear me out. I'm one of the few people you can't shut down, you can't control."

Surprise marched through those young-but-seen-too-much eyes.

"You're an excellent soldier, Dean. You know the drills, you know tactics. And for the most part, your team has your back because you've earned their respect. It's the mark of a real leader." Lance didn't like digging into the personal affairs of his men, but this time, personal got public—and militant. "I think you *do* have feelings for this girl. But maybe you can't see it because you're too scared to tempt the demons inside you."

Watters looked as if he'd puke.

"Which is exactly why I did bait you, why I laid the trap so you'd enter it. I knew you'd risk something you fight every day to avoid."

"Captivity," Watters said, his voice and expression grave as it slid to Lance. "If we do this. . .we go in. . .we aren't coming out."

Lance took his time responding so he could keep the panic from his own voice. "Yes." He sat in the chair and motioned for the captain to do the same. "You survived Nemazi once. You knew how to buy their favor and another day."

Seated, Watters held a hand over his fist, rubbing his knuckles.

"She needs you, Dean. You're the only one who can bring her out alive."

Bobbing his head, the man had tension roiling off him like thousand-degree heat waves. "You say I'm the only one who can bring her out alive, but you can't guarantee that I'll make it out alive this time."

Watching Watters wrestle the demons of his past carved a long, deep gouge through Lance's heart. He'd never—*never*—asked something so personal. "Nobody can, son." Lance's heart caught when Watters started shaking his head. Scrambling to think through a line of reasoning to convince this guy...and yet wrestling with the fact that he was—possibly—asking him to lay down his life.

Voice quiet and words raw, Watters said, "You know what I went through...."

Lance said nothing because they both knew that answer.

"They raped Ellen right in front of me." Stony face. Staring at nothing in particular. "Over and over..."

This time, Lance swallowed.

"They wanted to break me by breaking her." He leaned forward and propped his right forearm on his knee as he slid his gaze to Lance. "General—" A shuddered breath dragged through Watters. "I can't watch that happen again." The clock ticked...ticked... "Not to Zahrah."

"Then help me get her out of there."

"I...I have to think about this."

Disappointment chugged through Lance's veins. "We don't have time, son. Don't be afraid to sacrifice your life for hers."

After a caustic laugh, Watters got to his feet. "Dying doesn't scare me. In fact, I think I'd welcome it."

"Then what is it—what's stopping you?"

Hand on the knob, gaze on the floor, Watters paused. "Surviving." It seemed like he was staring into the past. To something painful. "Surviving if she doesn't. Remembering what I didn't stop. How I failed to protect her."

"Failed to protect her..." This was as much about '04 as it was about now. Lance met him at the door. "Dean, what happened to Ellen wasn't your fault."

His greenish-brown gaze hit Lance. "Wasn't it?"

CHAPTER 33

Somewhere in Afghanistan

Thudding pain hauled her from the stiff claws of sleep. Zahrah lifted her head, blinking through the semidarkness. Hard-packed dirt smeared out in a confusing mural of rock, dust, and shadows. *What. . . ?* She pushed her torso up off the floor.

Searing pain exploded between her eyes.

With a yelp, Zahrah dropped to the ground and clutched her head. With the stab of pain came the recollection: She'd been kidnapped then forced into that tunnel. That was the last thing she remembered. More gingerly this time, she lifted herself. Took in her new prison. Dank and dirty, it reeked. Reminded her of the diaper pails in the nursery at church when she worked Sunday school. Of the slums on the outskirts of Mazar-e, where mothers and children foraged for scraps of food in the waste piles.

A small rectangular window no longer than her leg and not even as wide as her arm stretched along the upper portion of one wall. Grayish in color, no light filtered through. Or maybe that gray *was* the light pressing in against a grimy window.

Propped against the wall, Zahrah felt protrusions digging into her spine. She ran her hand along the surface, feeling the rocks sandwiched with mud. No, too grainy. Maybe mortar? To avoid additional discomfort, she shifted until she could sit without aggravation. Well, the throbbing headache wasn't going anywhere. What happened to her head? It felt like the pain emanated from the back—

Pain shot through her, like a fork through her eye, as her fingers grazed a spot that felt stiff and hard. More gently this time, she fingered the spot. Dried blood crusted in her hair. A scab at the base of her skull, just above the beginning of her neck. Had someone hit her?

The injury told her she'd been out long enough for the cut or whatever to form a scab. What scared her most was that she had no idea where she was now. How she'd gotten here. Or what. . .what might've happened while she had been unconscious. Mentally, she checked herself, felt no other pains indicating. . .anything.

Had God protected her in that regard?

I choose to believe You did.

Like a chilled whisper came the question, *Why didn't he protect you from getting snatched?*

Zahrah struggled to her feet. Thoughts like that would drag her down a sinkhole of depression. That wouldn't serve her well in escaping or surviving. She had to keep her strength and wits up. Couldn't do that if she sat being morbid and depressed on the cold floor. Hand on the wall, she walked. The rippling, partially jagged texture of the stone wall gave way to a plastered one. She worked her hands around the area, straining in the darkening light—*it* is *getting darker, isn't it?*—to see the wall. Was this an interior barrier? Could she somehow break through it, given enough time?

She grunted. She didn't want enough time—she wanted out!

But no. It was just a wall, so she moved on. Another four feet. She stubbed her toe and turned left. Two steps later, she felt something hard beneath her hand. Cold. Smooth, mostly. Maybe a little rusted. Steel? Her fingers traced the outline of a , "Door," she whispered. Rats! No handle or lock. Not even braces for her to pry off. It bumped out several inches, but again, nothing to work.

With a grunt, she raised her fist to bang out her frustration. Then froze. No need to draw attention. Let them think she'd died in here.

Keep moving. Keep thinking.

Four more steps delivered her to the next juncture. She turned left and the smooth gave way to more stone. And then the wall with the window or grayish indention. On her toes, she reached up, fingertips barely grazing the lip. She strained, ignoring the thump against her temples, and—yes! Smooth glass.

Could she clean it? If she did, maybe she could see out, figure out her location. She reached for the hijab—and stilled, remembering her hair, the scab. *No hijab.*

Okay, so no hijab.

Maybe if she just wiped the glass. On tiptoe again, she tried.

"It will not do any good."

Zahrah flipped around and sucked in a breath. Hands against the uneven surface, she searched for the source of the voice. "Where are you?"

"Here," the man muttered. "To your left—the cell next to yours."

Cell? I'm in a prison!

"There is a small hole in the wall."

Inching closer, still half afraid the owner would jump out at her, she squinted. "How. . .how can you see me?"

"I can't," he said, his voice gravelly and weak. "I hear your movements. I've been here long enough, I trust my ears, not my eyes now."

Dread spilled into her stomach, hot and putrid. "H–how long have you been here?"

"What year is it?"

"2014."

The man groaned. *"Ya salaam."* A strange noise filtered through the darkness and stench.

Zahrah stumbled toward the noise, toward where the voice had been. She crouched. "Are you still there?"

The strange noise, almost like. . .*crying*. She used it to hone in on the hole he'd mentioned. Crouched near the base, she found the small opening. No bigger than a small apple.

Her heart clenched. *"Staa num tsa dhe?"* Asking his name wouldn't cure his broken heart, but maybe. . .

"Majeeb."

"*Khushala shum pa li do di*, Majeeb. I am Zahrah." Sharing names somehow shared hope. That's what it did for her.

"You sound like my Zuleika—sweet and young." He groaned and a thumping came from the other side. Was he beating his chest or the wall? "She probably thinks I am dead."

"How long have you been here, Majeeb?"

"Fourteen years."

—∽—

Camp Marmal Chapel
27 June—0630 Hours

Gone was the massive cross that once adorned the exterior of the Camp Marmal chapel, compliments of political correctness gone awry. But Dean didn't need a wooden cross on the outside to tell him what he'd find inside—solitude.

Sitting on a folding chair, he sat alone with his thoughts. His agony. He'd vowed—*vowed*—to never go back.

Serving in SOCOM was one thing. Knowingly and willingly surrendering everything and walking into that party—it was more certain he'd be captured than it was he'd walk out unscathed.

Hat in hand, he lifted the snapshot from the inside rim. Ellen had been a blond bombshell in ACUs. She had fire, she had tenacity. He'd admired that about her. Though a specialist like him at the time, she'd taken no flak from anyone, not even commanding officers. Then again, she didn't give anyone reason to either.

Before her. . .before watching her. . .die, Dean had still been idealistic. Even with his messed-up family history, his murderous brother, his druggie sister, he reached for the dream that one day he might want a family. One day he might find that *right girl.*

She'd flirted with him the first day they'd seen each other in mess. His buddy, Will, had the hots for her, so Dean tried to take a backseat. But watching his friend hit on her twisted him up bad inside. He'd been arguing with Will when he drove right into the ambush.

Dean tugged Zahrah's picture from his pant pocket. Unfolded it. And each fold felt like a wall around his heart. He clutched her picture and clamped his eyes shut. It'd be easier to convince himself not to go if he didn't stare into those eyes. If he didn't see her smile.

God. . .I can't do this. Shaking his head, he ripped the Velcro on his tac pant pocket. *I can't go back there.*

It was ambiguous in terms of location but exact in terms of experience. Feeling that razor-lined strap ripping the flesh from his back. The stinging rod they'd stabbed into his side. The electricity shredding his nerve endings. Even now, he ran his thumb pad along the end of his right ring finger and felt almost nothing, it'd been so damaged by the high voltage.

That's what they're doing to Zahrah.

Again, he clenched his eyes tight. They'd send someone else after her. If he didn't go, another A-team would be tapped. And that's better for her. Better for her chances of survival.

But that wouldn't happen till they discovered her whereabouts. And that might be the day after never. It'd taken them ten years to find bin Laden.

Double Z doesn't have ten days.

Trapped. . .just like that day in the built-in hamper with smelly socks and underwear.

Boom! Boom!

Dean flinched and jerked straight, locking away that memory. Served no one no good. No good. *No. Good.* He saw movement to his right and snapped in that direction. General Z-Day Zarrick stood there. Hands in his pockets, waiting.

Dean shook his head, glad he'd put Zahrah's picture back already.

"Where'd you get the picture of her?"

On his feet, Dean slid his baseball cap on, determined not to talk to this man. He shouldered enough blame on his own. He didn't need the deuce-and-a-half that Zarrick wanted to load him down with. He started for the door.

"What can I say to convince you to go in, bring her back?"

Dean slowed. Stopped. "She's better off without me."

"What kind of cockamamy line is that?" Zarrick stood next to him with amazing swiftness. "This a pity party? I thought you were a better soldier than that."

Dean gave a cockeyed nod. The general had just proved his point.

"You sorry piece—she'd be ashamed of you!"

The sword sliced through the last remnant of resolve Dean had.

"You don't deserve that praise my girl threw around about you." Zarrick pivoted. Shoved aside a nearby chair. Cursed.

Dean couldn't move. He wanted to, but his feet wouldn't obey.

"You know what they'll do to her?"

"Yes. Much of what they did to me." He met the man's gaze evenly.

"Ah," Zarrick said with a growl. "So that's it. You're yellow bellied. Chicken."

"I'm smart enough to know if I go in there and something goes wrong, I probably won't make it out of there alive."

Zarrick stomped toward him. "Do you care about my daughter at all, Dean Watters?"

Swallowing hard, Dean hauled his composure back into line as he met the man's steel blue eyes. "I respect her. A lot."

"Burnett is convinced you're the man to get her."

Dean hung his head a little lower. Everyone believed he could do it, but him.

"And it chaps my backside to say it, but I agree. I've gone through your record. After Jalalabad, you came back stronger than ever. You've led your team on over a hundred successful missions. Never lost a man."

"Incorrect," Dean growled.

"*After* you were made team commander. I'm not talking about those in your convoy. That wasn't your fault."

"I should've stopped it."

"And it's killing you that you didn't."

"Yes!"

"But you didn't, you sorry piece of dirt. You just watched!"

"I was chained to a wall!"

"Why didn't you do something? She was counting on you! Any other soldier worth his mettle would've saved her. Would've gotten her out of there. You failed, soldier. *Failed!*"

Dean couldn't breathe. Felt the burn in his eyes. In his throat.

Zarrick grabbed him by the shirt and threw him against the wall. "Is that the crap you believe? The poison you've ingested for ten years?"

Stunned, pain darting down his neck, Dean eyed the man. Fought the trembling in his chin. The tears demanding freedom.

Hands fisted with Dean's shirt, Zarrick shoved against his chest. "It's a lie! A downright lie!"

"She *died*."

"Did you quit? Did you give up?"

It was hard to shake his head, but he did.

"Then you didn't fail!" Zarrick shouted. He drew in a breath. Nodded. "The outcome was less than ideal, but you did your best. Is that right?"

"I. . .tried."

Zarrick released him. Smoothed out the crumpled shirt. Patted Dean's shoulder. "And I know by the way you stared at her picture before you knew I was here, you'll do the same for my girl."

Grief strangled Dean. "I can't watch her die."

"Neither can I." The general's words were thick and strained. "And I'll have your bars and a few other pieces if you screw up. That's why you're going to get her back alive." The guy was short in stature but long in character. No wonder he was Dean's hero. "Isn't that right, Captain?"

Fail. He'd fail. Again. But he'd try. "Yes, sir."

"She believes in you, and though I hate the sight of you for stealing my daughter's heart, I believe in you, too."

"Stealing my daughter's heart. . ." He wanted to deny it, but Dean had seen the way she looked at him. The way her smile brightened when she saw him. Truth was. . .her smile—no, *she* brightened everything in his world. He hadn't noticed that until now.

"What if I don't make it? What if I'm too late?"

"Then you better die in there and save me the trouble of killing you."

CHAPTER 34

Somewhere in Afghanistan
27 June—1750 Hours

Shouts reverberated through the walls. Zahrah opened her eyes, surprised to find a bluish-gray haze affording enough light for her to see her surroundings. Which weren't much to see. Stone walls. Steel door. Dirt floor. Pretty much as she'd detected with her exploration. After Majeeb stunned her with his length of stay, she couldn't pry any more conversation out of him, except for his admonishment that she rest. *"You will need your strength,"* he repeated many times.

She'd curled up against the wall, huddled by the hole, her only lifeline to humanity. Sad day when her hope came in the form of an ailing old man talking to her through a hole.

At least, she guessed him to be old by his voice.

Shouts and clanking resounded yet again.

"Food," Majeeb said with a cackle. "If you can call moldy *naan* and dirty water that. But," he said with firmness in his words, "you must eat it if you are to survive."

Zahrah found herself nodding, though she couldn't imagine she'd ever eat naan with mold. Her stomach growled its objection. She wrapped her arms around her waist. Over and over a metallic *shink* radiated through the walls. It came closer. . .closer. . .then faded farther. . .farther.

Did they miss me? Zahrah stood and wandered to the door. Pressed her ear against the rusted door, a shade of gray that reminded her of the Confederate gray. Only a little bluer. Fingers pressed to the cold metal door, she listened.

The sounds grew fainter. "Hello!" She banged on her door. "I'm in here! I need food!"

"No, no, *flower*. You'll anger them."

She turned, her hair dropping against her face. "But they didn't give me bread."

"Here. Come, sit. I share."

"No, you need your ration."

"I am old and do not need much." Even as the words reached her, a chunk of bread tumbled through the hole. "Hurry. Before the rats smell it."

Eyes wide, breath stalled, Zahrah stared at the naan that was more green than tan. Her stomach rebelled at the thought but then screamed in protest at *not* eating it. "Rats?"

"One is as big as a rabbit. I call him Zmaray."

Zahrah returned to the hole, lifted the bread, and fought the urge to cry as she sat down. "Lion?" Naming a rat after a lion. . .only in an Afghan prison.

"Wait until you see him, *gul*."

"Take your bread, Majeeb. You need it. I can hear the weakness in your voice."

"What you hear, gul, is old age."

"And stubbornness."

"I am Afghan, yes?"

Smiling, Zahrah flicked the bread back through the hole. "But so am I." Tilting her head against the uneven wall, she sighed. "I'm sure they'll find me. It's a mistake I'm here. I'm not a prisoner."

"Aren't you? How can you argue with the walls?"

How indeed? "I meant. . ." What did she mean? She wasn't even sure why she'd been snatched. She'd expected them to rape and kill her right away, but they'd been more intent on secreting her away.

"Imminent danger." Dean's words wouldn't leave her alone. He'd tried to warn her. And she rejected that warning. Zahrah traced the stone with her hand once more, fighting off the fear and depression. Would Dean find her? Had he found the surveillance video? Surely he had. Of course, it probably would've been smart to tell Fekiria about it.

Was her cousin going mad with worry? What about Daddy? She almost laughed. He was probably threatening dismemberment and death over her disappearance.

The bread leapt from the hole again. "Eat, flower. It is disgusting, but it will help."

She lifted the bread. Ached for the old man sacrificing it for her. And lifted the bread toward her lips.

The steel door groaned on its hinges.

Zahrah punched to her feet, ignoring the stab of pain from her head injury as light flooded her cell. Bright, warm glorious sunlight.

Two men stepped in. The older, rounder one glowered. Shook a fist and demanded to know where she got the bread.

Startled, Zahrah looked at the evidence in her hand. "It was a gift."

The man stalked toward her. "Who? Who gave you this?"

Zahrah said nothing. Would not betray the only man who'd given her hope.

"Never mind about the bread," Kamran's voice boomed through the cell from somewhere outside. "Bring her. He wants to see her."

The man slapped the bread from her hand.

They stuffed a hood over her head and yanked her from the cell. Right at first, ten paces, then a left. As she walked, the warmth of the sunlight broke through the gloom with intermittent regularity, as if they walked beneath arches or past windows or something. A prison with arches?

Only as they thrust her into a room did she realize she'd stopped noting her passage. Stumbling in and unable to see, she hesitated and slowly straightened, her gaze on the ground.

Old, dusty, brown boots stomped into view. Seconds later, the hood came off.

Zahrah blinked and her gaze locked on to a lanky man standing before large, grimy window with steel safety bars that dwarfed him. He wore a dark suit and held a phone to his ear, keeping his back to her. His distraction gave her a minute to take in the room, but she wished she hadn't. Plaster that had once probably been a bright coral—evidenced by a square of the brighter color left from a picture that had been removed—now looked like it had blue-green lace crawling up from the floor. Mold.

But it was the table that bothered her most.

No. Not the table. What sat on the table. A computer. And not just some refurbished computer from a large manufacturer.

"I see you recognize this."

Zahrah's gaze snapped to the man who'd been talking on his phone. He faced her, his eyes narrow slits. Chinese. She automatically stepped backward.

"You are very bright, Miss Zarrick. No doubt you suspect what I want from you."

"No." She backstepped—but this time got shoved forward. "I won't help you."

He smiled, his muddy-brown eyes vanishing. "I thought you might say that." He lifted his chin. "Bring him."

Heart racing, she waited what felt like an hour before two armed guards brought in a haggard man. Scraggly gray beard, unkempt clothes, and wild, frantic eyes.

"Do you know who this is, Miss Zarrick?" The Chinese man watched her. He stood her height—five foot nine—and had a lanky build. His black hair was tied back in a queue.

She shrugged. "How could I? I was locked alone in a cell—for no crime I've committed."

The Chinese man returned to the table. "What is your name, good sir?"

Pushed to his knees by his captors, the man curled in on himself. "I am Majeeb Yusufzai."

"Of what crime were you punished, Majeeb?"

He hung his head, gnarled fingers cradling his ratty hair. "Stealing."

Zahrah frowned. Grew uneasy as the Chinese man worked with something on the other side of the computer. When he lifted it and she saw the gun in his hand, she took a step forward.

Eyes on her, he walked toward the old man. "What did you steal Majeeb?"

"Bread. That is all. My children were hungry. My Zuleika—"

"Stealing is a crime—is it not? You stole from another Muslim. Does not the Qur'an speak against such things?"

Two things struck Zahrah—the Chinese man speaking of the Qur'an and the cold menace in the man's words.

Majeeb nodded, rocking back and forth.

"And what did you do this morning, Majeeb?"

The old man stilled. Lifted his head ever so slightly but didn't dare look the man in the eyes.

"You gave bread to a prisoner who did not have a ration—is that right?"

"She sounded so scared—"

"Stop it," Zahrah said.

"That is a crime, Majeeb. You know it's forbidden to share your rations." He locked gazes with Zahrah, aimed the gun at the elderly man.

"No!"

Her shout was lost in the weapon's report.

Shocked, Zahrah stared. Saw the blood. The crumpled man. Rushed to him with a scream. "Majeeb!" Tears streamed down her face as she dropped to her knees, sobbing.

CHAPTER 35

Sub-base Schwarzburg, Camp Marmal
Mazar-e Sharif, Balkh Province
28 June—0415 Hours

No. No way this can end good."

Dean held his peace, knowing his guys wouldn't like it. They were like brothers. Even Falcon, who'd betrayed him. Who wouldn't look him in the eye right now.

"If the guy from the school is involved and sees you," Hawk said. "It's over."

"He's right," Harrier said quietly. "You've been there, Dean. You ready for this?"

"No." He wouldn't lie to them. "I'm doing something I promised myself I'd never let happen again. I swore I'd kill myself before I let them take me alive again." The truth almost suffocated his ability to continue. "But we don't know where she is, and since Kamran saw me with Zahrah, if he sees me there, I believe he'll take the bait."

"We'll tag you—"

"No." Dean sighed. "If they suspect I'm being tracked, they will kill me rather than snatch me."

"That's why we use the shortwave bursts. We'll trail within a couple of miles. . . ."

"Might work."

"If you get caught, they'll play you against each other," Hawk said.

"I think that's the point." Titanis hadn't spoken till now.

Dean eyed the Aussie, wondering if he'd object, too.

"Captain Watters is right." Titanis stepped from his quiet shadow. "More than a week and we still don't know where she is. With Zmaray right around the corner, we are running out of time." He placed his fingers on the table. "This plan is crazy, but it's our best bet in finding Zahrah and getting her out before they pry open her brain and tear apart American and who knows what other countries' intelligence networks."

Dean nodded his appreciation.

"Brownnoser," Hawk said with a sneer. "Who asked you, anyway?"

"I did," Dean said. "He's part of the team, and his advice is as valuable to me as the rest of yours are." He cut his gaze to Falcon, who snorted, shook his head, then started for the door.

"While I'm out of commission, Falcon is in charge of Raptor." Dean held the guy's gaze. "I won't even pretend to like this mission. Nor will I promise that I'll make it back. But they've thrown the die. We can't ignore this. I've been held before. I know what's coming. I know what to expect."

"Knowing what to expect and having it happen to you. . ."

Dean nodded. He knew. *Lord, help me. I know.*

"Has anyone besides me noticed the bad guys seem to know everything we're doing?"

"When don't they?" Titanis said.

"Sal," Dean said, never losing Falcon as the conversation explored options. "What are your thoughts?"

"It's crazy stupid." Falcon rifled his longer-than-regs black hair. "I'll shoot straight—I don't think your mind is in the right place to do this."

"What's that mean?" Hawk demanded.

"No." Dean gave his longtime friend a nod. "Falcon's right. And the table's open for discussion—if anyone can come up with a better plan, I want to hear it. Because believe me, I don't want them ripping open my back again."

"Yeah, we'd have to get you inked all over again," Hawk said with a mean glare. "But at least, *I'd* wait till you weren't drugged up."

Dean had to own up. "This mission is hitting very close to home for me. But not for the reason believed. Not because I have feelings for Zahrah." He met the gaze of each man on his team. "I respect her. She's intelligent and nice, but I accepted long ago that I'd never get married or involved. This"—he swept a hand around the team—"is what's important to me. You are why I'm doing this."

"Come again?" Hawk asked. "Us over Double Z?"

"It's us, my brothers in arms, that I'm willing to lay down my life for." Dean nodded and looked around. "The—"

"Captain Watters," Brie Hastings shouted as she burst into the room. "Check the local news."

Frowning, Dean shifted and nodded to Harrier, who already held the remote and changed the channel. A CougarNews special sported a split screen with a news anchor on the left and none other than General Pete Zarrick on the right.

"Son of a—"

Dean held up a hand. "Turn it up."

". . .that's right. SOCOM is in close contact with me—"

"Yeah, try the same base," Hawk sniggered.

". . .and her fiancé is furious. You know how these spec ops guys are."

Dean's jaw slid open as a picture of him in a baseball cap flashed over the anchor.

"Holy crap!" Hawk shouted.

Pivoting, Dean glanced out the small window that gave him a view of the short hall. "Where is he?" He stomped out of the room.

Burnett emerged from his office as Dean stalked by. "Hey."

"Where is he? Zarrick just exposed me on Al Jazeera!"

"What he did," Burnett said, tugging Dean into his office, "is do us a favor."

"Explain that to me. Because I'm missing the whole—"

"Your face is out there. They know who you are!"

"That's the problem."

"No, it's the solution. As soon as we enter the palace tonight, they'll know who you are."

Dean lifted his chin.

"We wanted them to take you to her, to use you against her. . .and now, we are guaranteed that will happen."

CHAPTER 36

Somewhere in Afghanistan

Knees hugged to her chest, Zahrah sat in the corner farthest from the door. Farthest from the place where she'd been the cause of a man dying. Where she watched a man get shot. For no reason other than sharing his wretched moldy bread with her. Even now, the hunger pains gnawed at her stomach as forcefully as the gruesome memory.

Heel of her hand against her forehead, she cried. Fought the thoughts that urged her to rail against God. The guilt that plagued her for causing a man's death. Now. . .now Zuleika's husband *was* dead.

She tossed back her head, stone smacking her wound. Though Zahrah cringed, she welcomed the pain. Deserved it. "God, forgive me, but *why?*" Shaking her head didn't dislodge the burning question. "I oought Your will and You wanted me to stay! Why—why would You have me here to take Majeeb's life? He was so gentle and sweet. He wouldn't have died if I had left."

Tormenting questions like that would do no good. *"God's ways are not our ways."* How many times had her mom said that, and yet. . .yet her mom killed herself because she could not fathom why she'd had such a hard life. Frustrating. She'd left Zahrah alone. Left Jay. Though she tried to understand and encourage her mom, at the same time, Zahrah didn't understand what was so bad about her life. She had a husband who loved her—though he was gruff. A daughter who adored her. A son. . . Well, Jay was their father personified. Terse. Rash.

Steel groaned against steel.

As light shot through her cell, Zahrah stiffened and curled into a tighter huddle. A beefy guard with a foul smell—probably too long holed up here in this smelly prison—stood inside the door with Kamran, who leered at her. "Come."

At first, she did not move. Did not even meet his gaze.

"Get up!" He stomped into the cell.

Zahrah hunched and stiffened her arms around her knees.

He grabbed her arm and hauled her up, his grip burning as he jerked her toward the door. The momentum sent her sprawling into the fat guard. And his hands—his hands went wherever he wanted.

Zahrah jerked away. But not before her hand flew on its own—right across his face.

Shock stunned him for a split second. But not long enough. He slammed his fist into her face. Her neck snapped back and she crumpled.

"You piece of dirt," Kamran shouted. "You'll pay for that."

Zahrah expected to feel the full force of his fury against her body. Instead, she heard a meaty thud and saw the guard stumbling. "Remember," Kamran growled, "no one touches her but me!"

With that, she was hauled back up to the room by Kamran, who flung her at the desk. She saw the dark spot that stained the floor. Majeeb's lifeblood.

Footsteps joined them from behind.

"Are you ready to cooperate this time, Miss Zarrick?" The slick-suited Chinese guy sauntered around the dirty table, the long jacket puckering to enable his hands to slide into his pant pockets.

"I will never cooperate with terrorists." The words she heard almost didn't sound like her own. "Not when you murder innocent men to force my cooperation."

"Innocent?" The man scoffed. "Miss Zarrick, look around you—this is a prison. Where the guilty, the murderers live."

"Your premise is faulty—I am none of those, but I am here."

"Fair enough, but you are the exception." His smile almost seemed kind. "And quite the rare exception. But I'm afraid beauty is of no consequence. You have a job to perform here. And we are short on time."

"Who will you kill this time, Mr.—I don't even know your name."

He nodded. "Very fluid play, but I'm afraid you only need to know those around you call me Zmaray."

"The Lion."

He gave a cockeyed nod.

"I have no friends here, no one you can use to influence me to do whatever it is you want me to do," she said, eyeing the system on the table.

"But see, Miss Zarrick, I know that you are a softhearted person. You treasure life, you see it as valuable, so it does not matter who I choose. Someone as gentle as yourself is bred to protect innocent lives. It's why you came to your mother's country, to teach children." He strolled closer and held a hand out to Kamran.

Zahrah glanced to the side as the creepy man handed Zmaray a silenced weapon.

"Being the cause of someone's murder. . ." His left eye squinted a bit as he seemed to be affected by his own words. "It's painful. Makes you question your maker, your god, does it not?"

Her heart skipped a beat. Was there a listening device in her cell? She looked at him, certain her fear was evident on her face.

"Even for someone who would violate you so openly like this man." He aimed the weapon at the handsy guard.

"No!"

The beefy guard's cry gurgled in his throat. She buried her face in her hands. Tried to stop the tears as the sound of him drowning in his blood chipped at her willpower. She covered her ears, desperate to block out the sound.

"Who will be next, Zahrah? Who will you cause to die next?"

"Stop it," Zahrah shouted at Zmaray. "Stop this!"

With a look and arched eyebrow, he shifted toward the computer and held out a hand.

Trembling from the murder of the guard, from the callous disregard this man had for life, Zahrah took forever before she trusted herself to speak. "I will *not* do this. Ever!"

"Then you will continue to be responsible for the murders of innocent people."

"No. Not me—you! It's your doing. You don't have to do this."

"But I do. Your stubbornness forces my hand."

"What you ask of me"—she jutted her chin toward the table—"would cause the murder of hundreds if not thousands of Americans. The choice between one or two dead here or thousands of my father's people—" *Dean*. Her chin trembled. "I will *never* help you."

"Then Kamran will teach you to see things my way."

A misfire in her heart felt heavy against her breast. She started to look toward the man who'd made her skin crawl since the first day she saw him at the school but stopped herself. If she showed her fear, they'd know they'd won.

And they had, hadn't they?

The Chinese enemy—and that is how she must think of him, not as a lion, one with strength, agility, and power, but as an enemy—handed off the weapon and left the room.

Kamran hulked toward her.

Zahrah felt herself cowering inside but kept her spine straight. Chin high.

Raising his shoulders, he drew his arm up and backhanded her. The hit spun Zahrah around and flipped her off her feet. She scrambled back to her feet and pushed herself way from him. Around the corner of the table.

"A little cat and mouse?"

Zahrah dragged the computer toward her.

Kamran's lecherous grin faltered as he watched.

She hoisted it—*mercy!*—it weighed a ton. Which meant it'd make a bigger dent—in his head! And for all she was worth, she tossed it at him.

"You witch," he roared, scrambling to save the computer. He caught it, fumbling and almost dropping it. Then tossed it on the table as if it weighed no more than a tablet. Even as it scraped over the table, he hopped over it and lunged at her.

His fist connected with her face. With her side. He pinned her to the wall, crushing her chest against the stones. His thick arms bracing her shoulders against the plaster. "It's time to teach you," he said, grunting as he used his body to hold her prisoner against the wall. Her cheekbone scraped on the smelly wall. She struggled to get her palms flat on the plaster so she could push back. But even as she did, she realized her strength was no match for his. She cried out and writhed. "Help me!"

"No one here to help you," he breathed against her neck. "Not this time." The jiggle of his belt made her flail.

Then his hands slid along her hip.

Zahrah bucked. Slammed her wounded head into his nose.

He cursed. Slammed her harder against the wall.

Her tunic lifted. She felt his sweaty palm against her waist. Sliding down.

She slid her own hand up. . .up the wall. Then reached back. Dug her fingers into his face.

"Augh!"

He pressed himself against her.

Zahrah clenched a fistful of hair and yanked hard.

Pain exploded against the back of her head. Her forehead bounced off the wall. Stars sprinkled against her vision. She broke free and scrabbled away from him.

"Kamran!"

They both turned, Zahrah feeling the desperate need to don a dozen more tunics, wishing she could bleach the memory of him groping her. . . .

Belt in one hand, pants knotted and held tight in the other, Kamran glowered. Three red lines across his face bore testament to her fight.

The Chinese man stood at the entrance, his lip curled. "Must I teach everyone my ways? Torture is far more effective than rape."

"But not near as pleasurable," Kamran said, his face contorted in anger.

Zmaray snapped his fingers and two guards appeared. "Lock her up." To Kamran he said, "Come. We have a party to attend." He sneered at Zahrah. "You might want to sleep tonight, Miss Zarrick. Because tomorrow, everything changes. I *will* have your cooperation."

—⁓—

Presidential Residence, Balkh Province

"I have to admit," Jeffery Bain said as he lifted a champagne flute from a silver serving tray ushered through the room crowded with dignitaries, politicians, princes, and other partygoers, "you confuse me, Captain."

Dean snapped a glare to the journalist. "No rank."

"Oh, come. You can't honestly think that these men don't know you're American military." He tipped the crystal glass toward Dean's head. "Not with that buzz cut and the look of war on your face."

Dean glared again.

"Are you going to be this much fun all night?"

Monitoring Burnett talking up an Arab in a keffiyeh, Dean maintained a constant vigil. Nemazi had yet to show his face, and Dean wasn't sure if he should be glad or nervous.

"Look, in all seriousness." Bain leaned closer. "I'm not sure what you're up to here, but this is some kind of stupid."

"Welcome to the Army."

"Cap—"

"Dean."

"Dean," Bain corrected. "These men won't hesitate to kill you."

"I know."

"No," Bain muttered, his voice lowering. "You're not following me."

Dean met the man's brown eyes. Studied him—the knotted brows, the sweat in a chilled environment. Bain licked his lips and looked to the side. Dean's heart kick-started. "What do you know?"

"They know you're here."

"Who?" Dean's pulse sped.

"Everyone. Keep your eyes open. They'll probably try to take you."

That was the point of this mission. But it didn't make Dean happy. The only thing he could guarantee tonight was that he wouldn't walk out of here a free man. Whatever tomorrow brought—if he saw tomorrow—was out of his hands.

"Do you know anything about General Zarrick's daughter?"

Bain smiled. "Except that you're going to marry her?"

Dean said nothing as he slid his gaze around the room. Noticed the two men near a door watching him. They were trying to be all cool and low-key, but nothing screamed trouble like an Arab playing low-key.

"You must've won a lot of brownie points with Zarrick to get him to let you marry his daughter—and I've seen her. She's worth the death threat."

Dean scowled, which forced a bit of contriteness into the journo.

"Sorry." Bain sipped his drink as his gaze trolled the room. "My point is, it wasn't smart to announce your relationship on national television here. It painted a target on your big head."

"Tell me about it," Dean muttered.

"So the old man didn't have clearance?"

"Would it matter to Z-Day?"

Bain sniggered. "True, true."

"Jeff, darling, would you come meet Kismet?" said a woman who didn't look a day over thirty and yet had the same nose and eyes as Bain.

"Of course, Mother. If you'll excuse me," he said to Dean and started away, but not before turning back. "Watch yourself."

Dean gave a breathy snort, realizing he stood alone, though he technically was never more than five feet from Burnett. The reassurance felt hollow in light of what he faced—being captured. Everyone had advice for him, but he got stuck with the gig. The evening played on, Burnett chatting up dignitaries, his position obvious though he wore no uniform. One didn't end up in DIA and not have facial recognition among the local royalty and power players.

"Who is your friend, General Burnett?" A burly man who stood at least six-three looked straight at Dean. "He looks a bit nervous."

Burnett nodded. "You would too if someone just kidnapped your fiancée."

Dean's heart pounded as several of the men clucked their tongues and shook their heads.

Dogs. Every man in this room probably knew where they were keeping Zahrah. And that heated his veins.

He also didn't like this plan of attack, the one Z-Day and Burnett had concocted to hit this gathering head-on, leave little question who Dean was and what he wanted. Didn't like the open, direct line of talk. Bain had been right—the concentric rings of the target seemed to burn against his chest.

It was one thing to intentionally walk in here knowing he could get kidnapped. It was another to bait the enemy. If Burnett and Dean pushed too hard, the enemy could smell the trap. Walk away. Mission failed.

The thought made him itch to leave. To believe they *had* pushed too hard. It'd be easy. So easy to cross the marble floors, past the pillars and gauzy curtains, and stroll right out the front doors.

But Zahrah...

His fists balled.

"A glass of wine, sir?"

It took Dean a second to realize the server spoke to him. He finally gave a haphazard glance and shook his head.

"Very well, sir," the guy said as he walked past, bumped against Dean's shoulder.

Something slid into Dean's hand. Heat spread across his chest as he casually lifted it. Glanced at the paper. It read: *They know what you're planning.*

He drew straight, his gaze skipping around the room. His mind bungeed back to the server. Who was he? How did he know to give Dean the note? Who told him? Patrolling the perimeter with his gaze, Dean edged his way to the side. All too aware of the heavy firepower and itchy trigger fingers.

Crap. Why hadn't they let some of the guys come? He hated this—feeling naked without his team. Without the reassurance of them covering his six. He had nothing now. Nothing but a hollow feeling in the pit of his gut.

God. . . What? What did he pray? He walked into this knowingly. Did God's mercy cover idiocy? *Just help me find her.*

Only as his heart settled with a strange warmth that spread through his limbs did Dean realize Burnett wasn't in the room. Scanning the room, his gaze collided with a chilling pair of eyes.

Crap!

The cold emptiness in his gut boiled as he stared at the man. Behrooz Nemazi.

A door opened behind the man, who stared back unabashedly, and Dean's pulse thudded. Burnett being hustled down a hall by the burly guy and two men aiming guns at his head.

Dean lurched forward.

But suits surrounded him.

Instinct kicked in.

A weapon in his face, Dean grabbed the muzzle and jerked it toward himself even as he stepped into the fight. Rammed the heel of his hand into the guy's nose, sending the cartilage into his gray matter.

Something flew at him from the right. He ducked and wheeled around, his leg swiping the target's feet out from under him, and yanked the weapon free. Armed with the Kalashnikov in his right hand, Dean brought it up as he squared off with four more. He fired twice.

But a half-dozen men dropped on him. He punched and kicked, knowing he was supposed to surrender, but the adrenaline drove him. The panic of dying. The terror of facing torture and unimaginable pain.

A weapon stock drove into his face. He rolled with the momentum of the blow, pain booming across his cheekbone and knifing through his right eye, which he felt swelling shut as he came back up.

Another hit nailed his jaw. Split his lip. Blood glanced along his tongue.

His knees went out from under him.

Pain exploded across his neck. Seconds later, he blinked and found himself on the floor with what felt like a dozen men on his back. He grunted and tried to arch his back. In a blur of black, the world vanished.

CHAPTER 37

Presidential Residence, Balkh Province

Son of a biscuit—get off me!"

Lance struggled against the wrestler's hold that had his face pressed into a soft cushion, his arm strung up along his spine, straining the tendons and ligaments as the man held him down.

"It's better this way."

"You sorry piece—let me go. They'll take my guy. I can't let them!"

"It's better this way," the man repeated, his knee in the small of Lance's back. "Trust me."

"Not after this. Never again." Lance struggled.

"It's clear." One of the two who'd stabbed their Glocks into his side and ordered him to walk out without Dean returned, his face bearing a sweaty sheen. "We must hurry."

"I thought you were a friend," Lance growled to the man holding him hostage. The handsome Sikh had not exactly been an American ally but a source of credible information. He'd saved their rear ends more times than Lance cared to admit or record on paper. Takkar's skills and connections were as unfathomable as his rejection of radical Islam. Lance hadn't fully trusted him. Ever. But he hadn't expected this...this betrayal!

Tall, broad-shouldered, Sajjan Takkar stood unfazed, the white turban making him taller than his six-two height. "I am the only friend you have here, which is why you're still alive." Strong-arming Lance, he pressed forward, looking at Lance from behind. "Are you ready to play nice?"

"If by nice you mean punching your lights out—"

The man hauled him up and pushed him out the side door. They hurried down a service tunnel and into a waiting armored SUV.

"Don't do this," Lance shouted. "I can't leave. Let me go—I have a man inside there!"

"As for your man, that I cannot help you with, but right now, your country needs you."

"I can't serve my country by being a coward—what do you mean you can't help my man?"

"A *dead* coward isn't going to do you much good either." Takkar ushered Lance into the back of the SUV and climbed in behind him. "Go." The locks engaged as the SUV spun out of the driveway.

Lance pounded his fist against the window, cursing. "Take me back. Take me back right now!"

"They knew what you were doing."

"Of course they knew—we made sure they did."

"No. They knew you planted the information. They know your friend was not Zarrick's fiancé but a soldier on a mission."

Lance stilled. "No. . ."

He nodded gravely. "You are alive because I bought your life. They were going to kill you both."

"How. . .how did they know?" The vehicle drained of oxygen. His head spun. "They're going to kill him."

CHAPTER 38

Somewhere in Afghanistan

Sleep came in snatches. With the shouting, the wailing, the moaning, the hinges groaning, the guards shouting or banging on walls—or her guilty conscience screaming against the murders of two people—Zahrah embraced what little rest she could find. Against the heaviness of exhaustion and starvation, she leaned on the wall and gave a soft snort. Never thought she could sleep without a pillow, then she came to Afghanistan and to her kaka's house, where she was just grateful to sleep on a mattress on the floor.

Now, she'd kill for that mattress. Or a blanket. Anything to ward off the chill seeping into her bones despite the heat of summer. Arms folded over her chest, she fought off the memory of the near-rape. She pressed into the wall, wishing she could disappear into it.

What had the Chinese man meant about everything changing?

She wouldn't change her mind. At least, she hoped not. It was easy to say—even sitting here in prison—that she would not do anything that would violate her conscience. But when they resorted to torture, to rape...would she still be strong?

It scared her. She thought of how nearly she'd caved when Dean asked her to return to the States. Just to please him. Just to honor what *he* thought was best. Not because she was weak willed, but because she trusted him.

She let her mind follow the trail that led to Dean Watters. The only happy thought she could find in this dank, dark cell. His intensity. His focus. She saw a bit of the man he was in the work he did, digging out Ara's broken body. How he'd shown up and helped in a gruesome task when he could've just hidden out on the base. But he hadn't. He'd cared.

He's a good man.

She leaned her head back and stared up at the grimy window, etched by a halo of gray light that pushed past the filth clouding the glass. Why couldn't she have met Dean two years ago? How different things might have been! She certainly wouldn't be here. Maybe they'd be off in Greece or something.

Does he like Greece?

What would he do for fun? Maybe camping with his family.

Oh. Would his mom even like Zahrah? Or would his mom be the way her father was, hating every potential candidate for her affection?

She smiled at the way her father had growled that she didn't need to get messed up with some grunt. But in that same gruffness, she heard a tinge of respect not only that the man she talked about was like her father, but also that he was Special Forces.

Zahrah shook her head. *What are you doing?* Fantasizing. . . No, keeping hope alive. *God, I know You told me stay, so I'm just going to trust that You have a plan here.*

Funny thing about God's plans, they almost never matched the plan she'd laid out.

"Quickest way to make God laugh is to tell him your plan," her father had said many times.

To which she responded, "He's a lot like you, then?"

As fear gusted over her fond memories, Zahrah struggled to breathe without grief. *Please let me see Dean again.* A warm tear slid down her cheek. Even if it was with a dying breath. "Don't be so melodramatic." She huffed a laugh and pushed to her feet, walked the cell, determined to keep up her strength and wits.

" 'They that wait upon the Lord. . .' " She began Isaiah 40:31 as she made her circuit, not only to reassure herself with the promises in the Word, but also to challenge her mind. Stay alert. On about her twelfth circuit, she changed to the 23rd Psalm.

Her door groaned.

Zahrah's mind erupted with a thousand questions—would they break her this time? Is today the day she'd betray everything she knew and loved because she preferred her own pain relief to sacrifice?

No. She wouldn't. She wouldn't fail her country. *God help me.*

As the door squawked open, Zahrah tucked herself into the darkest corner and folded herself out of sight—as much as possible. She wouldn't make it easy for them. Ever.

A half-dozen men, clustered and struggling to navigate through the opening, crowded in.

Drawing in tighter on herself, she clenched her eyes.

Thud!

Rancid air whooshed over her.

Steel squeaked and protested then locks engaged.

Zahrah slowly braved a glance—had they really left her? What did they do? Sure enough, the door was closed. Her gaze dropped to a mound on the floor. A mattress? She twinged toward it but then froze.

A body!

She yanked back. Who had they murdered this time?

A grunt startled her. An arm dragged out from under the body. The palm pressed against the dirt. A man. . .he pushed up. Collapsed with a groan.

Zahrah couldn't move. Wouldn't. Whoever this was, they wanted her to care. And she wouldn't. Couldn't. Not again. Not watch him die. Because of her. Back of her hand to her mouth, she leaned into the shadow. Prayed this man, whoever he was, wouldn't see or notice her.

Again, the man pushed up. Again, he collapsed. Grunts and groans issued. He flopped onto his back. Sucked in a breath. He arched his back and froze.

Zahrah craned her neck. Had he died?

But a hand raised to his head as his chest slowly lowered. Released another long breathing grunt. Finally, his hand fell away. He rolled his head to the side as if checking his surroundings.

Her heart jammed into her windpipe. "Dean?" Her voice squeaked.

He lifted his head and looked in her direction—and that's when she saw the damage they'd done. His left eye vanished beneath the red and bloody swelling. A deep, angry cut slashed his right eyebrow. His lip was busted and bleeding.

Zahrah threw herself across the room. "Dean!" As she scrambled closer, he collapsed. "No!" Hovering over him, she felt the tears pouring down her cheeks. "Dean, please!" He couldn't show up and die here, not right in front of her. Not like Majeeb or the guard. She couldn't do that. Couldn't let Dean die. She pressed a finger to his throat, frantic to detect his pulse against the hammering of her own.

Strong and sure, his pulse thumped out the reassurance. Beaten to a pulp and lying there out cold, he had never looked more beautiful.

But dead, too. Hands trembling, she framed his face with her fingers. "Dean...*Dean?*"

He groaned and his head shifted in her hands.

"Dean," she whispered, bending close. "What are you doing here? You were supposed to rescue me." But he was here. For only one reason. To use him to secure her cooperation. Her eyes slid closed. Twenty minutes ago, she'd been convinced she'd never surrender to their demands. Now, she knew it was only a matter of time.

She shoved to her feet and hurled herself at the door. Banged against the steel. "Open this door! Get this man out of here! He's a"—she nearly choked on the words but forced herself for his sake to release them—"a child killer!"

CHAPTER 39

Somewhere in Afghanistan

Something hit his cheekbone. Soft, wet. Dean blinked, words sifting into his awareness. . .*rescue me.* . . . The voice collided with a mental image—Zahrah! Blinking, Dean groaned. She hovered over him, her hair tangled and hanging free. No hijab.

"You stupid, foolish. . .courageous man." He noticed she held his face. "Why. . .why did you come?"

Breathing through the pain, he grimaced. "To rescue you."

She snorted through a laugh. Face twisted in grief, she shook her head. "No." Shoved away from him. "I can't. . .do this." She stumbled to the door. "Get him out of here!"

Her screams yanked Dean off the floor. He didn't care how much his ribs hurt. He could still breathe, so he guessed they weren't broken, only bruised. Still, the fire hitting his lungs felt a lot like walking the fires of hell.

"Take him out. Right now!" She banged on the steel door.

"Stop," he tried to say, but his throat was dry, and the word died before it made it past his vocal cords.

The door flung back. An armed guard shoved Zahrah backward. "Shut up!"

"Get him out," Zahrah said as she stabbed a finger at Dean. "I don't want him in here. He's a child murderer!"

Stunned, Dean sat on his knees, bracing his side and hunching through the pain. Ignored the accusation. Hated that she thought of him that way.

"He stays," the guard said with a smirk.

Recognition flooded Dean. The man from the school, the one who'd threatened Zahrah. *He knows.* Kamran had been there when Raptor team had shown up, when he stepped in for Zahrah. The last nugget of hope crumbled. Strangled by the defeat, Dean struggled to his feet. Struggled past the blinding pain. When he lifted his chin, the man's smirk was gone. His weapon was up. Aimed at Dean.

Zahrah yelped. "No!" She reached for the weapon.

The man smirked and shoved her toward Dean. "You both stay."

The ruse he'd planned, to remain aloof, to keep distance between them, was futile. This was what the captors wanted, the reason they'd taken Dean. They knew. Knew he'd come for her. He tucked an arm in front of Zahrah and nudged her behind him.

Nodding with a sick smile, the man slid the door closed. Locked it.

"Why—why'd you do that?" Zahrah cried. "They'll kill you!"

"No. They won't." He shifted toward the wall.

"They will! They've killed everyone else—Majeeb, a guard, anyone I've looked at." Zahrah shoved her hands through her long brown hair. "Now, they're going to kill you, too."

"They won't."

"Are you listening to me?" She came closer. "They'll kill you just like they killed the old man who gave me a piece of moldy bread."

"They won't."

"They will!"

"No, they won't. Not me." Dean felt sick to his stomach.

"Why? Why are you so special?" Her sarcasm was coated with hot tear.

Had to choose his words carefully. "Because they know I mean something to you."

Zahrah stilled. Her face drained of color. She drew back. "How. . . how can they know that?"

"The guard who opened the door—"

"Kamran."

"Right." Dean gritted his teeth. "He's the one from the school, the one I interdicted at the school when he was mistreating you?"

She nodded.

"And he's the one who took you, right?"

Again, she nodded. Then squeezed her eyes closed and tilted her head back. "He followed me—sat in the parking lot."

"Probably wire-tapped you, too." Dean touched his swollen-shut eye as he stretched his jaw. "Your frantic demands to get rid of me just now probably cemented any suspicion he had about your feelings for me."

Pink tinged her cheeks. Twisted a knot in his stomach. Scraggly dark brown hair dangled as she shook her head, gaze at the ground. "But. . .but they've *killed* the others."

"To wear you down, test your resolve." Dean eased against the wall and slowly lowered himself to the ground. "But they'll use me to break you. And vice versa."

"It terrifies me what they will force me to do." She crumpled to her knees beside him. "I'm not strong. Not like you and my father. I can't do this. They'll break me. And then I'll be the cause of thousands of lives being lost. I might as well die now because I can't live with myself if I do that. I can't."

Dean heard her panic. Heard the cry of her heart in those words. He'd seen violence—he'd effected violence as a Special Forces operator against terrorists. . . She hadn't. He turned to her. Saw the wide eyes. The pale, damp skin. "Hey."

Zahrah's chin dimpled in and out again. "They'll make me kill my own people." Her wild brown eyes searched his face. "I never killed anyone!" She lifted her hands to him. "They'll cover my hands with blood of American soldiers, men like you—maybe even *you*."

"Hey!" He slid a hand around the back of her neck and pulled her attention to his. He held her face, his heart thumping hard. "Don't do this. Don't deliver your own judgment. You've done *nothing*." But he'd been here before. Not in this prison but in this situation. "And no matter what happens under duress, it's not your fault."

Tears slid down her face.

Dean tugged her neck to jog her free of that paralyzing stupor. "Got it?"

She gave a weak nod as she looked down again.

Dean let her go and settled back, too aware of his own involuntary reactions to being so close to her. "What do you know about this place?"

"Nothing."

"Have you been outside this cell?"

"Yes."

"What'd you see?"

"Halls, doors, stairs."

"So, two levels?"

She nodded. "They take me upstairs to a computer. Order me to hack it."

"What else did you see?"

"A. . .hole. A massive empty room cordoned off with only a rope. I don't think there's any stairs, but they don't allow me to investigate."

"Good."

"How is that good?"

"The more we notice about our surroundings, the more we improve our odds of getting out." He closed his eyes, closed out her vulnerability, her beauty. *So much like Ellen. . .yet stronger.*

Quiet drenched their cell worse than the stench that clogged his nostrils. He had to shift her away from this dark talk. "Besides, if I don't bring you back alive, your dad will hunt me down and kill me himself."

Her shoulders bunched as she gave a small laugh. Then she sat next to him with a long sigh.

"How often do they bring food or water?"

Zahrah drew her knees up. "I have no idea—it seems like it comes only when I feel like I might die from starvation."

"That's what they want you to think."

She nodded. "I wanted to lose a few pounds, but not like this."

"You don't need to lose weight."

—⁓—

His words sounded like one of those "I like you the way you are" comments, but Zahrah wasn't sure she dared hope it was true. Still, she looked to him. Despite the swelling and cuts, Dean was still handsome. Strong. Impenetrable.

And completely unreadable.

Earlier when he'd said, "Because they know I mean something to you," Zahrah didn't miss the fact that he'd said nothing of his feelings for her. If he had any. Wasn't that always like her? Always falling for the guys out of reach. The quarterback in high school. Her advisor in college, which still embarrassed her that she'd developed feelings for the thirty-something professor.

And here she was, pining after a man who wasn't that much older— maybe five or six years—but an eternity away in terms of experience and direction. No small humiliation that he'd figured out she liked him.

Her words, calling him a child killer, rang in her ears. She imagined that he'd done brutal things as a Special Forces operator. Endured the unimaginable. Protected innocents. Carried out lethal missions. And bore it like a warrior. Now, he sat here with his eyes closed, as if being a prisoner was of no consequence.

Zahrah's conscience tugged at her. "I don't think you're a child killer."

A miniscule smile flicked across his face. "I know."

"Those words. . .I just didn't want to watch them kill you."

A quieter, "I know."

And he knew she liked him. How long had he known that? When had she been so transparent? "Is there anything you don't know?"

This time a bigger smile tugged at his lips but didn't crinkle his eyes the way she'd seen one do before. He angled his head toward her, eyes still closed. "Yeah—how many men are here?"

Mentally walking through her experiences here, Zahrah looked toward the door. "I'm not sure. I've seen two or three when they've taken me upstairs."

"What's upstairs?"

"Not much. Most of it's empty or crumbling."

After a sigh of frustration, Dean ran his hand over his buzzed hair. "What else have you seen?"

"Not much, really. They've kept me in here, night and day."

"What about when they brought you here? What d'you see?"

"Nothing." She eased against the wall and rested her head against the stones. "One minute they'd forced me into a tunnel, the next, I woke up in here."

"So, why do they take you upstairs if there's nothing up there?"

"The computer." The face of the Chinese man popped into her mind. "And Zmaray."

Dean snapped toward her. "Zmaray?" The muscles between his eyebrows knotted and pulled together. "How do you know that name?"

She shrugged. "That's what they call him. Why, does it mean something to you?"

"Too much." He drew up his legs and rested his forearms on his knees, staring up at the grimy window.

"Aren't we past the whole confidential thing?"

"Can you prove this room isn't monitored?"

Pride dinged, Zahrah relented. She'd taken his refusal to speak about the operation personally, but he laid the truth bare: There were listening ears—she knew that for a fact—and he couldn't compromise anything else.

Dean lumbered to his feet, wincing as he held his side. "The best thing we can do is keep conversation casual. Give them nothing to use against us."

Grateful for his presence, she squashed her frustration over the way his conversation came across more like a drill sergeant and less like the Dean Watters who'd drawn her attention and affection. The one who'd put the baseball cap on Rashid. The captain who'd brought his men to help find Ara. The one who'd texted her as Kamran stormed into the apartment.

She eyed his clothes. Not the typical SFOC dress he normally wore. Black slacks and a white shirt, stained with blood, sweat, and dirt. "Where were you when they captured you?"

"At an event with General Burnett."

Surprise coiled around her.

He turned from the window and looked at her, something odd in his expression. "Listen, I need to say something." Pacing, he scratched the back of his head.

Zahrah tugged her legs to her chest and waited.

"I need you to know—those feelings you have for me. . ." The man had the stiff stare down better than her father. "I don't share those feelings, Zahrah."

Humiliated, she jerked her gaze to the pebbles at her bare feet.

"You understand?"

She managed a nod.

"I've never wanted to get married. Have no desire to get married." He shrugged. "I can't even remember the last time I went on a date."

Choking on her own embarrassment, she forced a swallow. Hated the heat creeping up her neck and into her face.

"I'm not saying this to be mean or hurt you, but here—where these people think they can break you through me, you need to know"—his chest rose and fell hard several times—"I'm not worth it. I can't now, and I won't ever, return those feelings."

Her vision blurred.

"I know you saw something in me, and I'm honored." He hunched in front of her. "This isn't personal, Zahrah. You're an incredible woman, but Special Forces is my life. I can't—*won't*—commit to a relationship knowing one day I could come home in a pine box." Vehemence laced his words. "I won't do that."

Throat raw, she nodded. "I get it." She didn't. Not really. Where was all that scientific talk from the books that said if a guy was into a girl, he'd find a way to be with her. Guess Dean just wasn't *that* into her.

"Do you?"

"Yeah," she whispered. "Though it's a pretty selfish way to live."

"Maybe, but it leaves my conscience clear."

Anger punched through her chest. "Does it?"

"Yes." Sincerity seeped through the green-flecked irises. "I'm sorry. This wasn't said to hurt you."

"Then was it said for?"

The door groaned open.

Dean pushed back onto his haunches, then stood straight, stiff against the pain obvious in his face.

Zahrah tensed as Kamran entered.

"It was said"—the Asian entered and dragged his gaze from Dean to Zahrah—"in the misguided belief that you would let go of your feelings for him. That our efforts here would be nullified."

Dean glared. "It was said because it's true."

Hands tucked in the pant pockets of his slick Italian suit, Zmaray gave Dean a smug smile. He lifted a hand out and flagged his fingers to someone behind him. "We will test your theory."

Two men entered, a metal bed frame carried between them. Another wheeled in a cart that held what looked like a battery and cables

"Z," Dean growled, his tension palpable.

But she couldn't take her eyes off the equipment. Or steady the rapid-fire of her heart as it vaulted into her throat as the guards set the bed in the middle of the room. The third drew the cart toward the bed, ran a long cord out of the room. This was bad. Very bad.

"*Zahrah!*"

Her stomach knotting, she flinched and darted a look to Dean.

The two guards who'd ushered in the bed stalked to Dean and wrestled him toward the rusted metal frame. They then ripped open Dean's dress shirt and yanked it off. A T-shirt hugged his toned torso, and they hauled that over his head.

"*Remember. . .*" Dean's voice carried the roar of a mighty lion. "I'm not worth it."

CHAPTER 40

Somewhere in Afghanistan

I'm not worth it!" Dean struggled against his captors. He didn't want her staring at the equipment. "Look at me, Zahrah. Right here."

Wide and glossy, her eyes finally drifted back to him. It felt slow. Too slow—like time had dropped into some suspended frame. Lips parted, terror gouged into the soft lines of her face, she shook her head, slowly at first then faster as she started backing up.

"It's okay. This doesn't matter." He fought the urge to curse, knowing the fire that would soon boil the water in his body. "*I* don't matter."

"It has come to our attention that your great hero has a tracking device in his body." This was the guy from the video, Lee Nianzu. He walked the cell with the casual grace of someone visiting a museum. "That presents a problem we must remedy."

Two guards hauled him backward toward the metal frame. Dean held no delusions. He was headed to torture. Pain and simple.

Big paws jammed beneath his arms, the guards shoved him back. He fought, but the metal frame clipped the back of his knees. He went down—hard. Wire ring supports dug into his shoulder blades and spine. Might go down, but not without a fight. Tugging hard, he managed to free his right arm as the guy attempted to secure the belt. Dean punched the guard on the left.

"Captain Watters," Nianzu called, his voice preternaturally calm.

Dean's gaze skidded to his right. To where the Asian assassin stood. With a gun to Zahrah's temple.

Dean froze—just long enough to give the thugs an advantage. They fell on him with their full weight, pinning him to the metal springs. "You won't kill an asset you need."

"Perhaps not, but I am not against making a lasting impression."

Zahrah's whimper was enough to do Dean in. He hadn't been

able to control things with Ellen, hadn't been able to shift the tide of torture, to stop her from behind hurt, killed. Remembering the splat of her blood on his face, the warmth. . . He breathed in. Out. In. Out. Had to center himself or he wouldn't survive what this man intended to do to him.

This would be over before it started. Zahrah would end up just like Ellen.

Augh! No, can't think like that.

God, she trusted You. Livid, he closed his eyes. *So where are You?*

Cuffs pinched his wrists as they were secured to the metal frame. His feet were strapped as well.

He fought the curses sailing through his brain. This was familiar. Too familiar. Trembling overtook his muscles, knowing what was coming. Crap, did he ever know! Even though his body betrayed him, his mind raced for Zahrah. He wanted her to know it was okay. He'd be okay. They wouldn't kill him. Not yet. Because he knew she wouldn't give in so easily. Zahrah was a smart girl, too aware of what divulging that information would mean.

A beeping swept over his body. A sensor, probably searching for the radio-transmitter signal. To his left, the repetitive beeping increased until it finally shrieked. He strained and saw a blue-gloved hand holding the black control over his forearm.

A dark shape hovered to the side. "Here, Captain."

Dean eyed the bit offered to him.

"We would not want you to die. . .so soon."

Ticked, he allowed the grit to be placed into his mouth. He clamped down and shot a look to Zahrah. Did she hear that? He wouldn't die. Not yet.

He expected her to turn away, but something flashed through her eyes. Her lips flattened and her gaze bore into his, surprising him.

The buzz at first almost wasn't noticeable. It carried up his arms and—grew! Fire! Pain. Dean ground down on the grit. Started to look away but remembered Zahrah's determination. He locked on to her as his body vibrated. Convulsed. He threw his head back, limbs thrashing and bouncing against the voltage. He howled around the grit.

A sulfurous smell mixed with a charcoal-like odor. Hair and flesh burning.

The electric shock stopped.

Body trembling, Dean shoved his gaze to the ceiling. Concentrated on breathing. On compartmentalizing the pain. On surviving. Ignoring Zahrah's whimpers.

"Again."

"No!" Zahrah cried out. "Ple—"

Volts shot across his skin, sizzling and crackling. The buzz fried his concentration. This time was way worse than before.

"Stop, stop!" Zahrah begged.

Dean worked harder to fight the pain, to not react. But it was futile. The involuntary thrashing of his flesh as it conducted the amps made it impossible. His brain lost the fight as darkness rushed in like a hungry shark, chomping into Dean's determination.

The fire stopped, reduced to a smoking simmer that left his limbs trembling, his chest heaving for a breath that didn't burn.

Quiet dropped on the room.

Air swirled, cool and acrid, with the scent of his burnt flesh and hair. Someone was close to him. He fought to open his eyes. The rubber-gloved doctor held a device over Dean, sweeping, searching for the sensor.

Dean swallowed against a dry tongue. So much for Raptor finding his location. So much for a delayed-activation sensor. *How* did they even know? It shouldn't have activated yet.

The man nodded and moved back to the cart, where instruments clanked. Hopefully, he was packing up. Permanently. But that'd be too good to be true. The bindings on his left wrist snapped free. Then his right. Hands hauled him off the rusted frame, pushed him to the side.

Legs rubbery, Dean sat on the edge for a second to get his bearings. Find his land legs.

The frame shifted beneath him. He tumbled forward—a dull awareness that the Oriental and his goons left doing nothing but annoying him. Knees buckled. Felt himself falling backward. Jerked forward. The room blurred.

Arms wrapped around his shoulders. Sweet and sweat mingled. Soft. Sweet. "Hey. It's okay." Zahrah eased him to the ground.

On his knees, Dean shifted. Didn't want to lose face, not in front of Zahrah. He struggled against his puppet legs. Teeth gritted, he winced as he flopped onto the hard-packed dirt.

Zahrah was there again, arms around his shoulder as she slowed his descent.

"I guess I'm getting old." Dean swallowed again, this time his throat a little less dry as he looked up at her. "You. . .you did good." He folded himself against the wall.

Concern smoothed from her face, replaced by a shaky smile teasing the edges of her lips. She tucked a strand of hair behind her ear as she looked down at him.

He closed his eyes. "Thanks." Relaxed, still feeling the buzz zipping through his veins.

"For what? I did nothing."

"Yeah." Dean tried to smile. "You didn't cry, didn't show them they were right."

—⁂—

Sub-base Schwarzburg, Camp Marmal
Mazar-e Sharif, Balkh Province

"I can't believe you did that."

Sajjan Takkar, his face sheer granite, betrayed nothing with his dark eyes. "It was necessary."

Lance tossed his phone on the desk in the semidarkened office. Only the hall light and a small desk lamp provided illumination. With a heavy exhale, he went for the fridge. "Do you realize the damage you did?"

"On the contrary," Takkar said, the epitome of calmness and confidence. "If I had not secured your safety, far greater damage would've resulted. I know you do not like that I intervened, but I could not let an asset like you die when I had the means and power to stop it."

"Asset? I'm not *your* asset—you're my spook!"

"I am owned by no government." Pride glinted in the man's eyes. "I did not say you are *my* asset."

"What you mean is that I can still be of benefit to you."

Takkar said nothing. He didn't have to. Lance had no misconceptions about where power truly existed. Who held the better hand. Lance popped the top of a Dr Pepper and took a greedy slurp, savoring the fizzle that trickled across his tongue. "Half the time, I'm not sure if you're working me or I'm working you."

"We are working. Together. For the mutual good."

Hiking a leg over the edge of his desk, he sighed. "I'm not going to kid you, Sajjan. I need that *mutual good* to swing in my favor in a really big way. I need them back—Watters and Zarrick's daughter."

Takkar turned toward the door. "I have done what I can."

Lance slammed the can on the desk. "What in Sam Hill does that mean?"

"It would be cliché to say you have no idea what you are dealing with." Olive skin and brown eyes seemed to grow darker. "But it is true. The players on this chessboard are"—he shook his head, concern digging into the practiced facade of indifference—"I have not seen a game this big in a long time."

"Is that supposed to scare me?" Though Lance tried to smile, he wavered and slipped beneath the surface of his exhaustion.

"Do not think you can throw brute force at this one and win, old friend. Your enemy in this game is experienced and lethal. They are not simply one step ahead. Not even two or three. They are a dozen. They know your every move. They know your countermoves. They have studied you. They have prepared for you."

Lance muttered a curse and slumped into the chair beside Takkar. "You sure know a lot about this 'they' you keep referring to."

Hands in his pant pockets, Takkar said nothing.

Defeat stunk up his office like a dead skunk. "What are you saying—give up? Because I'll tell you—that's not going to happen. I'm not leaving my man out there, and I'm sure not leaving Zahrah Zarrick for them to manipulate so they can systematically take down our secure network."

Takkar remained an immovable, impenetrable mountain of mystery.

"What's wrong with you?" Lance growled. Bit back another curse. "I've never seen you lay down your weapon and walk away like this."

"I have laid down nothing but the truth. The fight. . .is not only at your doorstep. It has invaded your base, your command center, your men."

"Tell me something I don't know!"

Takkar inclined his head in cockeyed way. "Very well. Do not think this is something you can solve quickly. Do not think even if you get them back, that this will be stopped."

Lance frowned.

"This operation—I've been reading the underpinnings of it for years. Whoever is behind this—and I would tell you if I knew—"

"You know who *they* are, but you stand there and lie to me, say you don't know."

Anger sparked in the dark eyes that always kept Lance wondering if the guy had switched sides. "It is not hard to finger the subordinates, the ones who will take the fall. They will be hard to find, but you *will* find them." Meaning flashed through his irises. "But the top player, the one driving this?" He gave a grave shake of his head. "I am not convinced he will ever be found."

"Not good enough. We have to kill this at the source or we remain compromised and vulnerable."

"The horseman of your apocalypse is headless, unidentifiable."

Lance tugged at his collar and straightened his tie, fidgeting against the omen cast by Sajjan Takkar. And as he did, something ominous wormed into Lance's mind. "Wait a cotton-pickin' minute—*invaded my base? The command center?*"

Coldness spilled into Lance's gut, and it wasn't his Dr Pepper this time. He swiped a hand across his brow, his mind racing. He traced the thoughts across the vinyl, across the chairs, his desk. "Mother of God, help us!" Dread replaced his rage. "We have a mole."

CHAPTER 41

Somewhere in Afghanistan
02 July

My father always told me I was stronger than any son he could've had."
Zahrah arched her back, stretching aching muscles and straining to
shake off the gloom hugging the shadows. "I'm not convinced."

"I am." Dean had been an impenetrable rock since the guards
dumped him in here three days ago. They'd beaten him and used elec-
troshock, and his determination, his focus, never wavered.

She sat close to him, hoping, praying she could siphon strength and
courage from the Special Forces warrior. They were almost shoulder to
shoulder against the cold stone wall. He with his legs bent and arms
over his knees. She with her legs crossed as she held the chunk of bread
the guards had tossed in minutes ago. She lifted it to her mouth—

"Hey." Dean reached over, took the bread, and tore it in half. Then
in fourths. "Ration it. They aren't dependable with sustenance, and as
we hold out, they will too."

Eyeing the pieces he'd returned to her hands, Zahrah thought of
Jesus. If He could feed the five thousand, surely He could feed Dean and
her. And maybe. . .maybe that's what he'd done by having Dean come.

"How. . .how do you do it?"

He shifted his head a bit so he could look at her. "Do what?"

Her gaze traced the walls, the dirt, the metal door. "Keep your wits.
Stay in control." When he didn't answer, only closed his eyes, Zahrah felt
foolish for asking. He sat there as if waiting in the chow line. He'd been
trained. That was the answer. "You make it look easy. I've been here a week
longer, watching them kill those men, people I didn't even know, and I
can't shake it. Then the way you were able to focus when they strapped
you to that bed—"

"Hey." Dean's head came off the wall and he turned to her, his features as stern as his tone. "Don't do that."

Confusion darted through her.

"Don't doubt yourself—you're right. You've been here longer, but I've also been a prisoner longer."

Zahrah scowled. "You've only been here—"

"Ten years ago, I was held for six weeks with my unit—what was left of my unit." He shifted as if saying that caused him pain. "We were ambushed. Death by IED."

"I–I'm sorry." And yet, she wasn't. That he survived the experience gave her even more hope. It meant he'd *been there, done that*. He put his training to use, and it'd worked for him. "How—?" She looked at the bread again. No, it wouldn't be right to ask that.

"It's okay. You want hope," he said. "We need every lifeline we can dig up in here since they have no rules of engagement. They don't fight fair." Dean nodded. "I was newb, barely wet behind the ears and on my first deployment."

"So, you weren't Special Forces then?"

He grunt-laughed and shook his head. "Signed up at seventeen, chomping at the bit to get away—" His lips snapped into a fine line. He looked to the side. Then back to where she laid out the bread crumbs in her lap on the long tunic. "It was an out, joining the Army. I had no goals of heroism or good deeds. The only good I wanted to do was for myself."

"What do you mean?"

"Joining was an escape."

The question hung on the tip of her tongue, but Zahrah had the incredible feeling of standing on sacred ground—that piece of information he'd bit down on was something he didn't talk about. At least, that was her best guess. But she wanted to know. "Escape from what?"

Another grunt-laugh. He sat there for a while then finally turned to her. Caught the back of her neck and tugged her close, so his mouth was almost on her ear. A tickle skidded down her neck and spine as he whispered, "They're listening in, but they know everything, Z. They know how you feel about me and that I'm here to get you out. They're going to use that against us. In every way possible."

Zahrah swallowed—hard.

"We need to play their game, but only better." He leaned back, his nose almost touching her as those green-flecked eyes searched hers. "One way or another, we'll get you out."

She took a shuddering breath and nodded.

"No matter how bad things look, do not lose hope."

A smile she couldn't stop seeped through her, soaking her weary muscles and heart. "I can't lose hope—God sent you."

"Yeah?" Dean snorted. "Just wait. You'll get to where you feel like you've lost everything."

She smiled bigger. "They can never take God from me—"

With a half shake of his head, Dean let out a huff and dropped back against the wall.

"What? What was that?"

"Nothing." He reached over and took her hand. A thrill raced through Zahrah as she looked at their intertwined fingers. "You're undauntable."

"I'm not sure that's a word."

"It should be—and right next to the definition is your picture with that chocolate hair, sans hijab."

Zahrah's hand went to her hair before she could stop it.

"Yeah, I probably shouldn't have said that."

"So you do know how to flirt."

Something zipped through Dean's face, but he looked away just as fast.

"You know, I can't figure out if it's a good thing or a bad thing you're here."

This time, he looked offended.

She laughed. "Don't get me wrong—I'm glad. I wouldn't want any other hero with me right now."

"I'm not a hero. I'm a sheepdog."

She smiled. "Some people are sheep, some are wolves, and then—"

"There's sheepdogs." He almost cracked a smile. "Hooah."

"My dad loved that." Why was he holding her hand? He'd never made a move like that before. "You're a lot like him."

"Is that supposed to be a compliment?"

She nudged his shoulder with hers. "Of course." And then without warning, she felt very shy. "He's the best man I know."

Voices drew close to the cell.

Like lightning, Dean was on his feet. He leapt to the corner, back to the wall, shoulder pointing to the door as it groaned open.

A guard stepped in, weapon lazily held in front of him.

Breath stuck in her throat, Zahrah froze.

Dean threw a hard right, followed with his left and snatched the weapon from the guard just as Dean's fist connected with his jaw. The guard spun and stumbled. With the butt of the weapon, Dean slammed it into the guard's face. His neck snapped back.

Another guard entered.

"Behind!" Zahrah yelped.

Angling, Dean dropped and swung his leg back. Caught the second guard's foot. He flipped him. Dean pounced, punching the guard. Again. Again. He'd moved so fast. Neutralized the guards in seconds. Hope surged. She might actually survive. Dean knew what he was doing. He kept his fight, his head in the game.

Dean's face, alight with the fight, jerked to her. He held out a hand. "C'm—"

Zahrah took a step.

A board swung out of nowhere. Smacked into the back of Dean's head. He pitched forward. Went to his knees. But didn't go down. Not all the way. He groaned and shook his head, apparently trying to shrug off the daze.

Zmaray entered. Aimed a gun at Dean. Fired.

By the time Zahrah's scream reached her vocal cords, it'd registered that the gun didn't have the normal *crack*. She looked at Dean, one leg tucked under him, a hand propping him up as he leaned heavily to the right. Swayed. Yanked a silver vial from his chest.

Dart gun?

She looked to Zmaray.

"Bring her." He started out. "And teach the captain a lesson."

—m—

Dean threw a hard right.

Met nothing. Sailed wildly. His feet tangled.

Everything hurt. Burned. Ached. A blinding blow cracked against the back of his head. Teeth rattled. Something warm and metallic squirted through his mouth. He pitched forward. On all fours, he spit the blood from his mouth. Coughed—and seized as pain racked his body.

In a split second, he saw the boot flying. Braced himself. Not enough. The room tilted. Spun. Went black. Another cough as the air whooshed from his lungs. He shook his head, the stones spinning crazily. Still, he wasn't going down without a fight. But when he pushed up, agony tore through his arm. He crashed against the wall, groaning.

"Do not think you will be the hero this time, Captain."

Vision blurred, hearing partially blocked, Dean squinted up at the man towering over him, his tunic spotted with Dean's blood.

"She will cooperate." Kamran squatted in front of him, the guards standing over Dean with the business end of their weapons hovering over Kamran's shoulders and aimed right at Dean. "And I have the great pleasure of making sure you are in pain to force her hand."

Dean spit at him.

With flared nostrils, he used his sleeve to wipe the spittle. "And I will take great pleasure—more than I do in beating you—in breaking her."

White-hot rage shot through Dean. He threw himself, agony and broken body, at Kamran.

The guy went backward. Fists. Feet. Shouts.

Crack!

Flying sideways, Dean howled through the fire that seared his back. His body convulsed, the pinpricks of a Taser throttling him full of electricity. The squawk and thud of the door shutting allowed Dean to relax. He visually cleared the room then let his head drop back. He stared up at the cement ceiling and stared at the light. Let that blur his realities. The past, the present, the fantasy.

Zahrah. Beautiful and free. Laughing, surrounded by children. Teaching them.

Ellen, at the base, playing basketball like one of the guys. Laughing. Alive.

Mom. He couldn't remember her laughing. But smiling, at some of his antics. Chewing him out—man, what he wouldn't do to hear her chew him out again. Because that'd mean she was alive.

Rolling onto his side took every morsel of strength he had left. But he did. And scooted so that he could see the door. Slowly, he surrendered the fight. His body needed rest. His mind needed it. Otherwise, he wouldn't find a way out of here. It was all up to him now that they'd fried the transmitter.

He couldn't cling to any false hopes. Zahrah's life, the entire military establishment depended on them getting out of here alive. Hoping the transmitter had emitted a signal before it'd been killed was a fool's dream. They would escape.

"Escape from what?"

Zahrah's innocent question rocked the vault he'd stored those answers in years ago. Her hand felt so small, so delicate yet strong in his. He had to convince these goons that she meant as much to him as he did to her. That's what their captors wanted. But he hated himself for it. Hated the way she hung on his every word. Hated the way she looked at him with those beautiful brown eyes. Hated how she'd responded when he took her hand. She had expectation filled with an unwritten promise of more.

But there couldn't be more. Not when he was faking it.

But she didn't know that. And he couldn't let her know that. Because under duress, she might tell them it wasn't real. He had to convince her it was real. He just wasn't sure how to do that.

Let it be real.

No. No, can't do that. Heaviness pulled and tugged at him, dragging him into a black abyss.

Voices thudded against his throbbing head. Holding his side, Dean opened his eyes. Couldn't see the door. But heard the keys rattling on the other side. Gritting through the fire and pinching in his side and chest, he hauled himself up.

The door shrieked open, the hinges badly in need of some lubricant.

Two guards dragged in a waif of a teen boy.

What was this?

They released him.

The boy dropped to his knees and stayed by the opening, head down, shoulders sagging. Short hair chopped at weird angles and angry red welts along his neck and arms.

"What is this?" Dean clambered to his feet, unsteady but determined. "Where's Zahrah. What have you done with her?"

Sniggers trailed the guards as they stepped out.

Clang! Thud!

The teen jumped at the noise of the locks reengaging, his head coming up just briefly. Brown eyes—

Dean's breath hitched. He pushed himself forward. "Zahrah?" Steeling himself against the pain, he squatted in front of her. *This is my fault.* He'd mentioned her hair. Psychological warfare. Break their minds and spirits. More than ever, Dean knew they were listening. Watching. Very closely. To find the straw that would break their will.

God, help us.

Her brown eyes rose to his. Morose. Disheartened.

Dean cupped her face. "This changes nothing. Hair is a dressing, like clothes."

A tear trickled down her cheek.

He was reminded of their conversation earlier. "You're still beautiful."

She sniffled. "But not beautiful enough for you."

Smothered by her words, Dean stilled. "You're the most beautiful woman I know."

Her eyes widened. She drew in a breath that she didn't release. "What? What's wrong?"

Her chin quivered. "They said you'd say that."

Dean inched closer. "Z, don't let them get in your head, okay?"

"But they know. . .they know everything I'm thinking."

"They want you to think that."

"No, they *know*. They know how I feel about you, know what I'll say—what you say." She held his arm, his hands still bracing her face, as she looked up at him. Watery brown eyes, like liquid chocolate, seeped through his defenses. "I'm so scared." Her lids slid shut, squeezing out more tears. "So scared of what they're going to make me do."

Dread poured through Dean as her words echoed through him. "No." He wanted to curse. She'd already surrendered her will. Expected them to win. "They can't make us do anything we don't want to do. Everything we say or do is a choice."

"But—"

"No." Dean pressed his forehead to hers. "Be resolute, Z. No matter what they do to me, or to you, you have to determine there is no line in the sand. Nothing that will make you stand in front of a thousand American soldiers and pull the trigger."

Zahrah pulled away from him. Pushed to her feet and stuffed herself in the corner. "That's not fair."

"No, it's not. But that is exactly what you're doing if you give them what they want. Think of the men on my team. Think of your father and his friends. All those upper echelon that you've had in your home. Friends. The men and women on the base who took care of Rashid."

She whimpered and slid down the wall, shaking her head.

Dean went to her and knelt again. "Z," he said, his breathing heavy. His conviction so raw, so vigorous, he could hardly breathe.

"I believe in you. It's why I came after you."

Her brows tugged together. "Came after me?"

"I knew when I walked into the president's home, that I would be captured."

She shook her head.

He tugged off his shirt, swiveled around in his hunched position, and showed her his bare back.

Zahrah gasped. "What—?"

Dean tensed at her touch. "That's what happened to me ten years ago. Scars from torture, from beatings, electric shock." Threading his hands through his shirt again, he turned back. "I knew what they could do to me. What they could do to you. I came here because I knew. . .I knew if you had something you cared about, you'd remember why you're fighting."

Head back against the bulging rocks, hair looking like something out of a zombie flick, she eyed him. "I can't figure you out, Dean. And I'm tired."

He dropped his gaze. Losing this fight with her now meant it was over.

"When you first arrived, you acted like I was just an American you came to rescue. Nothing more. Then you held my hand, as if I meant something." She shuddered. "Now, we're back to this—you came here because you knew *I* cared for *you*."

This was sliding downhill with a rocket-propelled assist.

"Am I just a mission to you, Dean?"

CHAPTER 42

12 July

Screaming hard-rock music punched Dean's answer out of the air. The walls shook with the booming bass and the shriek of a death metal lead singer's voice. Zahrah covered her ears, hunching against the deafening noise. "What are they doing?"

"More psychological warfare," Dean shouted just as the light popped off.

Fear coiled in Zahrah's stomach. Darkness. Thundering, shrieking music.

Something touched her hand. She jerked away.

In the blaring insanity, she heard, "Hold my hand!"

Reticent but desperate for a lifeline, she relaxed. Dean's strong hand enfolded around hers. Then a little tug. He wanted her to move. She followed in the darkness, walking. . . He led her around the perimeter of the room in a steady pace. She felt the vibration of the music against her breastbone, tickling her feet. How long they walked, she didn't know. Only that her legs and feet hurt. Her back ached.

She tugged back and eased along the wall, but Dean refused her the break she wanted. To just sit down. Vanish into the black, deafening void that roared for her submission. Her legs buckled. Dean tugged her onward. "Just let me go." But her voice couldn't compete with the music.

Then out of nowhere, Dean swung her around—right into his chest. His arm slipped around her waist and held her close. His feet shuffled around hers. They turned. *What is he—dancing!*

Zahrah resisted. Dance? When they were torturing her?

Words, mangled by the screaming of the metal music, brushed against her ear. "Let go. . .make own. . .fight back."

Laugh or cry, she couldn't decide. Brain signals blitzing—she was in his arms, he was holding her close, they were being tortured with darkness and loud music, but he was close, touching her—she struggled to know what to do.

"One-two-three," came his words against her ear, faint, and yet she felt his chest puff as he'd shouted them.

Insane! The dance he was trying to lead her in was a waltz. To metal music? Instead, she focused on the waltz he led her in. Swirling around the small room, turning. She laughed, but the din of the music swallowed it. But she had laughed. And it felt good. Though she wasn't a good dancer, it didn't matter.

And he twirled her. Round. . .round. . .round, back into his arms. Her head butted his. She stopped. "Sorry!" She'd spoken but couldn't be heard.

Dean pulled her back into his arms. His chest bounced against hers, and she realized he was laughing as they started another waltz. This time, she envisioned something from the animated movie *Anastasia*.

When he twirled her the last time, their grip broke. Hysterical laughter shot through her. She fell against the wall, laughing, holding her side.

A gust of air next to her told her of Dean's presence. Instinctively, she reached out. Touched—oh. His face. Stubble. His cheek bulged slightly—a smile. She could see him perfectly. The buzz cut, the sun-bronzed complexion. His strong brow that sometimes had that terse, intense, tugged-together look. The strong nose. Angled features. His green-flecked eyes.

He placed his hand over hers, a reassuring gesture. When his hand fell away, she felt the emptiness of it. The cold air. Yet she felt he was still near, so she leaned her head against his shoulder. Closed her eyes. Whispered a prayer of thanks that God had Dean here to keep her sane. Keep her laughing. Keep her hoping.

—⚬—

Undisclosed Location
14 July—1545 Hours

"Do not sit there and tell me we're doing nothing."

Booyah. Or wait, these grunts say hooah. Or is it oorah? Whatever. They grunt—which is why they're called grunts. Anyway, my man

Hawk is standing off with the general. And I'm ready for this show down. It's wicked cool watching the pawns on my chessboard try to take control. They have no clue there is no such thing.

"Stand down, Bledsoe," Burnett growls at the alpha male.

"He's right." Ah, so Falcon has finally grown a backbone. So the guy felt the Aussie was nudging him out of his top spot, huh? Sort of like Jesus' disciples vying for a seat at his right hand.

Oh don't get all sanctimonious on me. Everyone knows that Bible story.

"Dean's been gone two weeks and we have nothing. Have done nothing."

"We've been digging."

"Not good enough," Falcon snaps. "Since you made it out of there without a scratch, you've had your head in the sand."

Oh, ho-ho-hoooo! What's this, insubordination? Taking down the American military might be easier than I'd predicted.

"You sorry son of—"

"Listen." The Oz has spoken! "Division in the ranks will not bring back Watters or Zahrah."

"You got that right," Hawk says. "Action will bring them back."

"And what do you suppose we do, Bledsoe?"

I swear, I can see the steam pouring out of Burnett's ears. His face red. Even though this is a black-white feed.

The general motions crazily with his arms. "Randomly shoot targets?"

Bledsoe is about to blow! "No, find out how they knew Dean was bugged."

"What're you talking about? That's pretty simple to figure out. The signal—"

"Hadn't gone live." Bledsoe pointed to the wall. "When I did attempt activation, it was dead."

"Bad bug?"

"It's not the flu. It's a high-tech device. They knew and they fried it. Which means they had to fry Dean to do it."

"That's an assumption. And we all know what those do."

Yeah, I probably don't need to spell that out, but it's pretty funny. Because it's basically how I see these guys. So full of themselves, of their power. . .and I've made them power*less*.

"And how'd they know to retrieve you?" Hawk seemed to be on a witch hunt. Or maybe a spy hunt.

Speaking of. . .I'm still running the blurred image of that Sikh spy through my database. It'd net me another mill if I can hand that information over to the boss.

Annnd speaking of that, I flip the feeds and dive into the prison holding the honeymooning couple. I gotta admit—never saw it coming. Watters is holding out. I thought with his past, with his history as a POW, he'd have broken like a *watter*logged—pun totally intended—piece of wood. Instead, he'd not only held it together, but also helped the hottie do the same.

Which has to change. Because if it doesn't, they won't get what they want, and I won't get what I want.

My time is limited. I've got to find out who's holding Zmaray's chain, who's the bigwig behind all this. The one donating millions to Zmaray to pay me. Maybe if I demonstrate my abilities. . . So a few keystrokes and piggybacking back channels, which they have graciously—and foolishly—wired so I can remain in contact with them, diverts control of the power in that prison to my hot little fingertips.

"Ladies and gentlemen," I say in my best announcer-man voice, "may I have your attention please?"

And zap! Just like that, they are without power. I start counting, knowing they will be calling me soon enough.

Bzzz. Bzzz.

I smile as my phone rings. No, I'm afraid it won't be as easy that. "You'll have to come to me."

It's a death wish. But only if I didn't know it was coming.

—∞—

Somewhere in Afghanistan
14 July—1600 Hours

Quiet crashed into the cell.

Dean's eyes popped open at the sudden intrusion of silence. He had no idea how long the music had played, but it had to be hours with the way his nerves felt fried, his head throbbed. A weight lifted from his right shoulder, drawing his gaze.

Darkness forbid him from seeing.

"What. . . ?" came Zahrah's sleepy response to the quiet.

"Music stopped."

Shouts outside warned him of more than that. He stood and mentally mapped his route to the door. Hands on the steel, he listened.

Watch the doors. I can't see anything, so neither can they.

"I think they lost power."

"Can we get out?"

"Locks aren't electric." Hands guiding him in the blindness, Dean returned to the far wall. "Just means more darkness." He stretched his arms and legs. How long had he slept?

"How'd you know I could dance?" Her question held amusement and the hint of a smile.

Dean could see that smile in his mind's eye, in the many times she'd offered him one. Somehow, it already made him feel better. "I didn't. Just hoped that with all the military balls your father probably subjected you to, that you'd gained some experience."

She laughed. "I did. But what about you—military balls? Dates?"

"I went because it was expected. Never took a date, though."

"But you dance really well."

Another laugh. "I said I didn't take dates, not that I didn't dance."

"I'm not sure how to respond to that."

He laid on his back. "Don't."

He did some sit ups, cringing and grunting against the lingering pain.

"I know how to score points with the officers by being charming."

He did another set.

"My father met my mother at a benefit gala, much like the military balls. She said he was this young, dashing officer and her father the equivalent—in position and rank—of an Arab prince. She was the prize catch."

"Not sure I like hearing about this side of your father."

Zahrah chuckled. "I'm not sure he'd like me telling you."

"That I can guarantee." He alternated elbow-to-knee sit-ups as their ears slowly found equilibrium in the noise of the silence.

"My father fell in love with my mother that night. He said he knew the first they danced that he'd do anything for her."

"I bet her father liked that, what with all the social rules and protocols."

"True, but my grandfather desperately wanted out of Afghanistan. He. . ." She drew in a long breath. "Like me, he had knowledge that could be deadly."

"I thought that was your uncle."

"They are both intelligent men."

Her answer felt. . .off.

"My grandfather was so happy when my father showed interest in his daughter."

"Let me guess—they made a deal."

"It wasn't quite so sterile as that, but yes, eventually. My mother was harder to convince. She was afraid of new things, especially living in a place where she knew nobody and could not speak the language. Then the Afghan government found out about their plan to escape to America. They were watched, followed, threatened, beaten. . . ."

"Not much has changed, then."

"But my mother started finding red poppies on her windowsill in the mornings. She knew it was my father—"

"So he's an old softie."

Zahrah laughed. Man, he liked that sound. "I bet you wouldn't say that to his face."

"I sort of like living."

More laughter. "He brought the flowers because she'd told him they were her favorite flowers. She'd told him about a field near the mountains by their home. My mother knew it was his way of saying he was there, that he would take care of her, provide for her."

Dean cringed. "Can we *not* paint these Romeo images of your father in my head, please?"

"He is a hard man, but he is also a very good man. Like you."

"You saying I'm hard?" He kept the lightheartedness in his voice, not wanting her to hear how much her words hit him crossways. He'd never seen himself as hard. Focused maybe. Intense.

"I think you could become hard if you are not careful."

The arrow pierced straight and true. He thought of his brother, his father. . . But they needed lighthearted talk. "So, what happened with the poppies?"

"He kept leaving them for her. One night, she slipped out of her house and went to the field. My father was there with a truck. He said he'd waited there for her every night. He wanted her to go with him right then, but she refused to leave her father behind. So they made a plan—the next time he left a poppy, that would be their signal that it was time to leave. My mother never betrayed the plan to my grandfather. Instead, one night, she woke him and begged him to come to the field with her."

"He went?" Dean hated to sound incredulous, but that was a wild shot in the dark.

"He did." Zahrah sounded pleased. "He later told her he saw something in her eyes he'd never seen in a long time."

"What?" Dusting off his hands, Dean returned to the wall beside her.

"Love. Hope. Their lives had become so cruel, so hard, that she'd lost her will to live." In the darkness, she shifted, her feet dragging over the dirt floor heavily. "All the times I've heard or thought of that story, I could never relate. . .until now."

Dean tapped her leg. "Well, don't lose your will to live, okay? I don't have any poppies."

Light exploded through the room, burning his eyeballs. Dean pinched the bridge of his nose, letting his eyes adjust to the brightness behind closed lids. "Guess the power's back."

Zahrah looked pale, but maybe that was just the light. She'd shed weight since he'd seen her in Mazar-e. "And food."

Squinting, Dean turned toward the door.

"I'll get it," she said.

"Nah." Dean caught her hand. "I got it." He retrieved it, sniffed— "rye and mold"—and, keeping his back to her, tore the bread in half. Cradling the smaller piece in his hand, he passed the other to her. "Doubt this is what they meant by be sure to eat your greens."

"Ew," Zahrah moaned as she looked at the days-old bread.

"Remember, ration it."

She nodded and tore it into four pieces.

Dean slipped his into his pocket. He tucked a quarter-sized portion into his mouth and chewed slowly. Not to savor the flavor but to give the appearance of having more than he did. "When we get out of here, I might kill the next person who hands me a piece of rye."

"Or sourdough." Another favorite of their captors.

He knew what he had to do to keep her alive. Knew what he'd failed to do to save Ellen. He'd made those changes. The food. The dry, sometimes dark humor. Diverting the torture to himself. Drawing out the fighters to know what level of firepower to expect when they made a break for it. To cage his heart and harness his mind. Give her something to live for.

There was just one problem. One thing he'd screwed up. One parameter he dropped. One line crossed: He cared.

CHAPTER 43

Somewhere in Afghanistan
18 July—1320 Hours

Blood streamed in rivulets down the tattooed, scarred back of the Special Forces operator. Captain Dean Watters moaned as he rolled sideways then onto all fours. Hands propping him up, he steadied himself. Glared up through a bleeding temple.

At a dirty sink, Lee Nianzu flipped the knob. Water trickled out then faster. He scrubbed the crimson stains from his fingers. "Take him back. Remember, Captain, it is in your best interest to convince the woman to cooperate."

"Sorry," came the deep, raspy voice as he was cuffed and dragged to his feet. "Not going to happen."

"You take pleasure in pain?" Drying his hands with a towel, Nianzu faced the American soldier, who struggled to hold himself upright.

"Yeah." Teeth mottled with blood, he grinned. "It means I'm still alive."

Kamran growled. "We can change that."

"Bring it."

"What about Zahrah's pain?" Nianzu slid his hands in his silk-blend pant pockets as he considered the operator. "Do you take pleasure in her pain?"

His arrogance faltered. "If it means she's alive—"

"Come, Captain. You and I both know you would do anything to protect her, including drawing our attention, anger, and"—Nianzu looked around the large room with chains strung from the rafters, water hoses, metal bed frames, a tray of tools, leather straps—"efforts. Perhaps you are far too caught up in being the hero that you do not realize how far you have fallen."

His jaw lifted.

"I do not mean failed."

Confusion now.

"I mean, you have fallen prey to your own feelings, your own protective instincts. I cannot help but wonder what you would do, should"—he slid his gaze to Kamran—"someone hurt her."

A dark shadow filled the captain's face and eyes. "As you said, you and I both know what would happen."

Lethal venom dripped from those few words. The soldier all but promised to exact vengeance if the girl was hurt. So, the captain's heart had become engaged in the situation.

"But tell me, what are you, a known assassin, doing here? Doing someone's dirty work? Aren't you"—the captain sneered—"better than this?"

Impressive. Trying to draw out anger. But no. There would be no shift of his focus in his mission. Tedious, dull work, this torture. But it served a greater purpose. "Until next time, Captain." With a jut of his jaw, Nianzu ordered the guards to return the prisoner.

Years had gone into this effort, but nothing in that elaborate planning had prepared Nianzu to have things go so perfectly, so supremely on plan. Nor had he ever expected to find such sublime pawns as these two. He returned to the makeshift office, changed shirts, and slipped into a tie and jacket.

"Your plan is not working."

Nianzu stared at the six-foot-four Afghan towering over him. The Muslim might have brute strength, but he did not have speed. Or cunning.

"I say we separate them. The soldier is a danger to my men and this mission."

"He is key to breaking the girl."

"No." Kamran took a step forward, his meaty fist balled. "Look at the tapes, watch the cameras. She draws courage from him."

He'd seen it, too.

"Let me teach her a lesson." The man leered. "Or two. I will break her."

"She must come to this decision on her own, or her help will not be trustworthy."

A well-muscled shoulder lifted. "I will help her see it's in her best interest."

Nianzu returned to the window that held no glass. To the view that held no inspiration. His mind traveled the distance, both in miles back to his home country and the past to the night he dispatched General

Zhang Guiern. It had been so easy. Manipulating pieces on the chess-board. Maneuvering the wills of those who believed they had a choice. Believed they could outdo him.

Just like the American Special Forces operator who believed that in coming here, he could either rescue or protect Zahrah Zarrick.

It was simple. So very simple. So much that even he could not believe how easily it had worked.

"Captain Watters has grown stronger because he knows their time is short."

"All the more reason we not give him another day to consider the outcome."

"No." Nianzu jerked to Kamran. "You will *not* kill him. Kill him, we lose her completely."

"Or maybe she will feel she has nothing to lose."

Nianzu sneered. "She is much stronger, both in mind and heart, than any of your warriors, Kamran. Do not underestimate her." He went to the desk and lifted his briefcase. "I must return to China for a few days."

Already the greedy glint appeared in the man's eyes.

"You know how far my reach goes. Do not force my hand against you." With that, Nianzu strode out of the complex and slipped into the sleek black Mercedes. He lifted his phone from his pocket as the car pulled away from the complex. As the road smoothed out, the call connected.

"Boss Man!"

"Send me a link to the live feed of the prison."

"Feed from the—I have no idea. . ."

"Ah, you thought I was ignorant of your devices. Perhaps this will teach you, Boris, not to tempt my patience." He breathed in heavily. Then out. "The feed. Now. Or you will need a speech-to-text to finish your contract."

"I. . .coming your way."

Nianzu ended the call and checked his e-mail. The link slid into his inbox. He accessed it. Scanned through a few cameras until he found the right one.

He almost laughed. It had been too easy. It paid to know your friends, but it paid even more to know your enemies. Through the dark shadows of the passage that led to the cell holding Zahrah Zarrick and Captain Dean Watters, Kamran stalked with sick, malicious intent.

CHAPTER 44

Somewhere in Afghanistan
20 July

They're escalating," Dean ground out through bloodied lips.

They'd beaten him to a pulp. . .again. But still he hadn't bent his knee, his will. When would enough be enough for him? The question scared Zahrah because she realized "enough" would've come much sooner for her without Dean.

Stomach roiling, she knelt beside him, hand on his shoulder—one of the few spots not splattered in his blood. Even with the brutality, she couldn't ignore the tattooed wings spreading across his back. A dagger thrust upward along his spine. She had to drag her thoughts from the inked design. "Wh–what do you mean?"

"Our time is short." He held his side, his jaw muscle bouncing. "We have to find a way out. Now."

Her gaze flitted between his pulverized back, the tattooed wings and up-pointed dagger marred, to the door. Locked. Bolted. Guarded. "Why, what's happened?"

He shook his head, staring at the wall. "Just trust me on this. The first chance we get—we take it."

Uncertainty darted through her, along with a hefty dose of adrenaline.

Dean met her gaze, sweat and blood trickling down the sides of his face. His eye had swollen shut again. His other was bloodshot. He could convince her to scale a hundred-foot cliff. But she was still terrified.

"You can do it, Z. Have to."

He'd read her thoughts. Which unleashed all the fears swirling around them. "I. . .I can't fight like you."

He smirked. "Fight like *you*. Don't need brawn." He grimaced and arched his back slightly. "You need brain."

If he'd just give her a sign, an indication that she meant something other than "the strongest woman. . . ."

"Hey." His dirty, blood-crusted hand cupped her face. "Promise me. Promise you'll fight. And this won't be a nice, clean fight, Z. We fight hard till we get what we want."

"What's that?" A stupid question but she needed to hear him say it.

"Freedom." Conflict traced his brow. "I know you're not trained, but we have to hit them hard. It'll be 'kill or be killed.'"

She wilted. She'd do anything for him. But what if she fell short? What if he died because of something she did? "I'm scared."

He grinned through bloodied teeth. "You and me both. But I'm not going to let them win." Fierce determination tugged together his brow and tightened his jaw. "Not this time. Not with you."

Those three words pounded against her heart. "Dean..." Everything in her ached for him to say he cared about her. That she was more than a friend. Three weeks in this prison, all day every day with him. She'd known the first time she met him that he was special. That he stood head and shoulders above the rest. This time of captivity cemented that.

But those thoughts were foolish. They were faced with death. "I want to see my father again. My cousin."

He nodded.

"What about you? Do you want to see your family?"

Misery crowded his face. He tried to smile. "Raptor's the only family I have."

"What about your parents?"

"Dead." He lowered himself against the wall, grimacing as his raw back rested against the stones. "My brother killed them."

Zahrah blinked. The surprise she felt couldn't have been more pronounced. "Dean," she breathed, "I'm so sorry."

Eyes closing, he gave a slight nod. "They weren't the best parents, but they didn't deserve that." He stilled, his face going pale.

"What happened?" She traced his obvious injuries then tore a swatch off the hem of her tunic. Kneeling over him, she dabbed the mess from around his eyes.

"Donny was always in trouble. Came home from a party, drunk and ticked. Desi said Dad tried to punish him with the belt." Dean's expression grew distant as the past once more took hold of him. "Donny was as big and meaner than Dad. Their yelling woke me up. Scared me, both of them in a rage. When I heard the gunshots, I climbed into the dirty clothes pantry—it was one of those built-ins that had a small swinging part." He snorted. "I stayed in there with smelly socks and dirty underwear till the cops came. Even then, I was too scared to come out."

"Who's Desi?"

He blinked. Lifted his head a little higher, as if he'd just emerged from a pool of bad memories. "What?" He focused on her. And his skin seemed to go green.

"I'm sorry. I didn't mean—" Zahrah dropped the question as she tended him, unable to *not* admire his handsome features, despite the cuts, bruising, and swelling. Because there was so much more and more beautiful to Dean Watters than his looks.

"Nah, it's okay. I just. . .I've never told anyone about them."

When he looked into her eyes, in that moment she saw his meaning. *Felt* the meaning—he'd given her a gift in that deeply held secret. "So, you were young?"

"Eight." He winced as she tried to wipe clean his brow. "We got put in the foster system."

Zahrah stilled. "We?"

He smirked.

Always with the mysteries. "Is that—the tattoo on your back. Is that why you did that?"

"Nah." Head propped back, he closed his eyes. "Got the scars ten years ago. My first deployment. We were on a supply run, our caravan, when we got ambushed." A long sigh seemed to end the story and forced quiet into their cell. "She didn't make it."

"Who?"

"Private First Class Ellen Green. Prettiest thing in camos I'd ever seen. Sweet. . ."

Greedy green talons dug into Zahrah's heart. She'd never heard him talk about anyone like that. Ellen must've been something special to him. *Be a friend, Zahrah, not a jealous snit.* "What happened to her?"

"They raped her to death." Once more, Dean's face had gone stone hard. "Right in front of me."

Zahrah inhaled the terrible words and froze. Tears sprang to her eyes. So much made sense about him now. About his need to control. To protect her.

"I should've died a dozen times, but"—he shook his head, looking to the ceiling—"for whatever sick reason, God wanted me alive.

Everyone told me I had an angel watching my back."

Her mind snagged on the mental image snapped of the tattoo. "Angel's wings."

His lips twitched. "And a dagger. When I came back, I was ready to drive that dagger through the heart of any enemy." Dean let out another grunt, holding his side.

"Smart man to realize where your help came from."

"You're too smart for my own good."

"Yeah, someone tried to tell me that before, and I ignored his advice."

"Hey." Dean touched her face. "You had a purpose, remember?"

Zahrah stilled as his fingers traced her hacked-off hair, the side of her face. As she looked into his bloodshot right eye, she felt a dart of exhilaration and attraction. But also. . .the answer. The answer to the elusive sense of purpose that existed just below her awareness. "You."

Dean frowned a bit, his hand trailing down her arm. "What?"

Out of habit, as she'd always done when nervous, she tucked hair she didn't have behind her ear. "Remember, I told you there was another reason I was here, one I couldn't quite figure out?"

He hesitated as if anticipating her answer.

"It's you. You're the reason I'm here."

"No." He scowled. "No!" He punched to his feet.

Zahrah stood, holding the bloodied rag. "Why. . .why does that make you mad?"

He jerked toward her. "Have you seen me? Do you *know* me?"

"I. . .I think I do."

"Wrong!" Fury reddened his face. "Did you not hear what I just said about my family? I don't do relationships. I don't have a need or desire for one. Never have. My team—Raptor is what I live for."

"Dean—"

"No, no platitudes. Just get it out of your head. I'm not made for relationships. I'm not worth saving."

"That is not true!" She strode the half-dozen paces to the other side of the cell, where he stood by the door. "You're the best man I've ever met."

"Wrong. Get over your attraction because it won't happen. I'm not dating. I'm married to the Army. I won't marry anyone." He shook his head and shuffled around, his hand on the back of his neck. "I won't do that to anyone. I won't. . .let that happen."

"Then this"—she held out her hands to their cell—"is where you belong." Calmness replaced her surprise at the dialogue that had opened between them. She'd hit a nerve talking about family. "Because you were a captive to those wrong beliefs before you ever entered this prison. They have held you hostage, kept you in fear, and forced you to sacrifice what you want."

"Yeah?" he growled, his face a simmering pot of rage. "And what is that? You? Are you going to tell me *you* are what I want?"

Zahrah looked at him. Prayed for wisdom, prayed to see beyond the poison spewing from his anger and to see the wounds behind those words. Asked God to help her reach the man standing before her, the one who'd been so strong and quiet and now stood in rage of fear and panic. *God, help me help him. . .just like You planned.*

And like a cool breeze, she remembered. "When was the last time you talked to Desi?"

Dean jerked as if she'd slapped him. "What do you know about her?"

"Is she your sister?"

He froze. Then turned away. Facing the wall.

Zahrah went to his side, touched his arm. "You don't need bars, a crust of bread, and water to be a prisoner. If your past is holding you hostage, then it's time to break out."

His nostrils flared as his chest rose and fell unevenly. "You don't know what you're talking about." He breathed. In. Out. In. Out. "What about you?" he asked, his voice low and gravelly. "You're here. You're a prisoner."

Zahrah inched into the space between his chest and the wall. "I'm not a prisoner, Dean." She smiled, feeling the liberation of the words before she spoke them. "I'm right where God wants me."

Voices outside jerked Dean around. The broken soldier, the raw one, was gone. In his place was the one always in control. The one ready to do violence.

CHAPTER 45

Somewhere in Afghanistan
25 July

Too far away to do serious damage, Dean would let the players enter his domain. He'd assessed the threat. Knew if he was fast, if he moved with violence of intent, he could do this. He'd had enough. Enough idleness. Enough inaction. Enough...enough of her. This was it.

Too far away to take them upon entry. He'd have to just use the element of surprise.

Two guards entered. Fear—of him?—made their grips tight but sloppy. Sweat on their brows. Which meant their hands were probably sweaty, too. Easier to disarm.

Kamran stalked in. His breathing was...odd. His gaze on Zahrah.

Like a battering ram, knowledge of that man's intent struck Dean. He knew that look. Knew the hunger in the man's eyes as his gaze slid over Zahrah. Knew without any doubt what this sick perv had in mind.

Dean's anger slid up another notch as the men marched in. Weapons raised and aimed solely at Dean.

This is it. Had to end this now.

Dean grabbed the muzzle of the M16. Rolled his shoulder into the guard. Jerked back his elbow into the man's face. Slid his hand toward the handgun holstered at the guy's thigh. Yanked it up. Spun. Aimed it at the second guard. Fired.

The man, face frozen in shock, stumbled backward and fell across the door's threshold. As Dean came round to take on the second guard, in his periphery he saw Zahrah kick out—nail Kamran in the knee. The man howled as she came at him with a controlled punch.

Satisfied she could hold him for a second, Dean whipped around. Sent a double-tap through the temple of the first guard.

Shouts yanked him up. A half-dozen armed guards flooded the room.

"Secure him," Kamran shouted. Limping, he held Zahrah's neck in the crook of his arm, her feet off the ground as he hauled her out of the cell.

Dean flung himself sideways, right between two guards. He lunged. Dived into Kamran. The captor and Zahrah pitched into the wall. Zahrah's soft grunt pushed Dean to fight hard. This was it. They had to get out of here. This puke of an Afghan was going to do unmentionable things if he could get free. Dean couldn't allow that. Wouldn't.

He dragged himself on top of the man. Threw a hard right into the guy's nose.

Kamran sliced his hands into Dean's sides.

White-hot fire shot through Dean, fuzzed his vision. He gritted through the excruciating pain. Had a fist-hold on his tunic. Used it as a homing beacon. Kamran threw his own punch. Connected with Dean's jaw. Dean squeezed hard with his knees. Resisted being thrown. Dropped and pressed his forearm into the man's throat. Grunting and straining, Kamran struggled. Dean felt the power infusing him. The surge to make this guy take his *last* breath.

Crack!

Before Dean could react, he found himself slammed against the wall. Numbness spreading down his neck.

A blur of camo and gray uniforms descended on him.

Dean struck out.

A fist cracked across his jaw.

"Lock him up!"

Hands, so many of them, pawed at him. Dragged him. Dean scrambled for purchase, watching as Kamran stumbled backward, limping, his arms wrapped around Zahrah's midsection. She flailed against the man, her attention glued to Dean. She reached for him, screaming and kicking as another guard tried to assist the oversized Afghan.

"Dean!" Her shriek echoed through the dark, narrow passage and thunked right into his heart.

"Fight!" Dean howled as he threw a hard right, sending one backward. Coldcocked another. "Don't stop fighting!"

After another whack against his head, Dean's responses blurred. Slurred. He shook his head—and the world tilted. He felt himself falling. Or climbing. Something hard collided with his shoulder. He didn't care. Zahrah—had to get to her. He blinked. Gathered his senses.

Inside. He was *inside* the cell. Door sliding shut.

He threw himself at the barrier. Banged. Kicked. Cursed. Shouted. Cursed himself. Cursed God. Rammed his foot at the steel again and again. Everything hurt. Nothing hurt—not when he knew what was happening to Zahrah.

God gave her to you to protect.

And I failed. Just like always. See? This! This is why he didn't deserve someone like her. Why he didn't deserve to be happy.

The thought sobered him. Palms flat against the steel barrier, Dean stared at the rust. At the door. At nothing in particular. Drank heavily of the guilt. Of the defeat.

But his heart, something deeper than that—*his soul!*—clung to the first part. *God gave her to you.*

No. No, good things didn't belong to him. He didn't deserve them. If he couldn't protect his parents, if he couldn't save Ellen, he didn't deserve Zahrah.

A scream knifed the rank air. Drew Dean up tight. He listened, his heart sputtering. Knowing. . .*knowing* what was happening.

He kicked the door again. Roared. Hopped around. Drove a heel into the cement wall. "Where are You?" He shouted to the ceiling. To the sky. To God!

"You." The way she'd said that. The conviction that flooded her eyes and her words, her belief so utterly resolute that her real purpose for being in Afghanistan was Dean.

"No!" Condemnation drowned him. If it weren't for him, she'd have gone back. If it weren't for him, Zahrah would be home. Safe. Unhurt. Whole.

Dean's legs wobbled. Failure pushed him to the ground. His shoulders sagged. Head hung, he reached for the only tendril of hope. "God. . ."

Memories crashed in on him. Smells. Darkness. Gunshots. Desi screaming and crying. Head against the steel door, Dean let them come. Let the nightmare take him.

Running scared. Bullied at school. Bullied at home. His brother had a thing for power, just like their father. And Dean had had enough that night. More than enough. The Watters blood held poison and generational curses. Some genealogy charts held heroism and valor. His held violence and cowardice.

"Dean, you can't change what's inside on your own, son. It's an uphill battle that never ends." In his standard blues, Sergeant Elliott showed up to talk with Dean after his shift one night. It'd been a bad week—month. His foster brother had called him the brother of a murderer. Dean punched him. His foster mom called Sergeant Elliott. *"But with God, you can."*

It was then Dean asked a question he didn't even know existed within him. "What if you don't want to change?" He was sure Sergeant Elliott would come down hard on him. Reject him. Those were bad thoughts.

"Why don't you want to change, son?"

"Because—they're doing wrong. And getting away with it. That's wrong, too."

That's when Sergeant Elliott said the words that changed Dean's life. "There's a warrior in you, Dean. God only gives that gift to a rare few."

"Being a soldier like you?" Dean's heart raced at the thought back then—he'd wanted nothing more than to be like his hero, his mentor, who'd served as an Army Ranger. "Is that what you mean?"

With a smile as he stood to leave, Sergeant Elliott turned to him. "I know you'll work hard to be worthy of that gift."

And Dean had. A year later with Sergeant Elliott at his side, Dean signed up at seventeen for the Army. The Monday after his graduation, he was on a bus headed to Fort Benning for Basic.

If only he had Sergeant Elliott with him now. To give him some sage advice. But Dean was alone. And defeated.

A warrior...

If only.

CHAPTER 46

Somewhere in Afghanistan

The Lord is my rock, and my f–fortress. . .” Zahrah sobbed through her words as the bindings were cut from her wrists. The verse. How did it go next? She strained to focus on a comfort in her soul when her body screamed in agony. For God to make the words true. “A–nd m–my deliverer—yes. My deliverer.” *Please deliver me!*

Hand on the wall, Zahrah gingerly made her way back to the cell following the guard and praying God would block the event from her mind. That she’d stop hearing his grunts. Smelling his smell. His stink. His sweat. *Please. . .*

They turned right, down the long, anorexic corridor that led to the cell. To Dean.

She stumbled.

The guard turned with a scowl. “Hurry!” He motioned her onward. But she couldn’t move. Couldn’t go forward. Couldn’t return to Dean. Her shame hung like a water-drenched wool pashmina around her shoulders. He’d know.

Four guards crowded into the passage with them. As one worked the lock, the others took up positions. The door flung back. Shouts echoed through the hall, “Hands up, hands up! On the ground. On the ground!”

A short burst of gunfire made Zahrah jerk.

Blinking through her tears, her shame, she waited, propped against the wall. The guards parted and ordered her inside.

Zahrah couldn’t move. Remained in the shadows with her shame. She’d argued with Dean. He’d be angry. And now. . .now what would he think of her?

“Go,” the guard beside her said.

She shook her head.

A guard by the door stomped toward her. Grabbed her arm. "No," Zahrah snapped. Wrestled.

Another joined the rough one.

"No!"

They dragged her, her feet tangling with theirs. They tossed her into the cell. Scrabbling onto her knees even as the door groaned and squeaked shut, Zahrah snapped her gaze to the ground. Held herself tight. Ignored the pain between her legs as she knelt there.

It was so quiet. Felt so empty in the cell. Was Dean even here? Her gaze darted to the wall, to the side. There. To her left, just beyond her visual reach, she saw his knees.

Her courage—what was left of it—crumbled. She covered her face and a gut-birthed sob ripped away her last vestige of strength.

—∞—

His last words to her had been mean, defensive. Panicked. And now. . . now she bore the marks of a man possessed by lust. A fury unlike anything Dean had ever experienced coursed through his veins, hot and virulent. He'd kill Kamran when he saw him again.

Face shielded behind her hands, Zahrah's sobs pummeled Dean.

It took two squatted walks to reach her. He caught her shoulders. "Z. . ." What was there to say?

With a strangled cry, she seesawed her shoulders away.

He recognized the evasive move for what it was—reactionary from being raped. He wasn't letting go. Wouldn't go away. He held firm and tugged her to himself.

After brief resistance, Zahrah collapsed into his arms, face against his chest. Dean folded his arms around her shoulders, bouncing from the sobs. With one hand cupping the back of her head and the other tight across her upper back, Dean fought the urge to break something. Like the guy's neck. Her torso convulsed beneath her grief and pain. Dean braced against it, feeling every ounce of her agony.

He'd sworn—*sworn*—to never be in this position again. But he was. That angered him, but something more, bigger, battered him. Before when he'd made that vow, he told himself it wouldn't matter who else was involved. It shouldn't matter that it was Zahrah. It mattered that a wrong against a human had been perpetrated.

But he was wrong. It did matter that it was Zahrah weeping in his arms. It did matter that he'd not just failed—but failed *her*. This whole situation was somehow darker, bigger, worse. Why, he didn't know. Only that it was. That was enough.

Head tucked against hers, he searched for something to say. Something to make it right. But there was nothing to say. "I'm sorry." About the rape. About so much more.

Zahrah pushed her face center mass, curling into his hold.

"Shh," Dean said, leaning against the stone wall. His pain nothing compared to hers. He worked through the anger. This was what they wanted. For him to care. For him to convince her to do what they wanted. Anything to stop the pain, the trauma.

Fingers dug into his triceps and biceps as she clung to him, crying harder.

Deafening music screamed through the facility. An explosion of blinding light shot across his corneas. Zahrah curled more—if that was possible—into his arms, and Dean squeezed her securely in his embrace. Half afraid he'd hurt her, but more afraid she'd think he didn't care.

In a way, he was glad for the metal music. Glad for the inability to talk, to reveal his gaping inadequacy. There wasn't anything to say.

How many times had he reminded himself of that? And yet, he wanted to say something—*do* something to make her better.

Idealistic fantasy.

Though he could no longer hear her cries, he felt them in her shuddering diaphragm, bouncing shoulders, and the tears soaking his shirt. Dean drew up his left leg and used it to support her when his arms grew heavy. With no clock and the blinding light, there was no way to gauge how long they sat there. Him propped against the wall, her in his arms.

When the lights snapped off and darkness once again gripped them in its powerful talons, Dean closed his eyes. Attuned to her. To the fact the shudders were spaced between minutes of deafening silence. She'd fallen asleep, he guessed.

And he liked that. Liked that she felt safe enough with him to let down her guard. Liked that he could actually *do* something to give her even a small piece of comfort. Funny how sleeping on a cot or in a sleeping bag now seemed like a luxury when all they had was the floor.

Exhaustion dragged him down a dark hole. So fast that he blinked and once again the lone bulb overhead glowed. He lifted his head off the wall and glanced down at her. Eyes puffing from the earlier crying, lip cut, her cheekbone red and swollen.

"You knew," she said, her voice catching on a dry, parched throat at the end. She shifted, her head tilting back, but she made no effort to climb out of his hold. "You knew what he was going to do."

Dean gritted his teeth, remembering that leering look. Hated that she was right—he did know, and there wasn't a thing he could've done to stop it.

"I think"—she shuddered—"I've known since the first time I saw him." She drew in a ragged breath. "Just as I knew the first time I saw you that I'm safe with you. That you'd protect me."

Ineptitude squirmed against her declaration. "But I didn't. Couldn't."

Zahrah pushed up, her hand on the ground to his left. "You nearly killed yourself trying."

Breathing burned. "I *failed*."

"Dean," Zahrah said, her hand on his chest now. "You did everything you could."

He looked away.

"God put you in here to keep me going."

"God." He hated his condescension, but the anger at God for letting Zahrah get raped seared his better judgment. "A lot of good He did while that man—"Jaw clamped, he bit down on the words. Shifted direction. "How you can even mention God at this—?"

Her battered face glowed with sweat and a little something he didn't understand. Something. . .serene. " 'For none of us lives for ourselves alone, and none of us dies for ourselves alone. If we live, we live for the Lord; and if we die, we die for the Lord. So, whether we live or die, we belong to the Lord.'"

There she went again with that faith he couldn't fight. "You're one of the best people I know. Why would He let you be here, get raped and beaten?"

Zahrah's gaze slid down. "I. . .I don't know." She looked sad, grieved.

Dean felt like a jerk for even talking about this. "I'm sorry."

She smiled and looked down again. "I. . .I don't understand, and yes—I'm hurt, maybe even crushed." Her lip quivered. "But Dean, He gave me something very beautiful in all this, something I couldn't have imagined."

He cut his eyes to her, daring her to sway his opinion with some revelation.

"You."

Dean breathed a snort. "Lot of good I did. Where was God in that?"

"If I got angry with you for not protecting me—would that be fair?"

"Different ball game, Z."

"How?"

"Because—because I'm not all-powerful. I'm not omniscient."

"That's right." She held her piece for a minute. "You're not. So, can you just stop flinging mud at God, who is? Who knows the future, knows what is coming?"

"How can you be so calm—he raped you! I want to rip the guy's throat out, and given half a chance—"

"Calm?" She shook her head. "I'm not calm. I'm—" Her voice pitched. "I'm hurting in ways I never dreamed. He stole something from me I can never get back. I feel dirty and. . ." She shuddered. Blinked away tears—but it didn't work. They slipped free. "God knew what I'd face here. For whatever reason He didn't remove me from this situation. He gave me you." Tears glossed her eyes. "That means. . .so much." She cried more. "Let me. . .let me just enjoy that gift." Tears raced down her bruised cheek. "Please?"

Without thinking, he tugged her closer, and Zahrah collapsed into his embrace once more.

I so don't deserve this. . . .

"Thank you," she whispered, her words strangely warm against the now-chilled tear stain on his shirt.

Hand around the back of her head and arm essentially shielding her, he squeezed. Resisted the urge to kiss the top of her head. But he wanted to. With that came other promises. Ones he couldn't fulfill.

Or could he?

His brain buzzed with the thought. If they got out of here. . .

That wall, that vault where he'd stored his heart sent up a frozen steel barrier, preventing him from exploring those thoughts.

But could it work?

How? She was a missionary teacher. After her resolve just now, he couldn't imagine she'd go back to the States with her tail between her legs. Which meant she'd stay in country.

That might work.

No. He couldn't protect her.

Can't protect her if she's in the States.

"That's not your job, Dean. It belongs to God." Zahrah's words haunted him.

Steel hinges groaned as the door squawked open. In stepped Lee Nianzu. Dean swept Zahrah aside and punched to his feet, defenses and anger drawn.

CHAPTER 47

Somewhere in Afghanistan
26 July

It would do you well not to fight me," Zmaray said, his Chinese accent thickening his words as he held up a hand to Dean.

Hands stretched out behind him, Dean held Zahrah close to him. Like a shield.

She could tell the words had the opposite effect on Dean.

"Miss Zarrick." Zmaray's almond-shaped eyes came to her, spiking her pulse. "I apologize for the awful things Kamran did in my absence." He seemed to pout. "Perhaps this would not have happened, had you agreed to cooperate. Because that would mean we'd be elsewhere."

"Bull!" Dean charged.

Zmaray, faster than a strike of lightning, whipped up and around, and drove his heel into Dean's chest. He flew backward. A crack echoed through the room. He braced himself, shook his head, which had hit the wall, then crouched, ready to stop Zmaray.

In the space of the two seconds it took for Dean to pounce, Zahrah saw it. Saw the fanatical determination to get out of here. To stop at nothing to free them. To protect her, even if meant his own death. But then, where would she be? Alone?

Zahrah lunged forward. "Dean. Stop!" His mad fury scared her. She moved into his path, holding up her hands. "Please."

He barreled into her.

Zahrah held on, pushing back. "Please, please, Dean."

His touch to her back was warm, protective. Absently, he looked at her. "You hurt her again—"

"Dean." She kept her voice quiet, touched his face, once again bringing his gaze to hers. "It's okay."

"No. No it's not." To Zmaray, he snarled, "You act without honor, Nianzu. No matter what you say—if you cannot control your men, even in your absence, then you have no honor, no respect."

"Miss Zarrick." Zmaray's voice cracked like a whip.

"I'll be okay," she said to Dean.

"Z." He caught her hand at the last minute. Tortured hazel eyes held hers, hard and fast. It felt an eternity as he stood there, staring into her eyes. As if he wanted to say something. Again, his gaze struck Zmaray. Then hers. "You're the strongest woman I know. Stay strong."

Heart quickened by his words, she nodded. Turned and shuffled out of the cell. The clanking of the locks and the thud of the door brushed a cold chill down her spine. She glanced back, the emptiness of being separated from Dean acute.

A guard poked her in the back with his weapon.

Zahrah followed Zmaray to a room where he'd set up the system. He strolled to the table as if this were a walk in the park. He circled the table, his hand coming to rest on the tamperproof box. Hip propped against the table, he eyed her and smiled, his eyes narrowing closed. "I'm afraid things have become a bit dark for you here."

Zahrah lifted her chin and locked her gaze on the blackened window across the room.

"You are a very intelligent woman to have such an advanced degree, to understand things I cannot begin to comprehend." Zmaray came to the front and slumped back against the table, sitting on it with his hands on either side, so he was almost perfectly within her line of sight now.

She kept her gaze above his hairline.

"But what I cannot comprehend is how a woman with a gentle heart like yours can knowingly commit brutal acts against those you love."

Zahrah frowned. "What?"

A howl erupted from somewhere in the prison, the sound scraping down her spine like a cold blade. A gargling scream followed next.

Though she knew it's what Zmaray wanted and she shouldn't, Zahrah looked over her shoulder. Visualized back down the hall, to the right, to the left. . .Dean.

"He must be punished for killing my men, for fighting back. We will break him."

Zahrah swung her attention back to the Chinese man. *"Stay strong."* Dean's admonishment flooded her senses. Zmaray was saying things to sway her willingness to cooperate.

"I thought you might doubt me." He returned to the other side of the table, tapped in a few keystrokes, and then turned the monitor around. With one finger, he pushed a button. Sound drenched the room. Hands back in his pockets, he watched.

Zahrah didn't. She refused to.

"I've told them to break his fingers. One. . .by. . .one." Though she wasn't looking right at him, she could tell he was smiling. "I'm afraid they got a little carried away, it seems."

Her gaze betrayed her.

Arms stretched out in front, tied across a table, Dean strained not to scream. Not to howl. Even at the distance the camera stood back, the veins on his temples were visibly bulging. His face red. Spittle along the sides of his mouth as he gritted through the torture. The emblazoned wings on his back seemed especially pronounced in the video feed. *"He shall give his angels charge over you. . . ."*

A hammer swung down. *Crack! Thud!* Blended with his mangled cry.

Zahrah flinched. Bile rose in her throat, the crushing of his bones ringing in her ears.

"See? I knew you were not calloused the way Kamran said." Zmaray again returned to the front, where he sat beside the monitor. "This man who held you with such tenderness after you were brutalized—you see him in pain and already you're crying."

Zahrah's hand went to her cheek, startled to discover he was right.

"How much can you stand, Miss Zarrick? All you have to do is help us unlock the network. Just a few hours' work to buy his freedom, your freedom." He folded his arms. "I think you know the time is drawing near to find a compromise, yes?"

He stood and crossed the room to her. Stood before her, almost eye to eye. His spiced cologne tickled her nose. Or maybe it was the hair gel that smoothed back his hair. "In the cell, you saw that Captain Watters has lost his focus. He is in a rage. He does not think clearly. Your hope for escape, which solely depended on him"—he lifted her hand and unfurled her fingers—"now rests solely in your delicate fingers, Miss Zarrick."

It sounded like he was offering her a way out, a way to save Dean. "That's what evil men say—'do what we want and you can go free.'" She tried to keep her voice steady. "But then they kill you anyway."

"You are far more valuable to me alive."

What he didn't say was more alarming that what he did say. "What about Dean?"

He studied her face, intense and fierce. Muddy-brown eyes drilling holes through her crumbling strength and already glinting with victory he'd ripped from her hands. From Dean's.

He lifted a shoulder in a lazy shrug. "He is becoming a problem."

"You've tortured us, deprived us of nutrition—"

"And yet you're killing guards who are merely doing their job."

"Merely doing—"

"It does not look good for the captain, Miss Zarrick. I cannot guarantee his safety when he so willingly incites violence." Terse words belied his calm expression. "But we are here to discuss you." He motioned to her hands. "You hold the power."

"To what?"

"To change. . .everything. To save yourself. To save the man you love."

CHAPTER 48

Somewhere in Afghanistan
28 July

Pain pushed Dean in and out of consciousness. Broken fingers throbbed against his need for sleep—anything to mute the agony. Braced by two walls in a corner, he tried to stay awake. Tried to fight the fog of deprivation and his body's need to shut down so it could preserve and heal.

But Zahrah...

Noise outside the doors drew Dean straight. Forearm up, he braced it against his chest. Steeled himself as the door swung open.

Two guards rushed in, weapons aimed at him. They shouted in Pashto, "Get down! Down. On your knees."

The urge to fight filled him. No way would he bow any more knees to them.

Nostrils flared, Dean flattened his lips and felt the pinch of torn flesh. Trained to fight ambidextrously, he was stronger, faster, more accurate with his right. But he could still incapacitate with his left. And if that's what it took—

"Down!"

Dean stood.

A shout from outside tangled with the guards inside, the ones afraid of Dean. The ones demanding submission.

Zahrah stepped into view.

Dean stilled. Swayed as the guards backed out, changing places with Zahrah. The door shut. Even as the locks were engaging, Zahrah came to him. "Are you okay?" She flew right into his arms. No hesitation.

It felt good. Very good. He crushed her to himself and breathed deeply of her, relieved she wasn't hurt more. Relieved she was back. "Fine. You?"

Zahrah's gaze hit his arm and widened. "Your hand!"

Dean cupped her face. "Hey." But her attention was still glued to his swollen and shattered limb. He crouched so she'd look him in the eyes. "Hey, it's okay. I'll be okay. We'll get out of here."

The words seemed to tug more grief out of her.

"We will. I'll make sure."

After a faint nod, one in which she didn't look at him, she motioned to their corner, the spot they'd occupied together for many days and weeks. "Sit. You're hurt."

"I think we're beyond that." But he relented. Spine to the stone wall, he slid down, using his left hand as a guide. Zahrah's light touch never left his back and upper arm. Strange, how much comfort he drew from that simple gesture.

Sitting shoulder to shoulder, as had become their habit, Zahrah tore off a length of her tunic. And another.

"Keep doing that, you won't have much left."

"Is that a smile I hear in your voice?"

The laugh barely made it across his windpipe.

She worked the two ends into a knot. "Here." She scooted around to face him, legs bent underneath her. Motioning him closer, she said, "Lean forward."

Ah. A sling. A smile cracked his dark mood. Now who was taking care of whom?

Zahrah pushed up on her knees, leaning in to look behind him. Her cool, soft hands touched and teased the back of his neck. Dean closed his eyes as she worked. This wasn't something to enjoy.

She sat once more. "Not the best, but it'll do for now."

Floored at the way she tended him, worried over him, Dean adjusted the knot so it didn't rub the back of his neck. "It's great. Thanks." The trembling from holding his arm in place so movement didn't jar it eased.

It was weird—a good weird—to have her doting over him. Felt like. . .he wasn't sure what. Other than good. He hadn't had anyone take care of him since Sergeant Elliott's wife.

She shifted back into place, leaning against him. Dean drew up his legs and let his left arm dangle over them. Blood and scabs marred his knuckles. But at least he could feel his fingers. He'd need his right digits set or they'd heal wrong.

Quiet draped over them like a wool blanket. When would the lights go out again? Or the blaring music? Or blinding floodlights erupt? Meant to force him to remain vigilant and tense, the psychological torture had nothing on remembering when Kamran took Zahrah.

"He made me watch them breaking your fingers."

Dean snapped his gaze to hers. Even with the hacksaw hair job, she was beautiful. Strong. More than he could've imagined for a softhearted person like her. She loved people, cared for them, sacrificed for them.

Staring at the ground in front of them, she didn't move.

The toll of the last few weeks had spit and scratched her face, leaving indelible marks. Her olive complexion now seemed pale, sallow. A weight darkened her eyes. In his gut, something churned. A fear, one he'd known far too well. "Z." He gave his shoulder a bounce, gently lifting her head. "You okay?"

She bobbed her head lightly. "Do you know the story of Corrie ten Boom?"

Blinking, Dean tried to switch gears with her topic change. "Yeah. Sure. Who doesn't? Sergeant Elliott showed us the movie at the rec center."

Brown eyes peered up at him. "Sergeant Elliott?"

Dean sniffed. "Yeah. He's the reason I wanted to be in Special Forces. He'd served in Vietnam, then became a cop when he got back. The night my brother killed my parents, Sergeant Elliott was the first responder on the scene. He pulled me out of the hamper." Dean shook off the heaviness of that memory. "He became my mentor, even in the foster system."

"So, he was strong."

With a snort, Dean nodded. "You could say that."

"Like the ten Booms. They were so strong." She sighed. "So grounded in their faith. Was Sergeant Elliott a man of faith?"

He grinned. "Beat me with the Bible every chance he got." Dean laughed. "Seriously—he is the reason I'm not a total screwup now. I gave him grief and heartache. But he saw something in me."

"I see it, too—and I'm so thankful God put that man in your life. And Casper ten Boom, Corrie's father, saw something in the Jews worth saving—that God loved them. He wore the Jewish star band even though he wasn't Jewish. He once said he'd count it a high honor to die saving God's ancient people."

Her obsession with the ten Booms both worried and amused him. Worried because most of the ten Booms didn't have a happy ending. Amused because her tenacity wouldn't let her stop talking about it until she made her point. And she must have one because she wasn't letting go.

"They saved about eight hundred lives in the course of their efforts. Every day, knowing it could be their last. And for three of the four ten Booms, it would be." She tilted her head, chopped hair cute in a rebellious-girl kind of way like Desi had done as soon as she entered the foster system.

But rebellious wasn't Zahrah. She had too much sense for that. Dean pushed his mind around the pain in his arm and focused on Zahrah. Something was different. Wrong.

She peered up at him. "Did you know it was a clerical mistake that caused Corrie to survive? A mistake? No, it was a miracle from God."

He agreed, but something. . . "Z, what's this about?"

She slipped her hand beneath his arm and hooked it with her own. "It hurt me—really hurt—to watch you being tortured." Her words sounded distant. Stiff, as if hard to say. "It ripped my heart out."

Dean slid his arm around her shoulder, and she burrowed into his side. He cringed, a newly cracked bruise screeching against her weight. Dean gritted his teeth, not caring. Something was happening here. Something. . .not right. "I'm sorry. I know that feeling."

"I'm not sure I can handle it again." A warm, wet tear hit his upper arm. "Japan."

"What?"

"You know, some theorize that had Japan not bombed Pearl Harbor, America might not have entered the war in time to save England." She shook her head and sighed. "Can you imagine if Britain had fallen?"

"Z, you lost me. A lot of people lost their lives in that attack. Why are we talking about Japan?"

"I know. It was awful." She tugged her arm free. Sat there for agonizing minutes, staring down at her lap. But her eyes were on a race to some unseen finish line. "If. . ." She lifted her chin and looked right into his eyes. Those brown orbs of her so rich, so creamy like his favorite Toblerone chocolate. But melted. "If we got separated—"

"We won't."

"But if they do separate us," she said, angling toward him. She was on that race again—this time the course was his face.

Dean's pulse skipped a beat. "I won't let them."

She touched his cheek as her gaze roamed his features. "If we got separated, if somehow they took one of us. . ."

This was wrong. "Z, what—what did he say to you? What happened? Did he threaten you?"

"Would you find me, Dean?"

"I'd die trying!" He caught her waist, holding her close, his own heart thundering at the dark and dizzying conversation.

"Please—don't die." She placed her cold fingers on either side of his face, a tear slipping free from glossy eyes. Her lower lip trembled. "I don't have poppies."

He couldn't laugh. Something about this strangled his mind and his breathing. "Z—"

"I love you, Dean."

"Stop. Stop talking like this."

Zahrah smiled through her tears, her chin puckering with the grief that ripped through her beautiful face. "I saw strength in you that first day. Something so similar to what my father has, to the courage that enabled him to command thousands. You have that same strength. I knew it then. I think I even loved you that first day at the school when you took Rashid in your arms."

Dean shook his head. "Zahrah, listen to me—"

Instead, she leaned in, her eyes trained on his mouth, and kissed him.

Panic detonated in his chest. But—oh man. She tasted good. Sweet. Soft. Dean's heart crashed—*wrong! Something's wrong!* "Zahrah." He eased back.

"Find me," she whispered. Then stood.

Dean caught her hands. "Zahrah, what's going on? What's this about?" He couldn't let himself believe they'd broken her. Not now.

She touched his fingers. Turned and walked to the door. Rapped three times. "I'm ready."

Oh crap! Dean jumped to his feet. Stumbled. Pain in his side shoved him into the wall. His broken hand hit the cement. He cried out.

The door opened and Zahrah stepped out.

"Zahrah!" He lunged. "Don't do this! It's wrong—they'll kill everyone."

Steel slammed in his face.

"Zahrah!" His pulse jackknifed through the realization. *She's sacrificing herself!*

CHAPTER 49

Somewhere in Afghanistan
29 July

B egin." Zmaray pointed to the table where the computer waited.

Zahrah stood, hands clasped and an ocean of terror before her. "As I told you," she said, feeling the shudder of her grief sifting her courage. "I will not begin until you show me absolute proof that Dean is alive and back with his team."

His cheek muscle twitched. Anger. She'd seen it before. "Is it not enough that you saw them remove him alive?"

Peace flooded her, knowing she had the power now. He wanted her help. She could give it. But not until she saw Dean living and breathing on American-held ground. "No." She nodded toward the table. "Besides, what I need is not here."

He stalked toward her, his face red. His hand flew swift and hard.

Zahrah stumbled back from the blow across her face. Dazed, she shielded her face. But just as swift, she knew she was still in control. More in control that Zmaray. She'd angered him, which showed she'd hit a nerve. Angry because he no longer had control.

"Kamran!"

Zahrah sucked in a breath at the name. Then held it as booted feet thudded closer.

"I would remind you, Miss Zarrick." Zmaray moved back to the other side of the table, wiping his hands on a linen pocket napkin he'd extracted from his silk gray suit. "Control is an illusion. I may have granted your request to return Captain Watters, but I give no guarantees of your safety or well being until you"—he motioned to the computer—"fulfill your obligation."

Kamran stood over her, pressing into her personal space.

Swallowing, Zahrah kept her gaze on the Asian. "I will do what you ask, but not under threat of violence. I have asked for one thing—

reassurance that Captain Watters is alive and with his team."

"I am not an American soldier. I cannot walk in and take a picture—"

"You got this computer." It felt like breathing underwater, what with Zmaray's anger and Kamran's imposing presence. "Surely you can manage to take a picture of him, alive. *Clearly* alive. Then I need better equipment to analyze and break down the encryption, to stop the box from self-destructing."

"You could have told me this before."

True, she could've. But this served to delay, to evade the end game, which was her hacking and possibly bringing down the entire military network. Compromising the lives of not only the American military, but also America herself. But she saved Dean. At least, she hoped she had. And that he'd understand what she'd been trying to tell him.

Please. . .find me, Dean. Before it's too late. Before they make me do this. . .

—⁂—

Patrol Base Jaker, Nawa-I-Barakzayi, Afghanistan

Whoosh!

Glaring white seared his corneas. Dean grimaced and ducked. Dean squinted rapidly, trying to force his eyes to adjust.

The Marine frowned at him as several others gathered around, business ends of their weapons aimed at Dean's head, then pointed to the tape as if asking permission.

Dean nodded and his body swayed. He jerked straight. Then his body pulled him backward. Dizzy. . .he was dizzy.

The Marine ripped off the tape.

After the moment of prickling fire, Dean stretched his jaw. "Watters. . ." *Breathe.*

"He needs water!" a grunt shouted.

"No." Dean shook his head. Wet his lips. "Watters, Dean. . . Patrick. . .Captain." His vision was ghosting. "Four f–four—" His body surrendered.

—⁂—

"Dean?"

The voice sounded a thousand miles away, a gargle of noise beneath a thick gray fog. Dean swam through it, searching for the voice. "Where. . .?"

"You there, Watterboy?"

The familiar old nickname tugged him to the surface. He blinked a few times. Face swooned in and out of focus.

"Sleeping on the job, eh, Cap'n?"

"Hawk." Dean wanted to smile at the guy's jab, but speaking was harder than he thought. The name caught at the back of his throat. His eyes finally adjusted and he found himself surrounded by the team. In a hospital room.

"They got a tube in your mouth." Falcon explained.

"Guess they got tired of you yelling, too." Hawk never stopped. "Eagle went to the get the nurse."

Dean blinked. Eagle's back?

A nurse returned with Todd Archer, who gave him a nod of greeting.

"Captain Watters," the nurse said. "I'm going to remove the feeding tube. If you'll sit up," she said, taking hold of his left hand and tugging him upright. "Now, don't fight it."

"Don't fight?" Falcon sniggered. "That's all that guy does."

The tube came up, burning and inciting his gag reflex. Finally free of the tube, he coughed. His throat burned.

"Here," the nurse said. "Sip this slowly."

Dean nodded, easing back against the bed. Soft bed. Pillow. Luxuries compared to what he and— "Zahrah." Chest seizing with the memory of what she'd done, he tried to sit forward.

"Oy, easy there." Titanis moved in and held Dean back. "You were severely dehydrated and undernourished, with quite a mangled hand."

Dean glanced down at the temporary cast that ensconced his right forearm and fingers. "We have to get her back."

Falcon's dark eyes intensified. "What do you know?"

"Yes," came the booming voice of General Burnett. "Tell us what you know."

"Give the guy a break," Eagle said. "He just—"

"How's Zahrah?" Her father. Right behind Burnett. Eyes ignited with a lethal cocktail of fear and anger. No doubt ticked Dean had returned without Zahrah, which shot him up with fear that she wasn't alive.

"She's alive—or was." He grabbed the bed remote and raised the head so he was sitting upright.

"Why'd they throw you back?" Zarrick glared.

"I think. . .I think that was her doing." Dean tried to think through it all. "I think she made a deal."

"You telling me she turned traitor?"

Dean snapped his gaze to her father. "No, sir. Far from it. They tortured me and made her watch. I think she was afraid they'd kill me."

"So you're saying she's weak."

"I'm saying she's stronger than I ever realized. She asked me, right before she walked out of the cell, what I'd do if we got separated."

"So they kept you in the same cell?"

Dean looked at Burnett then he nodded. Prayed he didn't betray anything other than an affirmation. And that Burnett wouldn't ask what happened. Details of their torture.

"Go on."

"She wanted to know if I'd find her. I said I would. That's what she wanted—to know I'd die trying to find her. She's buying time, I think." Dean's heart thumped, echoing in the machine rigged to the finger cuff. "We have to go after her. Stop them before they force her to hack the network."

"So you know where she is, where they held you?"

The adrenaline bottomed out like a massive sinkhole beneath his desperation. "No." His mind scrambled for purchase on this tricky ground. "But—those men dropped me off from the back of a truck. That means it had to be within driving distance of the base. Wherever they're holding her, it can't be far." Dean swung his legs over the edge of the bed.

"Whoa, Cap'n," Hawk said. "I'm glad to see you, but there's only so much I *want* to see."

Gaping dressing gown. Dean stilled, testing his body. Searching for pain. Other than throbbing fingers and head. . . "I need clothes."

"I think you need to hold up for the docs to clear you," Falcon added.

"Then get them in here. She's on her own, and those guys aren't withholding any tactics to get what they want."

"You sure she didn't already break?"

"I think she broke, but not in the way I—or any of us—expected. She didn't go crazy. She became more focused. More strategic."

"That's my girl."

Dean eyed the beaming general. What would he do when he found out she'd been raped and beaten?

"We need to talk to cybersecurity guys. Find out how fast someone like Double Z can crack the code." Legs spread shoulder-width apart, Hawk folded his arms over his chest.

Falcon nodded. "I'm thinking it won't be long."

Hawk rubbed his clean-shaven jaw. "I mean, I could do it in a day or two, but she's got that advanced degree, so. . ."

"They need to know there was a tamperproof box at the prison." Dean eyed the team. Man, it was good to be back. Even if he was minus a hand and weak. "So she might've already made some progress."

A uniformed doctor entered, glancing around, and hesitated.

"We're on a timetable. Can't afford to lose time." Dean frowned. Looked at the guys. "How long have I been in here anyway?"

"Just a few hours."

"Good." Dean stayed there, his arm threaded to an IV and monitors still probing his vitals.

Hawk clapped a hand on the doc's shoulder, pitching him forward. "Sign him out, Doc. We got lives to save!"

CHAPTER 50

Sub-base Schwarzburg, Camp Marmal
Mazar-e Sharif, Balkh Province
30 July—05.30 Hours

One eye black and blue. The other morphing from purple to green and still swollen. His once-split lip patched with an angry red hue around the stitches. Right forearm in a short cast with three fingers casted as well, all dangling from a sling.

Watters stood at the table, staring at a map. The guy had run the gamut and returned changed. Not just the bloodied and broken body. He hoped the guy could get his head back in the game.

Lance joined him. Stared down the detailed map of the area, complete with known structures and hotbeds. "Anything familiar?"

With a sigh, Watters shook his head. "They didn't take us far from the cell. She talked about going upstairs, but whether that was ground level or a second story, I couldn't tell. They kept me down, out of sight. No windows save a high, narrow one."

"What about walls?" An analyst sat opposite the table, fingers poised over the keyboard.

"Half stone, half cement. It felt damp and hot. Not scorching, but enough that we knew it was a scorcher outside."

Russo joined them, knuckles on the table. "That's just about every building in a fifty-mile radius."

Watters huffed and pinched the bridge of his nose.

"There's gotta be something that stuck out."

"No. They were deliberate about keeping us in the dark—literally. Except when they blinded us with light." Watters traced the lines of the map. "I was taken out of the cell, down a hall and to the right where they beat me."

"You keep saying *cells*." Lieutenant Hastings emerged from the sidelines. "Was it really a cell, or just a room with a barred door?"

"I don't know. Something with several rooms, but they're all barred."

"So, maybe a converted building."

"Yeah. . .maybe." Watters's gaze bounced around the maps and possibilities, as if trying to recall something. "Zahrah said there was a big, open area upstairs—she called it a gaping hole."

Hastings moved with purpose. "Since you went missing, we've been working round the clock on possible holding locations. There's an old clothing factory here, and a school here."

"Not a school. Layout's wrong—not designed for flow."

Russo thumped the spot where the factory had been marked. "So the clothing factory?"

Watters seemed to hesitate.

"What're you thinking, son?" Lance sensed the burden the guy carried.

"If we're wrong—it's hours wasted." His gaze roved the map, the options. "But I don't have any better ideas."

"Uh, guys?"

Watters and Russo turned toward Black, who hadn't spoken or engaged on this planning session. He held up a piece of paper. "Just came in on the fax."

Lance took it. Stilled. "Is this some kind of joke? Where'd it come from?"

"Don't know. Fax just spit it out."

Watters frowned and nodded toward the paper. "What is it?"

"It's an address." Lance tossed it to Watters. "For the factory."

"We're not buying this, are we?" Watters scowled as he looked up from the paper. "How the heck did they know. . . ?" His gaze skidded around the room.

Lance glanced around, too, feeling hairy spiderlike legs skittering up his neck. The mole. But only the team was here. "Get your team and head out to the factory."

"But—"

"Now, Captain." Lance tugged out his phone as he glared at Watters.

Ticked, Watters seemed to finally get the hint. "Suit up!" He started for the doors.

Lance waited till the men left then walked to the door, flipped the lock, and lifted the phone to his ear. "Hastings, get me a sweep team." To the half-dozen service members in the briefing room, he met each of their gazes.

"All right, people. Settle in. It's going to be a long night." Which one had betrayed them? Who would face charges of treason against the United States? He set his hand on his holster. "Nobody's leaving till I'm satisfied and we have a mole strung up."

CHAPTER 51

Balkh Province, Afghanistan
30 July—1720 Hours

What do you think?"

Dusk huddled over the structure that was neither familiar nor unfamiliar. In fact, it looked like a dozen other structures Raptor had entered or passed during missions. Abandoned, in disrepair. "I don't know. I was kept belowground."

"Then let's go belowground," Falcon said.

"Hooah." Dean nodded to the team and resisted the urge to remind them of everything they'd discussed en route: They'd hacked off her hair, and the man they'd ID'd as Nianzu on the video was her captor. All others should be held for questioning if Zahrah wasn't found.

Heat and humidity chased them out of the MRAP and down the eerily empty street. Falcon had point, with Hawk behind him.

"Cameras on." Hastings's voice came through the staticky coms.

Dean reached up and activated his helmet cam. "Raptor Six Actual."

"Copy that, Raptor Six."

As they stacked up by a main door, the others followed suit with the cams. DIA and CID wanted as much intel as they could gather without getting their hands dirty. That was fine with Dean—less people in the way. If he hadn't been here—wherever "here" was—he'd be back watching from the other side of the monitor.

"Going in," Falcon said.

Parking lot vacant, doors hanging at angles, half-blown walls. None of it familiar. But he hadn't been topside, except maybe when they dragged him in—unconscious.

Positioned at the rear, Dean held his M9 up. Heartbeat whooshing in his hears, he prayed—*begged*—God to let this be it. Let them find Zahrah. Get her back alive, safe, unharmed, no more than she had been when she walked out of that cell.

They streamed into the darkened halls. The thick air told him there'd been no circulation in here for a while. He waited, itching to be active the way Falcon and Hawk were as the leads on this mission. Cursed Kamran for disarming him, almost literally, and breaking his hand. Didn't matter. They were trained to use both hands, so breaking one wouldn't disable the operator. Besides, he sure wasn't going to let a fracture stop him from completing this mission.

Three rooms were cleared as Dean waited in the hall, watching the main entry point, listening, attuned to the movement of his team.

"Clear."

A tap on his shoulder told them they were moving farther in. Dean pivoted and trailed the guys through a set of double doors. To the right, a hall presented itself. Straight ahead, a half-dozen more doors.

Falcon led the team to the right, clearing the rooms one after another. Dean trailed them as they moved, fluid. Swift. Room one. . .

They'd find her. He couldn't lose that thought, that hope. She was counting on him. *"I love you, Dean."*

He tripped.

Hawk eyeballed him as they made egress. "You okay?"

Dean nodded. He'd heard what she said but hadn't *heard*. Until now. Burdened with a sudden responsibility to honor what she felt, to honor *her*, Dean vowed he would find her. *God, You know where she is, and she believes in You—and your plan—resolutely. Let me be a part of that plan. Let me find her.*

He turned the corner, the other five still moving without hesitation. As he took a step toward the first room, his gaze struck a steel door. No sign. A broken knob. But what really snagged his attention were the parallel lines in the dirty floor leading beneath the door. Drag marks.

Dean waited as the team moved to the next door then eased closer to the barrier. Stood on the drag marks. His heart galloped. "Found something," he whispered into his coms.

Hawk and Falcon were on him in seconds, and in their eyes he saw that they understood. The team stacked up, everyone knowing they could open the door and it could blow. Or they could face a dozen armed gunmen. Or. . .emptiness.

Falcon fingered the knob. Twisted. . .

The door eased open.

Falcon nodded to Hawk. Then flung it open. Hawk rushed into the open area and cleared it. "Stairs," he whispered.

Heart in his throat, Dean stepped forward. A gust of warm, stale air hit him. Flooded his senses with memories, and alarm. "This is it." Adrenaline spiraled through him, his heart pounding and begging for a good ending.

They hustled down the stairs, expecting with every step for someone to move into the open. Shoot.

When they didn't, each step grew more ominous. What he wouldn't do to have his M4 in hand. They stacked up at a corner. Dean strained to hear a sound. A step. Crunch of boots. Chatter. A hinge squawking as they'd done when he was here less than twenty-four hours ago.

Hawk and Falcon turned the corner, pieing out to cover them as Harrier and Titanis moved in. Eagle right behind him then Dean. As he stepped into the new corridor, a cold rush of dread spilled down his back. This was definitely the right place. But it was dark. Empty. Abandoned.

Resisting the urge to rush past the men, cast off the life-saving clearing procedures, Dean eyed the cell. "First door, left."

Hawk looked at him. Stilled.

"That's the cell."

Falcon and Hawk took up position. Breached. The others flooded in. Dean couldn't move, afraid she was there. Dead.

"Clear," Hawk said, still in the cell.

Pulling in a ragged breath, Dean nodded to himself. She wasn't here. Good and bad. He crossed the threshold. Searched the shadows. Beams of light from the guy's shoulder lamps bounced and bobbed. Dean aimed his at the corner where they always sat. Where she'd professed her love then walked out as the sacrificial lamb.

"You're sure this was it?"

Stunned to find it empty, Dean nodded. "Yes."

As the others searched the building, Dean couldn't leave the cell. Couldn't shake the memories. The time with her. The thought of never seeing her again. He crouched against a wall, staring at the last spot they'd occupied together. Part of him still wanted to throttle her. Together they had a chance. Now. . .now it was all multiple guess.

She'd placed an incredible trust on his shoulders, believing he could find her. Believing he had what it took to get her back before it was too late.

So get moving, soldier!

"Captain."

Dean came off the wall and followed Hawk out of the cell.

"Found another flight of stairs." Hawk hustled up the flight of steps. "Team found just what you described—the gaping hole."

At the top of the stairs and to Dean's left, a platform of sorts just ended. Beyond it lay a cavernous room. "The factory floor."

"Nobody's here," Falcon said as he emerged from a room where a table sat.

"*. . .a computer on a table. . .*" The words Zahrah had spoken pulled him into the room. He walked the circumference, imagining her here. His boots crunched—then popped. Dean stepped back and lifted his boot to see what he'd stepped on. Something blue peeked up at him. He crouched and reached for it, stilling halfway there.

Turquoise. The bead was from Zahrah's bracelet that Rashid had given her the day at the funeral.

"Find something?" Hawk asked.

"A bead," Dean said, straightening.

"Double Z had a bracelet like that—the kid gave it to her after the funeral, right?"

Dean glared at Hawk.

Hands up, Hawk chuckled. "I was there the same day you were."

A door groaned and then thumped.

Hawk frowned.

Dean spun to the dirty window. Smashed his casted arm into one of the square panes. Outside, someone raced across the field toward a vehicle. "Got a rabbit!"

"Step back," Eagle said as he swung his sniper rifle into position at the window.

"We need him alive!"

CHAPTER 52

Balkh Province

Falcon and Hawk sprinted out of the room.

Eagle didn't falter. Two large, powerful strides carried him away from the door as he simultaneously took aim.

Seconds fell off the clock as Dean backed toward the exit, not willing to leave Eagle alone, but also not willing to lose the only person who could tell them where they'd taken Zahrah.

Crack!

A scream racked the air.

"Let's go," Dean shouted.

Eagle swung around and they both bolted down the hall. A glare of light streaked down the hall from the left. Dean chased it, breaking into the open in what felt like a heartbeat.

Dust plumed like a halo around a tangle of bodies.

"He's hit," Hawk said with a grunt.

Harrier sprinted toward them, already shrugging off his pack as he ran. He slid into them.

By the time Dean reached them, Harrier had a tourniquet around the leg of the man, who was laid out, tears streaming down his face as he reached toward his maimed leg that was missing a hunk of flesh.

Holstering his weapon, Dean glanced at Eagle.

Eagle gave a one-shouldered shrug. "He's alive."

On a knee, Dean leaned over the local. "Where did they take the woman?" he asked in Pashto.

Face screwed tight in pain, the man shook his head, crying.

Dean grabbed his collar. "Where is the girl?"

"They—" Arching backward, he gave a bloodcurdling scream. Then passed out.

Disgusted, ticked, and just plain exhausted, Dean stood. He shuffled toward the rusted-out Ford nearby. Kicked the fender. Kicked the tire. Every opportunity ripped out from under him. Every chance to succeed, he'd been defeated. Whatever chessboard God was up there playing with, Dean wanted to topple it. He bit down on a curse.

He got a good look at the guy from this angle and recognized him. "He was one of the guards." In fact, Dean remembered—this guy had been the one who brought Zahrah back after they'd hacked off her hair. "Let's get him back to the base. If we can get him drugged up, he might talk."

"How long do we have if she's cooperating?"

"She's not," Dean snapped.

On a knee, Hawk secured their prisoner's hands. "I'm not a cyber-geek, but I imagine no more than twenty-four hours."

—∞—

Camp Marmal, Mazar-e Sharif

Todd walked the hall of the sub-base command building. Though he'd been back a week, run a mission with the team, and it felt good and right, he still felt. . .off. He'd written up his AAR and submitted it. The routine of it all helped him not to think.

But then—if he didn't think of Amy, she'd vanish.

Before he knew what he'd done, Todd stood at the counter of Cup of Joe and asked for a coffee. With vanilla. Oh, and ice.

"You mean a latte?"

Todd hesitated. Was that right? Amy'd always ordered for him. "Sure."

A few minutes later, he crossed the base and headed back to the tent where Raptor bunked. Even before he entered, he noticed Dean lying on his cot. Todd tried to walk quietly, knowing the captain needed rest. The dark circles, bruises, cuts, broken bones—he'd been through a lot. And still went on that mission. Conducted himself as a true soldier, though a haunted one.

Dean didn't move. Maybe he actually managed to fall asleep.

Todd set the drink down on the ground and removed his vest and tactical shirt. A shower would be good about now.

"Sorry about Amy. She deserved better than dying like that."

Todd stilled then looked to his captain's cot. "That she did."

Still on his back, eyes closed, Dean still wasn't moving.

"Thanks."

"The team would've been there. . ."

"No worries. It was how she wanted it—quiet and family only. She was always like that, ya know, quiet and beautiful. But that girl could beat me three ways from Sunday without a word." Todd snorted then flinched. He must sound sappy. "Reckon that's TMI."

"No." Dean drew himself off the cot and sat on the edge, broken arm resting on his knee, eyeing something in his left hand. "No, it's not. A month ago, I would've said I couldn't imagine a loss like that. . ." He coughed into his hand. "Anyway, have they gotten anything out of the factory guard?"

"Doubt it," Todd said. "He was in surgery last I heard."

"You did good out there, nailing his leg like that."

What was with this talk? Dean wasn't himself. Had the days of captivity done a number on his mind? "Hey," Todd began as he eased onto his own cot. "What's this about?"

Dean closed his hand around whatever he held and bounced his fist. "She's out there." He shook his head. "And I have no idea where. They won't let me in the command bunker—told me to rest. I told them I could sleep when I'm dead."

Todd waited. Didn't seem right to talk just then. The captain had a weight to get off his chest.

He opened his hand and the small blue bracelet bead rolled around his palm. "She put her life in my hands, and I'm just. . .sitting here."

"Would doing nothin' for no justified reason make you feel better?"

Dean met his gaze evenly. Angrily.

Todd held up his hands, feeling like that'd do as much good as staring down an angry prized bull. "I get your pain. You can't be there, you can't do the one thing her life depends on—go after her. But you've been through a lot, and if you aren't rested up and got your strength back when we do know where to go, you'll be in no shape to lead the mission."

Dean lifted his broken arm. "Already there."

"Dean?" He waited till the captain looked him in the eye. "What is this—did they get to you, or did she?"

With a snort, Dean smirked. "Both, I guess."

"She mean that much to you?"

He rolled his palm and glanced at the bead again. "I. . .I don't know."

Then he smiled. "You'd like her. The two of you could have a Bible verse contest." His smile twisted into grief and vanished beneath a deep frown. "She was so convinced God wanted her to stay here. When we were in there together, she started talking about Japan and Corrie ten Boom."

Todd chuckled. "How are those connected?"

"I think she was trying to get me to let go of my anger at God over her getting raped."

The words barreled over him. Saw the way they tormented Dean. Felt the rawness of his answer. "God can handle your anger."

Another snort and smile, but this time with only half power. "You keep telling me that. But it doesn't make sense why He'd let someone like her go through all that."

"Dean, if I'm hearing this right, Zahrah put her life in God's hands, correct?"

Barely a nod.

"Just like when you signed up with Uncle Sam, you put your life in the hands of men like General Burnett."

Dean eyed him.

"You signed up for whatever came your way. Bullets, terrorists, IEDs. . .why?"

"To fight for those who can't."

Todd smiled. "Exactly. Zahrah's doing the same."

"Are you saying I can't fight? I think I did a pretty good job."

"You are in a battle that can't be fought with bullets and fists. This is a battle that demands complete surrender."

Dean scowled. "Surrender? I'm not so weak I have to surrender."

"Surrender isn't weakness, Dean. It's showing strength, recognizing the fight is beyond you." Todd scooted to the edge of his seat. "It's a paradox, really, because the act of surrender produces power and victory."

"Dude, if I didn't have the bruises and fractures to prove it, I'd say you're the one who was captured and tortured—right out of your mind."

"Zahrah wanted you to surrender the fight against God, right?"

Dean sagged. "She told me she wasn't a prisoner, that she was right where God wanted her. It was crazy. Like she wasn't afraid."

"That's because surrendered to God, she didn't have anything to fear or anything else to surrender to." Todd felt an infusion of inspiration. "Do you know who William Booth is?"

Dean shrugged.

"The founder of the Salvation Army. He said, 'The greatness of a man's power is the measure of his surrender.'" Todd lifted his latte and took a sip. "There was a song years back, a Christmas song, about a little girl who got fake pearls for Christmas. Then one year her father asked for them back. I don't remember the story exactly, but she wouldn't release the toy ones. Her father had real pearls for her, but until she surrendered the fake ones, he couldn't give her the real ones. Life is just like that—you're fighting so hard to stay in control, to fix things, but I think God has brought you to a place where it's time to surrender."

"Surrender what?"

Todd gave him a sympathetic smile. "Everything."

Dean jerked his gaze down.

"What's in your hand?"

As if he hadn't noticed it before, Dean turned his hand over and revealed a turquoise bead.

"Think maybe God wants you to let go, so you can have the real thing?"

He stared at it, unmoving, silent.

"You're fighting a fight you have no business fighting. If Zahrah gave her life to Christ to serve Him, that's her choice. And it's up to God what He does with that. Just like it's Burnett's choice to send you on a mission that could kill you. Just like it was His choice to free Amy of the pain and disease." Raw at the mention of his sweet wife he'd never see again, Todd took a breather. "When it's the wrong fight, fighting only wears you down."

Quiet reigned before Dean, head tucked, staring at the bead. Held it between his thumb and pointer finger. "I can't just leave her out there."

"I don't think you're supposed to. But I do think you need to get smart and stop blaming yourself and bearing guilt that doesn't belong to you. You said Zahrah put her life in your hands."

"She also said I was the reason she was supposed to be here in Afghanistan."

"Okay, then that means God has a plan."

Dean cut him a look. "I'd sure like that mission briefing about now."

"Then fight like a surrendered man—on your knees."

"You mean pray."

Nodding, Todd smiled. "I mean to say."

Hawk sprinted into the tent. "Factory dude's awake!"

CHAPTER 53

Somewhere in Afghanistan
01 August—1015 Hours

What one plans and what happens are often two very different things. Especially when held at gunpoint. Zahrah slid a glance to her right then her left, where armed guards stood over her. They'd let her sleep through the night—a first in. . .*how many weeks?*

Betraying Dean had been the only way to save him. To save her and—hopefully—the entire military community. Perhaps America herself. That is, if she could stall long enough for Dean to get here.

Could he find her? In the cell, she believed resolutely, with deprivation and hunger gnawing at her insides, that Dean could do it. As an elite warrior, he had the training.

"You've been here since dawn, Miss Zarrick."

Zahrah shifted on the seat, the chains binding her hands clanking. "It might speed my progress were I free"—she tugged the restraints to make her point—"to work without hindrance."

Zmaray stalked between the rows of tables. Zahrah sat at the front. A half-dozen cameras trained on different angles around the box on the table that stared her down. "You have had twelve hours, and. . .what? What have you accomplished?"

"Besides raw wrists," she said, hiding her fear behind the frustration of being chained to the task. "I believe I am close to unlocking the mechanism."

"You've had twelve hours!"

"And your team has had"—she squinted at him—"how long have they been working on this again? And nobody's cracked it?" She had to play her card, the only one she had over him. "You haven't proven to me that Dean is alive and with his team."

He stood on the other side, hate, spite, and fury spewing from his brown eyes. Jaw muscle popping, he reached into his breast pocket and withdrew a piece of paper. "This will have to do."

Zahrah took the sheet and unfolded it. The grainy image seemed to be a hospital room. A man with a bandage on his forehead and arm in a cast lay there. Whether alive, she couldn't ascertain. She held it out to him. "He could be dead for all I know."

"He is not." He nodded to the paper he wouldn't take back. "That is your proof. All I can and will provide."

"Not good enough."

Smirking, he tilted his head. "I think you need some motivation."

Unease squirmed through her stomach, upsetting the lamb and curry they'd given her for lunch. "Threatening me will not make me smarter."

"Oh, I think it will." Zmaray raised a hand.

A guard left the room.

Silence gaped across the once-humming room as they waited. Everyone shifted. Muttering scampered around the room, filling the silence with tension. Well, more than had previously been here.

Thwat.

A door swung open. In walked Kamran with a small—

Zahrah punched to her feet, her arms jerking taut against the chains. "Rashid!" She flashed a glare at Zmaray, but panic replaced the anger. "Don't do this. He's a child, for pity's sake!"

"Yes. An innocent child." Zmaray sauntered closer, his hands once again in the pockets of his suit pants.

Kamran led Rashid to the table and urged him into a chair at the end then chained him around the waist and arms.

"Rashid," Zahrah said, looking at the boy. "Are you okay?"

Wide, frightened eyes held hers. He gave a nod, but his chin trembled.

Zahrah held out her hand, but with the chains, she couldn't reach him. "Be brave, Rashid. It'll be okay."

Dean, where are you?

If he'd forgiven her, he had a monumental task in front of him since they'd brought her here. Wherever here was. "Pull your chair closer, Rashid."

"No," Kamran said.

"Leave him," Zahrah said, the snarl in her voice surprising even her. "He's hurting nothing and he's terrified."

"No. I'm brave. I can be brave." Rashid nodded to the computers. "Please, Miss Zarrick. Fix it so we can go home, yes?"

"His life is in your hands, Miss Zarrick." Zmaray stood before her then bent at the waist and placed his hands on the lip of the table. "I have seen how effective a little persuasion can be with you. Perhaps you will work more quickly so little Rashid here does not have to endure what you put Captain Watters through."

"You wouldn't—he's only a boy."

Almond eyes narrowing, Zmaray glowered. "Then you should work faster. You have one hour to free the computer!"

—⁓—

Somwhere in Afghanistan

Jogging down the hall behind Hawk and with Eagle on his tail, Dean could feel the hope surging through his veins. Was it a coincidence that he'd asked for a mission briefing from God and then Hawk showed up?

They flung through a set of double doors. Hawk slowed. Dean nearly collided with him. Sighted a commotion ahead.

Burnett and Zarrick emerged from the curtained-off area that was rapidly filling with medical personnel. Zarrick flung a medical tray out of his way. Kicked the thing down the hall. An orderly hopped over it to avoid getting hit.

"No, no," Dean said, rushing between Hawk and Eagle. "What happened?"

Zarrick turned away from Dean. Burnett seemed to crumple against the wall.

"Our asset killed himself." Titanis grunted. "Grabbed my weapon and. . ."

Dean stared at the area where the staff were vainly trying to save the Afghan man. Why. . .why would he kill himself? It didn't make sense.

Unless he knew something that could get him killed.

"Excuse me, sir," a nurse said as she wove around behind him.

Dean blinked, not realizing he'd entered.

A doctor stepped back. "Time of death: 1723 hours." He snapped off his medical gloves and deposited them in a bin off to the side.

Dead. Their only hope of finding of Zahrah—

God is our hope.

Strangest thing, but those words had Zahrah's voice behind it.

He couldn't fight Zahrah's faith.

Couldn't fight this man's death.

"The greatness of a man's power is the measure of his surrender."

Dean struggled to breathe. To dare to hope. There was nothing—absolutely nothing—he could do. And Zahrah was out there. Depending on him. Believing in him.

No, depending on God. Believing in God.

I'm just a tool. Dean fought the urge to throw a fit. Throw a fist through the wall. To curse and rail. But that'd definitely be a fight he had no business fighting. It didn't make sense. If he was tasked with saving Zahrah, a guy would think God would show him how to do that. Not close every doggone door he walked up to.

Zahrah. Zahrah was out there. Having god-knows-what happen to her.

Darkness clutched at him. Made him want to panic. Surrender? No way! He should be fighting harder to save her.

It's not your fight.

Dean roughed a hand over his face. *Okay God. . .I'm on my knees. Down to my last breath. I. . .I surrender. Is this what You want?*

"Who can read Pashto?"

Dean flinched at the question, snapping back to the present. The doctor stood over the body of the Afghan man, looking around the room. "I can," Dean heard himself say. "A little."

The doctor waved him closer to the bed. "He wrote something here. We can't read it."

Angling over the bed, Dean studied the Arabic scrawled on the sheet.

"Watters," Burnett said, "What is it?"

Dean's heart thumped at the characters. Was he reading it right? "Sadri Ali."

Hawk was there, hands tucked under his armpits. "The opium supplier we chased in Majorca?"

"Where is he based?" Dean asked.

Burnett pivoted. "Let's talk." And he was walking. Fast. Down the hall, the team following like magnetic particles in his wake.

Dean hopped to keep up, swinging the curtain aside as they hurried down the hall. Harrier and Falcon were with them now.

"Ali's based all over the place, but he's in town. Visiting a certain diplomat."

With a lunge, Dean walked evenly with the general. "Wait, you mean that house I was snatched from?"

"The one and the same."

Hope sped through Dean's veins, on fire at the possibilities. "Hold up." Dean stopped the general at a juncture. "We need to hit this now. Hard. Fast. Before they have a chance to know what's coming."

Hawk nodded. "Agreed."

"No record of the mission till we get back," Dean said. "They're always ahead of us, but this time, I want to make sure they're not."

"You think we have a mole?"

"We've got something, and Burnett's working on it." Dean looked at the team. "Nianzu was in the prison, trying to get Zahrah to help. If we can nail this opium supplier at the same time we kill this cyber threat—"

"That'd butter my biscuit," Eagle said with a grin.

"Ladies," Hawk said with a smirk to everyone, arms held wide. "Biscuits and gravy for chow tonight!" He clapped.

"Grab your gear. Meet at the airstrip in fifteen."

"A place like that, we're going to need backup." Burnett held up his hand. "Don't argue. It's smart strategy."

"You mean good politics."

"That, too. If they have her, that place will be armed to the teeth. I'm bringing in Ramsey's SEAL team."

"Someone just burned the biscuits," Hawk muttered and strode out.

Dean eyed the general. "As long as they know Raptor has point."

Burnett grinned. "Wouldn't have it any other way."

Dean turned and found himself facing General Zarrick. "I failed you once, sir. It won't happen again."

"Not a failure, son. A delay in delivery." He clapped Dean's shoulder. "We have to get her out of there before she does something she doesn't want to do."

CHAPTER 54

Somewhere in Afghanistan
01 August—1948 Hours

A triumphant cheer shot through the room.

"You have not disappointed, Miss Zarrick." His voice was slicker than a vat of oil and made her skin crawl.

I have *disappointed—myself.*

She sat back in her chair, fear of what she'd just done mirroring the excited thrum in the room. *God—help me!* Doing this violated everything she believed in. She'd been foolish to think she could do this, delay and stall until Dean showed up to save the day.

Superheroes weren't real.

"We can go home now, yes?" Rashid asked, excitement muddled by fear in his sparkling eyes.

Zahrah's heart tripped off the ledge it'd been sitting on. They were no closer to rescue. And within a day, she'd have the network hacked. Soldiers in danger. America exposed. All because she was stupidly naive, believing she could deceive Zmaray.

Her gaze drifted to where he stood with a phone pressed to his ear. His expression fell from excitement to defeat. . .to anger. "No," he said then a string of Mandarin dialogue she could not decipher. When their gazes met, he stilled then turned his back to her.

What is that about?

With the men in this room who were knowledgeable—yet not experts like her—surely one would notice. . .

"You did it—you made them happy. Now we can leave." Rashid hopped his chair closer. "Yes?"

"Afraid not, Rashid." Zmaray stood by the boy, hand on his shoulder. He crouched. "See, our Miss Zarrick has been using delay tactics."

Guilt swirled through her stomach.

"She is a very intelligent woman." Zmaray lifted a silver device in one hand. "And now that the box is off, she knows she can solve this puzzle very quickly. But she fell in love with a man. And she's very loyal to him and her country."

"Leave him alone," Zahrah said with a growl.

"So we need to make sure she does her very, very best." Back against Rashid's chest, Zmaray held out the hand and splayed the fingers. He slid a cigar cutter over Rashid's pointer finger.

"No!" Zahrah screamed. "Don't do this!"

Meaning spiraled through his gaze. "You have done this to him."

Zahrah wrenched. "Stop!"

The cutter closed around Rashid's finger.

The boy screamed.

Zahrah screamed. "Stop! Don't—no!"

Red sped down Rashid's finger.

"Please! Stop." Zahrah yanked and tugged against her chains, straining to intervene. "I'll do it. I'll do it. Just leave him!"

Rashid howled.

Zmaray slid the cutter off. Straightened. "Next time I will not be so compassionate." Chin lifted, anger in his eyes, he stared down his nose at her. "How long before you have it broken?"

Wiping the tears from her face and beneath her eyes, Zahrah looked at the computer. "A day, maybe two. I don't know how intricate the system is yet."

He leaned toward her. "You have two hours." His breath smelled of curry and wine. "For each hour you go over, Rashid pays."

CHAPTER 55

Residence, Balkh Province
01 August—2010 Hours

Thunder had nothing on the rotors of a Black Hawk. But stealth also had nothing on the technology that silenced the rotor wash to prevent giving away their presence. Grabbing a line, Dean fast-roped from the helo, a challenge with only one good hand. He dropped from the nylon cord and hit the ground hard. He stumbled, righted himself, and plucked the M9 from the holster at his waist.

The team swarmed into the compound.

Gunfire erupted.

Frantic, ongoing sprays of fire were answered by the operators' tight, controlled bursts of three to four shots at a time. Control. Precision. That's what told him they'd beat this. They had to.

With thirty operators descending on the compound, the bad guys didn't have a prayer. As they flooded into the night-darkened palace, Dean mentally mapped the route. His gaze hit the grand staircase that led to the upper level. That's where the party had been. Where they'd lured him into a lesser room, though still opulent. Where they'd ambushed him. Beaten him and dragged him out what must've been the servants' entrance. He'd been mostly unconscious, fading in and out.

Hawk, Falcon, and Eagle pied out through the main room. Moonlight pushed through curtain cracks and transom windows over the French doors. Patio lights glinted off the Olympic-sized pool.

Dean stuck close, but gave them room to operate.

Movement near the French doors drew Dean's attention. He aimed his gun that way. A sea of black-clad operators rushed through the doors.

SEALs. Dean let out the breath he'd been holding.

It was quiet here. Too quiet.

Through a tall, narrow door, Dean shifted to the side and turned to aim his gun at the door, watch the team's six as they moved and cleared it. His heartbeat whooshed in his ears, every sound amplified in the deathly quiet palace. The scritch of his tactical pants. The subtle squeak of tac boots.

"Occupants located orange three."

Upper level, third section.

"Secured."

Dean breathed a little easier knowing the innocents were locked down, narrowing the chances of finding the bad guys with each minute.

"Thermals show staff snoozing," came Eagle's voice. Laid up on a rooftop, he was monitoring the team's movement with a high-powered scope that showed infrared and bled through buildings.

Staff quarters lined the northeast wall, so seeing through those walls had been easy and essential. If they could secure the staff and prevent them from entering the active mission, Raptor reduced the risk of innocent casualties. They moved on. Two offices. A sitting room. A green room. Butler's pantry. Regular pantry. Kitchen. A room for refrigerators and dishwashers. Incredible when one considered the relative poverty of this country.

What took two hours to prep and plan had been executed in less than five minutes.

Their objective, they believed, would be in underground storage areas. Or third-level quarters, which the SEALs were clearing even as Raptor moved toward the kitchens.

The hall was narrow and cramped with artifacts and treasures. Dean narrowly missed toppling a statue. He grabbed it and stilled. A garish representation of a giraffe. Maybe. But he remembered it from them dragging him out.

"Levels two and three clear," came the final report.

Raptor went right. Only one more room.

But...Dean hesitated in the kitchen. A large metal island with a rack dangling over it. His gaze drifted to the right. To the bank of refrigerators. He walked to them. Opened one. Then the second. The third.

"Captain."

The fourth—he snapped back, weapon up, heart thrumming at the darkness that glared back. It wasn't a fridge. It was a door. "Got something."

The scritching of tac pants preceded a tap on his shoulder.

Dean nodded and held his stance as Hawk aimed his shoulder lamp into the darkness.

"Stairs."

Keying his mic, Dean followed Hawk into the underground passage. "Underground passage in the kitchen. Raptor going in." Behind him, Falcon, Harrier, and Titanis crammed into the space.

Light beams bounced and sparked against dust particles.

A half-dozen doors on either side. Raptor entered the first one. Dean held the tail because of his arm.

Harrier blurred to his right.

Dean swung that way, his mind coalescing the movement with the image his brain snapped. "Stop! U.S. military!" Even as he started that way, Hawk rounded him.

"What'd you see?"

"To the left. Someone ran left."

They rushed forward. Hawk cleared the corner and moved into the darkness. Dean with him, both with their NVGs and cameras active.

Something swung out at them. Popped Hawk in the head and knocked him to a knee. Dean eased back his trigger at the wielder. In the microscopic second of muzzle flash, he saw someone else dart into another room. He heard the thump of the wielder falling but pressed on.

Three quick strides delivered him into a wide room. He shoved himself to the right and against a wall, pieing.

Through his NVGs, he saw Hawk do the same on the left. As their lines of fire crossed, Dean stilled. Two glowing forms—no, three. A man with a gun to the head of— "Zahrah!" Dean shoved forward with renewed purpose, stalking right as Hawk continued. Flanking the guy. Forcing him to choose one or the other.

The gunman pressed the barrel harder against Zahrah's temple. "Stay back or she dies."

"Not going to happen," Dean shouted in Pashto, recognizing the man's voice as Kamran. Oh sweet justice! Would God really let him repay this man for the harm he'd done Zahrah? "Release her and the child. Now!"

"Dean," Zahrah said, her voice clear and focused. She wrapped her arms—were those chains on her?—around Rashid. "I'm ready."

His heart sped. Ready? It took a second for the understanding to register.

He gave her a nod, then glanced at the kid. "Rashid, is that you, recruit?"

The boy nodded with a whimper.

"You done good, Rashid. Looked out for her just like I asked." And he prayed—begged God to have Zahrah understand. *"Now!"*

Bending at the waist, Zahrah drove her elbow into her captor's stomach. When she did, it brought Kamran forward, giving Dean a clear head shot.

He fired—just as he saw the weapon pointed at him.

Deafening cracks peppered the stale air.

A strangled cry—from Zahrah!

Dean's heart stopped as time spun into a deathly slow motion. She pitched forward. Back arched. Eyes wide. She stumbled. He lunged into her path as gunfire exploded. Dean quickly eased her to the ground. "She's hit!"

Something loomed from the shadow. Dean whipped his weapon that direction. Verified the target in a split second. Fired. Twice.

Kamran Khan spun and raced for the door.

Dean focused on Zahrah. On her gushing wound. "Z, stay with me."

Her hand covered his, snapping his gaze back to hers. A slow smile came to her face as a sleepy-peaceful expression smoothed out the knot between her eyes.

A stream of bullets flew from Hawk's M4. "Take that!"

"Heads-up," came a voice through the coms. "Twenty or more coming your way in two trucks."

"Take them out," Riordan's command crackled through the coms.

Boom–boom!

Walls trembled. Dirt rained down.

"Z, stay with me. I'll get you out of here." When she didn't respond, Dean touched her face. "Z—with me?"

Zahrah blinked. "Rashid," she breathed, then her eyelids slid shut.

Rashid? "Hawk—the kid!" Dean checked to make sure she was still breathing—good. He spotted a small form huddled in the corner.

They had to clear out. The enemy knew they'd found her, and they weren't going to let her go easily. If he lifted her, he could risk permanent injury to her spine if the bullet was close. But if he didn't—

Dean scooped her into his arms, pushed to his feet. After another nod to Hawk, who had the boy, Dean started for the exit, where

Titanis and Falcon waited.

"Raptor coming out with objective plus one. Both wounded. Need medevac," Falcon said as he led the way, clearing each corner in a swift—but painfully slow to Dean—way.

A shooter appeared at the end of the hall.

Falcon fired but never stopped moving, even to step over the combatant's now-still form. Up the passage and back into the kitchen. There someone came at Titanis with a knife. The SAS soldier managed to turn the blade into the attacker's stomach and put him down. Falcon led them out the back door.

Light pushed against Dean's eyes. He struggled, his arm pounding, as he hurried toward a secure spot where he went to a knee and set Zahrah down. "Z." Eyes closed, she lay unresponsive. He ripped off his glove and jabbed two fingers against her carotid.

A second large boom detonated from the far side of the compound. Dean covered Zahrah against any falling debris. The gunfights, the shouts, all went silent.

Worrying over the gray pallor seizing Zahrah, Dean keyed his mic as he looked at the sky. "Mockingbird, where are those choppers?"

CHAPTER 56

Camp Marmal, Mazar-e Sharif
02 August—1345 Hours

Rhythmic beeping numbed his mind as Dean sat in the private room. Cold plastic dug into his legs after having occupied the chair for the last three hours. Forearms resting on his knees, he stared at the bed. At Zahrah propped on her side in the bed. Clinging to life.

"Anything?"

Dean glanced to the side. There stood General Peter Zarrick. Zahrah's father. Haggard but looking a bit better since Raptor returned her to American-held soil. "Nothing. Not yet."

"Since Nianzu escaped, Burnett and I are concerned they'll come after her again."

Dean nodded. He'd had those thoughts countless times. It's why there were round-the-clock guards. "Figured as much. Ticked we didn't find Sadri Ali. Those Chinese are slippery thugs." Dean's gaze went to Zahrah, lying in the bed. So vulnerable. "If they come after her again..."

"Official word on her injuries will be memory loss and limited loss of cognitive functions."

It took Dean a second to process the words. "In other words, when Nianzu reads the report, he'll believe Zahrah useless now."

"That's the plan anyway." General Zarrick nodded as he appraised Dean. "You did real good out there, son. Thank you."

Surprise drew Dean up.

"Thank you for bringing her back." He sighed. "But with the way you're sitting in here, pining over my girl, I guess you're looking to steal her from me."

"No, sir." Dean's heart thumped against what he immediately knew was a lie. "Well. . .maybe."

"I won't make it easy for you." Though gruff, the words had a tease to them.

"Wouldn't expect you to, sir."

"Good." He grinned. "Heading down for some java. Want some?"

"No, sir. Thank you."

Alone with his thoughts, Dean shifted his leg and felt something press against him. His hand stilled over the pocket, remembering the flower bed as he and the team loaded in the chopper. It was silly. Borderline stupid. He'd probably just throw it away.

C'mon, Z. Don't give up now, not when I realize how much I need you.

She'd taken a bullet to her back. Almost severed her spinal cord. Docs weren't sure how much neurological damage there would be. Dean didn't care. He just wanted her to wake up, set those beautiful eyes on him, and give him that killer smile. Maybe another kiss.

He glanced down. *God, I know You didn't bring her this far to die on me.* Somehow—yeah, he knew that. What he was supposed to do with this, with the budding feelings that had upended his whole life plan. . .

He wasn't even really sure what love was, but he had feeling it was a lot like this mess in his head over Zahrah right now. Terrified he'd screw it up and hurt her. And yet more terrified not to have a chance with her. In his pocket, he wrapped his hand around. . .a promise. Closed his eyes. *Just a chance.*

A sound drew his attention to her bed. She moved her foot and turned her head.

Dean was on his feet and at her side in a heartbeat. "Zahrah?" She moved her foot!

Beautiful brown eyes latched on to his face. She smiled. "Hey." Groggy and a bit unfocused, but beautiful.

"How do you feel?"

"Like I got shot."

"That might be because you did."

"But we got him, right?"

Dean faltered. "Kamran's dead. Nianzu has vanished."

She closed her eyes in a pained way.

"Hey." Dean touched her head. "The important thing is you're alive."

"Yes, that's a very good thing," she said. "You came for me."

He eased closer, leaning over the bed. "I told you I would—and I

347

said I promised not to die. You, on the other hand, I forgot to extract that promise from. You cut it close."

A small smile then worry crowded into her gray-rimmed eyes. "Rashid?"

"He's fine—we thought he was shot, but he was thrown into a table corner or something. Big knot on his head, but fine, poor kid."

She lifted a hand and touched his face. "Dean..."

He felt powerless beneath her touch, the soft whisper of her voice.

"I still love you," she said, her voice softer. More serious.

Dean wished he could say it back. He wanted to—was a cad for not returning the sentiment. But that was some serious commitment. One that scared the tar out of him. Casted arm over her head on her pillow, Dean bent down. "You picked a very thickheaded guy to feel that way about."

She smiled. "Yeah."

He wrapped his hand around hers, eyes less than an inch from hers, and tucked the promise there as he bent down. "Get better so we can talk." He pressed a kiss to her temple.

"Ah, good morning, Miss Zarrick." A dark-haired man entered the room. "I'm Doctor Prevost. How are you feeling?"

—⁓—

Heart in her throat, Zahrah felt the delicate bloom on her hand, unable to look at it right now. Unable to bear the disappointment if it wasn't what she thought it was. Dean still stood to her left, but he'd retreated as the doctor spoke.

"Sore. I'm very sore," she finally managed to answer.

Dr. Prevost lifted a plastic cup from the tray by her bed. "Here, sip some of this for me."

Grateful for the water, she wanted nothing more than for the doctor to leave the room. Dean to leave—she didn't want to look at what he'd tucked into her hand as he leaned over, smelling every bit the hero she'd fallen for months ago.

"I'd like to check your vitals and check your reflexes. Is that okay?"

Dean hedged closer. "I'll wait outside." He stepped into the hall and stood against the wall, hands tucked up under his armpits. Two other soldiers joined him.

"Can you move your toes, Miss Zarrick?"

She did, wondering.

"Your legs?"

She shifted her legs out, unable to ease onto her back because of the bullet wound.

"Good, good. With an injury, we want to be sure there isn't damage to the spinal column or nerves." He patted her shoulder. "In a few days, you should be okay lying on your back. Anything else hurt?"

Zahrah shook her head and drew her hands closer to her face. "No." When would he leave?

"Any questions or concerns?"

Just that you won't ever leave. "Nothing, I'm good. Tired." Would that work? Surreptitiously, she took a sniff between her fingers.

"All right, then. I'll leave you to rest."

Oh, thank goodness.

"And that's the most important thing right now—resting so your body can heal itself."

"Right."

"You've been through a lot, and that can really take its toll on the body and its ability to heal quickly and properly."

Zahrah groaned at his rambling—but coughed through it. "Sorry." Dean and the two men walked away from her room, and her heart hitched.

"Maybe more water?"

"No," she snipped. Then smiled. "Just rest."

"Very well," Dr. Prevost said as he scribbled on her chart. "I'll leave you to rest. If you need anything, just press the button."

"Thank you." Zahrah pressed her fingers curled around the gift from Dean to her face, waiting as the doctor left. As the door shut, she closed her eyes, feeling the warmth of her own breath pluming back in her face. Without a scent. Her heart raced. Could it be. . . ?

Braced, she eased her hand back and unfurled her fingers. In a flood of joy, quiet tears streamed down her cheeks as a bloom smiled back at her.

A red poppy.

EPILOGUE

Underestimating one's opponent is a mark of arrogance. And defeat.

I'm still there. They haven't won. It's a game, really. One in which they thought they had the upper hand. Where they believed themselves to be masters and me, the apprentice.

But this isn't over. Far from it. We've gained more ground than I could've thought possible. Take that pound of arrogance, add a dash of politicking, an ounce or two of mistakes and stupidity. Bake for a few weeks or months on high, and you have a well-seasoned terrorist plot.

True, I've made my own mistakes that have cost me time. Money. Resources. And names—they've known me as Boris. Scythe. Whatever I need them to believe about me so I can play under their radar without detection. Whatever makes them feel confident enough to start relaxing. Slipping up. Making more mistakes. It would only take one mistake to put us over. To put is *in* their system. Then, as the saying goes, "All hell would break loose." Imagine that—demons running amok. Of course, America would call them Muslims. Or Chinese. Or wait—their favorite—Islamic terrorists.

When my phone buzzes, I glance at the name on the ID as I pull the truck up to the gate. Flash my ID.

"Thank you, sir." The Marine signals for the barriers to be moved.

Phone to my ear, I ease out onto the street. "I'm here."

"They found your equipment."

"As expected. Took them longer than I thought."

—⚌—

Sub-base Command, Camp Marmal
13 February—0918 Hours

Lance stormed into the briefing room. Officers of all rank and branches stood in the semidarkened room, glued to the monitors. Explosions ignited on the screen, throwing bursts of light across the stricken faces. He spotted his aide and joined Hastings. "What's happening?"

"It's. . .awful." Hand over her mouth, Lieutenant Brie Hastings shook her head. "They never had a chance—walked right into a colossal ambush."

"Who?" Lance scrambled mentally to map out the chaos ripping through the feeds. "Who is that?"

Hastings blinked. Looked at him. "It's Charlie Company, Second Battalion."

"What in Sam Hill are they doing there?"

She turned to him. "Ramsey sent them."

"What is he doing ordering around an ODA team?" Generals were more facilitators of policy and mission-end goals. ODA leaders and analysts assembled packets of intel and planned mission specifics.

"No," came a vehement growl from the back. "This isn't me. I didn't send them."

An attractive blond in uniform turned stiffly. "Sir." Her name patch read: WALKER. A single bar velcroed to her chest identified her as a second lieutenant. "I got the order from your secured address."

Ramsey stormed forward. "You're crazy. I never sent an e-mail. That's not how it works." He pivoted to Lance.

"I can prove it." Whitaker turned and motioned toward a computer. "May I. . . ?" When the Asian major removed himself from the seat, Whitaker sat. A few keystrokes later, she was in. "I received the e-mail on 23 January." Her gaze scanned the e-mails. "I. . ." She frowned. "I don't understand. It was right here." Face unusually pale, she stood. "I have copies—I'd forwarded them to the appropriate deparments for the mission prep. I'll retrieve them."

"Sir!" someone from the front shouted. "Oh my—"

Gasps and shrieks severed conversation as an angry plume of fire and smoke vaulted into the sky.

"Mother of God, have mercy on us!" Burnett hurried back to his office, sensing Hastings bringing up the rear. "Get Raptor on the line." In his office, he heard his fax machine and glanced toward the corner where it sat on the credenza. A paper dropped into the tray. Lance lifted and read it.

Hey, Diddle Diddle.
The grunt and the riddle:
Which cow jumped the gun?
It's not over, General. In fact, it's just starting.

ABOUT THE AUTHOR

Ronie Kendig is an award-winning, bestselling author who grew up an Army brat. After twenty-plus years of marriage, she and her hunky hero husband have a full life with four children and a Maltese Menace in Northern Virginia. Author and speaker, Ronie loves engaging readers through her Rapid-Fire Fiction. Ronie can be found at www.roniekendig.com, on Facebook (www.facebook.com/rapidfirefiction), Twitter (@roniekendig), and Goodreads (www.goodreads.com/RonieK).

Coming soon from

RONIE KENDIG

THE QUIET PROFESSIONALS
BOOK 2